A Duchess a Day

He stared at her mouth, waiting impatiently for her to say the word.

Please tell me to stop.

Slowly, carefully, with fingers that shook, he reseated his hands on her waist. He met her gaze; their eyes locked. His expression was meant to convey entitlement and possession and strength.

She laughed.

She actually laughed. A light, musical sound. "Well," she said. "Come on, then."

Declan growled, and scooted her to the edge of the workbench in one forceful yank. She sucked in a little breath. She settled her hands on his forearms as she tipped her head up. The word *stop* seemed like the farthest thing from her mind.

Declan went slowly, carefully, closing the distance between them. With the pressure of a feather, he bussed her lips with a soft kiss. Once. Twice . . .

By Charis Michaels

Awakened by a Kiss

A DUCHESS A DAY

The Brides of Belgravia

ANY GROOM WILL DO

ALL DRESSED IN WHITE

YOU MAY KISS THE DUKE

The Bachelor Lords of London

THE EARL NEXT DOOR

THE VIRGIN AND THE VISCOUNT

ONE FOR THE ROGUE

Charis Michaels

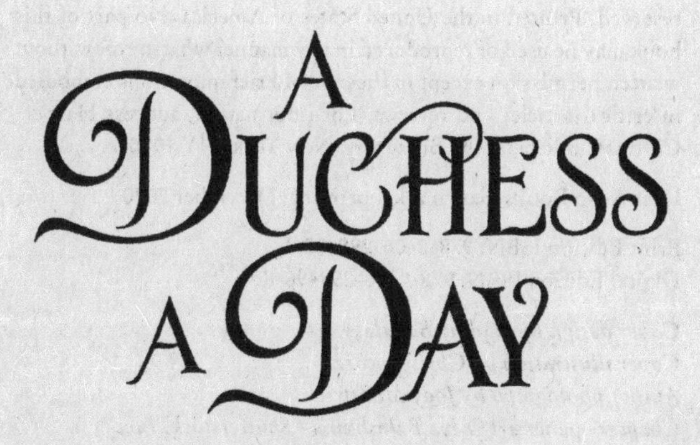

Awakened by a Kiss

An Imprint of HarperCollins*Publishers*

This is a work of fiction. Names, characters, places, and incidents are products of the author's imagination or are used fictitiously and are not to be construed as real. Any resemblance to actual events, locales, organizations, or persons, living or dead, is entirely coincidental.

First Avon Books mass market printing: December 2020

Print Edition ISBN: 978-0-06-298495-1
Digital Edition ISBN: 978-0-06-298496-8

Cover design by Nadine Badalaty
Cover illustration by Chris Cocozza
Author photograph by Jody McKitrick
Chapter opener art © Iya Balushkina / Shutterstock, Inc.

FIRST EDITION

20 21 22 23 24 QGM 10 9 8 7 6 5 4 3 2 1

For my father.
Thank you for sharing your knowledge
of apples for this book
and all the useful things you've taught me all my life.
I love you and I love learning from you.

A Duchess a Day

Chapter One

London, 1816

Newgate Prison was not for the faint of heart.

It was also not for the claustrophobic, the hygiene conscious, or anyone with a weak stomach.

Declan Shaw was none of these; in fact, he was a hardened mercenary (currently unemployed) and occasional spy (when the price was right). He'd seen a lot of hellholes in his life, but Newgate represented a new level of despair. After four months on the inside, he'd never been more motivated to get the bloody hell out.

Today, with no explanation, he'd been transferred from the subterranean general lockup to his own private cell. He was now in possession of a small barred window that looked out on a muddy mound. He'd been issued a weevil-infested mat and there was gruel twice a day, instead of once.

"Huntsman?"

And someone was calling his name.

"Huntsman?"

No, not his name. He was known to guards as "Prisoner 48736" or "Shaw" to fellow inmates. "Huntsman" was the alias by which he was known in professional circles, his mercenary brand, the name they called him on the London streets.

"Huntsman?" the voice called again.

"Aye," he called back. If he didn't claim it, someone else would. Everything was up for grabs in Newgate.

"Ah, yes, there you are," said a male voice, still yards away. From around the corner, the sharp *tap, tap, tapping* of delicate-heeled shoes punctuated an oddly singsongy male voice, followed by the heavy plod of guards' boots.

"Oh, just look at you," enthused the disembodied voice, "you *are* an imposing fellow. Size and bearing have done no favors in your plea for innocence, have they? None at all."

Declan leaned against the cell bars, straining to see through the smoky gloom. The silhouette of a stick man emerged, slight but with a bold stride. The man snapped his finger at a guard, demanding that a torch be brought closer. He studied Declan like a collector in a shop.

"You may leave us," he told the guards. "When I require you, I will call."

Narrowing his eyes at Declan, he said, "And how have you enjoyed your private cell, Huntsman?"

Declan had not, in fact, enjoyed the private cell.

The man continued, "I could not bear to call on you in the dungeon. They were kind enough to move you here so we could discuss business, assuming you are amenable." He flashed a hopeful smile.

He smiles too much for prison, Declan thought. "*What* business?"

"What indeed? You are known for such a wide variety of services, aren't you?"

"At the moment, I'm known for captivity."

"Quite so. But before the ghastly cock-up with the abduction, and the alleged murder, and that poor, wretched girl, your profession was . . ." The old man trailed off, studying Declan as if trying to envision him in some other setting. "Well, you were a sort of bodyguard, were you not? A tracker? *Mercenary*, I believe is the correct term? One of the finest in the country, according to my sources."

"My name *and* my trade," Declan observed. "You're full of information, Mr.—?"

"Oh, do forgive me." He frowned as if he'd used the wrong fork. "Titus Girdleston, at your service. I am the uncle and family steward of my nephew—His Grace, Bradley Girdleston, the Duke of Lusk."

Another pause. Declan waited.

"Are you familiar with the Girdleston family or His Grace, the duke?" the man prompted.

"No."

Declan saw no reason to hide his disdain for aristocrats in general and dukes in particular. He didn't do business with the nobility, not anymore, not since a certain royal duke had framed him for abduction and murder and stood idly by while Declan went to jail.

"No?" Girdleston repeated, his voice high and

contemplative, as if Declan had stated a philosophy he'd never considered.

"Don't work for dukes," Declan said.

"Oh, pity. Well, I suppose *I* am not a duke, and *I* would be your employer."

Declan sighed wearily and asked, "Employer for . . . ?"

"Oh, right—the job. Well, you see, I've come . . ." Girdleston raised his eyebrows, ". . . because my family has a job for you. There is a young woman traveling to London. She comes this very night, in fact. Her name is Lady Helena Lark, and she is the daughter of the Earl and Countess of Pembrook. She is betrothed to my dear nephew, the duke. In the weeks leading up to the wedding, she and her family will reside in our ducal residence, as their own London townhome is under construction. This close proximity will help the girl become more accustomed to her future role as duchess. It will also allow us to keep an eye on her. Which is precisely the job I'm looking to fill, Huntsman. I've come to hire you to *mind her,* for the lack of a better word. Keep a close eye on her from the moment she reaches London until she walks down the aisle to legally wed my nephew." He paused and looked knowingly at Declan.

Declan narrowed his eyes. *This is a joke.*

Girdleston cleared his throat and continued. "By 'mind her,' of course I mean guard her safety, see to her comfort in muddy lanes or crowded shops, make certain she's happy and looked after and—and this is where it gets a bit tricky, but no effort for you, I'm certain—keep her from bolting."

Declan couldn't help himself from asking. "Keep her from *what*?"

"Bolting," the old man confirmed solemnly. He let out a sigh. "There has been some confusion and hesitation on the part of the girl, I'm afraid. The union has been several years in the making, due mostly to her . . . lack of cooperation. But now we are all in agreement on the wedding and happy future of this couple. Her parents assure me we'll enjoy her full cooperation. That said, when she reaches the city, I should like to have a trusted man in place to safeguard against future incidents of . . ."

"Escape?" provided Declan. He actually felt sorry for whatever poor sod was hired. And the girl. If there was anything Declan understood, it was captivity.

"Oh, it's nothing so drastic as 'escape,' " Girdleston assured. "How shall I term it? The families on both sides of the marriage hope to remove incidents of *distraction*. Lady Helena's time in London will be devoted to activities that should delight any bride-to-be: shopping, tours of her new residences, and parties in her honor. I wish for her to remain focused throughout the proceedings, with her eyes set firmly on the prize of matrimony."

"Why isn't she *minded* by her own people? Parents or staff?" Declan asked on a sigh. The sooner he validated this man's problem, the sooner he would go away.

The old man nodded sagely. "Yes, wouldn't that be convenient? Unfortunately, I've found her family to be wholly ineffective when it comes to minding her. And her particular brand of . . . oh, let us call it 'spirited willfulness' has proven too much for chaperones or maids."

"So your natural next choice is an accused felon?" It couldn't *not* be said.

"Oh, your alleged crimes do not startle me, Huntsman," said Girdleston. "But I suppose you haven't heard. There's been the most astounding development in your case. Just this morning, in fact. The informers who accused you of abducting that poor girl have actually *changed* their claim. Dropped the charges, all of them. It's only just hap—"

"What?!" rasped Declan. Shock and disbelief shattered like glass inside his head. He lunged, straining against the iron bars.

Girdleston nodded, his white teeth shown through his smile. "The family of Miss Knightly Snow have heard rumors of a sighting. The girl has been spotted several times in the South of France. A cousin, I believe, has been sent to recover her. The family is trying to be discreet, I'm sure you understand—"

"Knightly Snow has been found?" Declan demanded. He was in prison because he'd been hired to escort her to France and she'd mysteriously disappeared instead. He'd known all along that she was alive, traipsing around the Continent of her own volition, not abducted, and certainly not dead. Most of all, he knew that whatever she was doing was not his bloody fault.

He'd simply not been able to prove it.

He'd proclaimed his innocence before his arrest; and since they'd locked him up, he'd spent hundreds of pounds on lawyers to exonerate him. And yet the accusation and charges persisted.

Until now.

"I want my lawyer," Declan said. No victim meant no crime, and no crime meant he was free. His skin tingled. Fuzzy stars crackled at the corner of his vision.

"In due time," assured Girdleston, making a clucking sound. "All in due time. First, I should hope my role as bearer of good news will inure you toward the offer I've made." A pause and knowing look. "About the potential of our *working together.*"

"What?" snapped Declan. "We've bollocks potential, mate. I want my lawyer. I want out of this cage. I want to see my father. The list is rather long, at the moment, of the things I want, Mr.—"

"I would not be too hasty about my offer, Huntsman," cut in Girdleston, "because I've come with more than news of the dropped charges. I've come with the potential of *money.*" He paused and raised his eyebrows.

Declan knew enough to say nothing.

"You'll forgive my presumption about your current financial situation," drawled Girdleston, "but I happen to know that you've spent months contesting your innocence. I also know you've paid lawyers and court fees, and God only knows the price of survival inside Newgate. Perhaps you will be set free, but will you be able to restore your life? Your livelihood?"

"Why do you care?" Declan gritted out.

"I don't care, to be honest," said the old man,

"except that your desperation fits perfectly with my need for a soldier-for-hire. And when I say 'hire,' Huntsman, please be aware that I can make your financial losses of the last year simply go away. *Poof.* Like it never happened. And then some."

Declan stared, forcing himself to listen. The shock and hope had dulled just enough. His survival instincts began to bristle, and he started to play the game.

He asked, "This girl? Your nephew's betrothed? You believe she'll consent to a 'hired minder' tailing her around London? To contain her . . . her—what was it? 'Spirited willfulness'?"

"Now we've begun to see eye to eye," said Girdleston, chuckling. "Actually, I believe Lady Helena may accept your presence more openly if you take on some service role in the household. An alternative identity, if you will. I was thinking you might fit well in the role of personal groom to the future duchess."

"Oh God," Declan breathed, turning away.

"I understand that you occasionally assume false identities or undertake some subterfuge in order to do your job more effectively," Girdleston said. "And your time in the army would have made you a proficient horseman. Given the correct livery and proper bearing, I believe you would make a convincing stable groom. And certainly this position will give you reason to follow the girl about and redirect her should she . . . veer off course. And you will be handsomely, handsomely compensated. Enough money, Huntsman, to never have to work again, if you so choose."

Declan considered this.

He considered a young woman who required an armed guard simply to get married.

He considered posing as a groom, wearing livery and adopting the bearing of a servant, whatever that meant.

He considered what kind of duke sent his uncle to hire an ex-convict to guard his future wife.

But most of all, he considered the payout. Girdleston had been dead-accurate about Declan's need to make considerable money, and fast. If it was only himself, Declan could easily live lean while he rebuilt his life. But he was not one man, alone—he had a duty to his father and sisters.

"How much?" Declan rasped. In the end, this was all that mattered.

Girdleston smiled. "£500, Huntsman. All payable upon delivery of this young woman into holy matrimony with my nephew the duke."

Declan made a choking sound and stifled it with a cough. He'd been thinking of a number in his head that would make the job worthwhile. The sum Girdleston named exceeded it by several hundred pounds. He studied the older man with new eyes. What was so important about this wedding that justified the outlay of £500?

"And if I fail?" Declan asked, perhaps the most important question of the day. "What if this woman evades me or makes trouble? What if something goes wrong? In my experience, disaster proliferates when females are involved. You wouldn't be making the offer if she was easy."

"Oh yes, of course," chuckled Girdleston. "Females, troublesome creatures, there is no doubt."

"I vowed after Knightly Snow never to take on another female client."

"Well then, I suggest that you not think of the client," urged Girdleston, "think of the lovely payment. If you succeed, you will be a rich man."

"I asked about failing, not succeeding."

"Oh, right," sniffed Girdleston, tightening his gloves. "How very thorough. If, for some reason, you *fail* to retain her, if you *fail* to see her down the aisle, you will receive nothing. Oh, and there is a chance . . ." he looked knowingly at Declan, ". . . that the informers who originally brought these charges of abduction and murder of Miss Snow might . . . *revive* their story?"

And there it was.

Declan gritted his teeth. He'd expected this. Of course the freedom and the money and the job were all linked.

"How can I be accused again," he said tightly, "if Knightly Snow has been found in France?"

"Well, there's been a *sighting,* I believe," said Girdleston. "I cannot say if they've actually *found* the chit. Or how long that might take. A cousin is searching, as I've said."

Declan swore under his breath and turned away. If he'd had more time, he would've been able to find her. But he'd been arrested, and expedited back to England, and languishing in the court and penal system since the girl went missing.

"Not to worry, Huntsman," the older man said. "I have every confidence in you. You can manage Lady Helena. I would not have come if you couldn't."

Declan pivoted to lean against the wall. He refused to look at the man's calm face as he (also calmly) drew him over a barrel.

Declan *hated* being drawn over a barrel.

But he was a survivor. He would not jeopardize this open cell door, nor the promise of £500. A large part of surviving was knowing when to say *no, thank you,* and when to make a deal with the devil. Declan had run out of options.

"I'll do it," he said, turning back. "Now get me the bloody hell out of this hellhole."

Chapter Two

Lady Helena Lark had run out of options.

She had feigned sickness, perpetrated madness, and applied to be a nun. She'd declared herself too young, too old, too thin, too pale, and too disagreeable in every possible way.

For the last six months, she had simply dug in her heels and said *no.*

Before that, she had run away. Five times.

But her parents' great wealth and influence had restored her every time. Today they had restored her to what appeared to be the point of no return. To London. To the townhome mansion of her betrothed.

Betrothed, Helena thought, rolling the word around in her head with a doomed inner voice. She took up the apple in her lap and frowned at it.

Consigned would be more accurate, she thought, taking a bite.

Bought and paid for.

Sold.

"Do strive for a pleasant expression, Helena," sighed her mother. "You've no choice but to marry the duke, you've known this all along." The countess said this in her most placid voice, the voice of someone who'd been patiently stating inevitability for five years.

"Perhaps I have no choice who I marry, but surely my expressions are my own," said Helena.

"Your life is very fortunate, darling," the countess continued, "ample reason to smile. But the fortune comes at a cost. In order to enjoy the homes and gowns and holidays and esteem, you must accept the responsibility. We *all* have a responsibility."

"You and Papa enjoy the wealth and position," Helena said idly. "I simply want to be left alone in Castle Wood. With my apple trees and the crofters. And I don't want to be married to a prize idiot, even if he is a duke."

"For God's sake, Helena, must you be so very dramatic?" droned her father. He squinted out the window at the bright stone facade of the duke's townhome. Yellow-liveried servants scurried to greet the approaching carriages. "Marriage to anyone, even the very devil, need not be the end of the world. You will have the ceremony and accommodate the duke in a few small ways, and then your life will go on. Except that you will be a duchess. Every girl aspires to this, but it has been *given* to you by birth. You are making a fuss over a minor detail, in the grand scheme."

"My life as I've known it will not go on," said Helena, thinking of the forest and her orchard. "And it is not a minor detail."

She took another bite of apple, wondering why she bothered to object. They'd traveled from their estate in Somerset for the sole purpose of marrying her off to the Duke of Lusk. The marriage joined two ancient families and (more importantly) tied the duke's limestone mines to barges on her family's stretch of the River Brue.

The wedding was an arranged match for which her parents had been waiting, immovably, unshakably, for five years. She'd fought the betrothal in every way imaginable, and they had been blind and deaf to it all. They had not punished or strong-armed or shamed. They had simply ignored her pleas and waited. Now some fluctuation in international markets caused a spike in the demand for limestone and, in their view, the wait was over.

Helena pressed her back into the carriage seat, refusing to moon out the window at the duke's London mansion. She'd seen the hulking townhome, thank you very much. In the weeks before the wedding she would come to know it very well.

How suspicious it was, Helena thought, that their own London townhome was suddenly undergoing renovations. Now they were forced to live as guests of the duke and his tyrant uncle. Her mother expected her to smile about it.

She finished her apple, the very last of the harvest. This time next year, if she was married to the duke, the apples would be gone—destroyed by heavy limestone wagons trundling down the terraced orchard to the river.

The great irony was that the Duke of Lusk, a man who was as ridiculous as he was inane, couldn't care less about the wedding. At best, he was wholly indifferent to her; at worst, he was openly bored. He was a thirty-year-old man-child controlled by his uncle.

But Helena would not be controlled, or lose her orchard, or leave the forest. And she would not smile.

But also, she reminded herself, she would not be difficult. The time for evasion had come and gone. The only solution now was to engineer some *lasting* means of escape—something that did not extract her so much as put an end to the betrothal once and for all.

Luckily, she had a plan.

If she could manage it.

If she could be pleasant enough, and forestall suspicion long enough, and be clever enough to pull together the necessary players.

If she could get the duke to jilt her for some other girl.

That was her plan, plain and simple. Well, actually, it was not entirely simple. Helena intended to find the most perfect, most provocative replacement fiancée for the duke, dangle this sparkling girl under his nose, and let love or passion or mutual ambition overtake them. When Lusk was entranced by someone else, he would finally stand up to his uncle and demand a wife he really wanted. And Helena would be free to slip away, back to the orchard and the forest that she loved.

The greatest challenge to her plan seemed to be finding the ideal girl to dazzle the duke. For this, Helena relied on Lusk's open delight in traits like buxomness, shapely calves, and round fannies.

Also, his penchant for all-night parties, drunkenness in the middle of the day, and dancers. Never once had Helena chatted with Lusk when he did not broach these favorite topics. For years, she'd complained about his tedious vulgarity, but her mother dismissed it as boyish prattle. Helena knew better; it was a window to his soul. Now she planned to open that window and crawl out.

The line of carriages had scarcely stopped in front of Lusk House when her parents popped open the door to descend. They'd tried (and failed) to conceal their open delight at the prospect of having a duchess in the family, and they would be crushed when the betrothal fell apart. But if Helena's plan succeeded, the duke's change of heart would be his own choice. What could she do if he'd fallen under the voluptuous spell of some other girl?

What indeed?

Move on with a life on her own terms.

The earl and countess convened in the street, smoothing silks and readjusting hats.

Helena's three younger sisters spilled from the second carriage and descended upon their mother with a barrage of complaints and requests and grasping governesses.

Her father's dogs thundered from the third carriage, along with aunts and cousins and stewards and her mother's maid.

Helena allowed the commotion to swallow her up. She'd learned through the years how to disappear in plain sight. It was ironic, really, how little the duchess-to-be mattered in her family's quest to claim a title. She was like the cart that transported them to the fair that they deserted in a ditch when the festivities were in plain sight.

But now the fair commenced. The heavy oak doors of Lusk House swung open and Titus Girdleston stepped importantly onto the stoop. Someone remembered to produce Helena, and they thrust her forward like a virginal sacrifice.

"Lusk House welcomes you, my Lord and Lady Pembrook, Lady Helena!" Girdleston boomed from the stoop, extending his arms like an opera singer. He clipped down the steps and greeted her father with a robust handshake and bowed over her mother's hand.

"Ah, Lady Helena, how delighted we are that you've finally come to London to stay," Girdleston said, turning his thin-lipped smile to her.

"Thank you, Uncle Titus," Helena said cordially. "A pleasure, I'm sure."

She must not draw undue attention. Her plan depended on it. Belligerence only elicited tighter control. It was essential that she give the illusion that she could be managed.

"But where is the duke?" she asked, the words out before she could stop them. She'd learned five years ago that her fiancé would not appear for arrivals or departures. In fact, the Duke of Lusk was only present when Girdleston forced him. Typically, she was glad for the void, but it amused her to point out this flagrant rudeness. Then again, she was not here to amuse herself; she was here to set herself free. She beamed an innocent smile.

"The duke has been detained," Girdleston rushed to explain. "Estate business, I'm afraid.

He will join us presently for supper." The older man narrowed his eyes, speaking to her parents. "But first, allow me to present the duke's attentive and well-trained staff."

He snapped his fingers and dozens of yellow-liveried servants scurried to form a presentation line that stretched from the carriages to the house.

Oh for God's sake, Helena thought, squinting at the endless wall of yellow.

"How delighted we are to have you as our guests," crowed Girdleston, "and we should like for you to think of our household as *your* household." He gestured to the servants as if he had formed them from his own rib.

Helena sighed, looking at the long line of retainers. She made no claim of penury or modest living; she was the daughter of an earl, after all. She'd been waited upon by servants her whole life. Her father's estate in Somerset was a grand manor house with boys to carry firewood and girls to scrape the ashes. As soon has she'd been old enough, Helena had elected to leave the main house and live with her grandmother, the dowager countess, in her summerhouse elsewhere on the estate. She far preferred the lively cottage tucked within the leafy boughs of Castle Wood to the mansion where her parents and sisters lived. There had been fewer servants there. A cook and housekeeper, a man to mind the livestock. And her grandmother. Oh, how she adored her dear Gran. She'd been the only family member who'd seen Helena's free spirit, her love of nature, her curiosity and independence.

A fever had taken her some five years ago, and Helena missed her with an ache that never seemed to go away. She'd scarcely been laid to rest when her parents began to entertain the notion of using Castle Wood and their stretch of the River Brue to expedite their neighbor's mining operation. Gran had forbidden the arrangement while she'd been alive, and she'd even bequeathed the wooded section of the earldom—known as Castle Wood—directly to Helena to protect it. But with Gran was gone, there was no stopping her father from marrying Helena to Lusk. When the duke was her husband, he could do what he wished with the forest and the river.

"Renovations are never convenient," Uncle Titus said now to the earl and countess, "but you couldn't have chosen a better time to rebuild your London townhome. The duke is delighted to host you here. After all, soon Lady Helena will reside here with us permanently."

Helena recoiled at the thought. She worked to keep her face serene.

"We've arranged a tour of the grounds and house tomorrow," Girdleston went on, leading them up the walk and into the house. "But now let us provide nourishment and give our future bride and groom a chance to reacquaint. I've requested a restorative menu. Nothing too rich after such a long journey. Right this way, if you please . . ." He gestured Helena's mother to precede him through the heavy oak doors.

Helena idled near the carriages, collecting two more of her apples from a crate in the carriage.

So the duke would attend the meal. Normally

she dreaded any scheduled contact with Lusk, but now every shared moment was an opportunity to more effectively matchmake.

Most young women, she knew, would pounce at the opportunity to become a duchess. When it came to foisting him off on some other girl, the title was his most significant draw. But surely Lusk had more to recommend himself than simply the dukedom. Some occupation or passion or quality that he'd been previously too drunk or immature to reveal?

"Helena, dear?" Girdleston called from inside the great hall. He beckoned her with the smooth, spooling gesture of a ghostly majordomo. "You'll be gratified to know that I've set aside a contingent of highly trained servants for your exclusive use, to make certain of your every comfort and safety."

He's what? Helena thought, following him up the front walk.

"Come, come," he pressed, "so I may introduce you to your *private* staff." A clutch of yellow-liveried servants formed a half circle behind him. "This is only a start. As duchess, you may wish to expand their number. Whatever you require, the duke has made your comfort his highest priority."

"Please do not trouble yourself," Helena called. "I'm so often in my orchard I hardly know what to do with my father's maids and footmen. I cannot imagine taking on the duke's." *I will not be hounded by Girdleston's spies.*

"'Tis no trouble at all, my lady," Girdleston continued, his voice sharp. "Let me introduce

Mrs. Danvers. A highly skilled lady's maid. Previously in the employ of the Countess of Polk, you will find Danvers to be tireless and—"

"I've traveled to London with my own maid," Helena interrupted while glancing at the hatchet-faced woman beside him. *Absolutely not.*

She looked to her family. Did no one find this odd?

Her fiancé could not be roused to say hello, but his puppeteer uncle was saddling her with strange staff?

"My maid has been in my service since girlhood, and I've no intention of retiring her."

"Yes, well, perhaps you will reconside—"

"I won't."

"But what of this personal footman, Thomas?" he tried again.

An elderly footman limped forward, making a slight bow and wincing in pain.

Helena smiled at the old footman and turned on Girdleston. "I couldn't possibly accept the responsibility of a personal footman. I am wholly self-sufficient, as you may remember. Any passing footman will do. I am unsettled by fussing servants."

A flash of anger pinched Girdleston's face, and he forged ahead, gesturing to a large man in an apron. "But surely you cannot object to a personal cook . . ."

"I am not particular about what I eat," Helena said.

"Well, perhaps a brief trial with the cook," Girdleston countered.

"That won't be necessary."

Girdleston's wide, furious eyes reminded her that she was not in control, not really. The angrier he was, the harder he was to evade. If her ultimate goal was to defeat him, she must show some cooperation and choose her battles.

She added, "I have always enjoyed the meals at Lusk House. Your existing chef is so talented."

She was just about to reiterate that she felt uncomfortable with private servants, but Girdleston continued. "But surely you will not reject this private groom . . ." He swept out his hand. "The duke will insist upon a personal groom to squire you around London, to look after your safety and comfort in and out of carriages, busy streets, and balls late at night."

His voice had taken on a simmering urgency, a pot about to boil over. "Surely you cannot deny a personal groom, my lady?" he said.

Helena was formulating another way to convey the word *no* when a broad man, dressed from shoulder to ankle in straining yellow velvet, stepped forward and bowed his head.

Helena's denial froze on her lips.

She blinked at the vast expanse of eye-popping yellow. Her first thought was that he did not *wear* the livery so much as stretch the lemony fabric over his muscled body. It did not fit, not even a little. His hands were huge, his boots were huge, and his very posture—still and substantial—seemed less like a servant and more like the castle guard.

He wasn't a giant, but he looked stronger than anyone in the room; he looked stronger than anyone Helena could ever remember meeting.

So much muscle straining against so much . . . yellow.

He did not appear chagrined or bashful. His eyes were soft brown, and he glanced at Helena with a passive detachment that she struggled to decipher. Not supplication, not hopefulness, not boredom—

He looked at her like he was gauging the height and weight of a chair that someone had asked him to move across the room. Had he looked to her face? She wasn't sure.

When, finally, he met her eyes, he humbly lowered his head in a half bow.

He looks . . . useful.

There was something about the combination of his vagueness and brawn. He had muscled arms, significant shoulders, powerful thighs. She would not ordinarily consider the thighs of a servant (or any man), but the impossible tautness of his golden britches made every part of him impossible *not* to see.

His face remained averted, but she could see his profile: strong jaw, reasonable nose, dark eyelashes.

Eyelashes?

She scolded herself for noticing (first) thighs and (now) eyelashes, especially when her very future was at stake. His eyes made no difference, but taken as a whole, she could not deny that he might come in handy.

She glanced at Girdleston and speculated about the loyalties of this "private groom." The man had certainly fallen into line when Uncle Titus beckoned, but he'd moved in a rote, just-following-orders sort of way. He'd seemed more compliant than complicit and he lacked the slow, knowing bearing or the shared looks of a collaborator. He seemed . . . *biddable.*

Perhaps he *was* just a groom. Perhaps he was a big, strong groom with more muscle than brain.

Perhaps he was exactly what she needed.

"This groom is meant to be for my private use alone?" Helena heard herself ask.

The look of ravenous hope on Girdleston's face almost made her laugh. It would certainly appease him if she consented.

"Precisely, my lady," said Girdleston. "Someone to ease your way around the city."

Helena *would* require help navigating London. She was a country girl, loath since girlhood to spend more than an afternoon in the capital, and now her first order of business was to rove Mayfair, ferreting out potential duchesses. If this groom could be used for her own purposes rather than . . . whatever purpose Girdleston intended, then she was being inadvertently given a most useful ally.

Helena looked back at the rejected circle of private servants. The maid had been an obvious spy, and the old footman was likely loyal to the dukedom. Helena had no doubt the private cook would slowly poison her. But the groom—the large, biddable simpleton of a groom—might be harmless. And useful.

"Yes, Uncle Titus," she said. "I do believe I can find use for a groom on the unfamiliar streets of London. How kind of you."

"But you may thank His Grace, my lady,"

gushed Girdleston, bowing slightly. Helena refused to acknowledge this and instead spoke to the groom. "Pray, what is your name, sir?"

The groom raised his head but he kept his brown eyes averted.

"Shaw, my lady."

His voice was lower than she'd thought, although she couldn't say what she'd expected. She'd struggled to hear him, and she suddenly wished very much to hear him again.

"Very good, Mr. Shaw," she said. "I am Lady Helena. I grow apples in Somerset. Would you like one?" She reached into her pocket and extended a shiny, speckled apple. Behind her, she heard her parents groan.

Girdleston chortled. "Shaw is not accustomed to receiving, er, food from his charges, Lady Helena. Pray do not trouble yourself."

The groom stared at the apple like it was a tiny cannon ball, its fuse just lit. He glanced up. For a split second, their eyes locked. Helena could have sworn his expression said, *You're joking.*

She blinked. Surely not. Surely he was simply nervous and confused.

Helena waited for him to look up again, to reveal himself, but he merely made another approximated bow and kept his gaze fixed to the floor.

Well, she thought. She pocketed the apple. There would be plenty of time to establish some rapport. It didn't matter. He need only to do what she said when she said it, lift heavy things, and unwittingly aid her plan to escape with her future.

"You mentioned the duke will join us for supper," Helena said brightly to Girdleston. "I do believe I am hungrier than I thought."

Chapter Three

Declan had not expected this.

Understatement of the century.

He had expected a rich gentleman's daughter. A patchwork of deficiencies. Some combination of demanding and childish or flighty and selfish, with the potential for daftness or madness thrown in.

In no scenario had he envisioned a captivating beauty, determined to undermine the bloody dukedom. He knew insubordination when he saw it. And brains.

When she'd entered the great hall, she'd spared not a look at the stained glass or the carved staircase or the chandelier. She ignored the servants. Unless Declan was mistaken, she was looking for a way out. Girdleston had summoned her, and she didn't obey him so much as charge him. Her posture was upright but not rigid; she was thin but not brittle.

Declan had blinked, telling himself it was his job to stare. *Looking at her* was his job.

I cannot not *look at her.*

Fine. Right. So look.

Her eyes were pale green, the color of a peridot, and her hair was the color of ink, not interrupted by auburn or mahogany or ash, arranged in a tidy bundle on the back of her head, half obscured by a small green hat.

She had dark lashes and brows, but her skin was the color of the inside of a shell, pale and luminescent. The contrast of light to ebony was stark and beautiful. A raven's feather in the ice.

In that moment, Declan comprehended the level of difficultly—nay, the level of impossibility—of this cursed job. It hit him like a bat to the chest. He was looking at Helena Lark as a woman, not a client.

And not just any woman, a stunningly beautiful, obviously clever woman. Only a fool or an amateur would fail to admit this.

This was a problem because—first, distraction. His regard for her, even as an appreciative observer, would interrupt his ability to "contain her." Second, beautiful, clever things incited sympathy, and he could not sympathize with this woman; he worked for her enemy. And third, Declan had made a habit of running in the opposite direction of Problem Women.

Females in Declan Shaw's life had fallen mostly into one of two categories: convenient and willing . . . and everyone else. Clients were always "everyone else" because he was a professional, and putting his hands on a client was bad for business. Nonclient females—*if* convenient and willing—were a respite between jobs, so long as they harbored no illusions about pinning him down. Declan had been a natural solider and an even more natural soldier-for-hire. He liked his job. He was good at his job. No woman had ever tempted him to interrupt his success and he preferred it that way.

But he'd never met a woman like Helena Lark. This realization shook him to the core. He would walk away from this job if he did not require Girdleston's money so desperately and if he was not afraid the man had the power to send him back to prison.

"Well done, Huntsman," said Girdleston, suddenly beside him. Declan jerked around, unnerved by the man's omnipresence. "God knows why she consented to you and not the others; her intentions are a maddening mystery to us all. But now you've had a glimpse of the impertinence we've faced."

What Declan had glimpsed was cleverness and contempt, but Girdleston had not hired him for his opinion. He said, "It was ambitious to press five servants on her at once."

"By the time she becomes duchess, I will have broken her of the notion that she will ever be alone."

Declan paused. He hadn't known of a larger plan to "break her"—not of solitude or anything else. He swore and glanced at the disappearing form of Lady Helena. She was last in line again, following her entourage.

He looked away. Something sharp and heavy broke off in his chest and lodged in the pit of his stomach. He forced himself to think of the money, and his sisters, and his father. The decision to go along was no decision at all. He had no choice.

"Now you will stand attendance in the dining room, listening and watching," said Girdleston. "You must familiarize yourself with her machinations and insubordinations."

"A groom in the dining room?" Declan asked. "That makes no sense. Let me—"

"I'll decide what is sensical, Huntsman," said Girdleston. "You've only just been assigned to her. There is much to learn if you're to be effective."

Declan wanted to tell him that he'd learned quite enough already, but he gritted his teeth and thought of prison. Slipping into the dining room, he took up space in a dark corner.

Chapter Four

"I beg your pardon," Helena said, one hour into the family meal. She pushed up from the long dining table, smiling serenely. Up and down the table, conversations fell silent.

"Will you excuse me to see the duke is settled somewhere more comfortable? His Grace is . . ." She looked down at the Duke of Lusk and corrected, "His Grace has finished his meal."

All eyes settled on the duke, who slouched in his chair like a pile of laundry. His head lulled to one side and his half-lidded gaze was fixed philosophically on the remains of the goose on his plate. He'd propped his right hand loosely on the arm of his chair, and the goblet of wine dangling from his fingers threatened, at any moment, to drop and shatter on the floor.

For a long moment, everyone froze, and Helena took pains to gaze upon the duke with affectionate concern. She placed a gentle hand on his sloped shoulder.

The duke's uncle was the first to animate, opening his mouth to object, but Helena dropped to kneel at the duke's side.

"Would Your Grace fancy a little nap before your evening ramble?" she whispered.

The duke snorted, blinked, and helpfully leaned into her cheek. Helena maintained a serene smile while he trailed a wet, breathy nuzzle along her neck. She forced herself to laugh.

"If we may be excused," she said to the table, "everyone else may enjoy the meal with no rush. I'm told there is to be cake. We are newly reunited, and this meal has lasted an age . . ."

In the duke's ear, she whispered, "Up you go. That's it. Come, come, *get up*."

By some miracle, the inebriated duke climbed to his feet, swaying slightly as she took his arm.

Girdleston also rose, his narrowed eyes sharp with irritation.

Helena's father chortled. "I knew they would get on eventually, Titus. She's very nurturing, my daughter. She will have a soothing effect on the boy."

"Yes . . ." said Girdleston, in tone that said *no*.

Helena splayed her hand on the duke's hollow chest and leaned in. "Where is your private study, Your Grace?" she whispered. "Let us seek out somewhere dark and cool and quiet."

The duke hiccupped and pointed to an opposite door and Helena shuffled them out. "Lovely," she whispered. "Steady now. There we are."

Over her shoulder, she called, "Please pay us no mind and enjoy the meal. I cannot remember ever having goose quite so savory. I wouldn't dream of missing cake. We will make our way back in time."

"Your Grace?" the duke's uncle called. "Are

you quite alright?"

"Private . . ." mumbled the duke, "dark and cool . . ."

"Let her serve this wifely purpose, Girdleston," scolded her father. "With Helena, we've found the key to her heart is some manner of diligent caregiving. You should see what she's done to the bog in the forest surrounding Castlereagh. She will look after him and the result will be better for us all."

From the corner of her eye, Helena saw Girdleston reclaim his seat, but not before he gave a subtle nod to the large groom in the corner. The groom fell into close step behind them, and Helena gritted her teeth, hurrying the duke along.

"Which way, Your Grace?" she whispered. The great hall was marked with doors in every direction.

"Bedchamber?" the duke drawled, and Helena bit her lip against the gale of wine and goose on his breath.

"No," she said patiently, "your study. We'll want somewhere close, don't you think? Just a quick nap. They will not allow us to stay away for long."

"I'm going out," he protested, but he allowed her to drag him. "Plans . . ."

"Of course, your lovely plans," she assured. "More reason to rest now."

"You're an eager little cabbage," he mumbled.

"Yes, that's me," she said absently, looking from door to door, "so very eager." The duke snorted, misting her with another cloud of alcohol and goose.

Helena held her breath. "The study, Your Grace? Can you not remember? Which way is it?"

He made a vague gesture that could indicate any direction and dropped his chin to his chest.

Helena swore and pivoted slowly, trying to remember the layout of the house from previous visits. She was just about to choose the first available corridor when a voice behind her said, "I'll take him."

Helena spun and came up short against a muscled, yellow-clad wall of male. Her newly appointed personal groom. Shill? Sham? She couldn't remember his name.

"I beg your pardon?" she said, stooping to redistribute the duke across her shoulders.

"I'll take him," the groom repeated.

"That won't be necessary, Mr. Shill. And, if you ple—"

"Shaw," he said, reaching out. "Declan Shaw."

Helena's eyes widened. She couldn't remember ever having a male servant introduce himself by his given name. Or follow her from room to room. Or try to take something—well, in this case some*one*—out of her own hands.

She rarely scolded servants, but she cleared her throat and raised her chin. "That won't be—"

The groom wasn't listening. He put his hands on his hips and cocked his head, watching the duke's limp form slowly slip from her grasp.

Helena held more tightly and changed tact. "How lucky you've happened along," she said brightly. "Could I trouble you to point me in the direction of the duke's private study?"

"Don't know."

She narrowed her eyes. "You do not know?"

"Your guess is as good as mine."

The duke slipped another four inches, and his boot began to slide. Shaw extended his own foot to stop it.

Helena broadened her stance and took tighter hold of Lusk. "Are you not—"

"I work in the mews," he said. "Typically."

"Typically?"

"I'm going to take him," he told her. Before she could refuse, he reached out and rolled the duke from her shoulder, draping the smaller man's arm behind his neck. The duke half leaned, half hung against him like a limp scarf.

A burst of laughter rose from the direction of the dining room, and Helena was reminded that she had so little time.

Frowning, she set out across the hall. "If you are not familiar with the layout of the house, we'll ask."

A maid rounded a corner and Helena inquired for the direction of the duke's study. The girl pointed left, and Helena asked her to return with a basin of water and cloths.

"Put him there, if you please," Helena directed when they reached the study.

A floor-to-ceiling window rose above a leather divan in the corner; the groom deposited Lusk in an inebriated sprawl. Helena took a candle from the hallway and hurried to light the lamps. Each flickering wick revealed polished mahogany, grommeted leather, and books—so many books.

Naturally, the study would keep pace with the grandeur of the house—more a library than a study, with a maze of bookshelves towering behind a giant desk.

When the room glowed with soft candlelight, Helena leaned over the duke. "Now, Your Grace, isn't that better?"

Lusk made a snorting noise and flopped onto his back.

The maid arrived then, and Helena applied a warm, damp cloth to the duke's eyes. "Simply rest, Your Grace," she soothed, and took up blanket for his legs. Within moments, the duke began to snore. Helena backed away, willing him to remain unconscious for at least ten minutes.

"Now what?" asked the groom beside her.

"Shhh." She shot him a look.

"Trust me, he's out for the night." The groom cocked an eyebrow. "But I assume that's what you want."

"You've no idea of what I want. You may go, Mr. Sham."

"I'll wait," he said.

"Wait? Wait for what?"

If she hadn't seen his eyes before, she saw them now. They were deep, molten brown. Gone was all trace of shyness or chagrin.

"You may go," she repeated firmly. She nodded to the door.

On the divan, the duke jerked, flopping one arm over his head. He stretched his other arm, flexed his fingers, and then flopped his hand in the area of Helena's skirt and made a clumsy grab for her leg. Helena skittered back.

"I stay," the groom said, stepping up. Helena stared at him in wonder.

He added, "In case you need me."

"I won't."

"You might."

Helena blinked at him. "Actually," she said, "I haven't the time to argue. Go or stay, I don't care."

If a voice in her head told her she should care, she did not hear it. She wasn't ready to admit that she'd been wrong to agree to this groom. It was too early in her plan to be making wrong decisions.

She looked around, noting that the study looked wholly unused. Exactly what she would expect from a man who did not manage his own estates, write his own correspondence, or enjoy anything so cerebral as "reading." There was a scattering of paper on the desk, and Helena lifted the top sheet.

"What's that?" asked the groom.

Helena glanced up. "You should be aware that I will go about my business without explaining myself." She looked at the paper in her hand, a bill for hair tonic, and then back to Shaw.

"You came to the library for some other reason than settling the duke," he said.

"And *you* came to the library for some other reason than conveying a drunken duke. I propose that I not ask why and you not ask why."

"I could be of more use," he said, "if I knew what you were doing."

"More use as my groom?"

"Of course."

She nodded knowingly. "Unless I am mistaken,

grooms manage horses and carriages and shopping and umbrellas. What use would I have of a groom in a library?"

"*Well,*" he began, the word heavy with facetiousness, "as I've said, if I *knew*—"

"Why were you in the dining room?" She'd dropped the paper and glared at him. "Why did you follow us?"

"I—" began Shaw, but he stopped.

She nodded to herself. Direct questions had that effect on all but the most astute liars. He didn't have the look of a liar, but that didn't mean he wasn't another of Girdleston's puppets. How could she have been so foolish as to accept anything or anyone offered by Titus Girdleston?

"Are you a spy?" she asked casually, returning to the papers. Certainly he behaved less and less like a groom.

"What?"

She took a deep breath, glanced at the sleeping duke, and lowered her voice. "You've admitted to a new post inside the house, despite your insistence that we all regard you as a groom. You've tailed me from dinner. And you are still here, *in the library*, where no groom ever need tread."

She came to the bottom of the stack and found only markers for gambling debts and bills for hair tonic and snuff boxes.

"Are you suggesting that you could have dragged the duke all this way yourself?" he asked.

"I could have managed. Never let it be said that I am ungrateful for your assistance. Thank you, Mr. Sham."

"It's *Shaw.*" A frustrated pause. "Look, sweetheart, I'm here to serve. Whatever you need." Another pause. "Obviously."

Helena felt color rise into her cheeks. No one had ever referred to her as anything but "my lady" or "Lady Helena," and she'd never been called "sweetheart," not once. She slid from the desk, twitchy and unsettled. Two parallel bookshelves stretched to the back of the room, and she disappeared between them, studying titles. First insubordination and impertinence and now *sweetheart*?

"What's to be found in the duke's study?" Shaw asked—same question, new variation. He was definitely a spy. How stupid and careless had she been? Acquiring *a spy* within ten minutes of her arrival? She cursed under her breath.

"Can you read, Mr. Shaw?" she asked.

"Yes, I read." His tone made it obvious that she'd insulted him. She told herself that she didn't care. She told herself that she would send him away, in earnest this time. She kept walking.

"You're searching for something?" he guessed.

"I'm searching, and you're spying," she said. "How astute we both are."

"I'm not a spy."

"No?" she asked. "So you've *not* been hired by Titus Girdleston to follow, and observe, and report like a *spy*?"

She reached the end of the shelf—a vast collection on dog breeds and animal husbandry—and turned, disappearing down another cavern of shelves.

"Nope . . ." He followed her.

"If you are not a spy," she said, "and you are not a groom—"

"I am a groom."

She whirled around. "You look nothing like a groom. You're too large, you show absolutely no deference, and you look ridiculous in livery. No man of your . . . your . . . bearing would pursue employment that stipulated *yellow velvet*. No groom would stalk me through a library."

"If you thought I was something other than a groom, then why did you agree to my service?"

Ah, the question of the century, she thought. *Second only to, Why am I arguing with you now?*

He persisted. "When Girdleston offered, why not refuse?"

She said, "You looked useful."

"I am useful."

"And you looked biddable."

"I'm—"

He struggled to confirm this. She wanted to laugh. If her time in the study had not been so incredibly risky, and fraught, and fleeting, she would have laughed. But every moment in Lusk House was risky, fraught, and fleeting and there was no time for laughter. There was also no time for this conversation, and yet—

"*You* thought I was stupid," he realized.

"Your face did not have the look of inherent cruelness," she corrected, speaking to the books. "Like the others. You did not look *mean*."

"You thought you could manage me," he corrected.

She looked up. "I *can* manage you."

"You cannot," he shot back. "And you should

know that I am very . . ." he swallowed, ". . . mean."

Now she did laugh, and they heard the duke stir. Helena clamped a hand over her mouth, looking at Shaw with wide eyes.

Shhh, he motioned, a finger to his lips. They leaned to see around the shelf. The duke rolled to his side, mashing his doughy face against the leather, and resumed snoring.

He whispered, "And I'm not a spy."

"Then what are you?"

He paused, staring into her eyes. She stared back, relishing the opportunity to study the handsome symmetry of his face. His jaw was angled, his nose exactly the right size, his mouth full but wholly masculine. She thought again of how he looked confident and commanding but not petty. He did not look like he would take advantage of her simply because he was big and strong and was employed by her sworn enemy. It was something about his eyes, she thought. He was the rare combination of fierceness and confidence and something more.

She wondered where Girdleston had found him. Most of the Lusk House servants were stiff and sour and had worked for the family for generations. Her impression on previous visits had been a sort of "stoic loyalty" among the staff. This man had the bearing of someone who . . . who might be only passing through.

Finally, Shaw spoke. "How about you tell me your purpose, and I'll tell you mine."

"I beg your pardon?" The words *Absolutely not* shot immediately to the tip of her tongue. And yet—

And yet she could not seem to say the words. He stood very close. So close her skirts brushed against his boot. Close enough to see a scar below his ear. She had the vague instinct to take a step back. *I should run,* she thought. Instead, she licked her upper lip. He stared at her mouth.

Slowly, he repeated, "How about you tell me your—"

"You first," she said, calling his bluff.

"No."

"Why not?"

"It is obvious what I am doing."

She laughed. "It is not."

"Even so. I proposed the deal. My rules."

"You are demanding," she said, "for a groom."

He flashed her a look: *And?*

And nothing, she thought. Everything about this exchange was inappropriate. She turned away, walking the length of the shelf, sliding a hand along the spines of Greek tragedies. How inappropriate: the unconscious duke, the dim warren of shelves, the family elsewhere in the house. Years later, she would ask herself why. Why not flee the library? Why not ignore him and go about her business in silence?

Her reason, she thought, then and now, was that she was so very weary of fleeing and silence.

He ambled behind her, coming up close, closer than before. How close, she wondered, would he come?

Close enough to whisper his purpose?

Close enough to touch?

The thought of touching him, of glancing her

hand on his arm, or shoulder, or broad back, became a mesmerizing distraction in an already distracting conversation.

Before this moment, Helena's proximity to men had been the bouncy distance of a quadrille or the itchy distance of apple-tree shoots, but now dancing and apple trees were the farthest things from her mind. Her senses were fixed on this man in a way she could scarcely understand. Her whole consciousness seemed to reach in his direction.

And he'd called her sweetheart.

And he'd looked at the duke with open disgust.

And he wanted to make a deal.

She stopped walking and leaned against the shelf, her back resting against the books. He came up beside her, close enough to smell—wind, and horses, and *man*. She felt as if she was hemmed in by his body, and she liked it.

He reached for a shelf above their heads and hooked his hand on the ledge. He looked down, and she turned her face up. They did not touch but they were nestled, like a soft chestnut inside its hard shell. They were a silent, matched pair of indecision and judgment. The air between them strummed with a strange, delicious tension. Helena felt light and twitchy and expectant.

By sheer force of will, she began with an obvious lie. "My business is . . . I'm making the duke comfortable until pudding."

"Hilarious," he said. "Try again."

She smothered a laugh and rolled from the shelf. She followed the aisle to the end. He was behind her in an instant, eliciting a senseless thrill. But hadn't Gran always said that senseless thrills were the very best kind? Why risk everything to avoid the duke if not to experience thrills that made no sense?

I want to tell him, she realized.

The reasons began to pile up like eggs in an apron. She was weary of running. She wanted to state her opposition to someone who would listen. Would Declan Shaw listen? He'd certainly asked her enough times. He was veritably begging her to tell him more.

So he might use it against me, she thought—her last useful thought; her swan song before she revealed all the things she'd wanted to say for years.

She stopped suddenly and spun. He was on her heels, he came up short, and they collided. He reached out and caught her. She felt his strength as if she'd bumped into a tree. She did not pull away.

"I won't marry the duke," she whispered. "In case there was any doubt."

There. She'd said it. The first damning thing.

"Why not?"

"No one *asks me* that."

"I'm asking."

She felt a shimmer inside of her. She looked up. "Because you are a spy."

"I am a groom."

Another laugh. "Neither spy nor groom would be privy to this answer."

"Tell me anyway," he whispered, tipping his head. He broadened his stance, giving her room. He did not let go.

The answer, she realized, was bursting to come out.

"I won't marry him because he is ridiculous. And drunk most of the time. Because he's made no effort to know me. Because the very little he *does* know about me, he doesn't like—a sentiment I share. Furthermore, the Somerset estates that will merge because of our marriage will represent a giant financial windfall for both families. His family's mines and my family's river will mean more efficient transport of limestone to the Bay of Bristol. Apparently, this arrangement has needed only a wedding to be realized. Two families who are already so very rich will become richer—but at the cost of an ancient forest very dear to me, and the crofters who currently call the forest home. I cultivate a very rare variety of apples, you see—"

"The apple you offered me?"

"Yes, and how unfortunate you refused it. I gave it to a footman. They are delicious. And the season is over."

"I wanted to take it."

She paused at this, studying his face. He was so very handsome her stomach somersaulted.

Slowly, she finished her admission. "Lastly, I will not marry him because my life is my own, and I value my right to choose a husband, not someone arranged by my parents. Or Titus Girdleston." She made a face of disgust.

Shaw looked away and blew out a weary breath.

"If you are a spy, and you expected me to be impulsive or recalcitrant or daft, you were wrong," she said.

He looked at the floor and then to her. His face was a complicated mix of concern and . . . conflict. Looking into his brown eyes was like reading a language she sort of knew, like when she could almost read Spanish because she spoke Italian. The words were different but the roots were the same. She could *just* make out his meaning.

"How do you intend to get out of it?" Shaw asked.

"Out of what?"

"The marriage."

She laughed. "How utterly reckless would I be to reveal that?"

"Forgive me if you strike me as the reckless sort."

She sniffed, edging backward and slipping from his grasp. The loss of heat and touch was immediate, like pulling a shade against the sun. She tried, "But why does it matter how?"

"Honestly? I'm . . . intrigued."

Something about those words elicited the oddest little flip in her belly, like she'd jumped a fence on horseback. She considered the notion of intriguing him. She thought of the months and years she'd schemed, working alone. No one else cared, except to oppose her.

If he is a spy, she thought, *his entire purpose is to oppose and thwart me.* She glanced up at him. He raised his eyebrows. He did not seem like an opponent.

He is the soul of opposition, she thought, but she heard herself say, "I'm going to find some other, more suitable girl for the duke to marry. I'm going to haul her in front of him and have her somehow . . . enchant him."

She swallowed hard. When she said it out loud, with Shaw staring so intently at her, with the unconscious duke just steps away, the plan sounded . . . ambitious.

She plowed on. "After he is enchanted by this . . . better girl, he will defy his uncle for the first time in life, and he will throw me over for her. The girl he really wants. That is my plan."

Shaw's brown eyes narrowed, searching her face. She thought again of how long it had been since anyone had considered what she said. Even the crofters in the forest, her closet allies, listened only to comply or revere. There was no consideration, they simply followed.

She could see him struggling to comprehend the plan—the finding, the hauling, the enchanting, the jilting. If he dismissed it, would she care? Would she lose heart if he naysayed or laughed?

"And how," he asked, "do you intend to realize this plan?"

"Well . . ." she said cautiously, acknowledging that he had not dismissed or laughed, acknowledging that he had asked for more. "First I must locate a group of suitable potential duchesses to tempt him." She glanced at the slumbering duke. "Five or six, perhaps seven—if so many potential duchesses exist."

He exhaled wearily. "And then?"

"I will determine the most suitable ones. I don't want to pass on my terrible future to an unsuspecting girl. It must be a young woman who can tolerate him, obviously. Who aspires to be the Duchess of Lusk so intensely she can abide all the rest. For life." She made a horrified face. "When I find this person, I will acquaint them. The duke seems most interested in provocative, sort of . . . er, festive women. I mentioned that he must be enchanted. Obviously."

"Obviously," Shaw repeated. "And what role does the library play in this plan?" He looked at the shelves around them.

"Oh," she said, glancing at the books, "I'd hoped to discover a little more about him—beyond his interests in provocation and festivities. If I understood his passions, assuming he has any, or what type of girls he enjoys—I mean, besides buxom and giggly and, er, half dressed, traits he has mentioned to me on more than one occasion—I could better seek out the correct, most tempting girl. I thought his library might hold some insight into his soul."

"You've asked me if I could bloody *read* and then comb through a library looking for the passions of *this person*?" He cocked a thumb at the snoring duke.

Lusk stretched and scratched his crotch with an idle hand. He belched softly and flopped onto his back, snoring at the ceiling.

Helena glanced at Shaw, checking his reaction. He looked at the duke with unmasked irritation, like a man looking at rainwater as it drips through his roof.

"Now you," she said, turning to him. "Who are you and why have you been assigned to me?"

Chapter Five

At least he had not told her.

"At the very bloody least," Declan said to himself, making a noise of disgust. Three hours had passed since the library, and he stood in the dark stables, brushing the golden coat of a gelding by the light of a single lantern.

Lady Helena had known he was a spy; she'd known within five minutes of their first stilted conversation. She didn't know he was, in fact, *more* than a spy, but she was a clever girl. It was only a matter of time. Declan had no reason to gloat about not telling her. He hadn't prevailed, he'd run out of time.

Girdleston had turned up in the library, interrupting their confessions. The snoring duke had been hauled away by his valet and Helena had been marched back to the dining room. Declan was given no choice but to follow.

He paused now, rubbing a hand over the horse's coat. Speaking softly to the gelding, he lifted his hoof to inspect a shoe. Lusk's horses were meticulously cared for, and this animal was no exception.

Lady Helena will be meticulously cared for, he thought.

Lady Helena is not a horse.

And this was his problem.

He'd not expected to feel sympathy for Lady Helena Lark. She was a client, and a nobleman's daughter, a class apart. Her unhappiness had nothing to do with himself or his family.

There had been no time for Declan to look in on his father and sisters when he left Newgate. He'd hurried to Lusk House and sent word by private messenger, an expense he could hardly afford. His father would be relieved by his freedom, and Declan prayed his anguish over his son's incarceration had not damaged his already frail health.

Peter Shaw had served King and Country for forty years in his role of tailor to the Royal Marines. He was a craftsman of the highest order, but years of squinting at a tiny needle and thread in the candlelight had left him nearly blind and riddled with headaches. Lifting heavy bolts of wool and stooping over a worktable had crippled his back. Peter Shaw's uniforms leant warmth and polish to the British Army, but tailor services never made anyone rich. Declan's father's pension barely kept him in food and fuel. He was old before his time, unwell, and struggling.

This was the year he'd planned to move Peter from London to the countryside. They'd been searching for a cottage, someplace with a warm hearth and a bed on the ground floor. Declan envisioned a temperate, peaceful shire, where he could walk to a nearby village, read in the sunshine, breathe clean air.

The plan would also benefit his two sisters, who would thrive in gentler, slower country lives and the opportunity to marry decent men away from the crime of London.

All of it had languished when Declan was arrested, and now it could only be realized if he earned Girdleston's payout. Meanwhile, Helena Lark would enjoy an aristocrat's life of luxury, whether she married the Duke of Lusk or not.

And yet—

And yet, he hadn't been able to get her out of his head. He saw her in his mind's eye, a series of hot, candlelit flashes. Lady Helena, leaning against a bookshelf, looking up with pale green eyes, her lips slightly parted. Lady Helena, moving through the library as if she was already mistress of the house, beckoning him, disappearing around the next aisle of books.

Declan swore and stepped back from the horse. He was just about to move to the sorrel in the next stall when he heard rustling in the doorway. He glanced up, expecting another groom. "Hello?" he called, stepping into the center aisle.

The door was empty. The night was dark, and he could just make out loose hay and autumn leaves swirling in the alley.

"Hel—"

"Shhh!" someone whispered, cutting him off. The sound was close. Distinctly feminine. Heart-poundingly familiar.

Declan went still. *Surely not. Surely,* surely *not.*

"Who's there?" he tried.

Instead of answering, Lady Helena Lark

stepped from the shadows.

Declan could not have been more shocked if she'd drifted from the rafters like a feather. He blinked twice, took a step forward, stopped. Words tumbled inside his head, too many to choose. His mouth was locked half open.

She wore white. A night rail so profuse with billowing fabric the very whiteness and fluffy volume seemed to reflect the moonlight like snow. She appeared almost strangled by the high white neck, her chin tickled by a veritable tide of frothy lace. The hem swamped her feet. Her hair had been braided into a single, thick plait, which hung heavily over her shoulder. She looked young and celestial and a little bit suffocated. She looked—

"Do not be alarmed," she said matter-of-factly.

"Too late," he rasped. He spoke haltingly. His voice cracked. "What are you doing?"

"Our conversation was cut short."

"What are you wearing?"

"A nightgown."

Declan took a moment to allow the answer to penetrate. Did she wish to shock him? To provoke?

"Fine," she said, letting out an exasperated sigh. "It's is a night rail and robe. My grandmother had it made for me before she died. I pull it out when I require a bit of costumed embellishment. It was exceedingly useful during the madwoman phase of my Resistance."

"What does that mean?"

She rolled her shoulders as if burdened by retelling a tedious bit of boring family lore. "One way of the ways I've tried to avoid this wedding was to feign madness."

"Naturally," he sighed.

"I know the gown is ridiculous," she pronounced, "but I rather like it. Especially because Girdleston does not. He caught sight of me sailing down a corridor one night and cried out, dropping a glass. It's a powerful tool actually. I haul it out whenever I wish to appear ghostly or unhinged. It is particularly effective when combined with a pantomime of sleepwalking. And then there is Lusk's reaction." She took up a billowy swath of fabric and fluffed it. "It's the virginal sort of . . . density of it, I believe. So, there's an added benefit."

Declan wondered what sort of man thought to run away when he saw this woman. In any garment. "So you've come alone? To the stables? Dressed like . . . like that. On purpose?" he asked.

She nodded. "In case I encountered anyone. This nightgown is a sort of shorthand for my intermittent madness. It unnerves people. No one likes the bother."

"I am not unnerved," he said. "Just to be clear."

Helena paused for a moment, considering this. A tantalizing pinkness warmed her cheeks. She cleared her throat.

"And of course I have a purpose," she said. "One thing you should know about me is that nothing I do is arbitrary."

"And your current purpose would be . . . ?" He scanned the alley through the open door behind her. She had to go back, of course. She had to conceal herself and go back.

"My purpose is," she said, "we had a deal, Mr. Shaw."

"Lady Helena. You cannot—"

"I know, I know," she said impatiently. "I may not leave my room," she recited. "I may not wear my nightclothes in the stable—"

"Stop," he said. "Turn around. Go back into the house."

"Not until we've spoken," she said breezily. She gathered up handfuls of her gown and trudged closer. Beneath her hem, she wore leather boots and drooping stockings. Her legs were bare above the ankles. His mind frosted over with desire.

"Where can we speak?" she asked, coming up to the first stall.

"We cannot speak," he said.

She stepped in front of a lantern, and the thick layers of white went magically translucent. He could make out the outline of her body as if she stood naked behind a thin sheet.

Explanations failed him. Strategy failed him. She was perfectly formed. Thin and long-legged, with small, pert breasts. So lovely and natural and unexpected. Declan couldn't remember ever seeing anything quite as lovely.

"Can we speak in a stall?" she suggested. "Have you learned which horse is the calmest?"

He thought of what creature, equine or other, could be calm in her presence.

"Oh," she crooned, looking to the next stall, "a palomino." She pulled an apple from her pocket and moved to the gate, clucking softly to the horse. The animal, half dozing, opened its eyes and caught sight of the shifting white gown and spooked, neighing nervously, crowding himself in the corner, stomping.

Declan swore. "You're frightening the horses."

"I'm not. I'm merely—"

In one fluid movement, he fastened his hands around her waist and lifted her up, backing them away from the anxious animal. Helena let out a little yelp, but he kept moving.

"You *are* mad," he said, gathering up arms and legs and yards of white fabric. The gown wrapped around his forearms, tangling him like a net. He struggled to find her body within the cottony vortex of it, the robe trailing behind them like a train. Swearing again, he hoisted her into his arms like a mermaid.

"I can walk," she said.

"But you weren't walking, were you? You were inciting a stampede. Horses don't like things they cannot understand."

But I do, he thought. He glanced down at her and then away. *God help me.*

She said nothing, allowing him to carry her. He stalked past the tack room, the bridle room, the blacksmith's station. His only plan was to remove her from the open stable door and the sleepy horses. The building ended with the carriage room and he slowed only long enough to nudge through the door.

"The other grooms have gone," she informed him. "I made certain. I am only seen when I wish to be seen."

"Shhh," Declan said, but he thought, *You must want me to see you very much.*

I see only you.

Darkness pervaded the carriage room. The corners were swallowed by shadows. The duke's four vehicles loomed like carriage-shaped voids. A distant window offered a dusty rectangle of silver moonlight. Declan blinked, willing his eyes to adjust. He closed the door gently with his hip and pivoted. For a long moment, he held her, listening, alert for any stray movement or sound.

In his arms, she breathed in and out. Her breath on his neck was a caress. It wrecked his concentration.

You were in jail too long, he told himself. Across the room, he could just make out a workbench, clean and level. He strode to it, plunking her down.

"You have five minutes," he said.

She jolted when her bottom hit the bench—*"Oof!"*—but did not resist. She reached out for balance, clasping his biceps with both hands.

"Five," he repeated, staring at her bare fingers on his arms. His own hands were buried in layers of white fabric, holding tightly to the curve of her waist.

"And what should I say in these five allotted minutes?"

"You're joking?"

"Yes," she said coolly, "I'm joking. It is such a lark when servants take me up and haul me into dark rooms to interrogate me. Which, by the way, is precisely the behavior of a spy."

"Not this again," he groaned.

"Of course, this."

"My lady . . ." he warned. His hands slid from

her waist. He stepped back.

She held up a hand. "Look, Shaw, I know you are not a groom. I know Girdleston assigned you to me for some restrictive, duplicitous reason. My work avoiding this wedding is too important for me not to know your assignment or the reason for it."

"Fine," he said. "*If* I was a spy, do you think I would tell you?"

"If you were a spy, a real spy, I don't think you would have allowed the library to go unchecked. And yet Girdleston appears to know nothing. *If* you were a spy, you would not be entertaining me in this stable—"

"I'm *not* entertaining you."

"You are not marching back to the house." She raised an eyebrow. "Please be aware: if you are spy, you are very bad at it."

"I am a groom," he tried.

"If you are a groom, you are familiar and entitled and bossy."

"Your five minutes are up."

"I need more time."

"And I need you safely back inside the house."

"These first five minutes were not the only reason I've come. I have something else to ask you."

"I have nothing else to tell you," he said, but in truth, he thought he could talk to her all night.

"It's not a question, it's a request. And your answer will inform all my other concerns. I need your help."

Declan went still. This sounded like a trap. "What help? The kind of help available from a stable groom?"

She shrugged. "Possibly. It's for tomorrow. There's a party I'm meant to attend with my mother and sisters."

"And what is proven if I refuse to help?"

She waved a dismissive hand. "Do not trouble yourself. The important thing is, if you do it, it will help me a great deal. And if you refuse, your loyalties will be revealed. And I can make do."

Declan tried to make sense of this. "How will my loyalties be revealed?"

She shrugged. "Will you listen to the request?"

"Do I have a choice?"

"You could haul me inside and hand me over to Girdleston. But that, too, would tell me so much."

Declan sighed. She'd known that she would be safe here with him. She'd known that Girdleston would not be informed. He was doomed. He was utterly doomed.

"Lovely," she said, forging ahead. "Here is my request. This party should include the usual trappings, tea and cake, with droves of gossipy women and piles of gifts. So many gifts, in fact, I believe we will require several carriages for the purpose of conveying them home. I cannot imagine that grooms will not be part of this . . . transport."

"The coachman mentioned this," he said cautiously.

"Right." She planted her hands on the bench, sending waves of billowing fabric puffing in drifts down her body. "Well, because you are my *private* groom, I should like to have you there to attend me. *Inside* this party."

"Inside a ladies' tea party?"

"Actually, it's a garden party," she mused. "That is, if the weather holds. Lady Canning's garden is a great source of vanity. If it is remotely mild and dry, apparently we will be outside. Either way, I shall need your help, but certainly this will be easier done if we are in the garden."

"*What* will be easier? What is my objective?"

"Are you asking for your faux objective, or your actual objective?"

Declan swore in his head and turned away. He looked at the glow of moonlight through the window and thought of his jail cell. He thought of his father and the small, fogged window of his bedroom beside his tailor shop. He thought of his own bloody survival. She was like a dervish, but if he concentrated, if he really concentrated, he could just see beyond the cyclone.

"I'm asking for *all* objectives," he said slowly, turning back. "What can you possibly expect a liveried groom to do inside a society party?"

Lady Helena's held up slim fingers and ticked off expectations. "One of my mother's gossipy friends has been invited. This is a great stroke of luck, as she is my greatest hope for building a list of potential duchesses for the duke."

Declan blinked, trying to dissipate the shadows. Was she asking him to be complicit? Was the question no longer *Are you a spy?* Was it *Help me run away*?

He began shaking his head.

No. No. No.

No.

Lady Helena forged on. "The woman won't rattle off the names outright, of course, but I feel certain I can dislodge them through gossip and flattery, et cetera."

He gritted out, "And my role?"

"You will be assisting with my many packages and parcels—all the gifts I shall receive because I am Lusk's bride-to-be."

"There are footmen for this."

"But only my personal groom can be trusted with our gifts," she amended. "And while you are inventorying and guarding the gifts, you will also be standing ready."

"Ready for what?"

"For me to sail by rather quickly and—"

"Oh God."

"—take down the names of the girls I learn from my mother's friend. To record any useful gossip I discern. I could never take down these notes while I'm circulating. I couldn't remember everything I hope to learn. I'm wholly unschooled in London gossip. These names and directions will have no value to me. It will be like a foreign language."

"*No.*"

"But you've hardly considered it," she countered. "The task is only to stand near the gifts, inventory them—or pretend to inventory, honestly, who cares—and I will whisper my findings to you each time I come 'round. We need only paper and pen, which I will provide in the morning. Think of your secret role as Girdleston's nonspy spy. What better way to keep an eye on me than to be within the bounds of the party."

He stared at her, disbelieving.

I must reveal nothing but detachment and invisibil-

ity and a closed door.

Too bloody late for that.

Finally, he said, "You are aware that grooms have no business inside parties. Nor do they take dictation. And even if they did, I am employed by Girdleston. You are actively trying to undermine him."

"You cannot possibly have loyalty to Lusk or Girdleston or the dukedom," she said. "That was plain to me in the library."

Declan opened his mouth, then closed it. She was correct, of course. He'd recoiled at the sight of the unconscious duke. Looking back, he'd *wanted* her to see his disgust.

"Make no mistake," she went on, "I know you have no loyalty to me, either. We've only just met." She raised an eyebrow and flicked the thick rope of her braid over her shoulder. It hit the workbench with a thump. His gaze slid from her head to her boots again, and his body responded. Desire surged like a falcon on a tether.

How could he be invigorated by the sight of her when he could barely see her? And what he saw was buried in ten yards of white cotton. Why was it impossible not to look?

I'm exhausted, he thought errantly. *I began the day in prison, I made a deal with the devil, and now I'm in hell—all in one day. Exhausted.*

But that was a lie. He was not exhausted.

He should be. Any sane man would be. Instead, he felt like a thick bolt of lightning had made prolonged contact with the top of his head. His heart thudded. Every nerve was alive to the sheer challenge of Helena Lark.

He was just about to tell her that her five minutes were up when a loud, shrill sound rent the night, freezing them in place.

Crreeakk—the unmistakable sound of a swinging stable gate.

In unison, their heads snapped to the door. Helena sucked in a gasp. Declan brought a finger to his lips. *Shhh*.

Silence. Night noises fell into a hush.

Declan cocked his head, straining to hear footsteps, or the clink of tack, or the jostling of a chain.

Heart drumming, every muscle poised to scoop her up and dive into the shadows, he scanned the dark room. He'd closed the door but had not locked it, which was a reckless, amateur mistake. Now the closed door obscured his hearing while the open lock left them unprotected. *Stupid, stupid, distracted, stupid*.

Slowly, sound by sound, the night reanimated. He heard hoofbeats in the distance. Gutters dripped. Insects clicked and whirred.

Helena sucked in a breath to speak. "I will—"

Declan leapt forward, wrapping an arm around her shoulder and pressing a hand over her mouth.

"Shhh," he whispered, speaking to the whirl of her ear.

She went tense. She breathed in a slow, shaky breath.

"Not yet," he whispered, his lips against her ear.

She nodded. Another moment passed. And another.

The night unspooled with no other sound

but the rapid draw of their mingled breath. Far away, someone laughed. A horse whinnied. London rumbled at a low shuffle. Declan's heartbeat slowed; he swallowed, and let out a breath.

Bone by bone, Helena's tenseness began to drain. She went soft and malleable beneath his hands. He'd been braced against her, but her shoulders relaxed. She was soft in his arms. Her neck bowed, tipping her chin into his wrist.

She was perched on the edge of the bench, her knees sticking out, and they parted just a little—just enough. His thighs slid between her legs; he was flush against the bench, her legs on either side of him. He need only scoop her up to hold her. She need only wrap her legs around his haunches to—

He held his breath, not trusting himself to move.

Softly, she murmured some word. He was reminded his hand covered her mouth. He released her. His palm settled on her thigh.

"It must have been nothing," he said softly. "The wind."

She licked her lips, nodded, rustled.

Move away, he ordered.

Move on.

Move your head from your loins.

Move your priorities into plain view.

Declan did not move.

One hand held her shoulder, the other clenched her thigh. The cotton was fine beneath his fingers and, idly, he rubbed circles into the warmth of her skin.

She looked up. He could just make out the

green of her eyes. She appeared . . . mystified, like she was walking through a dream.

Declan's control, already so thin, rapidly drained away. A very distant chant of *No, no, no* pecked his brain, an inconsequential bird in an inconsequential tree, miles away.

"This is new," she whispered, "in the way of resistance." She licked her lips. "I had not thought to seduce one of the grooms."

"Please do not say that," he rumbled. "This is not resistance, nor seduction. This is *not happening*."

"I believe it is happening," she said. "I've never been . . . *taken up* by a man before. It is a singular experience."

Declan opened his mouth to say something but realized that honestly there was nothing he could say. He thought of pulling away but did not have the strength. He thought of tossing her over his shoulder and hauling her to the house, but that ship had sailed. He didn't have the will to return h—

Suddenly he was struck by the glimmer of an idea.

A very bad but potentially effective idea.

It would be like dropping a heavy bundle down a hill instead of lugging it down on his back.

He stepped closer and repeated her last words. "A singular experience, you say?"

She narrowed her eyes, confused. Her lips formed the most irresistible almost-smile.

If she told him to stop, he would. If she looked alarmed or distressed, he would stop.

If she was afraid of him, she would not ask favors of him or test his loyalties.

If she was afraid of him, she would not seek him out in dark stables.

If she was afraid of him, she would not torture him.

He stared at her mouth, waiting impatiently for her to say the word.

Please tell me to stop.

Slowly, carefully, with fingers that shook, he reseated his hands on her waist. He met her gaze; their eyes locked. His expression was meant to convey entitlement and possession and strength.

She laughed.

She actually laughed. A light, musical sound. "Well," she said. "Come on, then."

Declan growled, and scooted her to the edge of the workbench in one forceful yank. She sucked in a little breath. She settled her hands on his forearms as she tipped her head up. The word *stop* seemed like the farthest thing from her mind.

Declan went slowly, carefully, closing the distance between them. With the pressure of a feather, he bussed her lips with a soft kiss. Once. Twice . . .

So soft. Oh God, so soft. His eyes drifted closed. He dipped again. On the third pass, he remained *right there,* his bottom lip pressed to the crease of her mouth. He nibbled, gave a teasing lick.

Helena smiled, trying to follow along. Her eager innocence was his undoing.

He wanted to devour her. Everything about her—her confidence, her cleverness and courage, her ridiculous grandmotherly gown—made him ravenous. She was so deliciously unschooled, uncertain but intoxicatingly eager.

She let out a little sound, the noise of delight and desire, and it was nearly his undoing. His hands moved, smoothing his palms from her waist up the curve of her back. He felt her braid against the back of his hand and fumbled for it, wrapping it around his knuckles. He tugged, ever so slightly. Lady Helena arched her neck and sighed.

She'd held her body taut and upright, straining for his lips, but now she moved in a languid sort of daze, coming alive under his hands. She turned her head to breathe and her cheek scraped the stubble of his beard. Her hands climbed from his neck and dug into his hair, squeezing, pressing his face down. She burrowed into his chest until there was nothing between them. The soft, slight weight of her imprinted on him like warm wind to a stiff sail. His chest swelled; she filled his consciousness. He was propelled while he stood stock-still.

The heartbeat in his ears accelerated, blotting out all sound. If every horse in the stable had been set free, he would not have heard. His vision was reduced to flashes of her skin and her gown and *her*. Every sense was alive with Helena Lark.

He tried to think, he *meant* to think, but he'd been plunged into a pool of desire, and he was too far from the surface to swim up. He wanted to drown.

She was such a quick learner. When he tipped his head one way, she canted the other. When he teased her with his tongue, she met him with her own. Her hands trailed from his hair, down his neck, off his shoulders, kneading all the way. When she reached his biceps, she dug in. Her right leg hooked behind his left knee, and Declan groaned into her mouth.

The embrace unspooled so slowly, so gently. It was like unwrapping a delicate, forbidden gift that belonged to someone else. He was no thief, but God, he wanted this. With shaking hands, he worked back layers of ribbon and tissue, careful not to unsettle what was inside.

All the while, she kissed and kissed and melted against him, and he went on basking in her until his bad idea felt like the very best idea he'd ever had.

HELENA LARK SHOULD not have thought of her grandmother during her first real kiss. She knew this. Thoughts of Gran were distracting and strange and a waste of very precious time. Even so, it was Rosemary Lark's voice she heard in the final lucid moments before desire swallowed her up.

Well done, Lena, said the sweet, aged voice. *I should expect nothing else.*

Or that was what Helena hoped she would say.

Gran had been a purveyor of darkened stables, ridiculous nightgowns, and men of dubious, groom-spy distinctions.

Helena felt another swipe of Shaw's mouth, and stopped thinking. Sensation shimmered over her like a net, and she knew only sound and feeling and breath.

How could she think when she was working so very hard to keep up with his mouth? His lips were there one moment, gone the next, there again. Oh, but the last kiss did not retreat; it was prolonged softness, then less soft, then not soft at all, but thrilling. His mouth canted slightly and they fit perfectly together, two halves of a whole; then he canted left and they fit again. It was soft and slick and fast and very, very slow. Desire filled her body like steamy water filling a copper tub: fogged brain, flushed chest, her insides a swirl of liquid heat.

While she melted, strength poured from him like a river over a wheel, and Helena spun and spun. Large hands roved her back. Her instinct was to fall back to be held, but she also wanted to climb him. He allowed for it all, holding her upright with muscled arms and thighs that felt like marble.

With concerted effort, she remembered to breathe. There was so much to *feel*. She explored the smooth, roped muscles of his back, sliding searching hands along his sides. When she reached his shoulders, she hooked her arms on both sides and pulled up, straining closer to his mouth.

When she finally turned her head to suck in air, Shaw dropped his mouth to her exposed neck, kissing a hot trail from beneath her ear to the fluffy collar of her robe.

"This isn't happening," he said against her chin.

"You have a distorted view of reality," she gasped. "I assure you, it is happening."

"You're afraid," he said, reclaiming her mouth. "I'm scaring you away."

"What?" she asked, barely hearing.

"So afraid," he moaned.

"Wai—" she breathed, but he captured her mouth again. Helena melted into the renewed kiss. His tongue was there now, a fascinating addition to the enterprise. She hung on and tried very hard to remember what he'd just said. Softly, in the back of her mind, his words called.

You're afraid.

Had he said this? She couldn't remember. She dropped her head against his neck and allowed him to trace hungry kisses behind her ear. He gathered her up, scooping hands beneath her bottom and pressing her to him. Helena had the errant thought that they absolutely, positively, must do all of this again, and very soon.

Meanwhile, the more he kissed her, the louder his last mumbled statement echoed in her head.

"Wait," she panted, breathing out the word at last.

Shaw's mouth froze a heartbeat from hers. He made a slight choking noise. He pulled back. His expression went from hot and half-lidded to stricken and terrified.

Without thinking, she pressed a hand over his mouth exactly as he had done.

"Wait, wait, wait," she repeated. She sounded like a stage director halting a bad scene.

Slowly, the strings of her mind began to strum like a functioning instrument. She swallowed hard. "Did you just say that I'm frightened?"

"Ah—" he stammered, his lips moving beneath

her palm. He looked as if she'd doused him with cold water.

"Right," she continued. "That's what I thought you said. First of all, shame on you. You cannot imagine how I've been bullied and threatened these last five years. And now you endeavor to scare me? Thank God you're so very bad at it. There is nothing about you that scares me. I hope this does not distress or unman you, but it's true." She took a deep breath. She flung her braid over her shoulder.

Shaw made another distressed sound beneath her palm, and she released him. He staggered two steps back, his brown eyes huge. He wiped his face with the back of his hand. "My lady—" he rasped.

She held up a hand. "Was that it? You kissed me to frighten me away?"

"I don't—" he began.

She continued, "If you wish to frighten me, then embody the figure of an incurious duke, sleep half the day, and stagger about at night in a drunken stupor. Have no concerns beyond your appearance and no interest beyond the next bacchanal. Then have a puppeteer uncle force us to marry. Now *that* would scare me."

Shaw walked in an agitated circle and then returned to her. He pointed a finger at her. "*You* are too honest, in case you are not aware." She stared at the tip of his finger until her eyes went a little cross, and he dropped it. She chuckled. None of her previous visits to London were ever this diverting.

"It is not necessary," he continued, "to share

your every experience with me. I am *reeling*, in fact, from your great wealth of heartfelt revelations."

"You're angry?" she asked. "Angry? Because you tried and failed to frighten me with a kiss? Stop."

She shoved from the table. "I suppose this means I may stop worrying that you might think I was trying to seduce you."

He made another choking sound. "I beg your pardon?"

She began winding her way through the carriages. "I'd asked you for the favor," she reminded. "But I would never cajole you by . . . by doing what we've just done."

"I do not feel *cajoled*," he bit out.

A lone window glowed moonlight on the far wall, and she went to it. "I would never try to manipulate you through . . . er, seduction." It could not be said enough.

"Rest easy, sweetheart, I cannot be seduced."

She glanced over her shoulder. He did not look un-seducible. His hair was tussled, his tunic was askew, his expression was strained. He looked like a bear staggering out of hibernation.

"Good," she said. There was a door beside the window, and she hurried to it.

"Good," he repeated.

"*I* know that *you* know that I wasn't plying you with my, er, charms."

"You're beautiful, my lady," he sighed, "but not *that* beautiful."

Helena paused with her hand an inch from the doorknob. She turned back to him. "I beg your pardon?"

"Nothing." A growl.

"That was unnecessarily rude."

"That was the point," he mumbled. "I am rude. I am terrible. I am not to be trifled with. I am . . ."

He muttered to himself and spun away, mussing his disheveled hair again. He snatched a coil of rope from a carriage and tossed it on a bench. He clamped his hands behind his head and turned away.

"You should go," he said, spinning back. "How did you leave the house?"

She glared and reached again for the door. "Good night, Mr. Shaw."

The cold moonlight hit her like a slap, and she sucked in a little breath. She looked right and left, checking the alley, and then picked her way along the side of the stable.

He followed. "It's risky for me to escort you, but I can follow from a distance. Tell me your plan."

"Go to the devil."

"My lady . . ."

She sighed. "There is a side door that leads to the cellar."

"*Of* course," he breathed. "Did you leave it unlocked?"

"*Of* course," she mimicked.

They reached the low wall that lined the Lusk garden and she said, "I'm expecting your help tomorrow. Pray, do not disappoint me."

Before he could answer, she scuttled over the wall. She heard him swear softly into the night.

"Take care inside the dark house," he called in a whisper. "Go immediately to bed. This never happened."

Helena ignored him. She crept through the moonlight garden and around the side of the terrace. Her mind was full. Her chest felt uneven; corners and crevices were rearranging themselves inside her heart. The cellar steps descended behind a stone ledge, and she hit them at a run, not looking back. She felt Declan Shaw's gaze on her until the heavy cellar door closed out the night.

What she did not know, what even Declan Shaw did not know, was that they were not alone. He was not the only one who watched her. A third person lurked in the garden that night, unseen to Helena or Declan or the chipmunks burrowing in the ivy. A cloaked figure, shoulders down, face obscured quietly, took in the impetuous heiress and the surly groom-spy and their fraught, silent, longing-filled good-bye.

Chapter Six

Declan waited all night to be sacked.

When morning dawned with no summons, he waited to be hauled to jail.

What in God's name have I done? The question beat in time to his breath, his footsteps, his heartbeat.

He'd left the stable in a haze, worried about Helena's progress and cagey with unsated desire. After the worry and the desire, regret slowly dawned—like misty cliffs seen from the deck of a boat. By the time the haze burned away, he was colliding with rock.

What. Have. I. Done?

He'd put his hands on a client. As violations went, it was previously unthinkable. He'd never once dallied with the provocative daughters of foreign merchants, nor the beguiling harem girls of generous sultans. Oh no, he'd waited until he was guarding the daughter of a bloody earl, and his job was to marry her off. And then he'd—

What have I done?

Gone and gotten yourself sacked, that's what.

Putting his hands on a client was a violation of

trust and safety and the opposite of his objective on this job.

When morning dawned with no termination, Declan embarked on the new day like a man who'd taken a dram of poison. At any moment, the deadly effects would hit.

But then breakfast came and went, morning chores—no accusations. Girdleston called for three carriages to muster in front of the house, with feathers and silks for the horses, dress livery for the grooms.

When they convened in Park Lane and the doors to Lusk House swung wide, family members spilled onto the stoop completely oblivious to him. He was indiscriminate groom Declan Shaw.

No one knew.

It felt like he'd somehow slipped from the hangman's noose. Actually, it felt like the noose held, but the gallows had splintered and he'd scrambled away. Now he ran through the streets with a rope around his neck.

But then Lady Helena emerged, stepping into the bright autumn sun, raising a gloved hand to shade her eyes, and all the rumination and regret drained away. Her family milled on the steps fussing over a dog, and she wound her way to the street like a bright petal dropped into a moving stream. Declan held his breath, watching her. His eyes burned and the broken-off thing in his chest sank lower, digging into his side. He reached for his metaphorical noose and tugged.

She'd worn indigo, a dark purple meant to be regal and majestic, something befitting a duchess, but it put Declan in mind of a mythical creature. A fairy, perhaps. Or a good witch. It was the color of the innermost petal of a wild iris, so very striking against the white mist of her skin. Her hair was loosely swept up and her posture was upright but languid. She did not appear violated or traumatized; she appeared . . . serene. She waited pleasantly in the street, allowing her family to precede her.

Declan forced himself not to look. He busied himself loading the women into a carriage, supporting elbows and holding parasols. He restrained the wolfhounds from bounding inside the vehicle. Loading women into a carriage was like shoving flapping birds into a small box.

Suddenly there she was. She turned and raised her pale-green gaze to his. Their eyes locked.

If he thought she would ignore him or scowl, he was wrong. If he thought he would see outrage or fear, he was also wrong.

Lady Helena fastened him with a look so familiar, so knowing and expectant, Declan glanced around to see if anyone else had seen.

But then the moment passed, and she affected a sort of exaggerated whirl of ruffled pelisse, and slinging reticule, and bobbing hat feather. When she was on the step, she managed to press a leather satchel into Declan's hands.

He shot her a questioning look. She cocked one eyebrow, another expression of emphasized familiarity. If no one noticed the first time, certainly they would now. He was given little choice but to stow the satchel on his shoulder and hand her up into the carriage.

A fellow groom offered to unburden him of the satchel and stow it in the boot, but Declan grunted some excuse. He slipped behind the carriage, heart in his throat, and opened the brass buckles.

It would contain a letter, he thought, condemning him for assault. It would be a warrant for his arrest. It would be some equestrian item from the stable that had tangled in her nightdress or stuck to her boot.

Instead, he found five pieces of parchment, an inkpot, and a quill. And a note.

Shaw,

Here are the items we discussed for taking inventory of the gifts. The weather has held, so the party will commence outside in Lady Canning's garden. When we arrive, please report to the gift table and stand ready.

Many thanks,
Lady Helena Lark

Chapter Seven

An hour later, Helena wound her way through Lady Canning's crowded garden, repeating the names of three potential duchesses in her head.

Miss Tasmin Lansing . . .

Lady Moira Ashington . . .

Miss Lisbette Twining . . .

She waved to her mother's maliciously chatty friend now drifting to a footman with a tray. The woman looked almost sated in the aftermath of whispering these incredibly specific and useful details. Of course she'd gushed a host of extraneous bits, but Helena had worked to remember only what she could use. She repeated the notes in her head as she checked the gift table. Shaw lurked, a golden-liveried pillar of disgust, towering above Lady Canning's rhododendrons and a lichen-covered statue of a satyr.

She'd set the odds of his cooperation at less than half. And by cooperation, she meant making the list and then also relinquishing it to her when it was finished. She knew well the tactic of playing along until the crucial moment and then refusing to follow through. It was precisely her current plan with Lusk.

But first things first: Shaw had turned up. It was a good sign. He alternately frowned and stared, his expression conveying barely concealed resentment. But he had come.

It was wrong, she knew, to feel an all-over sort of tingled rush at the sight of him. The sensations surely showed crimson or perhaps iridescent (was this possible?) on her face. She would later describe the feeling as "eruptive"—for all the good it would do her.

What would Gran say about the fizzing, sparking regard for a man who seemed only capable, at least at the moment, of glowering?

Miss Tasmin Lansing, Helena repeated, trying not to forget. *Lady Moira Ashington, Miss Lisbette Twining . . .*

She wondered if Shaw felt iridescent or tingling. He did not look like someone who remembered their time in the barn fondly . . . nor did he look like someone who experienced eruptive thinking.

But he'd come. She'd asked him for help, and he'd come.

Bracing herself for any myriad reactions, Helena repeated the names in her head and strode to the gift table.

"Chin up, Shaw," she said, careful to maintain an expression of businesslike aplomb. "I've a trove of information for you."

He stared at her as if she'd arrived in a damp toga. Slowly, he began to shake his head.

She chose to ignore this and eyed the many

packages and parcels on the gift table. She affected an expression of *Oh, I cannot wait to open these,* and gingerly fingered a floppy bow.

"Pretend I am instructing you about the gifts," she said, "but take down, if you please: Miss Tasmin Lansing, daughter of the Baron Whitney. When in London, they are in Bruton's Place, but she rides in Hyde Park on Wednesdays. She is determined to land a husband who outpaces the earl that her sister married. Brown hair, rather tall."

She sucked in a deep breath, ready for the next set of details, but he'd not moved. She whispered harshly, "*Write it down.* Miss Tasmin Lans—"

Shaw swore under his breath and snatched up the quill and paper. Without looking up, he began to scribble. She was swamped with relief.

She cleared her throat, searching her memory for the next piece. "Lady Moira Ashington, who is the daughter of Viscount Groveton. Apparently, she devotes much of her time to traveling back and forth from Bath to take the waters. But she's in London at the moment, and she makes a habit of calling on a certain country herbalist in Wandsworth. Sometimes as often as three times a week." Helena squeezed her eyes shut, trying to remember. "She is blonde and . . . and willowy. Rather thin. The family lives in Piccadilly. Despite her interest in, er, health treatments, she apparently covets wealth, prestige, and power as much as the next girl." Helena took a deep breath, swallowing hard.

"Just not as much as you," Shaw said, still scribbling.

"Right," she said absently, searching her memory. "Are you getting this? There is one more. Miss Lisbette Twining, who is the daughter of a wealthy merchant in . . . in textiles. They are in Cork Street. She is very beautiful, with brown hair and blue eyes. And apparently she has some history with Lusk. He may know her from his own circle of friends."

Shaw nodded and reinked his pen, writing it all down. Helena let out a relieved sigh, grateful she'd remembered the details long enough to repeat them. Even more relieved that Shaw was recording it. She'd been correct all along. Well, she'd been wildly reckless, foolhardy, and self-indulgent, but she had also been correct. That is, she would be correct, if he recorded the list and then relinquished it to her.

She repeated the names and footnotes again, speaking to the gifts. She scooped up a festooned bundle and stared at the card, trying to appear wistful and bridely.

"You cannot hover here," Shaw said lowly, still writing. "If you mean to lurk in the shadows, you might as well take your own dictation."

She replaced the bundle and tried to peek at his notes. He shot her an expression of *What are you doing?*

She frowned and turned back to the garden. "I need a reprieve after . . ." She gestured to the milling party. "Just two seconds. I hate these sorts of things."

"I'm a servant, not your reprieve," he said.

"You are not fifty women who think me ungrateful and disobedient and willful."

"These women have come here bearing enough gifts to provision Scotland in winter," he said. "If that's not approval, I don't know what it is."

"The gifts are another cog in the wheel that moves me along their aristocratic wedding mill," she said. "They are not the worst part of today, but their mountain of gifts is wasteful." She frowned at the heavily laden table.

He was quiet for a moment, and she reminded herself that he didn't care, not about the gifts or the terrible women. He wouldn't ask.

"What," he sighed, "is the worst part?"

She glanced at him, feeling another eruption in her chest. She said, "The worst part is that they pretend. They carry on as if we are all in accord."

"You could *be* in accord," he said. "With them—with all of it. England is awash in women who live full lives despite being married to . . . to—"

"Men for whom they have no respect? Men who are ignorant and dullards and drunk by noon?"

"I was going to say, their opposite."

"Lusk is not my opposite, he is my . . . my . . . abbreviation."

"Very poetic. What do you mean?"

"I *mean,* if I am forced to be his wife, my existence will be cut down to a sort of foggy, half-lived, shorthand version of what it could be. My drooped shoulders and blank expression will stand in for what my whole self would otherwise do."

She stepped away from the table. "I've but one life, Shaw. I will not waste it being bound to him. I will not."

The words came out more strident and desperate than she intended, but they were so deeply felt. She found herself propelled by emotion back into the party.

Her next strategy was to glean one name each from various women who had marriageable daughters and fellow debutantes this season. Competition is a great incubator of gossip, and ten minutes later, she returned with another name.

"Miss Jessica Marten," she told Shaw, bustling up. "Daughter of Sir Reginald Marten, who is apparently an esteemed Egyptologist. Her father has enlisted her as his private secretary and expects her to devote her life to his work, but she loathes academia in general and couldn't care less about Egypt. She never had a debut, but she has society friends, and she complains about her lot. She can be found most days at the National Gallery, pressed into service for her father. Apparently, she is on the hunt for the highest-ranking title she can find, as only marriage to a lord would free her from her father's work. Very red hair. Curls."

Shaw resisted less this time, scratching out the name before she could repeat it. Helena took a deep breath and paced around the gift table, her mind spinning. Four names. All of them were beautiful, according to the talk. She was encouraged. She would interview one potential duchess every day. A duchess a day. Until she found a girl perfect enough to make Lusk defy his uncle.

"You might endeavor to smile," Shaw said. "Feign some sort of frivolity."

He took up a velvet pouch tied with a red bow and held it out. "It's not a dead bird," he said. "It's gift. Show surprise and delight."

She reached out and snatched the pouch. "Thank you for helping me," she said.

"I'm not helping you. I'm keeping a closer watch. Isn't this how you convinced me?" He cocked a sardonic brow.

Helena's stomach lit up with a rain of shimmering sparks. She smiled at him, thinking of the stable. If she was being honest, Declan Shaw's very presence made the terrible party tolerable. He was funny and confident and solid. He had a strong, anchoring quality that gave her a boost every time she looked at him. She was far more interested in speaking to him than anyone else.

But perhaps that is why she'd asked him to come. Not to test his loyalties or take dictation, but simply to have an ally.

She dropped the pouch with a *thunk* and took up a crystal goblet. Raising her eyes, she stared at him over the rim. He held that stare and her stomach shimmered again.

After a moment he said, "I need to apologize for last night."

So he did think of the stable.

Helena frowned. "Please do not."

The stable had exhilarated Helena. It tapped into fresh reserves of her will to fight. It made her think beyond the canceled wedding, to a future where she might meet a man she really did wish to marry and a lifetime of exhilarating dark stables.

"We were reckless last night," she said. "I did

not seek you out to be . . . to be contentious."

"You're worried about *contention*?" He made a choking noise.

"Yes, of course. But here is not the place to discuss it." She couldn't entertain an apology. If he thought she was traumatized by kissing him, he was wrong. She'd come alive when she'd kissed him.

She moved away, wrinkling her nose. "I'm going back in," she sighed, but she didn't move.

"You steal away into the night," he marveled, "creep around dark stables with your groom, but *these women* you find challenging?"

"*These women*," she said, "have feasted on the gossip of my evasions these last five years, and now they feast on the gossip of me being brought to heel. They look innocent to you, don't they? Of course they do. Their voices are hushed, their movements are restricted. Do not be fooled. They achieve this through tight corsets and tighter breeding, but they will not bind and breed me. How right my grandmother was to warn me."

"And you believe they cannot see your disdain?"

"They don't care if I'm disdainful." Helena sighed, drifting away. "They only care if I do as I'm told."

With this, she melted back into the party. A half hour later, she returned with: "Lady Genevieve Vance, daughter of the Earl of Nooning. Classic English rose with blonde hair and blue eyes. She lives in Blenheim Street but can be frequently found in the shops; she has accounts all around Mayfair. Jewelry and hats are a particular favorite. She would leap at a chance for the Lusk fortune." Helena wrinkled up her nose. "Apparently."

"So terrible, a fortune," he mumbled, not looking up from his notes.

"Write it down," she whispered. "Lady Genevieve Vance, with the shopping and the money. *And* Lady Rodericka Newton, daughter of Viscount Jennings. Apparently she has a great wish for a high-ranking title simply because she loves to manage things. The family are from Yorkshire but they live in Curzon Street when they are in London. I can apparently encounter her at any society ball or function. She and her mother are said never to decline an invitation. She has black hair and hazel eyes."

Shaw was shaking his head, but he scribbled the notes. Helena forced herself to feign interest in the gifts. Snatching a box at random, she held it up and examined its peach-colored tissue and mossy ribbon. The longer the list grew, the more eager Helena became to have it in her possession.

"You've been very good to do this, Shaw," she said, looking up at the sky. "I— Your participation has exceeded my expectations. I cannot say what I expected, but it was not this."

"You and I both," he mumbled.

Dark rain clouds had begun to scuttle the sun and the garden was cast in dark shadows. A chilly wind descended, strewing linen napkins and fluttering hat feathers.

"I believe this party may meet an untimely end," she said, backing away. "I'd feel better if I had one more name. I cannot say when I'll have this opportunity again. Let me take one final turn."

A quarter hour later, she returned with, "Miss Joanna Keep. She resides in Cumberland Place but spends her days at her uncle's medical office in Wimpole Street. Apparently she is his apprentice. He's a surgeon of some merit. She has a fascination with sickness and healing and surgical theaters. They say she would do anything to marry a duke because of the access to hospitals she'd enjoy as duchess." Helena let out a deep breath. "I cannot imagine that Lusk would fancy someone quite so high-minded, but apparently she is very beautiful. Curly blonde hair, the usual."

Shaw stared at her a long moment, almost as if he thought she'd made the whole thing up.

"What?" she said. "Can you not take it down?"

He continued to look, his brown eyes blinking, and then took up the pen and scribbled. "That makes seven," he said.

She nodded, staring at the storm clouds. "It will have to be enough. This party will soon enjoy a very cold, very thorough soaking. Lady Canning has said she will move us inside, but hopefully rain will send everyone home instead."

And now, the moment of truth.

She held out a hand. "Thank you for helping me," she said. "I'll take the list now, if you please."

Shaw stared at her outstretched hand and over her shoulder. His expression was unreadable.

"Shaw?"

"Look smart," he whispered. "Your mother."

Helena turned to see the countess marching

across the garden, waving at guests as they disappeared into the house.

"Helena?" called the countess. Her sisters trailed behind like ducklings. "Helena, every time I look, you are in the shadows, talking to staff. Come away from there at once. The rain has held, but the sky may open at any moment. The guests are leaving and we must see them off."

"I'm reminding myself of the gifts, Mama," she called, "so I may thank departing guests. My groom Shaw has a list."

The countess reached them, shaking her head. "Do not touch a gift on this table, Shaw," ordered Lady Pembrook. "Titus has an elaborate protocol for ducal correspondence and the proper inventorying and displaying of gifts."

She looked at Helena. "Leave the staff to their work, Helena. Titus wishes to inspect everything, God knows why, and he will instruct the grooms."

The sky rumbled, eliciting a chorus of titters from Helena's sisters. Drops of intermittent rain began to pelt the lush garden. The countess made a noise of exasperation.

"Inside, all of you," Lady Pembrook snapped, herding the four girls into the house. She took Helena by the arm.

"But, Mama," Helena protested.

"But nothing. You've hovered over the gifts long enough. People will begin to think you're grasping. Come with me at once." She tugged Helena by the arm.

Casting a final glance over her shoulder, Helena mouthed the words, *I want that list.*

Chapter Eight

Declan had the overwhelming desire to take up the nearest wedding gift and lob it into Lady Canning's fountain. He took up a box and tested its weight. A vase? Candlesticks? It would hit the lily-strewn water with a satisfying splat.

He flipped it, hauling back, and—

"Ah, there you are," said Titus Girdleston, coming around the pillar of the garden gate. Declan snatched the package from the air.

Girdleston stepped to the table like a pirate surveying his trove. "We'll want the gifts loaded into the carriages before the rain. But take care that the presentation remains intact. Ribbons and trim and, of course, each card must be carefully preserved. We've brought trunks with straw to pack any loose ends. Most things will doubtless be fragile."

Declan stared at him.

Did the man have no desire to learn how the future duchess managed the party? Was he curious about why Declan now stood in the garden instead of in the mews? Would there be no accounting? No briefing?

Perhaps Helena was correct. Perhaps they only noticed her when she was running away.

Declan had told himself he'd do her bidding because it allowed him to keep watch on her. The closer he was, the better he could understand her plan. In theory, this was true. He'd gained her trust, and learned her game, and the evidence was tucked securely in his vest pocket. He'd done his bloody job.

The next obvious step was to hand the list to the old man.

Give him the list, Declan ordered in his head.

He did nothing.

He felt the heat of the parchment burning a hole in his pocket, and he wondered if he would allow it to simply burn him alive.

"You heard me, man," harrumphed Girdleston. "The weather will not hold. Carry on with the loading of these gifts."

Staring at him a moment more, Declan scooped up an armful of boxes and turned toward the gate.

"Not in a jumble," scolded Girdleston. *"One at the time."* The old man plucked each package from Declan's arms, relieving him of all but one box.

"Now it shall be protected," cooed Girdleston, dispatching him again. Declan said nothing and trudged away.

Two other grooms joined the procession, working quickly to outpace the rain. Girdleston watched from beneath a tightly clenched umbrella, stepping out to inspect this or that parcel and to hurry them along. The Chancellor of the

Exchequer, Declan thought, did not monitor Britain's coffers more closely than Titus Girdleston pouring over his nephew's gifts.

With each circuit, Declan said to himself, *Give him the list*.

Halfway through the job, he said the same.

The threatening rain, at last, began to pound the garden, and another groom scrambled to distribute overcoats. The coat was warm and dry, and Declan thought of the list in his pocket. What if it got wet? What if it disintegrated? It couldn't be helped.

But that felt like a coward's way out.

Perhaps he could give the list to Girdleston in private. Or Declan could use it himself to watch Lady Helena more closely. He'd only need to restrict her movements if the information on the list became actionable.

Not for the first time, he estimated at the odds of her locating these women. After that, of approaching them.

She will absolutely locate them and approach them, he thought, delivering the final gift to the carriage.

"Tom has the last of it, I think," said Nettle, an older groom who had been friendly since Declan's first day. "We could've managed with two carriages if the ladies could balance one or two packages in their laps."

Declan nodded and circled the third vehicle, checking the contents. He was just about to slam the door when he saw Girdleston stomping up the alley, his giant umbrella pumping.

Tell him, Declan ordered himself. His hand

went to the list in his pocket.

Tell him.

"Just in time!" called Girdleston. "We've missed the worst of the rain. I shall ride in the second carriage, and the third will be empty except for the balance of the gifts. The women will ride lead, as before. Let us pull 'round to the front of house. They should depart presently."

Declan hesitated. He could tell him without even explaining. He could thrust the parchment in Girdleston's direction and claim he didn't know what it meant. The old man would be confused and Helena could make up a lie.

If he did it now, it would be finished. He'd be doing his bloody job.

He opened his mouth to say something. The moment stretched, suspending in the damp air like a swinging rope at the top of its arc. No words came. He bit off his glove and put his hand to the list on his pocket. He paused—

And then suddenly Nettle was there, helping Girdleston into the carriage. The coachman clicked to his team. Grooms scurried to take positions.

The rope began its downward fall, taking the opportunity with it.

Declan swore and leapt onto the runner of the third vehicle.

There will be another time, he told himself.

If nothing else, at least his participation today was not nearly as bad as what he'd done last night.

Today amounted to a report that hadn't yet happened, he thought.

Today was shite bad timing.

Helena Lark is not my problem.

When the carriages lurched from the alley, Nettle dispatched Declan to the center of Brook Street to stop traffic in both directions. The rain increased, and he stood in the cold downpour, ignoring drivers and riders as they shouted profanity. When at last he'd managed to stop traffic, the carriages bounced into road-blocking positions before Lady Canning's front door.

Ten minutes later, the rain abated, and Lady Helena and her family clipped down the steps with heads ducked and skirts raised to avoid the mud.

Declan was careful to give the lead carriage a very wide berth, allowing other grooms to form the necessary phalanx of umbrellas and outstretched hands. Lady Helena, thank God, was obscured. It was better if he couldn't see her. Instead, he stood stoically in the splash of passing carts, soaking to the bone, and didn't look.

"I should like to ride with some of my gifts . . ."

Her voice rose above the drum of raindrops.

Declan squeezed his eyes shut.

"Do not bother yourself, Mama," she could be heard saying. "I prefer a moment alone after the crush of a party."

No, Declan thought, slinging rain from his eyes and squinting through the mist. Five yards away, Lady Pembrook and her daughters scrambled to the front carriage amid lingering rain. All daughters, save one.

Lady Helena picked her way to him in the wet street. Another groom darted after her, trying to shield her with an umbrella. Declan swore and met them halfway, taking the umbrella handle like a baton in a race. Lady Helena huddled close.

"I want," she said lowly, "my list."

Declan scanned the street, checking the location of her family, the other grooms, and Girdleston, who appeared to be tucked tightly inside the dryness of the second carriage. A cold wind had begun to churn the last spitting drops of rain. The street was a slurry of mud and dancing horses. The wind yanked Lady Helena's skirt, sending it twisting and dancing; raindrops speckled the indigo with dark dots. Her coiffeur was rapidly dissolving in the rain.

"Give it to me," she demanded, holding out an insistent indigo-gloved hand.

"I mean to tell Girdleston," Declan said, hustling her to the door of the carriage. He whipped it open and extended the steps. "Get in."

"*No*," she said, crossing her arms. "Shaw—no. Let us come to some agreement, make a deal. In exchange for the list."

"No," he said again. "Get inside the carriage."

"Give me the list, and I will make it worth your while," she said. Something like panic had begun to creep into her eyes. He looked away.

"It was ruined in the rain," he said. "We're going."

"I don't believe you. Let me see it."

"We cannot stand in the muddy street and quarrel about it, *get in*."

She ignored him. "You've already recorded the names. Why do the work of writing it all down only to refuse me now? Shaw—please. I'll not trouble you again if you simply *hand over the list*."

He swore and glanced over his shoulder. The second-to-last sister was being gingerly loaded into the front carriage. There was no time for this.

"At least listen to what I will trade," she pleaded.

He was shaking his head.

"I . . . I'll keep a prudent distance from you," she vowed. "No more garden parties. I'll not ask you to do anything a groom would not ordinarily do. I'll not impose on—"

"You'll not impose, and you'll not ask for more. You will keep your distance regardless." He took her by the elbow. "This is over, my lady."

She sucked in an outraged breath, but Declan cut her off. "I can save my job by giving him the list. He'll not understand it and you'll not be punished."

"Except every day for the rest of my life," she cried.

He refused to hear. "If I hand it over now, you may let go of this madcap plan before you've wasted any more effort."

"Wasted effort? You don't think I can manage it."

"Helena, please," he gritted out. "We are not allies or collaborators, but if we make an effort to be civil, we need not be enemies."

"Civil?" she said. "Was that our rapport in the stable last night? Civility?"

"You would not," he said.

"Would not what?"

He dropped her arm. He took two steps back. "What am I thinking? Of course you would!"

"Would *what*?" she demanded, confused. "You

think I'll tell Girdleston about the stable? Are you mad? That was a personal moment, between the two of us. You're the one running to 'Uncle Titus,' not me. Even after everything I've revealed, you don't trust me at all."

"I barely know you," he gritted out, and he wondered how he'd managed to find himself standing in the rain, hissing at a beautiful woman about trust. His cell at Newgate was beginning to hold fresh appeal.

"Well, that is your poor choice, because I'm a lovely girl. Really. And I've been nothing but honest with you. Which was your idea, by the way."

"*Too* honest," he growled. He took her elbow again. "But now you must get in the carriage. Your mother's vehicle is ready."

"Give me the list."

"Forget the list."

"Oh, Shaw," she breathed, the words coming out in dramatic, melodious rush. He swung around, surprised by her sudden change in tone.

She looked him in the eye and shook her head in two slow, determined shakes.

For years to come, Declan would remember her odd reaction.

She tugged her arm free of his grasp.

"What is it?" he asked, letting her go.

She took one step back, then another. Then another. She continued to shake her head.

He should have known. In that very strange moment, he should have known. He was a fool not to know.

When next she spoke, her voice had taken on a

new quality. "You asked for this," she said.

"For wh—"

Before he could finish the question, Lady Helena took two more determined steps backward, raised her eyebrows as if to say, *What did you expect?* and spun around to bolt down the street.

It happened so fast, and with such unexpected fervor, Declan actually froze. He blinked at her retreating form, a streak of purple and black hair and mud.

"Oy!" shouted another groom, spurring Declan from his trancelike state of immobilized disbelief. Reflex took over and Declan lunged, giving chase.

A rain-soaked dog darted into the road and he hurdled over it.

A hunched figure in a dark cloak shuffled between them, and he spun, nearly going down, but he righted himself with a hand to the mud.

She was quick but he reached her in five yards. When he was upon her, he did not hesitate; he wrapped an arm around her waist and yanked, pulling her off her feet, legs still churning, soaked skirt fanning out in a whirl of muddy rainwater.

"Oof," she said, her back colliding with his chest. He braced, prepared to restrict arms and legs, biting and scratching, but she did none of these. She clung to him instead, sagging arms and legs akimbo. She was wet seaweed in his arms.

He grunted, "What the bloody hell—"

"Put me down, put me down!" she cried, although her voice was still strange, and she did not sound distressed so much as loud. She sounded as if her voice was purposefully pitched to resound in the street.

In an entirely different voice, her real voice, she whispered, *"Give me the list."*

The contrast in her two demands was startling. *Put me down* came out in a shrill wail. *Give me the list* was a stone-cold threat.

"You're mad," he whispered back, the only thing he fully understood in this moment.

He made a move to lower her and set her to rights, but she held on. She hooked her left hand over his shoulder and snaked her right hand down his chest. It would be impossible to put her down in her tightly held position. He didn't restrain her so much as balanced the two of them off the ground.

While he staggered along, Helena snaked her hand beneath his greatcoat and began to feel around his ribs and chest for pockets. Declan grunted and missed another step. Her fingers fanned out against pectoral muscles, his stomach, his hip, searching, searching.

The chaos of the moment should have masked the feel of her hand—but no. This was no indiscriminate fumbling; she was methodically walking fingers up and down his body, and Declan felt every swipe and probe. His footsteps grew heavy, his brain went light. His world shrank to the swirl of her hand on his chest.

"You're joking," he rasped, trying again to set her down. She climbed higher and hung on with the opposite hand. Now she searched the other side of his body with torturous attention to detail.

"Where is it?" she demanded lowly.

"Shaw?" Girdleston's voice called through the rain.

Declan swore. He could just make it to the third carriage. He dropped against the side, reaching for leverage to peel her away. He'd just managed to catch her beneath the arms when her searching hand found his pocket and dipped in, locating the damp parchment. He could feel her smile against his throat when she closed her hand around it. She retracted the list, shoved it down her own bodice, and went limp.

"Shaw?" Girdleston called a second time. Declan rolled his head against the carriage, looking in the direction of his name.

"Let me go!" Helena cried, invoking the loud, strange voice again.

"I'm not holding you," Declan hissed, "you're holding me." She had draped herself across him like a wet sheet.

Girdleston was out of the second carriage, his umbrella clutched beside his face. "What in God's name . . . ?"

"Uncle Titus," exclaimed Lady Helena, her head hanging upside down, loose black hair trailing nearly to the mud, "tell your great lummox of groom to unhand me. He's ruined my dress."

"Perhaps your dress deserves to be ruined," scolded Girdleston, snapping his fingers. Two grooms rushed to peel her away.

To Declan's great surprise, she allowed it. They set her upright and she went about smoothing her skirt and wringing out sopping hair.

"But what were you thinking, running down the street in a downpour?" scolded Girdleston.

She made a dismissive gesture. "A gust of wind had blown away my . . . my—"

"A likely story, *the wind,*" spat Girdleston. "And here in front of Lady Canning's home, the carriages filled with gifts from her party. Appalling. If Shaw apprehended you, he is only doing his job."

"If his job is to *manhandle* me," countered Lady Helena, her eyes flashing.

And now Declan understood. His sole focus became surviving the next five minutes with his job intact.

"Shaw's duty," lectured Girdleston, "is to keep you safe and looked after, which he cannot do if you are sprinting down the street. Your parents promised me that this behavior was finished, my lady."

Helena opened her mouth to reply but Girdleston cut her off. "Shaw? Please escort Lady Helena to her mother and sisters. Excellent work, acting so quickly when *the wind blew away her . . . item.*"

"I do not wish to ride with my mother and sisters," Helena announced. "I will ride in this carriage. With my gifts." She jabbed the side of the third carriage with three firm taps.

"Very well," said Girdleston. "The sooner you are out of the street, the better. But please be aware that you can expect to see significantly more of Mr. Shaw in your future."

"I've no need of a ham-handed groom serving as my chaperon," she said, huffing up the steps into the carriage.

"Your behavior suggests otherwise, my lady. And for that, you will now have Mr. Shaw waiting attendance with increasing regularly. Depend upon it. This cannot happen again. Thank God the rain has obscured the worst of it and most decent people are safely inside."

Lady Helena, now nestled among boxes and trunks, slammed the carriage door shut.

Girdleston made a growling noise and turned to Declan. "Well done, Huntsman. Let us pray this is the worst of it. But do not let her out of your sight. Clearly she can only be trusted when she's locked inside her rooms at night. Let us *increase* your surveillance. Monitor her every waking hour. Starting now. Ride with her, walk with her, hound her every step. Make her as secure as your *own prison cell*."

The reference to Newgate made him go rigid.

"Yes, sir," Declan gritted out, but the older man was already stumping away.

"Carry on," Girdleston called, waving to the assembled grooms. "We have devoted enough time and spectacle to this street." He mumbled to himself and climbed into the middle carriage, shaking his head.

Declan, now stunned, angry, and soaking wet, jerked open the door to the carriage and climbed inside.

Chapter Nine

Helena squeezed herself on the carriage seat between a stained-glass lantern and a portrait of a Labrador retriever. With hands that shook, she peeled off wet gloves and pulled Shaw's list from her bodice. She could hear Girdleston's voice droning on outside the carriage, but she ignored it. She scanned the list, holding it gingerly away from her wet dress and dripping hair.

It was all there, only a little smeared from the rain. *Thank God.*

The door to the carriage swung open and she jerked her head up. Declan Shaw climbed into the vehicle and sat heavily on a closed trunk at her feet. Glaring at her, he slammed the door.

The Lusk carriages were generous in size and lavishly appointed, but Shaw's great height and breadth transformed it to a hatbox. He was dripping wet, and his greatcoat sluiced rainwater onto the floor. The carriage filled with the overheated scent of angry, wet, windblown male.

Helena's pounding heart affected a tight flip and set off racing again. She kept her expression neutral. She said, "You cannot seriously expect to ride in this carriage?"

"Me?" he asked, peeling off his wet hat and tossing it in a crystal dish. "Here?" He bit off a glove and ran a hand through his wet hair. "Yes. I can expect it."

She made a nervous laugh. "You're joking."

"I'm joking?" he asked. "*I'm* joking? I'm not the one running down the street like a lunatic. I'm not searching a man's body for a document that does not belong to me—"

"It does belong to me."

". . . while strangling him . . ."

"I wasn't strangling you, I was—"

"It doesn't matter," he said. "You may have won this round, but the rules have changed."

He began to shrug from his wet coat. His movements were irritated and jerky. He snagged his collar loose. He stomped mud from his boots.

Helena watched him, fascinated by the simple rituals. He was a giant in a carriage designed for a small man and his smaller uncle. The jostling gifts enjoyed more room than his spot on the trunk.

I want more of him, she thought.

More often.

I want more of him all the time.

She wanted him like a busy person who forgets to eat and realizes she's starving to death.

It was wrong, she knew—this want. How had her very essential and very tenuous fight been waylaid by something so self-indulgent and impossible?

She glanced at him. How indeed?

Forcing herself to do anything productive, she felt around her for her soggy hat, jerking it free. She told him, "I'm not sure what you mean by 'changed rules,' but I don't want to fight you."

Shaw didn't reply. The carriage lurched into motion and he nudged the curtain with a finger, studying the wet street outside.

"I assume Girdleston installed you in the carriage to restrict me?" she asked, taking up a handful of hair and squeezing it into a vase beside her foot.

He let the curtain fall. "Behold: the new rules. Isn't that what you wanted?"

"Look, it was not my initial goal to *bind you to me*, but you gave me no choice. I offered a simple truce and trade that would serve us both, but you would not cooperate."

"I do not," he said slowly, emphatically, "have the freedom to cooperate." His voice was too loud for the small carriage. It should have frightened her. She should feel chastened and chagrined. Instead, she wanted to challenge him.

"Why?" she demanded. "Why can you not cooperate? You adore the Lusk dukedom? You detest me? What is it?"

He said something under his breath, an oath, a curse. He opened his mouth and then closed it, clearly choosing his words. Finally, he said, "I cannot cooperate because I need Girdleston's money to provide for my family."

"Your wife and children?" she asked, her heart drumming. Oh God, did Declan Shaw have a wife and children?

"No. My father and my two sisters. I am not

married."

Helena's heart did another flip. She thought for a moment and asked, "Are they . . . destitute?"

"No, not destitute, but they rely on me for survival. Not the kind of survival you describe, which involves marrying a bloke you don't fancy, and living in one mansion instead of another."

"That is not—"

"I am not unsympathetic to what you want for yourself, but I must put my own family first. I must do the job I was hired to do. I cannot . . . *cooperate* with you."

"I'm sorry," she said softly, the honest truth. She wanted to reach out, to make some physical connection, but she dare not. This was not the library or barn. They were not trading barbs about his inaccurate title of groom. He did not appear open to her touch.

She paused, hoping to diffuse tension. It was her fault, of course. She'd pushed him, and marched him about, and forced him to drag her down the street. Now they were soaked to the bone and he was—

Well, the look of desperation on his face made a tear in her heart.

She'd wanted desperately to know what drove him. What of this father and the sisters? Was his mother deceased? And how had he come to work—

The carriage bounced to a stop. The clatter of cross traffic could be heard outside. Helena took a deep breath. "Why didn't you tell me about your family?" she asked quietly. "I've wanted you to tell me thei—"

"Here's the long and short of it, my lady," he said curtly. "Girdleston's money will be the difference between an easy life for my family or hardship. My father is old and frail, and I need to get him out of the city. London is expensive and competitive and the smoke is damaging to his lungs. My sisters work as seamstresses, but they do not enjoy it, and they're bored and restless. This attitude, combined with how pretty they are, has already led to trouble. I want to move all of them to sunny country village with decent people. I would wager that I want this *more* than you want *not* to be the Duchess of Lusk. I'm sorry." He leveled his brown eyes at her. "*That* is why I cannot cooperate."

"Declan," she said softly, "I'm so sorry."

"It doesn't matter." He ran a hand through his wet hair.

"It does matter," she countered. "Any gesture made in love for the good of people who struggle? That matters very much indeed. One might say it's all that matters."

"It doesn't matter for you," he corrected.

"Do not tell me what matters to me and what does not," she said. He didn't answer, and she sat a moment, lost in thought.

After a several beats, she said, "I . . . I actually believe I can solve this."

"You cannot."

"I can. I *live* in a forest. It's beautiful and fresh and peaceful. The village of Winscombe is not far by wagon. I walk the distance myself, twice a week. The River Brue, assuming it is not destroyed by Lusk's limestone barges, runs cool and clear, through the center of the wood. Crofters make their homes along the bank. I live in the summerhouse formerly occupied by my grandmother, but there are outbuildings that you might find suitable for your father and sisters. A falconry. A caretaker's cottage. A stable with a coachman's flat above it."

He stared at her.

"What? You don't believe me?"

"I don't believe that you may invite an old man and two young women to simply build a new life on the corner of an estate owned by an earl and inhabited by his highly disobedient daughter."

"I am not disobedient. I'm so very compliant. I am here, in London, jumping through every hoop."

"Except the last, most important one."

"Yes, but when my plan is realized, the lack of a wedding will not be my fault. If Lusk jilts me, what can I do? I will be given little choice but to return to Castle Wood."

"I can think of any number of impositions that a disappointed earl might level on a daughter who causes Lusk to marry someone else."

"He will not know," she said slowly, emphasizing each word. "And the summerhouse in Castle Wood belongs to me, don't you see?" She scooted to the end of the seat. Her knees bumped his arm and she almost, *almost*, grabbed him by the sleeve. She wanted him to reach for her. His palm on her thigh. His fingers around her ankle. How could he sit so close and not touch her? She would dissolve, she thought, if he did not. She would reach out. She couldn't bear *not* to touch him.

"My grandmother," she went on, "left me the summerhouse and all the outbuildings. My parents live in Castlereagh mansion, but it is more than a mile away. They've no use for the 'ruins in the forest' as they call us. They've no use for the forest at all, except during hunting season. Otherwise, they leave me alone. When Lusk jilts me, I may do what I like. I may grow my apples. *And* I may invite a new family to move onto the estate."

She threw up her hands. *"Let me help you."*

He said nothing, staring at her with his deep brown eyes.

She tried again. "Your family may take any building they would like. There may be work to repair it, but I will help them."

"Lady Helena," he began. He let out a weary breath. "You do not know me. You've not met my father. What if he is . . . he is terrible? What if my sisters are—"

"If they are, or if the forest does not suit them, then I will sell a piece of my grandmother's jewelry and give you the money."

"This is outrageous," he said.

"This is a trade," she said, circling back. Perhaps he would be more open if he saw the offer as a barter. "You help me in a few small ways—namely not reporting my scheme to Girdleston—and I shall provide for your family when I am restored to my home."

"Why can you not simply marry this rich git chosen by your parents? Then I will *earn* my money serving as your groom and provide for my family myself. Can you not do what is expected of you, Helena?"

"Oh, like you have done?" she asked.

"What exactly do you mean by that?"

"You're meant to guard me, spy on me, run me down," she said. "And yet you haven't even tried. I've revealed myself to you. I've made you complicit in several outrageous ways. And yet I am still . . . unchecked."

"I'm riding in your carriage to keep you from bolting out the door."

"Are you?" She glanced at the door.

"Don't you dare."

She went on. "At least now I know why you've been hired. You've just admitted it."

"I admitted nothing."

He was quiet for a moment, studying her face. She worried that the terms of the trade made it sound like a choice between something he did not want to do and abandoning his family. This was no choice at all. The truth was, she wanted to provide for his family, even if he would not help her. She knew this as well as she knew her own desire for the future. She *wanted* to help. Of course, it would be far easier to help if she could escape Lusk herself.

She said, "I know this feels like a decision—you will *decide* to help me or you won't—but I'm offering you more than a decision. I'm offering you a *solution*."

She reached out finally, and touched him. Two hands clutching one of his.

"It would give me great pleasure to welcome your father and sisters to Castle Wood. Have you been to Somerset?"

"Yes." A vague whisper.

"Well then, you know. It's paradise."

He closed his eyes and turned his face away, a man torn.

She spoke to his profile. "Something has motivated me to fight this wedding for five years, to make a fool of myself and risk safety and sanity. It has not, I assure you, been my freedom alone. It's has been to protect this forest and the orchard and the families who have lived in Castle Wood for generations. I would not have gone to such lengths if I was not protecting something wonderful." She held up her palms, fingers open, as if she delivered the truth to him in handfuls.

Declan said stonily, "It's more complicated than that. Lady Helena—"

"Very well," she said, dropping her hands. "I understand. You cannot help me. You will not allow me to try to help you. Stop the carriage, then. We are at an impasse. Take the list to Girdleston so that I may revise my pla—"

She was cut off by a jolt from the road. The fragile contents of the vehicle clattered like a china shop under cannon fire and Helena was pitched from her seat. One moment she'd been on the bench, the next she was launched into the air. She landed with an "*Oof*" against a wall of wet muscle.

Shaw caught her with lightning reflex. "I've got you," he said.

Helena went rigid, every fiber of her body attuned to the sudden closeness. For a long beat, she said nothing. She held herself upright and still, waiting for him to deposit her on the opposite seat. She waited for irritation or disgust. She waited for him to touch her.

Slowly, breath held, she glanced up. She blinked, licking her bottom lip. She would thank him, she thought. She would say, *I beg your pardon,* and slink away. She would tell him again to hand her over to Girdleston. She would—

She raised her lashes to look at him. The words were on the tip of her tongue. Their eyes met.

Shaw made a growling noise and descended on her mouth with a kiss. Helena barely had time to suck in breath before he pulled her close. They fell into the embrace like a stone dropped into a swirling stream. The carriage, the entourage, the world, were a torrent around them, and they sank and sank.

There were no words. No *are you comfortable* or *damn these wet clothes.* He ravished her with his mouth. He crushed her against him like he wanted to absorb her. The smell of rain and wind pervaded the carriage. Unsettled gifts tipped against them. The wheels bounced over uneven cobblestones, jostling them blissfully closer. Helena wrapped her arms around his shoulders and held on.

She'd done her duty at the party, she'd gotten her names, she'd offered his family sanctuary, but she was so very tired of duty and families and talking. What she really wanted was *this.*

When he pulled back to breathe, he panted, "I cannot give you over to Girdleston. I've tried, but I cannot."

She nodded, breathing hard. She grabbed his tunic in desperate hands. "I will not bolt," she told him. "It is imperative that I do as they wish until the very last moment. And then it will be the duke's choosing. You *will* get your payment."

"This is madness," he said, claiming her mouth again.

She shifted, climbing to her knees in his lap, scrambling to get closer. His hands went to her waist, steadying her. She hovered above him, hands on his shoulders, her hair falling around them in wet clumps.

"Come back," he begged, pulling her down.

She endeavored to slide her legs around his waist, but her dress was tangled and the fabric was wet, and she toppled back to his lap, laughing.

"But no more of this," he said, scraping his emerging beard across her cheek. *"No more."*

Her laughter continued and he said against her ear, "This will get you into trouble from which I cannot protect you."

"I don't need protecting," she gasped, digging her hands into his hair.

"If I help you, we must be meticulously careful. We cannot mishandle it. No matter our . . . our . . ."

She claimed his mouth again. "We will not mishandle it," she panted. "We will be professional. And mindful. We will get your family to Castle Wood. We will beat this . . ."

"Go," he said, but he pulled her closer. "Stay back."

"Yes," she said against his mouth.

"Honestly, Lady Helena," he mumbled, nibbling her mouth with repeated brisk, pecking kisses. "Go." He cupped the back of her head with his palm and tipped her, reclining her across his lap. He buried his face in her neck.

"I'm going," she moaned, on fire with pleasure.

Only when they heard a shout outside the carriage, when the vehicle slowed, when she heard the barking of her father's wolfhounds, did Helena have the presence of mind to pull away.

They both dropped their heads and breathed in. He held her loosely with one hand and secured the door handle with the other. She blinked at the ceiling, panting, willing the world to slide back into focus.

Slowly, she began to disentangle from Shaw. When she was steady, he fell against the opposite seat, his arms stretched wide like a brawler against the ropes. Helena picked her way back to her bench. Her mind returned in surges. She yanked her dress into place and tied back her hair. With shaking hands, she smoothed the redness from her face.

"You should follow my lead," she directed. She sifted through the packages on the seat, took up a silver teapot, and held it in her lap.

"Wait," he said, "do you mean conceding that you are *in charge*?"

"What? Well, yes."

He shook his head. "Let's be perfectly clear. This is a collaboration. Half and half. I'm risking the future of four people." He shoved his wet hat on his head and worked his fingers into his gloves. "We decide together."

"I was the mastermind of the plan from the start. I thought of it, and I'm seeing it through," she said. "Collaboration should honor that."

"Lady Helena," he said lowly, a warning.

"Shaw," she said, mimicking.

She was just about to tell him that she would *entertain* suggestions, when the door to the carriage whipped open.

Shaw shot her a look she could not decipher and jumped out.

Lady Helena closed her eyes. She patted her bodice, feeling around for the folded parchment. She took a deep breath. She was capable and motivated and prepared. She had not planned for a—what had he called it?—"collaboration," and certainly not with a man she almost trusted and urgently desired. But nothing about Declan Shaw frightened or stifled her. Nothing about Declan Shaw suffocated. Nothing else mattered.

She could do this.

You can have both. For a time. For now.

You'll sort it out.

"My lady," said Shaw, his voice supplicant and detached. His servant's voice. She looked up. His gloved hand extended into the carriage, palm up, ready to hand her out into the street.

Helena clutched the teapot and went.

Chapter Ten

"You summoned me, my lady?"

Two days later, Declan stood in the doorway to the Lusk House armory, his hat in his hands.

"Ah, yes, there you are, Shaw," said Lady Helena, not looking up. She was leaning over a glass case, studying a map. "You received my note, then? My schedule and our plan?"

Our *plan*? Declan thought, his temper rising. *Our. Plan.*

For two days, he'd been stewing over the notion of "our plan."

She'd described the next steps in a sealed letter delivered by a stable boy; the notion of "our plan" a resounding battle cry on nearly every page. The muscles in Declan's neck constricted every time he read it. He'd been so annoyed, in fact, he'd balled up the parchment and pitched it in the fire. The paper burned for five seconds before he'd scrambled to retrieve it.

And now here he was, reporting.

What a fitting metaphor for the last two days.

To his surprise, Lady Helena had departed the

wet carriage after the party with a totally new regard. Strict heiress-groom protocol had, apparently, become the order of the day. Icy detachment, no eye contact, words only to issue an order.

Fetch this.

Yes, my lady.

Hold that.

Yes, my lady.

Declan had been given little choice but to bend and stoop and respond to her myriad whims. Her sidelong glances had stopped. Knowing looks and moments alone were no more. There were only orders about heavy trunks and forgotten parcels and walking her father's dogs. She was a young heiress and he was a stable groom.

And now she would not even look at him?

No.

His voice was as hard as steel. "I do not recall *our* formulation of a plan." He put his hands on his hips and cocked his head. "You and I."

And now she finally looked up. Despite her new detachment, his reaction to her face was unchanged. Always. Every time. His breath caught, his heart seized, and the broken thing in his chest lost another piece.

She'd worn pale green today, the color of a caterpillar. Sun streamed through a window, reflecting light off the blackness of her hair.

Declan had taken up the useless habit of cataloging what she wore: the spring greens and ruby reds and pearlescent whites. Her canary-yellow cape. The black gloves. It was an intimacy he allowed himself because—

Well, actually, he deserved no intimacy.

What he deserved was to return to jail.

He'd been hired to contain her, and he'd kissed her within hours and began conspiring with her the next day.

Jail seemed more and more like an inevitability.

The night after Girdleston had locked him in the wet carriage with Helena, the old man had summoned him to his favorite room in Lusk House, the green salon. While Declan watched, Girdleston curated his prized collection of miniature cottages, buildings, and trees, a tiny toylike village arranged on a large table like a general's model battle. While he formed little walkways through the miniatures structures with a tiny rake, he'd asked Declan about Lady Helena's demeanor in the carriage.

It was the report and reckoning Declan had known would come. And what had he said?

"She was petulant and weepy but compliant. Sir."

If he thought it would pain him to lie, he was wrong. The words rolled off his tongue like a song.

Girdleston had been pleased, but he punctuated the visit with an explicit reminder that the payout and his freedom would be waiting for Declan *only* at the end of a job well done.

Now he stared at the subject of the job—a job at which he would fail. "Perhaps my notes outlined more of my *idea* for our plan?" Helena said carefully. "But the schedule is set in stone. These *will be* my errands for the week. Or rather, my mother's errands on which I will be dragged along. She never wavers once she's decided. Changes interrupt her wardrobe."

Declan considered this, trying to make sense of her expression, which had gone soft for the first time in two days. Her voice was light and familiar. She couldn't know this, but he loathed fickleness, loathed it even more than flat-out betrayal or the act of committing some wrong. One of the many things about the army that had suited him had been the very straightforward nature of a command.

"I have your notes," he said flatly, reaching into his pocket for the charred parchment.

Lady Helena's "plan" involved her sneaking from Lusk House every afternoon. She would track down the potential duchesses on the streets of London after her schedule of morning errands with her mother. Declan's role was to arrange mounts or hail hackneys, give advice about the route, and mind the horses.

Everything hinged on her mother's need for a daily afternoon nap.

Doubtless, she'd laid out only an abbreviated version, but Declan had seen enough to know her "plan" was shortsighted, high risk, and doomed to fail. She would be easily found out, hauled back, and burdened with tighter security. Declan would return to prison. His father would die an early death in the heartless chaos of London.

If she would not reconsider the plan—and her behavior of the last two days suggested she would not—Declan would be given no choice but to renege on their agreement.

Declan kicked his leg back, closing the door with his boot.

"Oh," piped Helena, raising up.

"*Oh*," he repeated. He stalked to her. "Hello. Remember me?"

"What? Of course I remem—"

"I thought we were collaborating."

"We *are* collaborating."

"No. A note telling me what I will do is not a collaboration. It is you ordering me about. I must be consulted. From the beginning. There is too much at stake to mishandle this."

"Well, look who is now keenly interested in not mishandling this," she said. "Previously I had to beg you to stand in the garden and take down a few names." She crossed her arms over her chest.

"The notion of stealing away from this house every afternoon is improbable and dangerous," he lectured. "Perhaps you could manage it once or twice, but not *seven times*."

"Alright," she said, and his brain misfired. He'd not expected her to agree.

He cleared his throat. "Do you have the list of potential duchesses from Lady Canning's party?"

"You need only ask." She slid a piece of parchment across the glass case.

He stared at her, suspicious of some duplicity or conceit. Her expression was open and bright. She looked interested. She looked so beautiful his heart lurched.

"If I remember correctly," he said, dropping her schedule beside the list, "these women can be found at known locales around the city. The errands and social calls on your mother's schedule are, likewise, scattered about town. Why not engineer some sort of encounter with as many as possible *while we are out*? If we are shrewd and crafty," he added. "And if your family and Lusk continue to ignore you. If a miracle occurs, this *may* work."

Slowly, Helena began to bob her head. "So we would scout the girls while we are on morning calls?"

"In theory—yes. Look, tomorrow you are meant to be in New Bond Street for a fitting. This girl . . ." he pointed to the duchess list, ". . . is said to frequent New Bond to shop nearly every day. This one . . ." he pointed down the list, ". . . goes to the country market in Wandsworth for medicinal herbs. You are scheduled to visit Lusk's farm in Wandsworth, not a mile from the market, on Tuesday. And on and on it goes. At least four of their known haunts align with your business in town. The others, we can improvise while your mother naps. A ride in Hyde Park would opportune this one." He pointed again. "These two you can approach at this Winter Solstice ball."

She made a face. "I was hoping to decline the Winter Solstice ball. It's a masquerade."

"If you can encounter these girls as a matter of course, you'll lower the risk of discovery. They'll be less confused when you turn up." He glanced at her. "It's a very long shot. We will need *incredible* luck on our side. But—"

"I love it." She beamed at him.

And just like that, Declan felt his fight drain away.

"Aren't you *clever,*" she went on, studying the notes more closely.

He forced his brain and mouth to work. "Right. So, tomorrow. The fitting in New Bond Street." He pointed at the map. "If your discoveries about these women can be believed, this girl . . . *Lady Genevieve* . . . would consider no other street for her compulsive shopping."

"Yes! Lady Genevieve," Helena enthused, rounding the case to stand beside him and peer at the map. The closeness conjured the smell of clean air and apple tarts. His vision blurred. He squeezed his eyes shut.

"Have you worked out what you will say when you approach these women?"

She nodded, the satin bow at the base of her neck sliding up and down her shoulders. Declan fought the urge to reach out and give it a gentle tug.

"I'll need to revise it now," she mused. "I am working on several renditions. I am not so hopeful as to think every girl is appropriate for Lusk. If they look all wrong, I'll not approach them. If they seem alarmed or put off by my vague suggestions, I'll retreat. I'll only move in if the girl has real potential. And, in the end, I'll invite the best candidates to meet the duke at Girdleston's birthday party next week."

"Can you invite strangers to Girdleston's party?"

"Oh, he invites half of London," she said dismissively, "the man has no real friends."

She looked again at the first girl on the list, Lady Genevieve Vance. "For this girl, I'll be prepared to dangle Lusk's great wealth. If she likes the shops, she'll want to hear of all his vast houses to redecorate."

"The conversations will be your purview," Declan said. "I'll always be nearby, but my actions and behavior will be limited to that of a servant and—"

"I'm sorry you have to serve me," she said, glancing up. "Truly."

I'm not. The words popped into his head.

I want only to serve you.

"Certainly you've put me through my paces these last few days." He cocked an eyebrow.

"Oh yes," she mused. "That. I was playacting, of course. Trying to calm everyone's nerves after the theatrics at Lady Canning's. I've found it's useful to be very, very good after I've caused a . . . a moment of high drama. To this lot, being 'good' means treating staff with undue wretchedness, sleeping 'til noon, and talking about the next item I hope to buy. So tedious." She glanced at him. "But surely you did not believe—"

"I can take an order, my lady. Remember I was in the army."

"But surely the tasks I set before you are not so demanding as the army's?" she said, laughing a little.

"You are nothing like the army," he said, glancing up and down her body with a heated look. "If you were, I would have never left. You may order me to do just about anything you like."

"Oh," she said, her eyes wide. Color shot to her cheeks.

"But don't cut me out of the plan making. The

service is for your wishes alone. The *plans* are a collaboration."

Helena stared at him a moment longer, her green eyes barely blinking. If nothing else, he had her full attention. His body responded with full attention. His pulse began to pound.

"You . . . you were correct to seize control of plan," she said finally, looking away. She sounded breathless. "I'll manage the recruitment, you the logistics."

She turned from the map and looked across the room. The armory walls were hung with a fortress of rifles, swords, and rapiers.

"Perhaps we should arm ourselves with some sort of weapon?" she said, her voice a little wavery. She was rambling. She cleared her throat. "These pieces are two hundred years old, but good enough for show, which is all we'd need. Why a London mansion requires an armory, I've no idea. If some valued item exists, Girdleston must have it. No one ever comes up here. That's why I chose this room to meet you."

He turned, too, leaning his elbows on the case beside her. "Enterprising choice." The words were out before he could stop them. Flirtatious words, even after he'd forbidden flirtation. He couldn't resist. She was too close, too unsettled by his proclamation about the plans. He wasn't lying when he said she could order him about, but he could dish out his own form of authority.

She rambled on. "I hadn't thought of our need for showy weapons, but—"

"We won't need weapons," he said. "Everything that we do should look and feel very close to the task at hand. We play along with whatever we're meant to be doing. Tomorrow you'll be in New Bond Street to buy dresses—"

"Actually, tomorrow I'm meant to be fitted for my trousseau," she said, turning to him. She raised her eyebrows as if to say, *Who's flirting now?*

"Right." He swallowed. *Who indeed.*

He continued, "Fine. Do whatever your mother expects on the errand. Stay as close to the truth as possible. We must be watchful and nimble, able to take advantage of unaccounted time or distractions."

Helena nodded and turned back to her paperwork, fingering the edges of the map. Her expression was uncertain. "What you mean is, be subtle. I'm a failure at subtlety, I'm afraid."

"You finessed these names from the women at the party," he said. "I don't doubt you for a second. I would not have risked my job if I did not believe you could manage your part." *And my freedom,* he added in his head. *And my future.*

He tried not to examine why, exactly, he'd done it. He didn't want to know.

He went on, "The wild cards are these girls. We've no way of knowing if they'll be remotely appropriate, or willing, or discreet."

She looked around the room again. "Another reason to arm ourselves. Perhaps just a small dagger? If they are uncooperative. To sort of . . . brandish?" She gave a tired smile.

"Remember," he said, "we are not mounting an offensive against Girdleston; we are undermining *his* offensive. We are sabotaging. Sabotage means hiding in plain sight. It's targeted disruption, although in secret. And trust no one else, unless they can be bribed. Money is the only thing you can trust."

"Oh, actually, I thought of that. Even before I was a *saboteur,* I relied heavily on bribes. We'll use this for bribes as needed." She plunked a weighty velvet purse on the case.

"But, Shaw?" she asked.

It occurred to him that he loved to hear his name on her lips.

She continued, "You've said to trust no one, but I want you to know that we may trust each other. I trusted you from the first moment, I don't know why."

He turned his head, gazing at her. She was so certain of herself. So hopeful. And so lovely. It almost hurt to look at her.

"Declan?" she asked softly.

And now his Christian name. He was doomed.

She put a hand on his arm and he squeezed his eyes shut.

He mustn't. They must not.

"Declan?"

He felt the weight of her hand on his sleeve. He need only straighten his arm to slide her palm down. Their fingers would lock. The slightest tug, and she would fall against him.

He opened his eyes.

She was staring at his mouth.

"Bloody hell," he rasped. He loomed closer.

"So serious," she whispered. "Always so serious."

"Helena."

She licked her lips, and Declan could taste her. She inched forward. She raised her face to him.

"We cannot risk it," he whispered, forcing the words out.

"Can we not?" Playfulness. Her eyes were smiling.

"No. We cannot. The *plan* is the priority. Above all. Keep you from Lusk. Find some better situation for my father and sisters."

She nodded. They were inches apart.

"I am a groom and you are the future wife of my employer, and we are embarking on a tenuous plan that puts us both in jeopardy. If we are found out—"

"If you are my groom, I have a task."

"Oh God."

"You've just said you are happy to do anything I ask."

"In service," he corrected, his voice cracking a little. Now who was unsettled and wavery?

"So serve me."

"Helena," he breathed.

"Just once more," she said. Not a question.

"If we are found out . . ." he repeated, but he was already leaning. Every cell reached for her, his need had crystalized, hard as a diamond. If the armory doors flew open and the entire household flooded in, he would not stop.

"Last time," she whispered. He felt her breath on his cheek. Her eyes drooped closed. She made a small noise of pleasure before he even touched her mouth.

When their lips met, Declan felt as if he'd been fitted into the most secure, most wonderful place on the earth. The crevice of a grassy hill in the sun. A hollowed-out rock, smooth from the tide. He existed, body and soul, to tuck her against his chest.

She paused, waiting, and Declan let her wait. One beat, two beats. He breathed her in. When finally he moved, he went slowly, savoring, leading her into a last kiss that would sustain them. A kiss that celebrated The Now. Nothing more, nothing less. They would savor this forbidden thing once more, and then commit to do it no more.

"I could not be more serious, Helena," he said, turning his face against the silky skin of her neck. "No more. This is the last."

He found her mouth again, increasing the intensity, invoking his tongue, sweeping his hands up her back. With wide fingers and open palms, he memorized the dip of her waist, the run of her ribs, the lush roundness of the sides of her breasts.

"Last time," she agreed breathlessly. She kissed him like she had something to prove. He'd taught her, and she'd understood. She was proficient, so much more than proficient. She was the perfect mix of seductive and playful, and *killing him*.

Her kiss asked the question: *What are you going to do about that?*

His brain answered, *I cannot ever kiss you again*.

The reality of this sank in like teeth into a forbidden apple. Sweet but so, so fleeting. He devoured her like this really was the last time.

He'd almost said, *You and I may never be together, regardless.*

He'd almost said, *Just because you don't marry Lusk, does not mean you will marry me.*

He'd almost said, *I am a mercenary and you are a gentleman's daughter, and we have no future.*

But the words would not come.

Every true thing did not need to be said.

The strange tangle of regret and longing dulled his desire—a good thing, ultimately, because he'd almost said too much.

"I want you to know," he finally breathed, "I've never taken advantage of a client. Not ever."

This truth. It was easier. He tucked her closer and breathed in.

"And I want you to know I've never kissed a servant," Helena said blithely, far less serious about honor and professionalism.

He chuckled into her neck and pulled her tighter still; he wanted to imprint her on his body, the searing outline of one last embrace.

"We'll need more of the lofty heiress charade," he said into her hair.

"What?"

"You fooled even me, and it's exactly what everyone expects. You were correct. Every inch the future duchess, issuing orders to your groom." He dropped a line of kisses on her neck.

"I've noticed you enjoy it," she mused, dropping her head back.

"Have you?" he rumbled, but he thought, *Oh God, yes.*

She laughed and craned to reach his mouth again. He kissed her hard, trying to swallow her whole, and she kept up, tilting her head and digging her fingers into his hair. His body was as hard as granite. He'd never wanted anything more than he wanted to pull Helena Lark to the floor and finish this. It was a dangerous want, more dangerous than their plan and her future and his freedom.

He pulled his mouth away and gasped for breath. "The end," he panted, and she made a little sobbing noise.

"Helena," he breathed, kissing her once more, hard and final. "My lady. The end."

He stepped away. It felt like rolling from a warm, soft riverbank into a cold, hard current. It felt like more than he could take.

She stared at him through blinking eyes. "Then go," she said.

Chapter Eleven

Helena arrived in New Bond Street with a full contingent of sisters, her mother, and a matronly cousin of Lusk's called Maude. Declan Shaw clung on the outboard runner of the second carriage, one of four grooms.

A day had passed since the armory and they'd not spoken again. Declan Shaw had kissed her like a man sentenced to death and then gone.

He was good, she told herself, very good. As cold as the Thames in February. He'd gone so far as to affect a mix-up, pretending he couldn't distinguish her from her sisters.

Helena had played along, making a show of exasperation, ignoring him with equal opaqueness. It was part strategy, part self-preservation. There was nothing small about her flourishing desire for Declan Shaw. She wanted Declan Shaw almost as much as she did not want the Duke of Lusk. As desires went, it was reckless and disruptive and dangerous to both Declan and herself. He' been correct to remove himself from the kiss in the armory; it was right to pretend he could not distinguish her from her sister Joan.

And now she would do her part, and win Lady Genevieve Vance to Helena's side.

But first, they must locate her.

New Bond Street clattered with carriages and the snorts and whinnies of horses. Shopgirls swept stoops and wiped broad windows on the parallel rows of smart shops. Shoppers in colorful silks and fluttering hats moved with a sort of choreographed formality. They seemed to browse for the benefit of each other as much as commerce.

When they were out of the carriage, Helena embarked upon immediate separation from her mother and Lusk's cousin.

"Would you see Madame first, Mama?" she asked, looking to the modiste's door. "I should like to take a turn up 'round the shops before the midday crush."

"Lovely, darling," her mother had said, eager for her own time with Madame. "I'll take the first fitting. But mind your sisters, will you? Their squabbling has awakened that terrible throbbing behind my left temple. It was an error in judgment to bring only one governess."

Helena had planned for this, but she feigned irritation as she gathered her sisters and dispatched the youngest girl's governess to retrieve forgotten parasols from the carriage. Her sisters were fourteen, seventeen, and eighteen; well old enough to relish time to themselves in New Bond Street.

"Theresa, Joan, Camille," Helena called when their mother had gone, "how would you fancy a refreshment before your appointment with Madame? A little lemon ice, perhaps, to sustain you through hours of pinning and prodding?"

Her sisters' bickering and preening fell silent and three heads swiveled in her direction.

"What refreshment?" challenged Joan, her oldest sister.

"Why, there is a café just there," said Helena, pointing. "You see? On the corner? Fromley's Emporium, it's called. The duke has told me Fromley's is known for the loveliest lemon ices in all of London. The grandest ladies and gentlemen pop in for tea as a respite from shopping."

"Since when do you converse with the duke?" asked Theresa.

"He is my betrothed," defended Helena, "of course we converse."

Three sets of green eyes stared at her with open suspicion.

Helena ignored them. "Perhaps you're not hearing me. I've got two shillings for each of you. Indulge in whatever the café has on offer. Settle in at a window table and examine the fashionable ladies and gentlemen."

"What do you care for fashionable ladies and gentlemen?" asked Joan.

"*I* won't be there. I've my own errand in the street. You're old enough to enjoy the café without me. When Theresa's governess returns from the carriage, she will accompany you. And I'll send a groom to watch over you."

Helena glanced around. Shaw had gone to settle the carriages. Only Nettle hovered on the periphery of their group.

"You hate shopping," said Camille, the shrewdest of her sisters.

"I do not hate shopping, and I'm in search of a gift. For the duke."

Now the girls burst into laughter.

"Ah, yes. Hilarious." Helena shook her head and led them to the café. "You won't convince me that you're not interested in a London café. I won't believe it."

The girls quieted and followed her, casting sidelong glances amongst themselves. After a moment, Joan said, "You cannot simply leave us. We're not like you, accustomed to tromping around in the forest alone. We are meant to be ladies."

"First of all, I said the governess will be with you. Miss Turtle."

"Miss *Tuttle*," Theresa corrected.

"Miss *Tuttle*," repeated Helena. "Second, I don't tromp in the forest. I tend my apples and ride my horse and shop in the village, just as you do. If ever you chose to *visit me* and see the beauty of Castle Wood for yourselves, you would know this. How sad it has made me that you no longer come to the forest. Your preference is the manor house with Mama and Papa, I understand. But—"

"It's not a preference, Helena," said Camille matter-of-factly. "Mama and Papa do not allow us to visit you."

Helena paused, surprised by this admission. Visits from by her sisters had dwindled after their grandmother died, and Helena had been too grief-stricken and busy with the orchard to pursue them. When she called to the manor house, the girls' reception of her had been cool and distracted. They very clearly sided with their parents on the topic of merging families with the Duke of Lusk. Helena had begun to view them as disinterested bystanders at best; at worst, traitors.

Honestly, she'd been so wrapped up in her own deliverance she'd given very little thought to the girls. She could only save herself. Or could she?

"What reason do they give," Helena asked, "for not allowing you to visit the forest?"

Camille shrugged. "They don't want to lose us to it, as they lost you."

Helena made a bitter laugh. "They've not lost me. I'm a mile away."

"Are you not? Lost to them?" Camille asked, watching her closely.

"I am lost as any pawn, perhaps."

"And *this*," said Joan, "is why we are not allowed to call on you."

"Girls," Helena said, looking each off them in the eye, "mind yourselves. Be thoughtful about the men they propose under the guise of 'your own good.' Perhaps you've not been committed to arranged marriages like me—in this, perhaps, they've learned their lesson—but that doesn't mean you will have say over your lives. Begin now," she said firmly. "Assert some say over your own lives."

"This is the strong-headedness they do not want," said Camille, still watching her closely.

"You are a bad influence," recited Theresa, clearly a commonly heard refrain.

"I am an *influence*," Helena corrected, "this I'll not deny. But you are old enough to decide for yourselves if I am a bad one. The truth is, I miss you very much. Perhaps I've indulged in my private sanctuary of the forest for too long. If I manage to return, I shall contrive to get you there more often. But you mustn't believe what Mama and Papa say about exploring the world around you. You'll still be *ladies* in the forest. Certainly, you may enjoy lemon ices in a busy café for ten minutes. *I* am a lady. I'm . . . er, marrying a duke, aren't I?"

"Are you?" asked Camille.

Helena narrowed her eyes but said nothing. Joan crossed her arms over her chest. Her expression said their parents were correct; for Joan, the indoctrination had already begun. Theresa barely listened, looking at the activity of the street. But Camille stared back with a level gaze, studying Helena like a door she wanted to unlock. Helena bit her lip, wishing she had more time. Later, she told herself. Soon but not now. If she could escape Lusk and gain a real relationship with her sisters in the process, she would have success beyond her wildest dreams.

"Can you stay together?" Helena said now. She shot Camille a heartfelt look. "And follow Miss Tuttle's lead on how to place your order and settle the bill. And keep in sight of the groom."

"The groom called *Shaw*?" This from Joan, a note of challenge in her voice.

Helena paused.

"Careful," Theresa said, giggling.

"*No*," said Helena, leading them down the street, "not Shaw. He is my private groom and he will remain with me. Mr. Nettle will attend you."

They reached the café and Helena paused, digging for coins in her reticule. The sisters gathered cautiously, straightening hats and tightened gloves. Miss Tuttle returned with the girls' forgotten parasols, and she spoke briefly to the governess and bade Nettle to watch over them. The girls muttered vague gratitude and farewells and hurried inside, already bickering about who would sit closest to the window.

When she was finally, blessedly, alone, Helena turned back to the street.

Her plan had been to make one quick but thorough circuit, and then retire to the modiste's for her fitting while Shaw kept watch. After the fitting, she would make some excuse and circuit the street again.

Lady Genevieve. Blonde. Beautiful. Dresses to be noticed, she repeated in her head, raising a gloved hand to shade her face.

"It's ambitious, I think," said a male voice behind her, "to stand in one spot and hope she happens along."

Shaw. Helena's lungs were a sieve. He made her breathless simply by turning up.

"Ah," she said, not looking back. "There you are." Her voice was steady and controlled, but her heartbeat ran away.

"My sisters are occupied for twenty minutes, thirty if we are lucky. My mother is with the modiste. Shall we walk?"

She glanced at him, forcing herself to look imperious and demanding. She would not stare at his mouth.

"You'll have to keep behind me," she said. "And

carry this." She shrugged from a plum-colored velvet cloak and draped it across his arms.

"*Yes*, my lady," he said. Three simple words, words she'd heard from servants all her life. Did she imagine the note of . . . suggestion when he said them?

A charged sort of energy buzzed from along the back of her neck and slid down her shoulders. She sucked in a little breath and shaded her eyes again. She would be as cold as the Thames in February, just like Shaw.

"I assume you have made considerations if this girl isn't alone," Shaw said lowly.

"You assume correctly."

"I reckon she'll be in the company of a relative," he guessed, "or companion."

"Don't worry, I've thought of this."

They came to the intersection of Conduit Street, and Shaw stepped into the road to block the intersection so she could pass. Helena checked every female face. Nothing. Wrong age, wrong class, wrong coloring. There were blonde women, but they pushed prams or walked arm in arm with friends—almost correct but not exactly.

Helena went on. "Let me to tell you what I intend to say to her, if we see her. I stayed up half the night, making a sort of conversational map of each irresistible detail of the exclusive invitation I'm offering. I'll lure them in, bit by bit."

"I trust you."

"They've been singled out partly because of their very great desire for a title. And the title of duchess is the very best of all, save princess. I've pinned the whole thing on their very great desire for a duke. Every girl wants a duke."

"Every girl except you," he sighed.

"For example," Helena pressed on, "I will introduce myself, along with the added detail that I am engaged to the Duke of Lusk. After this revelation, I will watch very closely for a reaction. It forces either a congratulations or question about the wedding. If I detect even the slightest bit of hesitation or judgment or envy, that will be my cue to say something like, 'Oh, thank you. What a pity I cannot sleep nights for being worried about how I will manage as duchess . . .'

"And if *this* sparks a look of shrewd interest, along with the not-so-innocent question of, 'Why ever not?' I will follow with, 'Oh, the very great responsibility of it all. There are so many properties and a great number of social commitments. The shopping alone . . .' My expression will show something like 'winsome dread.' " She affected an expression of winsome dread.

"Thank God I've no part of this bit," Declan mumbled.

She continued, stepping around an old woman with a bird in a cage. "And if she shows concern—not authentic concern but kind of *mercenary* concern—I will say, 'Honestly, I'm worried that I might not be up to the task . . .'

"And on it on it will go," she finished. "I will be *nimble* and *opportunistic*. Just as you have said. Sage words, from a groom."

"God help us."

"In the end, if my cues and leading questions take us down the path to a place of their bald-faced interest, I will simply tell them: I'm trying to pawn him off. And then I will invite them to Girdleston's birthday party. Next week. There they may get a look at the duke and . . . and give it a go. They will *dazzle* him."

"Again," said Declan, "God help us."

"Do not worry. You underestimate the irresistible prospect of a duke simply . . . theirs for the taking. I chose these girls because they are primed to pounce. And if ever they appear less than *transfixed* with the idea of having someone like Lusk for themselves . . . then I will abandon the conversation."

A line of schoolboys snaked their way down the walk, and Helena stepped to the side. "It's a lot of 'ifs,' I know. But this is why I meant to approach so many young women."

They reached the end of New Bond with no sign of anyone remotely fitting the description of Lady Genevieve. Helena cursed their limited timing and crossed to the other side of the street.

"I've seen four blonde women," Shaw reported. "But the age is wrong. Or the dress."

Helena stared at the row of shingles hanging beneath the awnings of shop after shop after shop. "She could appear at any time."

"Look in windows," he instructed. "And inside passing carriages. There's no guarantee she'll march down the street."

Helena nodded, stepping up to a window. The display beyond the glass dripped with ribbons and lace, a blizzard of accoutrements styled in white-and-pink drifts. Her sisters had been mistaken when they said she didn't enjoy shopping. In fact, fashion was a hobby, and she rather enjoyed dresses and hats and ribbons—not the latest styles, not the ostentation of London, but playing with color and texture and looking distinctive in pretty things. Her grandmother had patronized a dressmaker in Winscombe, and the two of them had worked together on dresses that suited Helena's skin and figure, that drew inspiration from summer greens and winter whites. Helena's mother had insisted upon a few London-made pieces, her trousseau among them, but when Helena and her lady's maid pulled together her wardrobe, they reached for her gowns from the village dressmaker.

Now she squinted through the glass, trying to make out the customers inside. In a sudden *whoosh*, the door of another shop flew open, emitting an upright gentleman with stomping boots and swinging cane. Helena gasped and bumped into him.

"I beg your pardon, sir," she said, jumping back.

The man whirled around. "Mind yourself!" His snarl bared a wet glob of tobacco and a gold tooth.

Helena shrank back, and Shaw was there suddenly, inserting his large body between them.

"Careful, my lady," he sang in a low, almost playful sort of whistle.

Helena hopped back just as Shaw affected a half pivot, half stumble. The unsteadiness caused him to appear clumsy, although his control and balance was obvious to her. Moreover, she saw the look in his eyes: cool, shrewd, intentional.

"I've never seen the likes of this," the man bellowed. "Drunken revelers in New Bond Street." He raised his cane as if to strike, but Shaw's hand shot out and clasped the polished wood, stopping it midarc.

"Careful, governor," Shaw said, spinning neatly away. He gave the cane a little twerk, and the man yelped in pain. In one fluid movement, the cane flicked from the man's grasp and pitched into the air.

"Let me get that for you, gov," Shaw said, snatching it from above his head as if the man himself had tossed it. He caught it with one hand, spun it like a baton, and pressed it to the man's chest.

It happened so quickly his deft movements were barely perceptible, even to Helena. It looked almost like a dance, and he'd done it one-handed, with her cloak flapping gently across his left arm.

Who is he? she marveled.

Stepping back, she nearly collided again, this time with a small figure in a dark cloak.

"I beg your pardon," she said again, craning around. The person's face was obscured by a flowing velvet hood. Helena saw only the tip of a nose. She stepped closer, trying to make out a face, but the figure hurried away, disappearing into the crowd.

She looked back to Shaw. He was bowing with exaggerated humility as the gentleman glared and shook his wrist.

Shaw ignored the outrage, tipped his hat, and backed away. The gentleman spun and strode in the opposite direction, grumbling some indecipherable complaint.

Shaw stepped to her. "Are you hurt?"

"I'm perfectly well," she said, gaping at him. He'd moved like an acrobat and fought like a fencing master. It was unlike anything she'd ever seen.

"If you're certain," he said, "let's walk."

Helena walked. "Shaw? How did you manage that?"

Shaw was silent. He adjusted his hat.

"Declan?" she asked again.

"What?"

"Tell me what you've just—"

"My lady," he warned, "you are meant to be looking—"

"I'm perfectly capable of walking and talking *and* looking. If I simply stride down the street, gaping at everyone, I'll look mad."

"This endeavor is mad," he mumbled.

She whirled on him. "This was your idea and, foolish me, I believed it to be rather inspired. But now, I cannot say. I'd like some credentials. Immediately. In fact, I can't believe I've allowed the Great Secret of your identity to languish between us for so long. I'll not take another step until you tell me how a lowly stable groom understands the fine points of sabotage. And stalking young women. And disarming crazed gentleman in the street."

"Now?" he whispered harshly, moving her from the flow of pedestrians.

"Yes," she said. *"Right now."*

He looked right and left. He took a deep breath. "Fine. If you must know. My true profession is . . . is as a mercenary."

Helena laughed a little. He was making a joke. He was—

His face remained passive. He cocked an eyebrow.

"I beg your pardon?"

"I work," he said, "as a mercenary. Do you know what that is?"

"Ah . . ."

"It's a soldier-for-hire," he said. "A bodyguard. Paid security. I track people and things. I'm called 'The Huntsman' in professional circles because I specialize in finding people who do not wish to be found. Not unlike Lady Genevieve Bloody Vance, for all the good it's doing us."

Helena stopped and gaped at him. She could not be more shocked if he'd admitted he was King George.

"A mercenary?" she repeated.

"Yes." He began again to walk.

"How did you . . . fall into this line of work?"

"I studied it in university."

"Hilarious."

"I was a solider. The Royal Army. For many years—twelve. I fought in France, the Peninsula. When I had the opportunity to leave soldiering, I took it. My family needed me in London. I'd only been home a month when a former officer asked me to help him locate a wayward son who'd skipped off to the Continent. I'd been useful in reconnaissance in the war."

"And did you find him?"

"I did."

"Of course you did." So much now made sense. "No wonder I feel safe with you."

"Oh no," he said, waving away this notion. "I am not safe. I am very dangerous. I'm lethal. Everyone says it." He actually sounded irritated. Helena stifled a smile.

"Have you ever been hired to 'mind' someone before?"

"No."

"Have you ever posed as a servant before?"

"Yes—no. I can't remember."

"Have you ever . . . shot someone?"

"I've been to war, my lady."

"Have you ever—"

"Whatever you're thinking," he cut in, "I've done it.

They'd come to the end of the street. Her sisters could be seen preening through the front window of the adjacent café. Shoppers—none of them Lady Genevieve—came and went. Helena pulled an apple from her pocket and took a bite. Her hand shook. He'd fought and killed and guarded and now he was her groom, and she'd asked him to . . . to . . . help her get herself jilted.

And he'd *agreed*.

Helena tried to comprehend what his profession meant to her personally, as a woman—as a woman he'd touched and kissed. Likely, he kissed breathless women in stables and carriages all the time.

What could an earl's virgin daughter mean to him? Was it better that he was a mercenary and not a groom?

She couldn't know.

And also she couldn't devote any more of this fleeting day to thinking about it.

She forced herself to ask, "It's bad that we've seen no sign of Lady G, isn't it? In your professional opinion?" In her head she added, *As a mercenary?*

"The probability of encountering her was always very slim," he said, gazing down the street. "Finding any of these girls, especially the first day out? I put the odds at ten percent. But the outing isn't over. Your fitting will take time; convening six women to depart New Bond Street will take time. It was always a complicated plan, but we have more time. For now, collect your sisters and go to Madame Layfette's. I'll keep watch."

DECLAN HEARD LADY Genevieve before he saw her. A trill of laughter, pitched too loud to be borne of amusement. A whoop. The delicate clapping of gloved hands.

Nothing in New Bond Street was that amusing. He shoved off the wall beside Madame Layfette's shop.

A carriage, shiny and well sprung, had come to a stop five yards away. Footmen and grooms hurried to secure steps and mollify horses. Declan took a step closer, his breath held.

From the open door, a hat emerged, ivory with crimson trim.

Next, a head, popping out like a mole from a hole. Her laughing smile was so broad it made him blink. She looked as if she'd arrived at a delightful party already in progress. When she turned her head, he saw coil upon coil of white-blonde plaits tucked neatly beneath the hat.

Her body was compact, a little plump, but with

all the correct geography, sheathed in a cherry-red dress. The color alone demanded attention, a bold choice for which she was obviously prepared, and it fit her like the casing of a sausage. She clutched a small dog to her chest, its neck tied with a magenta bow.

Lady Genevieve Vance. It could be no other. New Bond Street was awash in fashionable ladies, yet this girl shone brighter, and laughed louder. Men stopped walking to stare. Women turned to study the gown and the hat and the dog, their subtlety and reserve given over to open curiosity. Her staff played their part, scurrying about as if the royal family had arrived.

Declan adopted his best air of biddable servant on orders and melted into the crowds of New Bond Street. He trudged past the window of Madame Layfette's. There was no sign of Helena in the showroom. Lady Pembrook, the earl's cousin, and at least one sister were bent over counters or peered at unfurled bolts of fabric. He could think of no subterfuge that would admit him, and certainly no way to get word to Lady Helena.

He changed course and circled behind the shop to the alley. The rear door was propped open by a brick; beyond the door, an empty corridor stretched the length of the building. Unintelligible voices mumbled through walls and industrious footfalls clattered on distant stairs. Declan considered his limited options, mindful of the minutes ticking away. If Helena was being fitted, she would be in a room along this corridor.

Within moments, a serving boy appeared, lugging a bundle of firewood. Declan saw opportunity and gave a low whistle. When the boy looked back, Declan flipped a shiny coin into the air.

Five minutes and sixpence later, the boy had informed Declan that, yes, the black-haired young lady was being fitted. She'd been installed in the middle dressing rooms, but the boy didn't know with whom. Madame Layfette had apparently become very upset when the lady hadn't made the proper show of delight over the color or style of a new garment. The modiste had fled to the basement with three seamstresses, determined to improve the design.

When the boy turned to go, Declan followed, slipping inside and pressing his ear to the middle door. Before he could detect any sound, Helena's middle sister, Miss Camille Lark, emerged, straightening her hat. Declan froze half a beat, rolled off the door, and conjured his best servant's expression.

"Shaw," said Camille Lark.

"Miss," said Declan, looking at the floor.

"Can I *help* you?" Her expression was intrigued amusement.

"I've a message. For Lady Helena."

"Ah. One can only hope you can distinguish which one of us she is. I'm guessing that you can."

"Miss."

"Let me give the message to her," Camille said.

More confusion, he tried to affect the expression of being torn. "I dunno, miss. I was told the message is private in nature. The young lady, a friend of her ladyship, bade me give it to her in person."

"A friend?" challenged Camille. "Lady Helena hasn't any friends. She doesn't like the bother."

Declan forced a blank expression. Her family knew her so very little.

He continued. "If you please, miss, I've been told she's here. If you—"

He let the question trail off. There was a fine line between being in a strange place at the wrong time and purposefully breaking the rules.

"She is here," affirmed Camille carefully. She pointed to a closed door. "Although I cannot say she is accustomed to visits from male staff whilst being fitted by a modiste." She raised an eyebrow. A challenge.

Declan took a gamble.

Keeping his face neutral, he said, "Likely you are right, miss. Perhaps you could ask her?"

Camille stared at him a long moment and then said, "Perhaps I could."

She moved to the door and slipped inside. When she emerged a half minute later, her expression was the slightest bit conspiratorial.

"Go on, then," she said. "Be quick about it. Madame Layfette is in rare form, thanks to Helena. My sister specializes in giving people fits."

Declan gave a curt nod and watched the younger woman walk away. When he was certain she'd gone, he edged to the crack in the door.

"My lady?" he whispered.

"Shaw? Come in!"

Declan slipped inside, shut the door, and turned the lock.

Pivoting a half circle, he scanned the room. Lady Helena was on the dais in the corner, her familiar black hair and cream skin a blur in his peripheral vision.

He moved on, seeing bolts of fabric, a trolley of sewing tools, a cat asleep on a cushion by the grate.

"She's here," he said, taking the long way to the window and positioning himself sideways to peer out. "I'm certain it's her. Arrived not five minutes ago. Young. Blonde. Expensive looking. And believe or not, she's *alone.* I saw her go into—"

He stopped.

His attention was finally, unerringly, fixed on Helena.

She was half dressed in loose, diaphanous green silk. Her hair down and her feet bare. He saw the perfect outline of her body through the silk, every shade and texture, every dip and swell. She was a fantasy standing before him.

Declan's mind went blank.

"What?" Helena asked, baring a shoulder as she stooped to collect a swath of silk and step from the dais. The movement sent lingerie billowing and flowing like froth on a clear sea. Through the fabric, he saw long thin legs, a flat belly, and small breasts with dusky pink tips.

"You saw her go . . . ?" she prompted.

Declan fought to keep up. He fought to remember anything but the overwhelming sight of her, mostly naked, before him.

"But did she go far?" Helena asked. "How did she look? Was she beautiful?"

There is no beauty beyond you, he thought. He could not form the words.

"Declan?" she demanded.

"I . . . I cannot form words," he admitted.

"What?" she snapped. "But why not? Are you—"

And then she followed his eyes, looking down at the outline of her body in the green silk.

"Oh," she said. Her head popped up, her eyes wide. Color rose in her cheeks.

"Yes," she said. Her voice was raspy. "Perhaps it's not so very bad." Her nipples hardened into pebbles beneath the thin fabric, and Declan's mouth went dry.

"Not bad at all," he agreed. He took a step toward her.

"I've told Madame that I hate it. She flew into a rage and they've gone to make some change." She licked her lips, staring at his mouth. "Lucky for us. She's only been gone five minutes. So we may . . ."

She splayed a hand on her neck, the languid sort of gesture of someone who needed to feel touch.

Declan would kill, he thought, to fulfill that need.

"I'm glad someone will see it, I suppose," she went on. "I would never wear it in the company of Lusk."

Declan took another step toward her. His brain snagged on the words *Lusk* and *wear it in the company of*, and he heard little else. He was filled with the kind of violent opposition that starts wars.

"Helena," he breathed.

"Yes?" A whisper.

"Helena," he repeated. Lust was an iron stake,

pinning him to this moment. He saw only her.

"We mustn't." Another whisper. She began shaking her head. Her hair swayed down her back in a soft, black curtain. "*You* made this mandate. In the armory, you said no more. And in the carriage. Every time is the last time—that is what you say."

"I shouldn't be here," he rasped.

"It should be only you," she said, and Declan's heart squeezed.

She went on. "I want . . . I want one hour when it is only you and me. A very long, very private hour. But—" She drew a long, ragged breath. "We are less alone in this moment than we've been since the beginning. Madame could return any moment."

"Yes." He couldn't look away.

"Yes." A thoughtful smile. "So . . . let us endeavor to stay on task?"

"Yes."

She made a purposeful turn, presenting him with a knee-weakening view of her anterior.

She spoke to a nearby chair. "Tell me about Lady Genevieve?"

Declan's brain still had not caught up. He watched her trudge to the chair and sink into it, gathering the frothy green silk around her like suds in a bath.

In his mind's eye, Declan saw himself coming to her, dropping to his knees before the chair, dipping a hand into—

"Declan!" she insisted.

Declan spun and faced the wall. "She's here—yes. Lady Genevieve. In the street. I've just seen her."

"Yes, yes, but how does she look?"

"Ah." He stared at the wall. "She has a dog."

"What? A dog? What care have we for a dog? *Is she the sort of girl who might appeal to Lusk?"*

Declan shrugged his shoulders. "She looked very . . . happy. She smiles unceasingly. She has a bit of a lunatic smile."

He turned, forcing himself to look only at her face.

"Unceasing, lunatic smile. I need more. I must see her myself."

She shoved from the chair and began to pace. "But how can I get outside to see her? Madame won't return my dress until she is satisfied with this . . ." she gathered up a puff of green silk and flounced it, ". . . and I can hardly go out wearing transparent green silk."

He stared at her, watching the fabric settle around her body.

Helena put a stiff palm over eyes and blew out a frustrated breath. Speaking slowly, she said, "If you do not say something or plan something, I will sort it out myself."

"Right," he said. "Forgive me. I was unprepared for your—"

"Yes, yes, I'm only half dressed—"

"You consider this *half* dressed—"

"Declan!"

"Yes, alright," he said, snapping to. "Here's the plan. I'll find a seamstress and bribe her. We'll have her bring you something else to wear, a . . . matron's robe or something loose and shroud-like that won't require a corset or petticoats.

The inventory in this shop should offer several choices."

"Yes, yes. *Thank you.*" Her impatience was clear, but she listened.

"When you've changed, I'll steal you into the alley, and you can approach the girl in the stationer's shop, assuming she's still there."

"Very great assumption," she said. "Good. Fine. Let's give it a go. But can you really locate something else for me to wear?"

Declan could. He prowled the corridor until he game upon a seamstress. He bribed her with half a crown to produce some suitable dress. Next, he bade the same girl to stand guard at the dressing room while Declan and Helena slipped out. She was to warn any inquirers that Lady Helena was indisposed and not to disturb her for at least twenty minutes. Finally, the same girl agreed to clear the corridor when they returned and allow them to slip back inside without detection.

Every piece of the plan, from the jittery seamstress, to the heavy gray wool dowager's gown, to the chance that Lady Genevieve was still nearby, felt tenuous and combustible and highly, highly unlikely. In all his years of stealth and tracking, Declan had never embarked on anything so wildly extemporaneous and risky.

But Helena moved through the motions with a patient, deliberate sense of calm. Her determination was as cold and hard as steel. These women were her last hand. If it didn't work, she had nothing.

Declan had not *not* believed her so much as hadn't understood the lengths to which she was willing to go. Even her sprint through the rain in front of Lady Canning's had seemed more like an elaborate show of protest than a high-stakes piece of a larger plan.

Now, as he stole her out the back door and into the muddy alley, her jaw set, her voice light and reassuring to the blotchy seamstress who watched them go, she had the bearing of someone bent on survival. It rivaled his own resolve to exonerate his name or the will of any soldier he'd ever seen fighting to the death on a field of battle.

"You can speak with her inside the stationer's shop," he told Helena quickly. "It's a large shop with a maze of shelves and counters. But you'll have more time and privacy if she can be drawn outside. Duck between shops or settle on a bench. Say the script, just as you told me. You'll be brilliant."

"Or I'll be laughed from the shop," she said, and she smiled at him, her green eyes full of excitement and hope. Declan's heart lurched again. He experienced the strange feel of slowly ripping in two, the old, self-serving, solitary part of himself separating from the part that was consumed with an untouchable, unattainable woman, so far out of his class.

But now she was gone. The bell on the stationer's shop door jingled, and Helena and her pile of gray wool trailed into the dim interior.

Declan looked right and left, his adrenaline pumping as if he'd been pursuing a highwayman. He tried to peer into the shop window, but saw only his reflection. He blinked at his face, a man doing a highly reckless, improbable thing on the pretense of exoneration and family. What a liar.

Swallowing hard, he slouched into the subordinate posture of a servant. He strolled past Madame's window and checked the showroom. The Lark women were clustered around an open box of baubles. Camille Lark looked up, catching his gaze.

Declan took a deep breath and circled back. He returned to the alley and checked the seamstress who stood guard. No one had come.

Again in the street, he made another circuit, taking the long way around, returning to the stationer's shop from the other direction. When at last the door came into view, he faltered. He could not trust his eyes.

Helena emerged from the shop with Lady Genevieve on her arm. The two young women walked together, their heads bent in conversation. The smile on Lady Genevieve's face had the sharp, cold point of a scythe. Her expression was so avaricious it sent a chill up Declan's spine. Behind the duo, the girl's forgotten dog whimpered and trotted along.

Declan trailed them half a block, keeping back fifteen yards. When they reversed their course, he kept pace in the alley, out of view. He caught sight of them at each gap between buildings. They walked close together, oblivious to passersby.

When he turned the corner at the modiste's shop, Lady Genevieve was gone and Helena stood by the edge of the building alone.

"What's happened?" he asked, darting to her.

Helena turned and beamed up into his face. "She'll do it," she said. "She very keen to be a duchess—to put it mildly. She wants to have a go."

Chapter Twelve

Seven Duchesses (Potential)

Happy ✓

The next day dawned cold and gray, with the windy threat of a rain. By eight o'clock, the garden outside Helena's window had been drummed into a wet tangle of gold and red. Undeterred, Helena continued to dress. She *would* travel to Wandsworth today, she *would* meet the next potential duchess, she would—

The note came with breakfast, a fastidiously folded rectangle balanced on her tray. She flipped it open with a sigh.

My lady,

How crestfallen we are over today's inclement weather. Such an unreliable time of year. Because of this, the duke and I are grappling with a postponement of today's planned outing.

His Grace does look so very forward to squiring you about his Home Farm, but he would not expose you to what is certain to be slow travel on muddy roads, not to mention a cold drenching the moment you step foot from the carriage. I am thinking also of your family.

Would you wait and tour the farm another, fairer day?

Yours,
Uncle Titus

Helena's scowled at the note. She'd never understood why the duke sent notes back and forth through his uncle. Why didn't he write himself if he thought it was too wet to ride?

Because he doesn't want to go, she thought. *In any weather.*

If they did not go as planned, the day would be shot; they would not go anywhere at all. There were only nine days until "Uncle Titus's" blasted birthday. She didn't have rainy days to spare.

Helena had never heard of Wandsworth nor realized that wealthy London aristocrats enjoyed "home farms" on the outskirts of London, but Shaw had known, and he'd made the connection between their tour of Lusk's farm and another of their potential duchesses, Lady Moira Ashington. Wandsworth boasted a large market, and Lady Moira was a devoted customer of a so-called "healer" who peddled her drafts and poultices from a market stall.

Taking up pen and parchment, she wrote:

Sir,

I am grateful to Lusk for thinking of my comfort. The onset of winter can be an adjustment. However, I am a country girl at heart and undeterred by wet roads.

Pity, too, because the Home Farm tour was of particular interest to me. I can feel hemmed in if I remain in London overlong, and that says nothing of my relentless curiosity of the natural world. Considering this, I can honestly say that I'd prefer a wet tour of the farm to no tour at all. My family is simply happy to be included.

But please do not let my enthusiasm inconvenience the duke. Of course we can wait for sunshine. Or, if Lusk prefers, I am happy to ride to Wandsworth alone. Thinking back, I cannot remember our ever discussing his Home Farm, which leads me to believe he may be ambivalent about the property. Meanwhile, it will be a rare treat for me.

I remain, as ever, His Grace's humble and willing guest.

Signed,
Lady Helena Lark

She folded the parchment and thrust it at her lady's maid, Meg.

Be nimble and opportunistic, she thought.

Stay as close to the truth as possible.

Shaw's advice, combined with her own turn of phrase, elicited a reply from Girdleston within a half hour.

"My warmest cloak, Meg," Helena told her lady's maid, tossing Girdleston's note into the fire. "The trip is on. I'll need something to keep out the wet. The crimson?"

Her suggestion of ambivalence from Lusk had done it. They would persevere. The trip was on.

A half hour later, Helena was being handed into the lead carriage. Girdleston designated that the future bride and groom should ride alone together except for "one of your dear sisters. Just a small nod to propriety . . ."

And so Camille rode beside Helena, immersed in a book. Outside, rain drummed on the roof of the carriage. Declan Shaw was an outrider on her vehicle; she could see his powerful bicep through her window. She'd just managed to swing out the glass when Lusk climbed inside.

"Your Grace," she said.

The duke made no answer. He flashed her a resentful look and collapsed onto the opposite seat. In irritated, exaggerated movements, he began to unscrew the lid of a metal flask. He took an elaborate swig, leveling her with flat, tired eyes.

She'd tried again. "Thank you for pressing on to Wandsworth despite the rain. Perhaps the storm has already passed into the south."

He took another long swig from the flask and smacked his lips. *"Perhaps the storm has passed into the south,"* he repeated in a nasally, singsongy voice.

He was mocking her. Helena blinked at the unexpected cruelty. Camille looked up from her book. The duke raised his brows at the two of them, daring a challenge, and then fell back against the seat. He tipped his face to the ceiling.

"I know what let's do!" he said in an obnoxious voice, too loud for the small carriage. "Let us drag ourselves to the most godforsaken part of London in the freezing rain to look at goats!" He laughed.

Helena looked at Camille. Her sister stared back with an expression of confused horror.

As a rule, the Duke of Lusk was not biting or sartorial or even particularly lucid. It occurred to Helena that, for once, he must be sober. Beneath the liquor and snuff, was Bradley Girdleston simply . . . hateful? A cold tremor of anxiety stiffened the back of her neck.

Beside her, Camille slid a gloved hand over her arm. Helena blinked at it, unaccustomed to any show of warmth from her sisters. She smiled at Camille and turned back to the duke.

"How fortunate you are to cultivate your own produce, even in the city," she said. "But surely you cannot begrudge a property that puts food on your table and wine in your cellar?"

He took another swig from his flask, still staring at the ceiling. "I do begrudge it. Farms? Don't care. Farm *homes*? Don't like. Wandsworth? I'd rather drown."

Helena swallowed hard, pressing on. "Well, I've heard the house is lovely. Perhaps you can find a comfortable spot near a warm fire while I nose around the orchard and hothouses. I've been told a stream on the edge of the property runs so thick with trout you can stand on the bank and see them jump."

"I wouldn't know," he intoned in that too-loud

voice.

She tried again. "Are you fond of the ale from your brewery?"

"Less talking," he mumbled. "More *not*-talking." He never lifted his head.

Helena nodded and looked away. It was always like this. She'd tried for years to appeal to him about their obvious unsuitability, about the control exerted over him by his uncle, about any earnest topic at all. She'd even asked him why he continued to welcome a fiancée who repeatedly ran away. He'd always ignored her, or deflected the questions, or passed out. There was usually more giggling or belching or pretending he could not hear her, but perhaps he was beginning to feel the pinch of their encroaching wedding. Perhaps the foolishness was being burned away and only panic remained. Certainly, she felt something akin to panic. She'd not expected to find harshness at the core of Bradley Girdleston, but then again, she'd not really known the duke at all.

After a half hour passed in silence, they reached the sprawling acreage of Lusk's Home Farm. The rain had distilled to a patchy fog that hung in the air like wet smoke. Servants formed a half-moon from the door of the house, fidgety and beaming, clearly unaccustomed to a visit from His Grace.

Good, Helena thought. *Let them leap to do his bidding. Divert everyone so I might ride out in peace.*

She pushed the carriage curtain aside. "Oh, I cannot wait to see it all," she said for the tenth time. "And look, the rain has stopped."

The duke rolled his head from the carriage

seat, squinting out the window. "Surely you cannot mean to traipse around in the fog, watching laborers muck about?"

"In fact, I do, Your Grace, if you are not opposed. I've my journals to take notes." She patted a stack of reference books and blank journals beside her. "But you needn't trouble yourself. I'll take a groom to assist me."

The duke rubbed his face with long, thin fingers and pressed the heels of his hands into his eye sockets. "What's gone and made you so agreeable all of a sudden?"

Helena paused. "I beg your pardon?"

"You were less annoying when you were running away," he grumbled more to himself than anyone else.

Before she could answer, his leg shot out, kicking the carriage door open with a bang. "Do what you like," he said. "If memory serves, there is a milkmaid here who I favor." He laughed. "She's the only reason I consented to make the trip."

The carriage had scarcely stopped before the duke unfolded himself from the seat and slid from the door. His shiny boots hit the mud with a sucking sound, and he let out a curse. The staff hurried to unroll rugs and extend umbrellas while Helena gathered her books.

"Helena?" said Camille, still motionless beside her.

"Hurry, Cami," Helena urged. "He'll not tolerate the countryside forever. How much time can one milkmaid occupy?"

"Helena?"

"Bring your novel, to be sure. Oh, how I wish

Mama and Papa and the other girls hadn't come. They'll be bored out of their minds."

"*Helena,*" her sister said a third time.

Helena turned, her arms filled with books.

"Whatever will you do?" her sister whispered.

Helena stared. She'd learned never to expect authenticity from her family; real concern was virtually unknown.

"Do not worry yourself," she tried.

"You cannot run away again."

"No. I don't suppose I can. But I will take care of it."

"What do you mean? But how?"

"I've . . . I've something else plann—"

"With Shaw? Your groom?"

Helena paused. Could she confide in Camille? A week ago, she would have said no. But since New Bond Street, a flicker of hope had begun to burn in her chest. Carefully, she said, "Shaw works for me, yes. He's rather useful and—"

"Do not trust him, Lena," Camille said.

Helena went still. "Trust him for what?"

"For anything. He's Girdleston's pawn. How could he be any other? We all saw 'Uncle Titus' attach him to you. I've been shocked at how quickly you've . . . you've accepted him. In fact, I've been shocked at your complete change of course. Even the duke is suspicious of you."

"The duke cares only for his own amusements."

"He's just said he preferred it when you were running away. And he will care a great deal when you invoke the wrath of Girdleston, which you are bound to do if you've made a confidant of his groom." She took a deep breath. "Unless . . ."

A pause. Camille inclined her head.

"Unless what?" asked Helena.

"Unless you've come 'round to their way of thinking. Unless you can reconcile yourself to some sort of agreement, and marry Lusk, but live separate lives—"

"No," said Helena, turning back to the door. The flame of hope began to sputter. Perhaps there was no kinship, no understanding.

"Helena, wait," Camille called again.

Helena's heart lurched. She hadn't realized how deeply she longed for someone in her family to care.

"I'm . . . I'm sorry if I've said the wrong thing," her sister said. "I'm merely worried. Lusk is terrible—truly. You've said so all along, of course, but I was too young to understand. And Mama and Papa tell us constantly that Good Daughters marry dukes when they are on offer. I thought I wanted to be good, but now I . . . I want to be like you."

Helena's throat constricted. She looked at her sister through hot tears.

"But not if it means you're ruined or trapped," said Camille, "not for me or for you. I don't understand why you're suddenly . . . going along? Excited about his stupid farm? The turnaround is alarming."

"You are mistaken," Helena informed her slowly. "Everyone prefers my agreeability. No one wants the union spoiled by my running away."

Camille shook her head. "*I* wanted you to run. And whatever you're doing instead frightens me.

Lusk is a fool, but the dukedom is very powerful."

"You worry because, if I don't marry, your chances for a titled husband will be very low indeed. You and the other girls want—"

"No," Camille cut in. "I'm worried for *you*."

Helena studied her sister's face, searching for some duplicity. She saw only gentleness and concern. "Camille," she whispered.

"I trust you, Lena, but I'm worried about a conspiracy with a servant furnished to you *by* Girdleston. What are you thinking, Lena?"

Helena clutched the books to her chest and slid toward the door. "You do not know him."

"That is for certain. So . . . you do have some understanding?"

"I cannot say what I have. But I am grateful for your concern. I've not relied upon anyone since Gran, and it's been a lonely road. I . . . I would love to rely on you. And to be relied upon. Please trust me. And if you really want to help, can you keep Mama and Papa occupied while I'm out in the fields?"

"Yes. Alright," Camille called softly, watching her disembark. "Take care, Lena."

Helena shot her a grateful look and hurried on.

"MY SISTER THINKS I cannot trust you," Helena told Declan two hours later. They were winding their way through parked wagons and grazing horses on the edge of Wandsworth's country market.

Declan had allotted twenty minutes to search the market, locate Lady Moira, and return to their mounts. It was ambitious, but in Declan's view, it was just as important to return Helena to the group as it was to approach these women.

"Which sister?" he asked. None of the Lark sisters had shown the slightest interest in Helena's regard for servants.

"Camille," she said.

Declan nodded. Of all the sisters, Camille Lark was the shrewdest. "You've not told her? About our plan?"

"Oh no, but she knows something's afoot. She's not stupid. She's seen our . . . our rapport, I assume? And she warned me against trusting you."

"Because she believes I'll, what?"

"I cannot say. Betray me to Girdleston, I suppose." She glanced at him. Her face was uncertain. She didn't accuse him so much examine his reaction.

His reaction was extreme frustration, but he kept quiet. He counted to ten.

The Lark sisters had no way of gauging Declan's loyalty, but Helena should have no doubt. He'd put his family's future in jeopardy to help her. He'd also done nothing but aid and abet her. Since the beginning. Today alone, he'd trailed her through the many acres of Lusk's Home Farm in his silent role as biddable groom. He held the umbrella while she spoke of late frosts with the duke's horticulturist, bee migration with the duke's beekeeper, and wool with the sheepherder.

He'd bribed a stable boy to saddle two mounts and interrupted her discussions so they could finally slip away.

And now here they were. The whole thing had been beautifully played. Her interest in agriculture, her family's abject lack of interest, even the rain. They'd manipulated the situation despite the implicit risk, but they'd done it together. There was no call for lack of trust.

"If I was going to betray you to Girdleston," Declan said, "I would have already done it. I've gone too deep for that now. My fate is tied to yours."

"You mean your family's fate," she corrected.

"Right," he said. He was reminded that he'd not been completely honest. He hadn't told her about the threat of returning to jail.

"Forgive me for raising the topic," she said. "I don't doubt your loyalty, Declan. Camille believes herself cleverer than she is, perhaps."

Declan nodded. He wasn't worried, not about her loyalty or her discretion, but they would have to be more careful around Camille. If nothing else, she'd introduced a new worry. Had Declan revealed enough about his situation to make Helena feel safe?

The muddy crush of the Wandsworth market came into view, and Helena was caught up in distant music and bursts of laughter, the smell of smoke and pasties. She craned to see over horses and carts, her face happy and curious. He stared at her pretty profile, gratified by her open delight. She'd shown disdain for so many things—the garden party, the trousseau, Lusk House in general. But the market captivated her. The broken-off thing in his chest lost another sharp, heavy chunk.

"Our best chance of finding the herbalist is walking up and down every row," he said, tugging her between a carriage and a pen of goats.

The market's outer perimeter was a large circle of wagons and tents. Once inside, rows and rows of vendors stretched the muddy field. A dark, smoky forest loomed in the distance and a crude bandstand and musicians dominated the far end. In the center, a bonfire puffed smoke. The booths spilled over with autumn vegetables, chopped wood, candles, loaves of fresh bread.

Helena pulled free of Declan's hand and spun in a slow circle, drinking in the swirl of colors and aromas. Children darted around her, chasing a dog.

Declan cleared his throat. "We're looking at every booth for an herbalist," he reminded her, pointing to the first row. "We're searching every person for signs of wealth and privilege. An heiress will be far easier to spot in a country market than New Bond Street."

"Yes, of course," she said, following him at a slow pace.

"But we must look," he reminded.

"I *am* looking," she insisted, but she was staring at a table piled high with chunks of soap, each bar pressed with a sprig of lavender.

He hustled her along and they rounded first one row, then another. When they rounded the third row, Declan heard himself say, "My last client was also a young woman."

Helena stopped walking. "I beg your pardon?"

He didn't look at her. The words were out before he'd considered them.

"I was hired by the palace to escort her from England to France," he said. "I want you to feel fully informed. After what your sister said. You should not fear betrayal from me, Helena."

"I've not felt betrayed," she said quietly, walking again. "But I have wanted to know more."

They rounded the corner of the next row. He wondered if he'd said enough.

"By 'palace,' do you mean St. James Palace?" she asked.

"Yes."

"The girl wasn't . . . one of the royal princesses?"

"No. She was the daughter of a viscount from Cornwall. She'd entered into a courtship with one of the king's sons. William, Duke of Clarence and St. Andrews."

"William?" marveled Helena. "It's said that one day he will be king."

"Yes. That is what is said. And his brothers, the other royal dukes, did not feel this girl was the correct consort for the future king. They've someone else in mind. When his brothers could not dissuade him of the courtship to this woman, they hired me to . . . deliver her to a holiday in the South of France. She had an aunt with a villa near Nice. The French seaside was meant to be far enough away to allow the royal duke to consider some other girl."

"The brothers tore the duke and his lady apart?"

"I cannot say how everyone felt or what hearts were broken or otherwise. The girl—her name was Knightly Snow—"

"Nightly Snow?" laughed Helena.

"With a *K*, as in Knight. Miss Knightly Snow. She knew full well she was being extracted from the duke so that some other woman could be installed." Declan thought of Knightly Snow and his stomach curdled.

He sighed, continuing. "She was a . . . provocative, mercurial sort of woman. She loved parties and society and adventure. From what I could gather during our very short time together, she was excited about the prospect of a holiday in France. She had a volatile bent—I saw her behave with outrageous temper to both staff and strangers on more than one occasion. Not to mention, I believe she and the royal duke quarreled quite a bit, before she took her leave. I also believe they paid her."

"Who paid her?"

"The royal dukes."

"Paid her for what?"

"To go away."

"And you were her escort."

"Unfortunately, yes."

"You did not fancy the job?"

"Worse job I ever had."

"Worse than me?"

He laughed. "You have no idea."

"Was she a . . . pretty girl?"

He glanced at her. She stared straight ahead.

"She was," began Declan, "curved and cinched and powdered and rogued. She craved attention and knew how to get it." He made a face. "No, I did not find her pretty. She was—" A weary sigh. "The journey to France was an exercise in frustration, mostly due to multiple wagons of luxuries related to her comfort. Her list of essential 'accommodations' made travel slow and burdensome. Longest journey of my life." He rolled his neck, remembering the extreme inconvenience of every mile.

"And now you are my . . . groom," Helena marveled. "You went from escorting the sweetheart of a royal duke to watching over me. Girdleston hires only the best, I suppose."

He made a noncommittal sound and steered her around a cage of chickens. Helena didn't need to know that he'd been unlocked from prison to do this job; she didn't need to know he would likely return there if they failed. Her pressure to succeed was already significant. He'd said enough.

"There are extenuating . . . circumstances with Girdleston and me," he finally said. "But if you're clearly valuable to the dukedom, of this I have no doubt. Girdleston is determined to shackle you to Lusk. I am guessing that the river on your family's land must be very highly valued."

"Thousands of pounds a year," she said sadly. "A fortune, or so I'm told. At the moment, the limestone in the duke's mines must be hauled to Bath by wagon. It is slow and expensive, and they sell it only within the region.

"But if," she continued, "the limestone can be moved on *my* river, they can float it as far as Bristol. From there, it can be shipped around the world. It would be a huge windfall for both of our families but it would destroy the forest and my orchard especially. The apples are on terraced land that borders the river, and the line of wagons would wind through the center of it. They would actually have to chop every tree."

Declan speculated, "If they must do it—"

"They must *not* do it," she insisted.

"Yes, alright, but if they *wish* to do it, why hinge the thing on the marriage of two unwilling people? Why not simply draw up some agreement between the families?"

"My grandparents, the previous earl and countess, forbade the disruption of the forest, and my father promised not to make any changes when he became earl. After Grandfather died and my grandmother saw the type of earl her son would become, she installed a second fail-safe to protect the forest by willing it *to me.*

"The loophole Gran could not foresee is, if Lusk is my husband, then the land will be *his* purview. And he may do as he likes. Or as his uncle likes. My father feels he is getting the profits from the mining agreement without breaking the exact language of the promise to his mother. His conscious is clear. Such a coward."

"But you are not," Declan said. Her position was as unfair as the false accusations about Knightly Snow.

Helena's jaw was set. "No. I am not." She glanced at him. "Thank you, for siding with me. And telling me about Knightly Snow. I'm . . . I'm sorry I raised Camille's fears about betraying me. You do not deserve to be doubted, least of all by me."

"Well, betrayal is afoot. I betrayed the very letter of my employment within hours of being hired."

"Why? I wonder." She slid him a shy smile.

"Good question."

"Because you were immediately persuaded by me?"

"Because . . . it's a bollocks job. Because everyone has a price, but mine is higher than saddling you with Lusk."

It was the truth, he thought. Why not admit it?

Helena considered this, and he added, "And yes. Because of you."

She laughed. "Because I am relentless?"

Now it was his turn to consider. She was relentless and irresistible and, most of all, doing the right thing.

"Aye," he finally consented. "Relentless. That's why."

Declan was still smiling when, scanning the crowd, he caught a glimpse of dirty-blonde hair and a dove-gray hat some five yards ahead. The smile froze on his lips. He pulled Helena to the side and looked again.

Damn! He'd not imagined it.

"Bloody, bleeding hell," he gritted out, ducking down. He dropped her hand and grabbed her around the waist, dragging her inside a basket tent.

Helena yelped, scrambling to stay upright. "What are you d—"

"Lusk," Declan whispered. "He's here. Two stalls down. Quiet, quiet, quiet." He held a finger to his lips, boring his eyes into hers. "We've got to move."

Lusk is here? She mouthed the words.

He nodded. They were at the rear of the tent and he felt around for a gap in the cloth. When he found it, he ducked and stole the two of them through. The alley behind the stalls was webbed with stakes and rope. Declan picked his way to the end, pulling her by the hand. They checked each tent for another gap; his goal was to wind his way as far from Lusk as possible without using the rows.

He found an opening five yards down and checked the vendor within. A cheesemonger's stall. He pulled her through and Declan wound them through wheels of cheese and a tethered cow.

At the entrance, he waited, watching the crowd. It was impossible here to hop from tent to tent; the rows gave way to the open area of the bonfire. He waited for a boisterous group of musicians to stroll by and fell in with their group. Helena laughed, clapping a hand over her mouth, and hurried to keep up.

"Did the duke see you?" she whispered.

"No."

"But what was his business *here*?"

"God only knows," he said. "He had two girls with him."

Helena thought about this. "Milkmaids?"

"Probably."

"Did he look . . . happy?"

"He did not look unhappy." In truth, he'd looked deliriously happy with two buxom village girls on either side.

"Perhaps I should be interviewing milkmaids," Helena said. She shook her head. "I could never subject a milkmaid to Lusk."

Now they'd reached the crackling bonfire. The glowing, hissing stack threw off heat from yards away, and sparks spiraled to the sky. Helena slowed, holding her hands to the warmth, but Declan pulled her along.

"Sorry, sweetheart." He tugged her from one cluster of people to the next, his eyes always behind them.

When the outermost circle of booths came into view, he picked up the pace, turned left, then—

Lusk again.

He stopped dead and she collided with his back.

Heart thudding, Declan tucked Helena carefully behind him and reversed course, moving them again. A stack of barrels was piled on the edge of a row, and Declan ducked behind them, pressing against the rough wood. He peeked around the edge at the footpath. Lusk was steps away.

"Damn," he hissed, sliding the opposite way. He dropped into a crouch.

What now? Helena mouthed, crouching beside him. Her eyes were bright, cheeks were flushed. She looked excited and hopeful and startlingly beautiful.

Declan forced himself to focus. "The fastest route to the horses is through a side field with very few people," he whispered. "We can move quickly, but I'm worried about my livery. It was foolish to embark on the market without covering the yellow. I stand out like a torch in the dark. Even if I make the entire jaunt by hopping booth to booth, I must blend in."

He looked around. An adjacent stall was decorated with fluttering strips of fabric, jangling metal trinkets, and bead garland. Rusted farm tools, antique furniture, and an Edwardian gown on a form flanked the opening. Colorful fishing buoys were tangled in a heap on the ground. Empty wine bottles had been embedded into the ground to form a walkway. An old sign read "Mr. Godfrey's Treasure Trove. Fripperies, Baubles, Oddities, and Relics."

He looked at Helena, brows raised, and inclined his head. *There?*

Helena nodded.

Checking the crowded row, he mouthed a countdown—*Three, two, one.*

They bolted.

He looked left but darted right, obscuring his face. Helena followed as if she'd been evading men in crowded markets all her life. They didn't stop until they were secluded by the flaps of the stall.

Declan looked around. Thankfully, the booth was empty. The sides were strung with animal pelts, antique clothing, cloudy tentacles of discarded chandelier, and faded oil paintings of tropical plants. Fluffy peacock fans hung from the ceiling. The floor was littered with clay pots. A teetering shelf bulged with scientific specimens in glass jars and old books.

"What is this place?" she whispered.

"Do not know, do not care," said Declan, searching for anything to drape over his livery. A weathered oilcloth coat hung from a peg and he snatched it off. "I can manage with this." He whirled it over his shoulders.

Whistling could be heard from behind a curtain and Declan called out, "Shopkeep?"

"Just a moment!" came the reply, then more whistling, then something shattered. Declan growled and darted to the entrance, peering out. Helena browsed behind him. When he looked back, she was fingering the crystal beads on a tear-shaped reticule.

"Ah, the Prussian officer's coat," said a voice behind them. "An excellent choice."

They whirled around. A large man with shrewd eyes and a kind smile bellied up to the counter at the rear of the stall. "How fine it looks with your . . ." he squinted, ". . . golden tunic."

"How much?" Declan asked.

"Sadly, I don't operate in pounds and shillings, sir. Godfrey's Treasure Trove only does business *in trade.*"

"You're joking," Declan said. "A merchant who refuses *money*?"

"But I am a very special merchant, my good sir." He gestured to the colorful walls and hodgepodge of items spilling from the shelf. "My treasures are both payment *and* inventory. Never fear, customers are typically able to locate some tradable item on their very person."

Declan looked at Helena. She held out her hands in a gesture of *Don't look to me.*

"If it's lady's jewelry you're after," said Declan, "you should think again. She doesn't bother with it. And jewels are hardly an even trade for this coat. It's dank and moth-eaten and fifty years old."

"Jewelry is sometimes sufficient," mused Mr. Godfrey, "but never my first choice. Rather expected, isn't it? I prefer to deal in the realm of the . . . *extraordinary*." He made a fanning gesture with both hands.

"I've a comb?" Helena said, stepping up. She pulled an ivory comb from her hair and clattered it on the counter. Her hair swung behind her in a long, damp curtain.

Godfrey examined the comb with suspicion, tapping the tines with a conductor's wand he pulled from behind his ear. "Anything else?" he wheedled.

"You're looking for weaponry?" Declan guessed, his eyes narrowing. They didn't have time for this.

"Not necessarily," said Mr. Godfrey. "I've been known to accept the odd war hammer or hurling star, but only if they're imprinted with the date and country of origin. What more could you have?"

Helena and Declan shared a look. Their list of offers was fast and impatient and so ridiculous Helena was laughing by the end.

"Botany reference book?" She held out a field guide from her pocket.

"Not unless it's *Viennese*," said Mr. Godfrey.

"Livery tunic?" Declan asked.

"I'm overinventoried in yellow," said Mr. Godfrey.

"Leather gloves?" Helena wiggled her fingers.

"Too small." Mr. Godfrey crinkled up his nose.

"Crimson cloak?"

"Too wet."

"Ladies' boots?" She pointed to her toe.

"Too modern."

"Belt with attached sheaths for blades?" Declan hated to part with his belt, but he was desperate. He reached beneath his tunic, revealing the broad leather belt strung with concealed daggers.

"I'd prefer something that is *not* an article of clothing."

"But not money?" Declan ground out. "We have little more than the clothes on our backs and these few trifling suggestions."

"Oh, surely not?" enthused Mr. Godfrey.

Helena laughed again but then covered her mouth with her hand. Declan spun away. "Have I *mentioned* that we are in an extreme hurry?"

Helena began patting herself down. When her fingers reached the pocket of her cloak, she pulled out a leather pouch.

"But would you consider this little sachet of apple seeds?" she asked.

"What an interesting thought . . ." mused Mr. Godfrey, his eyes brightening. He held out his hands like a child anticipating a treat.

Helena laid the pouch on the counter. "These are seeds from my orchard in Somerset. The apples are a new variety cultivated by my grandmother. The fruit is a beautiful red, it ripens late in the season, and the taste is a perfect mix of tart and sweet."

"And the seeds are poisonous!" exclaimed Mr. Godfrey gleefully.

"What?" Declan turned back.

"Oh yes, there is that," Helena said, working open the pouch. "When ground into a fine dust, apple seeds can be used as a mild cyanide. Not a deadly dose, but certainly the dust would make a person ill." She tapped a few seeds onto the counter. "Or," she said brightly, "you may plant them and grow a lovely apple tree?"

"A mild cyanide," cooed Mr. Godfrey, poking the seeds with his wand.

"Why do you have these?" Declan asked her lowly.

Helena shrugged again. "I tossed them into my trunk when I came to London—a talisman of my grandmother, I suppose. And then I brought them to Lusk's farm in case I needed to impress the horticulturist."

"But can you part with them?"

"Actually, I feel as if Gran gave them to me for this very purpose," Helena said.

"Excellent," boomed Mr. Godfrey. "A lovely addition to my inventory. And many thanks to you. Do enjoy the coat." He scooped up the seeds and closed a chubby fist over the pouch.

Declan's hand came down like an ax. "Not so fast." He held the man in place.

To Helena he said, "You're certain?"

The smile she gave him, gratefulness and kinship and something more, something misty and personal, a look just for him, caused his throat to go tight.

She nodded.

Declan released Godfrey and gave him a curt nod. "Thank you. If anyone asks, you never saw us." To Helena he said, "Let's go."

Helena was calling a polite farewell to Godfrey while Declan peeked out of the entrance.

Damn! He clamped the tent shut and spun. "Lusk is outside," he said.

"*No.*"

"*Yes,*" Declan said.

To the shopkeeper, he called, "Is there another way out?"

"You'd be amazed," sang Mr. Godfrey, "at the number of customers who ask this very question. It happens so often I've constructed a side entrance for this purpose." The large man pulled the rear curtain and gestured to a flap that led to the alley behind his stall.

"Thank you," said Declan, taking Helena by the hand. "Any idea who your neighbors are? To the back?"

"But of course," said Mr. Godfrey. "It's dear Mr. Jones-Tussle. We set up near each other when we can. Old friends, don't you know."

"Please tell me," grumbled Declan, slipping into the alley, "that Mr. Jones-Tussle sells Japanese screens or giant hats."

"No," said Godfrey, "textiles."

"Close enough," said Declan, and he pulled Helena into the opposite tent.

Chapter Thirteen

They were laughing when they spilled into the textile booth. Declan held her behind him, looking around. The tent was empty. And styled like a harem room. Heavy woven tapestries hung from the walls; the floor was piled with pillows. The dirt was padded by carpets. Colorful yarn weavings hung from the spokes of the tent.

Helena grabbed his shoulders from behind. "Where did you see Lusk?" she asked breathlessly, her lips close to his ear.

"Across from Godfrey's stall. He was two yards away." He turned his face to hers, his heart thudding.

She nudged closer to his ear. "It's a little exciting," she whispered, "to evade him." She brushed his cheek with her nose. His hat fell.

"Helena," he rasped. A very weak warning.

She released his shoulders and pulled off her gloves and was back again in a heartbeat. She pressed into his back, sliding her hands over his shoulders and down his chest. "Everything you do is exciting."

"Helena, we mustn't," he rasped. "This tent is

not private. This . . . interlude is not part of the plan. *This* is the opposite of the plan."

"I hate the plan." Her lips were so close to his mouth.

"The plan is your idea." He felt behind him, grabbing her hip.

"But you designed it."

She kissed him. She couldn't reach his lips, but almost. She kissed the side of his mouth, his cheek, his ear.

Declan turned his head to meet her. The kiss was meant to be quick and finalizing. But she licked him. She went up on her toes, almost climbing his back. One kiss became two, became ten.

He growled and twisted, grabbing her by the waist and sliding her into his arms.

"It's not a bad plan," he said, kissing her properly, "all things considered."

"It's a lovely plan," she breathed. "I'm thrilled by the plan . . ."

And now she jumped up, straddling him. He caught her bottom with two hands.

"You thrill me," she laughed.

Declan bounced her in his hands, finding the exact perfect alignment of her body. They were suspended there, reveling in the rare combination of familiar and fleeting. He knew her body, even when he should not. They'd done this before, but they shouldn't do it now. It was reckless and pulse-pounding and she was impossible to resist.

"Do you know," she panted between kisses, "I was actually worried I'd be bored when I came to London."

"Easily bored, are you?" he teased, but in his head he thought, *I am a diversion to her.*

And then, *Does it matter?* He delved his tongue into her mouth. He'd pleasured scores of women in his life and never cared about it beyond their mutual release. This could be no different. He could be her diversion.

"Running away was a suitable distraction." She sighed, digging her hands beneath his collar to find heated skin. "But I'd no idea how diverting compliance would be."

"I've got news for you, sweetheart. This is not compliance." He shifted her into one hand and bit off a glove, shifted her again and bit off the other. Every readjustment pressed her tantalizingly against his need. Helena squirmed and moaned into his mouth, setting off an explosion of sensation. Declan kissed her harder, kissed her breathless. He kissed her until his legs shook and he was forced to widen his stance to support them. Her roving hands slid between them, seeking the heavy bulge of his erection.

"But can I . . . ?" she breathed into his ear. "Is this alr—"

Declan moaned and went down one knee, pulling her with him. Plush cushions were stacked nearby. He need only fall back to sprawl her across him.

"Declan," she breathed, "I need . . ." She closed her fingers around him. All useful thought ceased. Her touch was a pulsing burn of pleasure.

"Declan," she pleaded.

"What—?!" ranted a voice from beyond Declan's haze of desire.

He froze.

"What is the meaning of—"

Helena giggled against his mouth. Declan swore in his head. He looked in the direction of the sound.

Sunlight spilled through the raised flap of the tent. An angry textiles merchant glowered at their entwined bodies.

Declan looked back to Helena. She bit her lip. Her expression was the blushing, bemused embodiment of *Oh dear.*

In that moment, he would have traded Newgate to kiss her one more time.

But he pivoted sideways, tumbling Helena gently onto a pile of cushions and blocking her from view.

"Easy, mate," Declan called to the merchant, and disentangled from Helena. He vaulted to his feet.

"I've got a guinea for five more minutes." Declan dug into his pocket and came up with a jingle of coins.

"I run a respectable business," the merchant insisted, staring at the coins.

"Of course you do," Declan agreed, tossing the gold, "and a successful one. Which is why you'll not pass up the opportunity to turn your easiest profit of the week. Five minutes."

The merchant grumbled but closed his hand over the coins and went away. Declan secured the tent flap and turned back to Helena. She was flushed and tousled but smiling, working her hands into her gloves.

"Five minutes?" she asked. "You could have bought us an hour."

"We do not have an hour," he said, tugging on his own gloves. "We don't have five minutes."

"You are a terrible groom," she sighed, tucking back her hair.

Yes, but what of the diversion? he thought. Before he could stop himself, he said, "Liked that, did you?" It came out with more curtness than he'd anticipated.

"What?" Helena paused, looking confused. "What do you mean?"

"The kiss?" He looked away.

"Was that 'a kiss'?" she laughed.

"Kiss*es*," he corrected.

"Of course I liked it. But, Declan, how could you not know this? Are you upset? Have I done something wrong? Have I displeased you?"

Declan considered this, putting on his hat. She pleased him in every way. This situation was not her fault. She'd been very clear from the beginning. She wanted his help. He'd not conceived of helping her exactly *this way,* but he had no right to complain. So what if she found him exciting and desirable? If it was adventure she craved, he could give her that.

"I am the opposite of displeased," he said, peeking out of the tent. "I live to serve."

"But that was not serving," she insisted. "That was—"

He stopped her by raising a flat palm. He turned back. "You would not believe this," he said. "I think we may have stumbled upon Lady

Moira."

HELENA RACED TO the tent door, her heart in her throat. Peering out, she saw two liveried footmen in royal blue standing sentry outside of a deep stall. Their smart uniforms stood out like toy soldiers in the crowd of tan wool. Beside the tent was a sign that read "Herbal Remedies and Cure-Alls."

Helena snatched Declan's hand, strumming with excitement. Oh, to leave the market with the connection they'd come for. Squeezing his hand, she examined the tent, waiting for some sign of a lady to match the liveried servants.

For a long moment, nothing happened. Declan warned her that the textile merchant would soon evict them. He suggested that the herbalist's booth, currently devoid of any activity, might be shuttered. She vowed to dart across the row and charge the booth herself, but he restrained her.

He was just about to engage one of the footmen when a sallow young woman emerged from the tent with a full basket over her arm. She spoke briefly to one of the footmen, handed off the basket, and pulled a heavy linen kerchief from her pocket. She glanced at the sky, holding the kerchief to her face.

"Oh," said Helena. The excitement draining away.

Declan said, "That's her?"

Helena stepped outside the textile booth, staring at the girl. Her thin hair was pulled tightly from her face. A hat designed for warmth (not fashion) obscured much of her face. Thick gloves turned her hands into woolly mitts. A heavy wrap swallowed her shoulders, and she shrugged deeply, burrowing within heavy folds.

She was wrong. Entirely. This couldn't be the correct girl.

Helena was just about to step up and ask some innocuous question when a footman said, "Very good, Lady Moira," and retreated inside the herbalist's tent. The young woman embarked on a sneezing fit, clutching her kerchief like a holy shroud.

Helena blinked. It was her. She was exactly the girl they'd come to find, but she was all wrong. Helena started to shake. She was chilled to the bone. The warm buzz of her encounter with Declan was a distant memory. Fatigue and disappointment pressed in. Her wet garments weighed a stone.

"She's all wrong," she said hollowly.

"Probably." Declan stepped beside her.

"Too thin," she said. "Too hesitant. Is her complexion . . . gray?"

She glanced at Declan. "Lusk has a clear preference for milkmaids. He wants robust and supple. This girl needs a doctor, not a husband. We . . . we should go."

"Yes," Declan said. He was looking right and left, scanning the crowd.

But Helena couldn't move. Lady Genevieve, the young heiress in New Bond Street, had been so perfect. Pert and flashy and ambitious. When Helena had given her a candid review of Lusk's many perceived shortcomings, the girl had been unfazed.

This young woman's wheezing could be heard across the row and over the thrum of shoppers.

"I cannot remember which gossip thought Lady Moira was on the hunt for a wealthy duke," Helena said. "They were wrong. I would never subject her to Lusk."

"If you're certain . . ." Declan said, but he'd already moved on. He took her by the hand and pulled her down the row, walking quickly, head down, eyes everywhere.

A figure in a dark velvet cloak nearly collided with them and Declan paused, studying the person.

"I think I saw that same black cloak in Lady Canning's street," he said. He turned to watch the figure scuttle away. "Did you see them?"

"I don't know," sighed Helena, barely noticing. "I don't care. I'm so disappointed. Please, can we go?"

"Aye," Declan said, watching the cloaked figure disappear into the crowd. "Let's get you home."

Chapter Fourteen

Seven Duchesses (Potential)

Happy ✓
~~Sneezy~~

A day later, Declan stalked the length of Wimpole Street, waiting for Helena to finish her mother's morning call. He had but one thought. *I need a day off.*

Actually, that was inaccurate. What he really needed was to banish the damnable Knightly Snow situation from his life.

Since that would not magically happen, not with him committed to Girdleston and unable to travel to France to track the girl down, he would gladly accept a day away.

He wanted to see his father. He wanted to look in on his horse and impress upon the hostler that he would, one day, buy the stallion back. He needed to see his lawyers.

He wanted freedom from Girdleston's frequent summons to the green salon, where he made vague threats about money and Newgate as he piddled with his toy village.

Mostly, he wanted distance from *her.*

The level of . . . *intimacy* they shared (there was no better word) had gone from inappropriate and reckless to something like all-consuming. What had begun like a drizzle now felt like a torrent.

It was some combination of the threat of discovery that was a swirl of adrenaline and lust. At night, when he slept, his mind spun carnal dreams in hot, yearning flashes: her hands on him in the tent at the market, the smell of her hair, the texture of her lips.

But it wasn't only her body. He found himself pacing with frustrated impatience simply to speak with her. She was curious and clever and interesting. She asked the correct questions. She was not squeamish or self-involved. Her love of the natural world was refreshing and her fascination with science was contagious. He wanted only to be near her.

He could blame prison for his lack of physical self-control. He'd needed a woman, and Helena Lark was the very embodiment of desirable female. But must he also want to *talk to her* so bloody much?

He needed a day away to garner his self-control. To steel himself. To refocus. Everything had begun to feel like some destiny bollocks, a happily-ever-after that could not happen.

Helena Lark was completely unavailable to him.

Even if, by some extreme miracle, they thwarted the wedding.

Even if Girdleston did not to send him back to

jail.

Even if she housed his father and sisters in her idyllic forest.

Declan Shaw was the son of a tailor, a soldier-for-hire by trade, and Helena was the daughter of an earl. She saw him as diverting and exciting but hardly a man she might someday marry.

And he hadn't even revealed to her that he was also an ex-convict.

They had no future beyond the scheme.

Their intimacy must to stop.

He didn't need a day away, he needed a lifetime.

Today was devoted to a woman called Miss Joanna Keep, who, according to Helena's notes, passed her time working, improbably, as an apprentice in a medical practice. The doctor was her uncle, Dr. Curtis Keep, a surgeon of some merit in Wimpole Street.

Declan had seen Cavendish Square on Helena's schedule and made the connection. Wimpole Street, with its flourishing array of doctors, surgeons, osteopaths, chemists, and therapeutic specialists, was just around the corner. They'd devised a plan on the sprint back to Lusk's Home Farm. At the very least, this potential duchess existed in a fixed spot on the map. No prowling about markets or shops. Whether she was suitable for Lusk? They'd learned yesterday that simply finding the girl was no guarantee.

After two laps to observe Miss Keep's alleged office, Declan returned to the duke's carriage. It was parked in front of the townhome that contained Helena, her mother, the sisters, and another Lusk cousin. Nettle and the coachman idled in the street, waiting attendance. The call itself was meant to be brief. Lady Linney, the host, was an acquaintance of Helena's mother but not a bosom friend. They'd hoped to stay only a half hour.

Declan nodded to Nettle. "Any sign?"

The older man shook his head.

He was just about to take another circuit when Lady Linney's door opened and Helena's mother and sisters spilled onto the stoop. Declan came to attention, watching them bustle down the steps in a spectrum of autumnal silk and spirited chatter. Helena was last as always—the most beautiful one, as ever. Today she wore a rust-colored dress with turquoise trim, ivory lace, and a caramel-colored hat. A small peacock feather extended from the brim, winging the side of her head. The affect was distinctive and arresting, far more stylish than the gauzy, modish pinks and creams of the others. Declan forced an expression of neutral indifference and waited for her to pretend to break her distinctive, arresting ankle. That had been the plan.

She caught his gaze. He quirked an eyebrow. She gave a nearly imperceptible shake of her head. *No.*

No? No—what?

No, she would not fake an ailment? No, they should not broach the medical office?

"The baroness puts on such a show," Helena's mother was saying, shrugging into her pelisse. "Overly solicitous in my view. La, just look at her, waving at us from the door. Her butler must wonder why he makes any effort." The countess smiled and waved to the house.

"It's all a bit much," she said. " 'Show deference to the dukedom'—which is appropriate, I suppose. But where is the subtlety?" She tsked at the Lusk cousin, a dour woman named Burris.

"We shall have to grow accustomed to it," the countess went on, "when we have a duchess in the family. So much posturing."

"Really, Mother," sighed Helena, stomping into the carriage, "the baroness and her daughters were simply being nice. Every person you encounter is not vying to impress you."

"Least of all you," said the countess, climbing in behind her. "Would it have killed you to answer a single question about the wedding?"

Declan tried again to catch Helena's eye, but she had disappeared into the vehicle and squabbled with her sisters about seating. He was given little choice but to take up position on the runner and hold on.

The first corner was Weymouth and Wimpole. Dr. Keep's surgical office was halfway down the street. They were there in a matter of seconds. Declan wondered what injuries could be sustained inside a moving carriage. They'd discussed a turned ankle or a fainting spell, something from which Helena could easily recover. But she was meant to succumb *before* they were speeding away. He leaned, trying to catch Helena's eye through the window. To his left, the clinic grew smaller and smaller. Their opportunity was slipping away. They'd not be back this—

Suddenly, the glass pane to the carriage window slapped open. Helena stuck out her head and called, *"Stop the carriage!"*

Declan swung away, barely managing to hang on. "Hold!" he shouted.

"Stop, stop, stop," Helena sputtered, sticking her head almost entirely out. She clutched the pane with tight, gloved fingers.

"I am . . . *not well,*" she gasped, pinching her lips together.

Declan didn't fake his alarm. Bloody hell. This girl—

"Stop the carriage," she called again, her voice winded and gaspy.

The carriage stopped, horses dancing a clatter on the street. Nettle rushed to open the door.

Inside the carriage, pandemonium reigned. Her sisters pressed back, their outraged protests a tangle of *Don'ts—!* and *Get-backs—!* The countess clutched a kerchief over her nose and mouth. The cousin appeared stunned.

"Really, Helena," her mother hissed, "can you not wait until we reach Lusk House?"

"I cannot help when I am struck by intestinal distress," Helena exclaimed, laying her head against the cool glass of the window.

"Mother, get her out!" said her sister Joan. "If she is sick in this small space, we'll all be . . . be—"

"Mama!" chimed the other sisters, kerchiefs now flying to faces and skirts pulled back. "The silks!"

"I'll go," called Helena, crawling drunkenly to the door. "I'm going." She lurched down the steps. "I need air. I need air."

A large planter of chrysanthemums stood nearby, and she staggered to it, gripping the sides, bowing over the orange blooms.

Lady Pembrook gasped. "For God's sake, Helena, comport yourself. You cannot mean to be sick in the street?"

"I cannot help when I fall ill, Mama," she said breathily.

Declan would not have believed this performance if he'd not seen it with his own eyes. "My lady," he said to the countess, "I see the office of a doctor just there." He pointed to Dr. Keep's door. "With your permission, I will take Lady Helena inside and seek care."

"What?" Lady Pembrook squinted at the shiny placard beside the smart green door. "Oh, so it is."

She glanced to Helena again, now hanging sideways off the planter, still clinging to the rim. She looked like a strong wind had blown her sideways.

"I'm afraid there is no other help for it," said the countess, withdrawing into the vehicle. "I cannot allow her to carry on in the street. We must think of the duke's dear cousin. Yes, yes, Shaw—take her inside. If she must be so . . . overcome, what choice do we have?"

She looked again at the planter, and Helena drooped in the direction of the flowers, her face nearly touching the petals. The peacock feather fell forward and hung limply in the chrysanthemums, a bird downed in flight.

"Take her, take her," hissed the countess. "I'm sorry I cannot accompany her, but I am highly susceptible to infection and would, doubtless, succumb. And I'll not leave one of her sisters and have them stricken, too."

"I'll stay with her, Mama," said her sister Camille from inside the carriage.

"You will not," said the countess. "She's too ill to risk our good health. I'll send Meg, her maid, as soon as we reach Lusk House. Helena will prefer the care of a trained servant."

"Very good, ma'am," said Declan, carefully detaching Helena from the planter. "I know this practice, and they will take excellent care. Perhaps it is merely something she ate."

"Carry on, coachman!" the countess said wearily, tapping the carriage wall. "Watch for Meg within the hour!"

The carriage door slammed shut.

"*Go*," Helena said, slumping against him. "Go, go, go."

IT SEEMED UNNECESSARY to carry on the charade inside the clean, modern clinic, and Helena straightened up and smoothed her hair. In the clipped cordial tones of a future duchess, she asked if she might speak to an employee, Miss Joanna Keep. Winking at Declan, she straightened her peacock feather.

She was so bloody good at this. Another piece broke off inside his chest.

"If I'd feigned calamity so near to the baroness's house," she said, "Lady Linney would have insisted I return. And the ankle would have been wholly insufficient. I had to portray some condition that would make my mother flee."

"That was accomplished, I'd say."

"I'm not the only one in the family with the proclivity to bolt."

"I cased this building while you were with the baroness. There was no sign of a young woman 'apprentice.' If this girl is all wrong, I hope you can feign an exit as quickly as you feigned an entrance."

"She won't be wrong. I can feel it. And if she is, I'll ask for a sleeping draft and we'll go."

Five minutes later, Helena was taking tea behind the last door in a long corridor of examination rooms. Miss Joanna Keep, an attentive young woman with sunny blonde hair and intelligent eyes, sat across from her, munching a biscuit. Declan leaned against the wall outside the door.

"I apologize for dropping in on you with no appointment," Helena told Miss Joanna Keep. "Thank you for receiving me. I've wanted to call on you for some time, but I couldn't be certain when I would manage it. I . . . I had to feign illness to break away from my family, I'm afraid."

"Oh yes, well," began Miss Keep, "you are in good company. We see numerous cases of feigned illness in this clinic. Mostly elderly patients who simply need attention; but also young women who actually need medical care, but for some condition more confidential than their little act."

"Is that something you accommodate here, Miss Keep? Confidential conditions?"

"We do. Anything you say to me will be kept in strict confidence. I'm so very gratified that you asked for me by name, because confidentiality is a priority to me. I . . . I had rather hoped that word of my discretion would get 'round. And now . . . here you are."

"Yes," said Helena, "here I am. But I'm afraid my business does not pertain to a condition, real or imagined . . ."

Helena paused, looking around the room. A tidy desk was tucked into the corner and bookshelves lined one wall. An easel held diagrams of the human body.

"You're employed here at the medical office, Miss Keep?" Helena asked.

"Yes—in a manner. I've not been given a salary, if that is what you mean. But I'm in the office every day, and I see to the tasks that my uncle, Dr. Keep, sets out for me. It's some combination of clerical work and nursing and housekeeping. On occasion, he permits me to observe his work. And, very rarely, I see patients alone. Like you."

"You are interested in medicine?"

"It is my only interest," said Miss Keep, smiling.

Helena returned her smile, studying the natural, unembellished beauty of her face, her slender frame, her blonde curls. She was pretty enough for any man certainly, but she spoke with a steady, reserved softness. She was thoughtful and serious. Her movements were economic, with no flourish or flutter. Her dress was plain slate blue, the color of a frozen pond. Her hair was practical, and her eyes were . . . her eyes were engaged and curious and settled. She did not appear to search her brain for the next exciting topic. She simply . . . sipped her tea and waited.

Helena liked her immensely, which was annoying, because it made no difference if she liked Joanna Keep or any of them. She was meant to be ruthless about enlisting the correct girls. She was meant to be earning her freedom, not making friends.

But no friend or even potential friend of Helena's would be the key to her freedom. Anyone who was a friend to Helena should flee the Lusk dukedom, not endeavor to wheedle her way into it.

Joanna Keep would have to transform into a different sort of girl in order to ensnare the Duke of Lusk. It was wrong. It was all very wrong. Helena let out a disappointed sigh.

Miss Keep asked, "But if you are not ill, are you interested in science? Or medicine, Lady Helena?"

Helena shook her head. "Please call me Helena. Actually—no. Well, my passion is horticulture, so science—yes. Humans—not really. But it just so happens, I am betrothed to a duke. His fortune and standing lend itself to . . . to philanthropy. Duchesses have money and influence to spare, and they can, that is—if they *choose*—they may use that money for things like the advancement of the medical arts."

She stared into her teacup. Even staying close to the truth, it was difficult for Helena to misrepresent any part of herself or her motives.

That said, she must see the visit to its proper end. She must be certain. She'd pretended to be sick in a plant, for God's sake.

"Philanthropy?" whispered Miss Keep. "Oh, please, please do consider me. I am grateful for my place in this clinic, truly I am, but I can only learn so much from my uncle. He does not teach me so much as demonstrate, anything more I must look up on my own. If I had a benefactress, I could hire proper instructors. Perhaps I could buy my way into a teaching hospital. If I had the sponsorship of a duke, I could realize my dream of making a place for female doctors at hospitals."

She sounded breathless. Her cheeks were flushed. She set down her cup with a clatter and used her hands for emphasis. Helena's heart began to beat faster. Perhaps she *would* suit.

"Does this sound like the type of work," Miss Keep asked, palms up, fingers wide, "that your future husband would be interested in supporting?"

"Ah . . ." hedged Helena. "Actually, I am wondering if you would not have more access to the money and influence if *you* were a duchess yourself?" A nervous laugh.

"I beg your pardon?" Miss Keep's face twisted with confusion. "How would I become a duchess? My father is a gentleman but our family does not keep company with any dukes. I refused my own Season because I'm a failure at socializing. I've never even made the acquaintance of a duke."

Helena replaced her cup. "Well, Miss Keep, that is the heart of the reason I've come."

And then she told her. It took five minutes. She rattled it all off, barely drawing breath. Miss

Keep watched her with wide, disbelieving eyes.

When she was finished, both Helena and Miss Keep slumped in their chairs, staring at a diagram of the human ear. Helena's mind spun—*What if?*

Miss Keep looked as if she'd experienced Helena's fake intestinal distress.

"You're certain you understand?" Helena asked. "Lusk is terrible. Harmless but terrible. His uncle is also terrible, but less harmless. Even so, as the Duchess of Lusk, you could appeal to the duke and his uncle for tens of thousands of pounds to buy whatever instruction you wished. You could use your standing to pursue privileges for women doctors at hospitals. *If* you could tolerate Lusk—and that is a very considerable 'if.'

"Girdleston will not live forever," Helena added, "and it is my great hope that, one day, Lusk will . . . will *grow up.*"

She looked at Miss Keep and made a face. "But I cannot guarantee it."

"I am not afraid of either of these men," Miss Keep proclaimed. "I never intended to marry, so a husband who pursues his own diversions sounds inconsequential to me. *If* the arrangement comes with money and influence and I may enjoy the freedom to study."

She got up from her chair and walked to her desk. "But what I don't know is if I can win him over. If he is as you describe."

"He is," Helena said on a sigh, but she was thinking, *She cannot. And is it fair of me to encourage her to try?*

For better or for worse, Helena pressed on. "It's

only the initial attraction that you would need to get perfectly right. For this, you would need to enchant him, in a way. And quickly—in fact, you'd have to make a very strong first impression in one afternoon. There's a party at Lusk House next week, and I'll invite all of the potential duchesses there to . . . in a manner . . . beguile him."

"Other women?"

"I know, it sounds arcane—it is a little arcane—but I've had to cast a wide net, and to do so quickly. My plan is to bring all the potential duchesses together at this event. Whichever girl seems to spark his interest would have a fortnight to further ensnare him. He must throw me over before the wedding in January. It's all very dire, I'm afraid. But someone will be the Duchess of Lusk in the end—only, it cannot be me."

"Oh," said Miss Keep, looking overwhelmed.

"Look, Miss Keep, you are very beautiful, but do you think you could flirt? Could you cozen up and appeal to him and . . . *bewitch him* for a time?"

"If it meant my hospital, I could try," she said, but she sounded very uncertain. She sounded like a bold child accepting a dare.

Helena slumped lower in her seat.

After a moment, Miss Keep said, "But what do you mean by the notion of *flirting*?"

Helena opened her mouth to answer but before she could, Declan rolled off the wall and leaned his head through the open door.

"Maid's come," he said.

Helena nodded, looking up, and she was struck with an idea. Unorthodox. Bold and provocative.

But what part of her scheme was not all of these things?

She said, "I need a favor, Shaw. Will you come in?"

To Miss Keep, she said, "My groom is very obliging."

Declan asked, "In the office?" He looked confused.

"Come. Sit." Helena rose. "Right here." She stood behind her chair and patted it with three taps.

Cautiously, Declan entered the small room. The very breadth of his muscled body put the spindly table and fragile tea service in jeopardy. The chair creaked when he sat.

Miss Keep took up a piece of parchment and pen and resettled into her chair. She stared at Helena as if she would explain some complicated magic trick.

"Shaw?" Helena asked, coming up behind him in the chair. "Will you help me demonstrate *flirting* to Miss Keep?" She settled both hands on his shoulders.

Declan reeled around. "Ah, no," he said. His expression said, *You wouldn't.*

Helena ignored him. "I'm no expert," she continued, dropping her face to beside his, dangling her wrists over his shoulders, "but based on what I have seen, you must touch unnecessarily at every opportunity."

Slowly, wiggling her fingers over his chest, she began to tug at the fingers of her gloves.

Miss Keep madly scribbled notes.

"Did you say that my maid, Meg, has arrived?"

Helena asked sweetly, speaking close to his face.

"Ah . . . ?" said Declan.

Helena dropped her limp gloves onto his thighs. He stared down at them as if something had died in his lap.

She leaned farther, encircling his neck with her hands. "Is she concerned?"

"Who?" Declan's voice cracked.

"Meg."

"No," he said flatly. "She's confused. But not as confused as I am."

Helena laughed, pressing her forehead to his, a quick nuzzle, and then slid away. She circled the chair to sit down in his lap.

Declan jumped as if something had bitten him.

She ignored this and shimmied deeper into his lap. She wrapped an arm around his neck and pressed her palm on his chest. Did Lusk's women drape themselves across him? Helena couldn't say. But if she had the freedom to be playful and affectionate with Declan, she would sit in his lap. She'd wanted to be in Declan's arms since they'd left the market. Helena's longing was real and urgent and ever present. Miss Keep would have to pretend all of these.

She told the other woman, "You hold eye contact for prolonged periods of time."

Helena gazed up at Declan. He stared back as if she'd burst into flames.

Miss Keep scribbled more.

"And you laugh at everything he says," Helena added.

"My lady . . . ?" Declan rasped. His voice was a warning.

Helena frowned. "Obviously, it would be difficult to laugh at something like *my lady,* but can you see what I mean?"

She slumped a little in his arms, happy, in spite of herself, to be so near to him. "You ruffle his hair. You say things that are funny and spirited. You suggest that the two of you embark on outings or adventures that are provocative or unorthodox. Like . . . ice skating at night. Or swimming in winter."

Now Helena was simply guessing.

She glanced at Miss Keep, and the other woman stared back with a look of applied absorption, forcing herself to understand. Beneath it all was a pale, tight panic. It was as if she'd just learned that her hospital was on the other side of deep canyon, and all she had to do was flap her wings and fly to it.

"And this is how *you* landed the duke?" Miss Keep asked. "In the beginning?"

Now Helena laughed. "Good God, no. My parents arranged the betrothal. Lusk and I cannot abide each other. I could not fake a flirtation with him if my life depended on it. Nor would I want to. And honestly, Miss Keep? I'm not certain you could either. I . . . I'm not certain you are the correct girl for this proposition."

Helena climbed from Declan's lap and dusted her hands together. Declan shoved from the chair.

"If I was a duchess," Miss Keep ventured, "I would be so much closer to realizing the work of my life." The words sounded forced. Her face was pinched with reluctance. She studied her notes, looking at the words like the recipe for poison.

"Wanting to be *a* duchess will not be the same as becoming the *Duchess of Lusk*," said Helena. "You're a smart woman, clearly, and your aspirations are not merely noble, they are necessary. The world needs more doctors of every stripe. Who knows what you might accomplish all on your own? Quite a lot, I predict. And without having to sell your soul to the Girdleston family to do it."

"I . . . I am so impatient for opportunities," Miss Keep said.

"I believe you," said Helena, "and I am sorry. But this was less of an opportunity, and more of a . . . terrible trade. I don't believe it is the best trade for you. Will you forgive me for wasting your time? I . . . I had to be certain."

Miss Keep closed her eyes, looked at the floor, and nodded.

As Helena and Declan made their way to the door, Miss Keep made assurances that she would not tell a soul that Helena Lark was in the clinic for any other reason than stomach distress.

Helena believed her, and she overwhelmed her with thanks and well wishes. At the last minute, Helena suggested that she might call on one Lady Moira Ashington to inquire about a consultation. If the girl was buying herbal remedies in Wandsworth, clearly she was open to alternative treatments. Even, perhaps, a young woman doctor.

When she said her final good-bye, Declan was already in the street. Helena collected a confused

Meg and embarked upon the waiting carriage, her heart heavy.

When they reached the carriage steps, Declan was shaking his head.

"What was that?" he growled.

"I know," she sighed. "I know, I know, I know. I'm sorry." And she *was* sorry. She'd been reckless with their plan and precipitous with Miss Keep's rejection. The interviews were rife with anxiety and complications. The margin of error was significant.

Declan did not respond and she climbed wearily into the carriage with Meg.

Not seen to any of them was the lurking figure in the black cloak hovering on the corner.

Chapter Fifteen

Seven Duchesses (Potential)

Happy ✓
~~Sneezy~~
~~Doc~~

Helena was sorry?

Sorry.

Sorry for what? Declan wondered.

Sorry for jeopardizing his wholesale betrayal of Girdleston by flaunting their obvious intimacy a woman they'd only just met?

Sorry for allowing a perfectly willing candidate to simply walk away?

Sorry for making him want her through it all?

It was impossible to guess at her regret, and they were given no opportunity to discuss any of it, as she was locked inside the carriage with her maid, and then her sister Camille rushed to receive her when they reached Lusk House.

Declan went through the motions of stable chores with jerky, agitated precision. He ate dinner with the other grooms in stony silence. Girdleston summoned him to the green salon for his nightly threatening. This time, thank God, he also paid him: £75 and a bottle of brandy. Declan gave the liquor to Nettle and wrote a long-overdue letter to his father.

Da,

Still on the new job in Mayfair.

Busy but well.

You would be appalled—they've given me the most jaundiced shade of yellow livery, and the fit is terrible. I look like a walking daffodil.

Beyond that, they feed me well, and they stable the finest horses and the most modern carriages. The client is . . .

Declan paused, his pen hovering above the page.

The client is beautiful and clever and demanding.

The client leaps from one bold, erratic gesture to the next.

The client is trapped.

The client is relentless.

The client thrills me.

The client embodies something I've never wanted but now struggle to do without.

The client has hair as black as ebony and green eyes.

The client terrifies me.

The client is killing me.

The client is more than I can handle.

The client may send me back to prison, and I don't even care.

The client needs me.

The client may deliver us all.
He could hardly write any of these.
He settled on:

The client is a spirited young woman who requires my full attention. I'm sorry there's not been a spare afternoon that I may visit you.

Before I post this, there is one more thing. I may have managed a new situation for you and the girls. It is a forest cottage in Somerset. There is a village nearby and a river. I've not visited the site, but I've been to Somerset, and it's lovely.

We cannot rely upon it, and I only mention it because you must be prepared to relocate quickly if I can make it come to pass.

Tell the girls. I know Somerset would be a significant change, but we've been over this. The good reasons far outweigh the bad.

I am sorry to tell you this by letter instead of a visit from me, which is long overdue. You are never far from my mind, and I have enclosed money for firewood and lantern oil and meat. It is more than usual, so please take care not to squander it. It is important that you keep some savings, Da. The next bundle is not guaranteed. Provision for the winter, buy the girls some frivolous treat, but ration. I'm sorry it is not more. I'm sorry for everything that has happened these last nine months.

Your son,
Declan

The mere act of writing the words imbued Declan with a new sense of purpose and a fresh stab of guilt.

Yes, Helena's family was shackling her to a future she did not want, but what of the future of his family? Where had his loyalties gone?

She'd made him so angry at the medical office. He'd felt like a passenger, watching a reckless coachman steer his team along the crumbling edge of a high cliff. And she expected him to enjoy the ride.

Tomorrow, he would speak with her. He would remind her that decisions about these women were made *together*. And that, *always*, they were discreet. With everyone. The intimacy they shared was not on display. In fact, the intimacy that they shared must stop. He was not her London diversion.

He would not touch her again—not tomorrow, not ever.

Chapter Sixteen

Helena was slated to visit the British Museum in Bloomsbury Street the next day. She would tour the exhibits, sketch the artifacts, and speak to a docent about becoming a patron. It was Thursday, and there were no scheduled family outings; this visit was purely for herself.

And to scout the next potential duchess.

The candidate was Miss Jessica Marten, a young woman who was said to haunt the museum most days, assisting her father with research and transcription. Helena's new priority was disliking the girl herself but finding her perfect for Lusk.

Despite the coldness of the morning, Helena elected to walk from Lusk House to the museum. She'd known Declan was out of sorts when they'd left Miss Keep the day before, and she'd worried about it all night. She would not ride in anxious solitude inside the carriage while he glowered outside, not when they could walk and talk.

She took care with her appearance, wearing a crimson dress with burgundy trim. She chose mauve gloves and hat, and Meg plaited her hair and pinned the braids in looping coils at the back of her head. She had a faint matador-ish look when she descended the stairs for breakfast. Considering Declan's mood, this felt appropriate.

She sent for Shaw immediately after breakfast. Girdleston hovered in the grand hall, peppering her with questions about where she intended to go on foot with no proper chaperone. Helena cheerfully informed him that she wished to research fossilized plants at the British Museum. She'd asked Lusk to escort her, she reported regretfully, but alas, the duke declined.

When Declan appeared, she stacked his arms with sketch pads, reference books, drawing materials, and a living specimen of *Malus domestica* in a clay pot. The final touch was admitting to Girdleston that she had (begrudgingly) begun to rely upon his groom—and they set off.

"You're angry," she said, striding in the direction of Cumberland Gate.

"Yes," he agreed, "I am angry."

They made the corner at Oxford Street, walking east. The cold air stung her eyes, but she did not feel chilled. She felt only him, his silence and rigid displeasure. A sharp animosity crackled with every *clip, clip, clip* of his steps. He radiated frustration.

"Should I begin to toss out guesses?" she asked.

"You truly do not know?"

Helena stopped walking and he almost collided with her. She pivoted to face him. "Truly, I do not know."

"Fine," he said, guiding her from the bustle of pedestrian traffic. "You were too cavalier and familiar in your 'flirting lesson' with Miss Keep yesterday. It put the plan in jeopardy and our collaboration at risk. As your groom, I am powerless to do anything more than say, 'Yes, my lady,' and follow your lead. I was forced to comply, and I didn't like it."

"Why not? Because the demonstration dissuaded her?"

"Because you *sat in my lap* and *cooed in my ear* for the benefit of someone you'd known ten minutes. Lap-sitting and ear-cooing is not the behavior of an heiress and her groom, and certainly not the behavior of an heiress and her 'minder.' What if Girdleston learned of the stunt?"

"He won't. Miss Keep can be trusted."

"We have no idea about Miss Keep; you'd never met her in your life."

"I don't need to meet her to recognize an earnest girl with serious pursuits, desperate to gain some control of her future."

They were on a schedule, and Helena resumed their progress down Oxford Street. "Joanna Keep lives in a world where she's at the mercy of almost every man and any woman older than she is. She could gain control through shallowness or manipulation, but she has not. If I thought Miss Keep was inauthentic or a schemer, I would have been more prudent. I also would have happily dangled her before Lusk without a second thought. But she is clever and earnest and genuine. She is better than Lusk deserves. And we can trust her."

A trio of boys darted in front of Helena, their hats overturned and filled with stolen eggs. One boy tripped and fell, making a mess of yokes and shells and a string of profanity. Helena tsked and stepped around the mess.

"My situation is not exactly like Miss Keep's," she went on, winding her way through scrambling boys, "but I am more like her than most young women. Enough to know that she'll not gossip about me. I'm vying for some control over destiny, just as she is. The flirting demonstration was for her benefit, and as strange as it was, I believe it was useful. She will not betray the favor."

"You hope she will not," Declan said.

"I have very good instincts about people. Look how right I was about you. I trusted you on the first night."

"That was sheer luck. One-in-a-million chance that Girdleston posted me to your detail instead of any of a hundred men who would've delivered you to him on the spot."

"You call it luck, I call it a gut feeling." She closed her eyes and took a deep breath. She felt strongly about her intuition, but she was beginning to believe this wasn't a quarrel about her instincts; it was about her taking advantage.

"Look," she said, opening her eyes. "I can acknowledge that it was . . ." and now she searched for the correct word, ". . . exploitive to summon you and drape myself upon you. I was trying to be *nimble*. And *opportunistic*." She walked a few steps, thinking about his complaint. Heat crept up her neck; she felt her face go red. His point was valid. As her groom, he was at her mercy. In full view of the public, he must do what she said.

She stopped walking. She pivoted back. "Perhaps now I can see that it may have been . . . poor form to portray the lesson in flirtation. Oh, Declan, I'm so sorry." She bit her lip until it stung.

Declan stopped short and stared at her. He began shaking his head.

"What?" she demanded.

He walked around her.

"Do you *reject* my apology?" she called.

"No, I don't reject it. I—" He made a growling noise.

"You what?" She followed him.

"You are too trusting," he said. "And too *honest*."

They were striding down Oxford Street at a fast clip. Declan must have realized their appearance and paused, ducked his head, and allowed her to precede him.

"This was a mistake," he said to her. "You shouldn't have apologized. It was better when we were at odds."

"Who is better off without an apology?" She walked without seeing where she went.

"Look," he sighed, "*Lady Helena*, our plan can continue—obviously we have no choice now but to see it through—but you and I? We cannot be so . . . so enmeshed."

She missed a step, momentarily unable to comprehend. "What do you mean, 'enmeshed'?"

"It's my fault," he said. "I've indulged too much. I . . . I never should have touched you. And I've revealed too much. If we quarrel, we quarrel. There's no need for apologies. Perhaps we simply do not get on."

Helena was speechless. She rolled his statement around in her head.

"Do not get on?" she repeated blankly. "Is that what you think?"

"I think it's best if we do not examine it from every angle. Instead, we restrain. We cannot touch, my lady. Ours should be a very simple groom-charge relationship."

"But you are not really a groom, and I'm not really your charge. We have this very important thing we are doing, and . . . and there is more. Do you deny there is more?"

They'd reached the busy corner of Oxford Street and Bloomsbury. To their left, the museum sprawled like a marble plateau in the center of an expansive lawn. Carriages and wagons clattered around them. The museum grounds milled with the lazy day-trippers. Declan gestured to the looming building and led them along the network of walkways to the front steps.

Helena followed, eyes narrowed, heart pounding. A knot had begun to form in her throat, cinching tighter and tighter with every step.

When they were up the steps, Declan led them down the front colonnade and ducked behind a marble column.

Taking a deep breath, he said, "Let us simply *start again.*"

"Start this conversation again?" she asked. She was so confused. She knew he was angry but she hadn't expected him to proclaim them "ill suited." Helena had waited half her life to feel as connected to another person as she felt to Declan. He validated her intelligence and humor and desired her. They were *of the same mind*. Her attraction to him was physical, yes, but it was also in her heart and in her head. After a lifetime of sprinting uphill to escape, she finally felt like she was coasting downward to *arrive somewhere.* She was falling in love with him.

And now this?

Declan repeated, "My lady—"

"Can you not call me Helena?"

"My lady," he repeated, swallowing hard. He paused.

Helena waited, studying his face. He no longer looked angry, he looked . . . anguished. Helena could relate, she also felt anguish; she felt anguish and heartsick and the cold fear of losing him. But she would not stand in the shadows and silently stew about it. She reviewed the conversation in her mind. What had he said? He'd said he'd indulged, that he never should have touched her, that he'd *revealed too much.*

She cleared her throat, banishing the tears. "You said," she began, "that you'd 'revealed too much.' About what, exactly, have you revealed so very much? You share cryptic details of your mysterious life in drips and drabs, usually in an odd moment in a crowded street."

"You've just said you chose me on instinct," he countered. "Why should you know anything about me at all?"

"Instinct said you would take notes at a party," she shot back. "*Which you did.* Don't oversimplify. We are—" A deep breath. "Surely we can agree that now we are *allies.* At the very least. Is it not common for *allies* to know a thing or two about each other? Certainly I have been an open book. And that says nothing of the other ways we are . . . connected."

Declan said nothing, staring down at her.

She amended, "No—forgive me, not 'connected.' 'Enmeshed.' "

He let out a deep breath. Finally, he said, "When I discuss my life, it draws us closer."

"Oh no, not that."

"Exactly. *Not that*. It leads nowhere, Helena. Not for us. I can reveal a handful of personal details to you if you like. But there's very little to say. My life is very meager and plain compared to yours."

"I live in the forest," she said. "I tend an orchard. I am not put off by meager."

"You are the daughter of a wealthy earl, Helena. I am your *servant*. Honestly, that should be the end of it." A long pause. "And the physical intimacy must stop. Every time I touch you, I am crossing a very dangerous, very significant line."

She blinked at him, trying to understand. *Crossing a line?* Was *she* the line? Had she behaved so inappropriately in the presence of Miss Keep? Did he simply not fancy her? Or not fancy her enough to risk being discovered?

She looked away. Her heart lodged into her chest and slid down, slicing her open. She wanted to sit. She wanted to run. She wanted her grandmother to tell her what to do.

She took a deep breath. She would neither sit nor run, of course. And she had no one to counsel her but herself.

She looked up to Declan and said slowly, "I've been terribly thick, haven't I? Clueless, really. You are handsome and strong, and you agree to my plans and validate my need to escape Lusk.

You collaborate and praise and make me feel as if I matter. You exude confidence even in that ridiculous yellow livery—and you should be confident. You are so very proficient and clever and thoughtful. You look out for me as no one has.

"Taken altogether," she said sadly, "I've misinterpreted the situation. I didn't know. I've . . . I've rather hurled myself in your direction, and you don't like it. And now you are trying to pull away. The . . . er, ardor I feel is not mutual."

The pain of realizing these words, and in nearly the same moment she expressed them, was almost too much, and Helena held out one hand as if to stop the march of time.

She added, "I understand. I am relentless but not without pride."

She took a step back.

She finished, "How foolish. Of course. *Of course.*"

Tears of humiliation and hurt had begun to blur the blue-gray shadows of the colonnade.

"Helena, stop," he said firmly. He set down the stack of books and the plant and stepped to her. He placed her outstretched hand on his chest, just over his heart.

"Hmm?" said Helena, wiping her eye.

Declan took a deep breath and began again. "Congratulations. You've said the one thing that would cause me to take it all back. Well, take most of it back."

"About crossing the line?"

"About not apologizing. About being better off at odds."

"Am I the line?" she whispered.

"You, my lady, are the compulsion. *My* compulsion. You are the reason I go through my day—what I wish, and what do, and the person about whom I cannot stop thinking. You are my first thought in the morning and the dream in which I make love at night. My desire for you is a fierce, pounding wave against a rock. You are not the line, you are the thing I'm risking my future to protect. But I will not ruin *your* future along the way."

"What?" Helena's breath lodged somewhere in her windpipe.

"As reversals go," he said, "this feels very comprehensive."

"What?" she repeated, higher, airier. Had he just professed himself to her? She wanted to call back his words and examined the meaning of each one.

He wanted her. She was his day and his night.

"I am not pushing you away because I do not like you, Helena," he said. "I am pushing you away because—"

"Don't say it." The words gushed out. Suddenly, she knew. He was about to offer an excuse as old as time. Shakespeare must have said it. Likely, Adam said it to Eve before she offered him the apple.

"Because," he continued, "I like you too much."

He said it anyway.

She fought the urge to take him by the lapels and shake him. Instead, she said, "And why is it wrong to like me so much? In the day and in the night, et cetera, et cetera?"

"Helena."

"No. Now I urge you to say it. I want to hear the words."

"What future have we?" he asked, his eyes grim and serious. "A mercenary and an heiress."

"*I* am a farmer," she corrected.

"You are engaged to a duke."

"A duke who I am about to pass off to some other unlucky girl."

"And then your parents will betroth you to someone else."

She was shaking her head, but he continued. "Heiresses do not build their lives with mercenaries, Helena."

"This heiress will not marry a duke," she said firmly. A shimmer of hope rained in Helena's chest.

She pressed on. "I have vowed not to marry him from the beginning. If I can manage *not* marrying who I want, then I can manage the opposite." Helena realized this sounded dangerously like a wedding proposal. She felt her face flush red. There was challenging and then there was stalking.

She cleared her throat and said, "My parents arranged my marriage to Lusk when I was scarcely nineteen years old. I have made the five ensuing years pure hell for all of them. They will not do it again. Depend on it. When this betrothal is finished, they will not care what I do. They will move on to Joan—or Camille, God save her. I am too much work."

"You think you want me, Helena, but you've been blinded by the thrill of escaping Lusk. We are dashing through markets and slinking away from your parents. It is exciting. I am a diverting adventure. You will not want me for all time."

"Do. Not. Tell. Me. What. I. Want," she said. "I am so very weary of other people informing me how I feel or what I want. I am not a child. I know my own mind and my own heart."

Declan jerked off his hat and ran a hand through his hair. He said, "There are obstacles in my . . . my situation that you do not know," he said. He turned in an agitated circle.

"So tell me," she said, trying to tamp down what felt like growing euphoria. What more about his "situation" could matter if he'd admitted he cared for her? She repeated, "Tell me."

He was shaking his head. "It's tied up in this job and my father and the future. There's already enough pressure on you to end the engagement. My problems are not yours. My problems are so very far beneath you. One of the many tenants of my person that is beneath you. I refuse to pile on to your worries."

"More than the money?" she repeated. She reached out and put a gloved hand on his bicep.

He nodded. The worry in his brown eyes cracked her heart. He said grimly, "More than the money."

Helena nodded. His expression said, *Leave it.* For the moment, she would leave it. She held his arm, digging her fingers in. She wanted to rip the yellow sleeve from his tunic and lash him with it. But she did not press.

"But . . . mostly this is about my rank?" she asked quietly. She let her hand slide away.

"The differences in our lives are colossal, Helena. No matter how well we get on."

"If *you* were the son of an earl and I was, say . . . the governess or a nursemaid, would you proclaim it impossible for us to . . . enmesh?"

"It's not the same, and you know it," he said. "Nor is it our situation."

"Perhaps not, but I am one-half of our collaboration, and I've been completely honest with you from our very first meeting—"

"Too honest."

"—and so I'll be completely honest with you now. I do not subscribe to your fears about the future. Not about you being a mercenary and myself an heiress, and not about being blinded by adventure. But even if I *was* afraid—which I am not—I would never allow fear to stand in the way of . . . of our potential. I hope I do not overstep by saying that I believe we hold very great potential."

"And what if I said that *I* am the other half of this collaboration, and I have an opposing view?"

"I would say that I am the person on the receiving end of your rejection, and I don't like it."

"That is the heiress talking, giving an order—pronouncing what she wants."

"I *will* say what I want," she countered. "You'd not found issue with this until now, and here is my point. If something about me—my outspokenness, my tendency to march people around, my small feet, my black hair . . ." she grabbed her braids with both hands, ". . . is not to your liking, then fine, say this and detach yourself. I can accept actual rejection if it is founded in distaste. But I cannot abide the other way."

"Helena," he sighed, "wouldn't you like to fall in love with a reasonable gentleman, someone who can provide you with the sort of life to which you were born? Who will inherit a beautiful home and pass it on to your children? Who will see them properly educated and guarantee their standing in the world? Not every aristocrat is as pitiful as Lusk. I've served in battle with many honorable, decent men of rank. You've never had the opportunity to meet a reasonable gentleman."

"I don't want a reasonable gentleman," she said, stooping to snatch the potted apple. In her head, she finished, *I want you.*

She wouldn't say it. She'd said enough—too much. But at least now she knew. He was not angry or disinterested, he simply could not see a way out.

Helena had spent her entire adult life searching for ways out. There was always a way.

She took a deep breath. "Look, I do not mean to dismiss your worry for my future or your esteemed plans for my children, but I reject your caution. And I reject your rejection."

"I didn't reject you, Helena."

"You tried to, and I cannot accept it." She stepped around him and then turned back. "But one thing at a time, shall we? First, I must consider this poor girl and dangle the dukedom in front of her. If I can foist Lusk off on someone else and not hate myself for it, dealing with your fear of heiresses will be a summer's day."

And then she whirled around and strode to the door of the museum.

DECLAN FORCED HIMSELF to be vigilant in the dark catacombs of the British Museum. His brain was in a fog. Helena wound her way through windowless corridors and up dim stairwells, the black smoke of lanterns snaking to a ceiling. His thoughts traveled a similar circuitous path.

What had just happened?

He'd begun the day indignant and determined to put her at arm's length. Now he was spouting declarations about days and nights and dreams—and it was almost as if he'd issued a challenge to her. He'd all but dared her to believe in a future together.

At least he'd not told her about the threat of prison. If their plan didn't work, or if Girdleston found out, at least she wouldn't have the added pressure of keeping him out of Newgate.

It was one thing for her to develop an . . . an affection for a mercenary, quite another for her to fall for a convict.

Helena held a map of the museum to a lantern, studying the route to the Egyptian Hall. She didn't ask for his help. She wouldn't need it, and also reading a map together would feel very forced in this moment.

Poking her head through an open doorway, she frowned at an exhibit of ancient crockery, and strode out down an opposite hall.

"We're very close," she whispered, brushing past him.

Declan followed, replaying their conversation. What he had expected? That she would simply agree with him? When had she ever simply agreed? She'd had too many people dictating her future for too long. She wanted to decide. She should decide.

But it felt shortsighted and unstainable for her to settle on *him*.

She was headstrong and knew her own mind, but could she conceive of the life he could give her—or (more accurately) not give her? Compensation for mercenary work was decent—a living wage to be sure—and he demanded a very high fee, but his savings had vanished. If he was fully exonerated (and that was a significant *if*), he would start again from nothing. She was strong and resilient and claimed to have her own living, but could he saddle her with a husband who would rebuild from nothing? If he was not locked away forever?

No, I cannot, he thought, watching her slender back as she wound through the dark halls.

He'd not ply her from Lusk only to bind her to a possible convict who could not feed his horse.

And anyway, "binding her to him" was a very great assumption. She desired him, of this he had no doubt. She did not want him to push her away—she'd made that perfectly clear. But did she wish to marry him? Was *he* the future that she saw for herself? Or was she caught up in fierce attraction and untried desire?

Did she want him forever . . . or simply for now?

He dare not ask. He didn't want to know. If she was wise—if they would both use their heads and not their . . . and not any other parts—they would concentrate only on *now*.

And keep their hands off.

Now she'd located the Egyptian Hall, a long,

dim room flanked by sphynxes and a labyrinth of glass cases containing mummified bodies. Helena strode boldly forth, seemingly unphased by the vaguely human-shaped cocoons lying still beneath the glass. A handful of other museum-goers milled in the distance, studying the placards or holding guidebooks to the lantern light. Helena stuck her head inside anterooms and book-lined alcoves until, at last, she came upon an open door that led into what appeared to be an off-limits staff room, illuminated with high lantern light and dominated by a long table, strewn with open books and unfurled parchment.

In a stiff chair in the center of the table slumped a young woman with fiery red hair and an ink-stained apron. She appeared to be asleep across an open book.

Helena shot Declan a hopeful smile and stepped through the door. She cleared her throat. She gave a chair a gentle shove. The loud screeching sound of wood on stone rang through the hall. The woman did not stir.

Declan scanned the room for potential threat and found it empty except for bookshelves and open cases of artifacts. Another door on the opposite end was shut. Helena inched closer to the woman with intentionally loud steps. The sleeping girl began to snore.

Helena stepped closer and said, "I beg your pardon."

At last, the girl jerked up with a start, blinked three times, and stared down at the open book before her. She frowned.

"I'm sorry to disturb you," ventured Helena.

The girl turned her face, squinting her eyes at the intrusion. "Oh. Sorry," she said. "There are no exhibits in this room. This area is devoted to research for faculty and staff. If you're looking for the sarcophagi, they're actually—"

"Are you, by chance, Miss Jessica Marten?" Helena cut in.

The girl paused, looking confused. "I am Jessica Marten."

"Oh, lovely," said Helena. "I am Lady Helena Lark, and I've been searching for you . . ."

Declan drifted just outside the door to stand guard, hearing their conversation in snatches.

"Forgive my intrusion, but we have a friend in common, and she said I might find you here," Helena began.

"No friend of mine would knowingly send someone to this or any museum," said Miss Marten tiredly. "Forgive me, Lady—"

"Helena."

"Right, Lady Helena. It's been very long week and it's only Thursday. You'll forgive me, I'm in a foul mood."

"Oh . . ." said Helena. "Have you been met with some . . . frustration? In your work?"

"Well, the work that I do is entirely my father's," she said, stifling a yawn, "and it is the very soul of frustration. This week and every week."

"You don't enjoy the research that you do on behalf of your father? I can only imagine the reward of collaborating with a historian of such merit."

"I can see how one might make that assumption," said Miss Marten tiredly. "But if they'd spent years of their life—as I have been forced to do—in a dim, smoky museum among mummified bodies and ancient texts, they might not feel the same way."

"But it is not your choice to assist your father?"

"Ah, no."

"But he . . . forces you to assist him?"

"What can I say? He began my training very young; now I'm the only one who knows the languages, knows his filing system, knows the ghouls who run the research library. Who else is there to do it? Until I have something better to do—such as a proper husband and family of my own—I am expected to be here, transcribing hieroglyphics, until my mind is numb and my eyes are shot." Another yawn.

"You are unmarried?" asked Helena.

"It's difficult to locate a husband in the bowels of the British Museum. Most of the men here have been mummified. Figuratively or literally."

"You enjoyed no debut Season, I take it?" asked Helena.

There was a pause. Miss Marten said, "No. I did not enjoy a debut. My father did not find a London Season to be a useful allocation of time or money. When we are in London, we must be here. Rapidly expiring of boredom." She slammed the book shut. "I'm sorry, what friend did you say sent you? How can I help you?"

"Oh, right. Well, honestly, I cannot remember the friend. A woman I met at a party. And the reason I am here is to offer you a proposition . . ."

The conversation went from there and Declan shook his head, impressed by her cool mastery of the art of saying just enough. She carefully drew out a kind of exhausted honesty from Miss Marten—her desire to crawl from beneath the thumb of her father and the boredom of her current life—and her willingness to do anything to become a duchess.

Helena was so good at it Declan marveled that she devoted so much of her life to apples and forests. He was just about to step away for a closer look at the fox-like face of the stone carving when he caught sight of a smudged figure across the room. His eyes followed the movement. It was a hurried person in a dark velvet cloak, cutting a fast line to the far door.

The hair on the back of his neck stood on end. It was the cloaked figure from the market. He took a step closer, looking again. Yes, he was certain.

The hood was up, which was wholly unnecessary in the dim museum, and the figure shuffled along with a fast but not necessarily stealthy pace.

Declan began to follow, not chasing but also not allowing this person to duck into a dark corner or dissolve into the gloom.

It was impossible to distinguish gender or age. The figure had no apparent purpose in the museum—he or she wasn't hunched over an exhibit or gazing at statuary. It was as if the person was using the halls of the museum to get from one point to another.

Or as if they were following him. Or Helena.

Declan's stomach pitched in outrage at the thought. He glanced back at Helena through the open door. Miss Marten had her head facedown on the desk, slowly shaking it back and forth, the universal symbol for *I can't take it*, and Helena stood over her, gently speaking to her, a hand on her shoulder.

Fine, good, they were in the midst of their discussion. He could be spared. Declan left Helena to it.

The cloaked person ducked from the Egyptian Hall before Declan could reach the door. He sped up, walking just shy of a jog. His yellow livery made him appear phosphorescent in the murky museum and he wished for the officer's coat.

When he reached the door outside the hall, the landing was empty. Declan swore, looking in any of three possible directions. He cocked his head and listened.

From the stairwell, he heard descending footsteps and the muted slide of the cloak trailing down steps. Declan followed, reaching the ground floor in time to see the shadow of the draped figure sliding from view.

He swore and leapt the last five steps, scanning the corridor.

Nothing.

The corridor emptied into a library, a cavernous, shelf-lined room that was crowded with patrons, including a squirming line of schoolboys and scrum of nuns. More than half the patrons were dressed in black.

Declan rushed in, mentally dividing the room into quadrants and searching each space—nothing.

If he had an hour to track this person, to speak to people, to scout entrances and exits and case the building, likely he could find them. But he'd left Helena alone for too long. If the cloaked figure doubled back and approached Helena from the opposite direction, she shouldn't be alone.

Taking a final look around the library, Declan jogged back to the Egyptian Hall. When he rounded the sphynx, Helena rushed into view. Her smile lit up the dark museum.

"We've a second potential girl," she exclaimed. "She wants it so very much."

Chapter Seventeen

The Seven Duchesses (Potential)

Happy ✓
~~Sneezy~~
~~Doc~~
Sleepy ✓

There were no outings for Helena the next day, not alone or with her mother. The household, and in fact all of London society, was preoccupied with the inaugural event of the Season, a masquerade ball known as Winter Solstice. The ball would take place that night, the longest of the year, but the day was devoted to perfecting costumes and masks.

As with all London parties, Helena had wanted to decline, but the ball promised access to two of the potential duchesses. She could observe the girls, possibly even approach them.

Two hours before the ball, Helena stood before her bed, staring at a spectrum of pink satin, trying to sort out some costume. She hadn't wanted to bother with fittings and refused to have something commissioned. Girdleston had been appalled and offered to send up a few possibilities. Helena reluctantly agreed. What did it matter what she wore?

"What do you think, Meg?" she sighed, looking at her maid.

"I can't say that one stands out as the obvious choice," said Meg charitably. "They are so opposite from your usual style, aren't they? It's as if Mr. Girdleston doesn't know you at all."

"Imagine that," said Helena.

"But this is the point of a masquerade, I suppose," the maid said. "You'd do justice to any of them, honestly."

There was a knock on the door. Helena assumed it was tea, but when Meg opened the door, her middle sister, Camille, stepped into the room.

"Hallo," Camille began boldly, her face overly bright.

"Hello yourself," Helena said cautiously. She was not accustomed to friendly visits from her sisters. "Is something the matter?"

Camille shook her head. "I came to see what you would wear to the ball."

Helena narrowed her eyes, trying to decipher Camille's expression. Her sister had never paid any mind to Helena's wardrobe before.

She turned to the dresses on the bed. "Meg and I have come to understand that Girdleston favors me in pink."

"Oh," her sister said, frowning at the dresses. "Does he instruct what you wear?" She sounded horrified.

"Not typically, thank God, but he is very determined that my costume might complement the duke's. I would rather die than match Lusk, but he's sent up these options."

The dresses splayed across the bed were pink, pinker, and glowing pink. The first was a pig-colored affair with exposed pantaloons, ribboned staff, straw hat, and wooden clogs. A Georgian-era goose girl?

The second was a bright pink profusion of ruffles sewn with a swarm of beaded butterflies. A coordinated mask represented the full wingspan of a pink-and-yellow butterfly, its exaggerated antenna affecting long eyebrows.

The final dress was a sugary pink confection with tiers and tiers of poufs that would make Helena feel like a wedding cake.

"These dresses give me a toothache," said Camille.

Helena laughed and eyed her sister. Were they actually having a warm conversation? Camille's comments were clever—Camille had always been clever—but her joke had the underlying tone of conciliation. Her sister was trying to say the correct things. Helena's heart felt soft and light.

"I quite agree," Helena said slowly. She turned to Meg. "The pinks are out of the question. But could we do something with my old aquamarine silk?"

She pulled a turquoise gown from the wardrobe, one of the last pieces her grandmother bought her before she'd died. Helena's preference to stay in most evenings meant that her more formal gowns languished. The turquoise silk had always been a favorite, ethereal and mysterious and wholly unique. The blue-green fabric shimmered with an iridescent cast, and gauzy silk strips in three shades of aqua trailed from the shoulders and hips.

"Much better," agreed Camille. "And you should wear your hair entirely down, loose and wild."

"Perhaps I shall," mused Helena.

Meg cut in, "I could weave fresh flowers in your hair, my lady. Just think of spring, when the apples are in full bloom and the blossoms everywhere, including your hair. So pretty. The hothouse will not have apple blossoms, but I'll work with whatever the gardeners have on hand."

"Brilliant, Meg. That solves it. If anyone asks, I'm Demeter, Goddess of the Harvest."

"What is Lusk's costume?" asked Camille.

"Who knows. A Swarm of Locust, possibly? That would be fitting."

The three women laughed, and Meg began to pack away the rejected pinks. Helena drifted to the window and collapsed, peering into the garden. "Tonight will be cold," she said. "Perhaps I won't stifle in the crush of the ballroom."

"I don't see how you tolerate it," said Camille, "going to these things on Lusk's arm. You don't enjoy London parties, and you don't enjoy Lusk. How do you manage?" She settled on the edge of the bed.

Helena shrugged. "I decline most invitations. When we do go out, I am friendly to the point of irritation. You saw this in the carriage to

Wandsworth. Hope springs eternal that he will become so annoyed that he'll tell Girdleston he won't have me."

"He won't," said Camille.

"And then I wait for him to abandon me," Helena concluded. "Which he always does. Almost immediately. He has his own friends, his cards, his drink. We arrive together, but I leave alone."

Camille nodded, toying with the embroidery on the coverlet.

"I'm sorry that I cannot carry on with this system for the rest of my life," said Helena softly. "If I could, you and the girls would benefit from the dukedom."

"Stop," said Camille. "I would not benefit. Not at the price of your misery. And anyway, I don't care about dukedoms."

"Truly?" asked Helena, her eyes stinging with tears.

"Truly," said Camille. "And I'm sorry that you ever believed this of me. Joan cannot see why you resist the wedding, but I can."

"I'm grateful. And I don't blame Joan, not really. Mama and Papa have planted the notion of prosperity and rank, and it has taken root. The idea, I believe, is that we should marry well and live two lives. A title and money on the one hand, and lovers or whatever else we wish to pursue on the other. I'm so glad that you can see beyond it."

Camille was nodding her head. "The duplicity and resentment would kill you or me."

"Let us live," pronounced Helena, her voice cracking.

"You first," chuckled Camille. "I'm following

your lead. But I still worry for you. I wish I could be of more use to you tonight at the masquerade."

Camille's debut in London society was not until next year's Season, so she and Theresa would remain at home.

"And what would you do to be useful?" asked Helena nervously. Her maid Meg was still in the room, pressing wrinkles from her gown.

"Whatever you have planned. To end the wedding."

"What makes you think I've something planned?"

"I'm not stupid, Helena." She rolled off the bed. "I don't blame you for not telling me. It's not as if we've been . . . close."

"I should like us to be close," Helena said lowly. To Meg, she said, "Would you mind checking for flowers, Meg? I love your idea for my hair."

The maid bobbed her head and quit the room.

Despite their solitude, Helena whispered, "I'm grateful, Camille. Truly—more than you know. But you needn't worry—"

"Stop," Camille cut in. "It's one thing to run away, quite another to . . . Well, I cannot guess what you've concocted."

Her sister began to prowl the room. She looked determined and calculating and very sincere. Helena could feel herself beginning to trust. Her heart opened and beat in a newer, gladder way. She'd wanted this for so very long.

"Assuming that I have undertaken some . . ." Helena began, clearing her throat, ". . . some *sabotage* of the wedding to Lusk—not admitting anything, but assuming—yes, sometimes I am anxious."

In truth, Helena's emotions were a painful jumble of fear and hope and anxiety and doubt. Her belly roiled with nerves. She slept poorly and barely ate. Her plan could unravel or explode at any moment. The girls they chose could lose heart or be failures at seduction. The girls they didn't choose could gossip about being approached. The duke could ignore the potential duchesses, or he could love them but still refuse to throw her over.

There were so many more things that could go wrong and only one very improbable thing that could go right.

And then, underlying it all, superseding it all, was Declan.

Totally unexpected, but now wholly central.

He'd begun as a means to an end, and now, in Helena's mind, he seemed like the very embodiment of "the end."

She'd fallen in love with him, of this she had no doubt. Her realization of this had been like discovering she was soaking wet even as she'd willingly waded into a stream. She'd wanted to sample the coolness and current and now she was being swept away.

And it *wasn't* because he was the only man she'd been allowed to consider, and it wasn't because he was strong and sensual and exciting.

It was because he was all the things that Lusk was not, plus a host of things she'd never dreamed she needed. Opinionated, interested, courageous, sacrificing, clever. The list of why she loved him was very long.

And it begged the question: Why endeavor to enact this plan, if he wasn't there in the end?

"What of Shaw?" asked Camille.

Helena looked up. If before her sister had seemed astute and observant, now she seemed positively clairvoyant.

"Camille," sighed Helena.

It was one thing to admit that she resisted the duke. All of London had heard of her resistance. It was quite another to admit that she'd fallen in love with her groom.

"Do you . . . love him?" her sister pressed.

"*Camille,*" Helena repeated. "Shaw is a servant."

"If that is true," said Camille, "he's the boldest, most arrogant and entitled servant I've ever seen. Not to mention strapping. And clearly he operates very safely inside your confidence."

"You're mistaken."

"I'm not," Camille sang. "You're simply fortunate that I'm the only one paying attention. I'm not sure why that is. I'm only seventeen."

"You are easily passing for thirty in this moment."

Camille ignored her. "What I don't understand is why Girdleston doesn't suspect something."

"When I bolted from Lady Canning's party and Shaw recovered me, Girdleston ordered him to never leave my side. The old man bound us together. Shaw's attention is his job."

Camille turned away, wagging her finger. "Not so very much attention. Not so willingly, both of you. Can you not feign indifference to him, Lena? And tell him to stop staring at you like you're . . . you're a winged angel from the heavenly host."

"How have you seen this?" asked Helena, dragging herself up from the window.

"You're not the only clever Lark sister."

"Quite so," Helena chuckled. She beamed at her sister. "I'm so glad you came to my room."

Camille nodded. "It occurred to me that I had a choice to make. Before we'd left Somerset, I thought I could either go along with Mama and Papa as Joan did, or I could do what my head and my heart has been telling me for some time. I'm of the same mind as you, Lena. I want to be like you. I want to make my own choices and live as I want to live. *I* want to fall in love with my own version of a handsome groom."

Helena made a choking sound. "Well, perhaps let us take this new independence one step at the time. I'm not—"

"Do not," sighed Camille, "spare me the subterfuge. Have you made arrangements for Shaw to be with you at the ball?"

Helena was uncertain of how to answer this—and not only because it meant taking Camille into her confidence. She and Declan had gone back and forth about it. Declan felt Helena should allow Lusk to escort her in the ducal carriage. In his view, this was the most prudent, least-suspicious way to arrive. Helena had recoiled at the notion and they'd quarreled about it on the walk home from the museum. In the end, Declan promised that he would find his own way inside the ball. He would be near her but not immediately beside her. That she would be safe. He was a mercenary, after all.

Helena looked at her sister now. "Probably,"

she said.

"Good for you," said Camille.

Helena collapsed on the bed, staring at the molded ceiling. "It's a masquerade. Everyone will be caught up in the pageantry and half of the guests will be obscured by masks. It will be a blur of crystals and plumage and women standing too close to candelabras while their headdresses catch flame. He could don any number of costumes and not be detected. Or, what's more likely, he may infiltrate the ranks of the hosts' footmen."

"Oh, Lena. Forget *your* love for him. Obviously, *he* loves *you*."

"You are too young to speak of love," Helena said flippantly, dropping an arm over her eyes.

These were just words to say, of course. Perhaps Camille knew more of love than any of them. Their parents hadn't properly modeled love, not the love she wanted.

Camille had no reply, and Helena regretted being dismissive. She tried again. "Shaw has some concerns about our differences in rank. Apparently."

"I cannot say I am surprised," Camille said. "I would be concerned if he did not."

"Why?"

"Well, I'd regard him as a fortune hunter for one," said Camille. "If he did not bring up rank, it might mean he intends to slide himself into the prosperity of Papa's earldom. You know, sort of, *Oh? Were you a fabulously wealthy earl's daughter? Will marriage into your family position me for a life of luxury? I hadn't noticed.* When he resists, he's acknowledging that being a lady is a significant part of your identity."

"He has no intention of sliding," Helena said. "I assure you. He doesn't like aristocrats."

"And also, it would be selfish and unfeeling of him not to question what your life will be like if you marry outside the peerage. He is, after all, a stable groom."

"He is more than a groom actually."

"Do tell."

Helena shook her head. "Never you mind. What matters is the house left to me by Gran. And the orchard. They matter very much. I can provide for us both, no matter if he's a servant or the man in the moon."

"I'm not saying it's impossible," said Camille. "I'm simply glad he's being honest. And asking you to consider the ramifications."

Considering ramifications seemed like the only thing Declan wanted to do. They'd discussed it before they'd entered the museum. On the walk home. He'd sent a note by stable boy.

And Helena *had* thought about it, dismissing his reservations now as she had then.

"I've nothing more to say about the topic of Declan Shaw," Helena told her sister, "except that, yes, we have specific things we want to accomplish, and I hope he will be nearby tonight. I've no other allies, and he will fortify me—if he does not actively help me. Which he may do. God only knows what will happen." She picked up the butterfly mask and held it to her face.

"I've thought you'd done a very noble job, all on your own. These last five years."

"I cannot run away forever," said Helena. "And anyway, I need his help. But moreover, I simply want him."

She didn't say the rest, but she thought, *I want to be with him more than any other combination of ways I can be. I want him more than I want to be alone. More than I want my family. More than I want to be in the forest.*

She wanted him.

She loved him.

She could acknowledge that now. And Camille could guess it—clearly. Which was something she probably needed to address.

"Please don't tell anyone, Cam," said Helena, dropping the mask.

"I won't. You have my word." Camille smiled sadly at her sister. "I'm sorry Papa is selling you to gain shares in the duke's limestone mine."

"Yes," sighed Helena. "So am I. But it's not official until I walk down the aisle. So. There is still time." She stepped to her sister. "And I appear to be acquiring unlikely allies right and left. Thank you for listening to me. For warning me."

"Thank you for being true to yourself. All along."

She was just about to embrace her when Meg bustled into the room with an armful of fresh flowers. "We're in luck," chirped the maid. "There were anemones. Oh, but I've learned some other news. The duke's valet was polishing his boots belowstairs. He told me Lusk is going to the ball dressed as a man-shaped slab of Somerset limestone."

Chapter Eighteen

Declan infiltrated the masquerade ball as the Huntsman.

It had been his father's idea. With Helena occupied throughout the day, he'd asked Girdleston for a day off and gone to his father's shop in Savile Row.

After an avalanche of questions from his sisters about Somerset, and Castle Wood, and if the village had assemblies of handsome men, the three of them worked together to construct a costume.

His "Huntsman" identity wasn't known outside of military and security circles, but his father knew his reputation—fierce, skilled, dangerous—and he chose black leather and buckskin. His sisters added touches that invoked legendary heroes like Robin Hood and King Arthur. The resulting costume amounted to a hooded vest in thin black leather, no shirt (everyone but Declan was in agreement about this), broad belt and dagger, black buckskins, and layered strips of leather bindings wrapped around wrists, biceps, and thighs. If he fell into the Thames, the weight of wet leather would pull him under.

But he wasn't bound for the Thames, he was bound for the bloody Winter Solstice Masquerade, and God help him, he was desperate to get inside. He wanted to see Helena safe and protected and . . . and—

And he'd simply wanted her. The devil himself could not have kept him out.

As ridiculous as the costume felt, the throng outside the ball parted ways when he arrived. Women tittered in delight and men could not hide their deference when they looked him up and down. Something about the black leather and bare muscled biceps, the deep hood and thin black mask, lent an air of scintillating menace to his otherwise uncredentialed presence. No one questioned him; in fact, he was regarded a bit like the only interesting guest invited to Sunday dinner.

He'd called in a favor to an old army comrade and finagled an invitation. His friend, a retired officer, had also given him a fake name and foreign title to feed to the herald on the ballroom stairs. No one had questioned a thing.

An hour after the first guests arrived, Declan stood in the ballroom doorway. The cavernous room, a two-level space with ballroom below and balconies above, was illuminated by thousands of glittering candles. Orchestral music soared over a raucous crowd that dripped in jewels and floated in silk.

He saw a woman dressed as a provocative milkmaid pulling a dazed calf on a ribboned lead. Another woman had secured a festooned birdcage to the top of her head and live birds thrashed about inside. Several men wore elaborate hat-mask combinations that transformed their faces into a velvet panther or a feathered falcon. Countless guests wore assimilated togas, some of them dampened to cling to their bodies. Most guests wore masks, some beaded and feathered on long sticks; others, like Declan's, were strips of silk tied with holes for eyes.

Because of his work, this was not Declan's first ball, or even his first masquerade. But he'd never been to an event where decadence and indulgence were so clearly the order of the night. He saw diamonds affixed to cheeks and swirling in the bottom of champagne glasses. He saw expensive French wine sloshed on the floor. Each cluster of guests seemed to throb with their own brand of sensuality, their anatomy, both male and female, girded, groomed, or gauzed to invite the eye. Furniture was strewn with languid couples. Terrace doors were thrown open to the night, despite the chill, and guests disappeared into the dark garden.

Declan stalked the rooms, forcing himself to walk at an amble. He'd been unable to locate Helena. Every time he rounded a corner and did not see her, his heart rate increased. He could feel his face hardening into what his sisters referred to as his "death stare." He was sweating, which was remarkable, because he hadn't been allowed to wear a shirt. But he must not panic. She was here. She would hate everything about this, of course. She would be searching for him, anxious that they had not connected. But he would find her.

She'd managed perfectly well before he'd—

He clipped down steps, and then there she was.

She stood next to a young woman dressed as Cleopatra. Helena looked more beautiful than ever he had seen her. She wore no mask. Her hair fell long and loose down her back, dotted with bright, dewy blossoms. Her dress was the color of early spring at dusk, when the acrid green of new growth turned blue-green. While other gowns in the room poufed and flounced, Helena's skimmed her slender body, sleek and spare. The neckline was daringly low, showing off an expanse of creamy skin and the contour of her breasts. A waterfall of teal and turquoise silk fell from her shoulders and hips. She looked like a forest nymph—no. She looked like the *ruler* of the nymphs.

He glanced around, checking the reaction of other guests. Women slowed and cast her with appraising once-overs. She slid the heavy mane of her hair from shoulder to back, and men stared openly at her exposed décolletage and startlingly beautiful face.

Declan own mouth went dry, watching. He wanted her. Now. Later tonight. Tomorrow. Forever. He wanted to scoop her up and carry her away.

He wanted—

Helena looked up and their eyes locked. She went very still. She blinked. She cocked her head. She mouthed his name.

Declan.

Not a question. She knew.

He began to walk; he didn't look away.

Helena took a deep breath and excused herself from Cleopatra.

A large easel had been arranged in a corner to display the painting of a dog. Helena stepped up, examining the art, and Declan stepped behind it.

"You've come," she said to the dog.

"Yes," he said. He kept well behind the easel, his face averted from the ballroom. He felt like he hadn't seen her in a year. He felt as if they'd never parted. He felt as if his whole purpose in the world was to find her at this party and carry her away.

"You look . . . remarkable," she said flatly, speaking to the dog. "You were always handsome, but I was not prepared for how you would look outside of the—" She glanced at him, hungry eyes raking him from hood to boot. Declan's body tightened.

She finished, "—how you would look outside."

"Ah," he said, not prepared for her praise.

"Clearly the yellow livery is more like a costume, and this black leather is your usual attire?" She couldn't help laughing. "Please tell me this is your usual attire."

"Ah," he repeated dumbly, looking down.

"Can I . . . touch you?"

He opened his mouth to make another wordless sound, but she added, "Surely here, among this . . ." she looked around, ". . . frivolity and excess and the obscured vision of so many masks, no one would—"

She stopped and swallowed hard. "My God, I have to touch you."

Declan's reason and caution shattered. His

hand lashed out, snatched her by the wrist, and pulled them from the painting.

Without thinking, he led her around the dancing, past two anterooms, stopping at the last room in the row. It was set up for an impromptu musicale, with pianoforte, harp, and several lutes. Chairs formed a half circle around the instruments. The room was empty except for a man gently plucking strings on the harp.

"Get out," Declan said.

"I b-beg your—" the man stammered.

"Get *out,*" Declan repeated, and the man fled.

When they were alone, Declan swiftly, silently, pulled the double doors shut and locked them.

When he turned to face Helena, she leapt into his arms.

He caught her up, his chest exploding with the luminating delight of holding her. She was like coming home and stumbling upon the best, most unexpected paradise ever, all in the same embrace.

He buried his face in her hair, breathing in the familiar, sweet apple smell. He squeezed her until she cried out, a shrill, breathy giggle.

He spun. Pressing her back against the closed doors. "Can you touch me?" he growled, repeating her words.

She laughed. "It was my only thought." She gave him the tiniest, softest kiss. She reached up and slid his flimsy mask away. He blinked, looking at her with no obstruction.

"You are magnificent," she whispered. "I . . . I can't believe you're mine." She made a noise of distress and bit her bottom lip. "That is, I can't believe you are *my groom*."

With every word, his heart expanded, and that said nothing of his body. He was as hard as stone. He spun again, turning her in one deft movement, collapsing his own back against the door and pulling her against him. Helena made a noise of surprise and delight. They never broke the kiss.

While he devoured her mouth, his hands massaged their way down her body. Her gown was fitted and restrictive; he tried to grab her hip through the silk, but the fabric had no give. He fumbled, tracing the outline of her hip, and then he dipped low, catching the hem and sliding up the skirt. When he rose, he grazed his hands over long, silk-stocking-covered legs until he bunched the skirt at her thighs. Now he could scoop beneath the fabric and grab her bottom. He pressed her against him and Helena groaned.

He pulled away, panting. "*You* are magnificent. Why do you ever tie your hair back?"

"So I don't look like a child," she laughed, cocking one knee on his hip.

He grabbed the underside of her thigh and hitched her closer. "You look nothing like a child," he said. "You look like a seductress. You look like you belong in the forest, ruling over flora and fauna and wood and stream. You look like you belong so very far from this place."

She kissed him, dragging her fingers through his hair. "It's terrible," she agreed. "I hate it."

"I worried for you," he said, between kisses. "I was so bloody worried." He released her leg and gathered her to him, his hands on her back. He reclined her in his arms, holding her out so he could look at her. She smiled gently, one hand on his face. Her long, black hair fell almost to the floor. He leaned to kiss her exposed throat, the tops of her breasts, her ear, her lips.

"I cannot say I'm enjoying the ball," she said softly, "although it's certainly improved since you arrived."

He growled again and yanked her up, reclaiming her mouth. "You slay me."

"If you feel slayed, I think the yellow velvet is to blame. This black leather, I must say, takes your already significant stature and makes it all the more imposing. You look masterful. I love it."

Another kiss.

"Declan?" she said.

His brain barely functioned, but something about the sound of his name made his skin go hot. He kissed her again, the kiss so deep they almost tipped sideways.

"Declan?" she repeated.

His heart thundered in his ears. Another kiss. His tongue. Her eyelids, her cheeks, her lips again. His hands returned to the silk stockings beneath her dress. Her perfectly formed bottom filled his hands.

"I love you," she whispered. She twined her hands around his neck. "It's terribly inconvenient, I know, but it could not *not* be said. We've risked everything for these five minutes. Let us make it worth more than stolen kisses."

"Helena," he moaned. Her words were a swirl in his head. His brain was caught somewhere between lust and terror, but he was cogent enough to not say more than her name. Her name could not hurt him. Or her. Or this moment.

"It's true," she said, pressing on. "It's not fair or useful, but I do." She laid her head against his chest. He felt the soft, warm skin of her cheek on his bare shoulder. Her hair fell over his arm. He grabbed a loose handful, filling his fingers with the flower-strewn locks. He held on to her as if he would sink into the ground if he let go. They embraced like the world was falling apart.

"We cannot stay here," she finally said. She looked up. Her green eyes were very bright.

"Yes," he whispered. He kissed her again.

"Anyone could have seen us come in," she said.

"No one saw," he said, but he'd no guarantee of this. He'd all but dragged her here. He'd considered nothing but his need to have her in his arms.

"We cannot indulge in recklessness now," she said.

He laughed. "I've never been so reckless in my life until I met you."

"I'm going back out," she said, sliding her hands away. Stepping back. He let her go. He clenched his fists at his sides. She smoothed her hair and flowers molted to the floor.

"Did you see the woman with whom I was speaking?" she asked. Her voice was raspy. She glanced at him and then away, blushing slightly. She looked happy but a little uncertain. He felt like glass in a storm. One strong gust and he would shatter. *I love you.*

Helena went on, "The tall girl, dressed as Cleopatra? That was one of the two potential girls. Lady Rodericka Newton."

Declan couldn't remember any woman beyond Helena.

"She'll not suit, I'm afraid," Helena went on, shaking her head, smoothing the silk strips that fringed her gown. "She comes across as . . . sort of . . . humorless? Domineering, I'd say. When you came upon us, she was giving me advice on how I might improve my costume."

"You're joking," he said. "Your costume is the best of the night."

"Thank you." She smiled with genuine pleasure. Declan's heart shattered.

She went on, "She'd already informed me that she'd made a list of music she felt the band should play, including the order of songs, and given it to the conductor. She's found fault with the temperature of soup and lectured several footmen."

"A bashful sort of girl, is she?" Declan asked.

"Bashful?" Helena laughed. "Oh yes, definitely. She's under the impression that she's somehow responsible for this ball, and she barely knows the hosts. She said she and her mother would make some recommendations for future events, but they were only invited because her father is a viscount from Yorkshire and they are new to town."

"She wasn't sensual enough for Lusk," Declan said, turning to crack the door and peek out.

"Look who's taken note of sensual women at this ball," Helena teased.

Declan closed the door and turned back, sweeping her into his arms. "I only see you, sweetheart." He dipped her back and kissed her.

"From the beginning, I have only seen you. God help me."

When she was breathless, he lifted her upright and checked the door again. "I will go first. It makes no sense for me to be alone in a music room. If you are discovered, at least you can pretend to play a musical instrument."

"I am a rather accomplished pianist."

"Really?"

"Sadly, no," she said. "I'm terrible. But I can pretend."

Declan returned to the door. "After five minutes—don't rush it—wander out. Have you seen the other potential girl?"

She nodded. "Earlier. She was lounging in a room down this corridor."

"Which?"

"The second—no, the third room."

"With all the smoke and the couches?" Declan looked at her.

"Yes. I saw her rather clearly; it had to be her. She's pretty. But she was surrounded by friends, and the room . . . unnerved me for some reason. I couldn't invent a reason to go in."

"The smoke in that room was opium. Let us *not* have you go in, shall we? Wait her out instead? Surely she'll emerge eventually."

"Yes, yes," Helena said, adjusting her dress. "Far preferred. Will you be nearby?"

"Always." The word was out before he could stop it, and her face lit up.

Declan's heart lurched and turned back to the door. "I'm going," he said.

"So you say." A giggle.

Declan shot her a look—if only she knew how badly he wanted to lock the door and never leave. Securing his mask, he gazed at her another long moment and went.

He made an easy slow circuit of the dance floor and anterooms, checking first the location of Lusk, who was in the card room. Helena's parents were at the drinks table upstairs. Girdleston was smoking with men on the terrace. No one seemed to notice Helena's absence. He marveled that someone so incredibly important to so many people was also so widely ignored. It made no sense. He'd been trying for days to put her out of his mind—his life and the lives of people he loved depended on his ability to forget her—and he could not.

When he made his way to the row of rooms beside the dance floor, Helena was there. She hovered outside the murky room that reeked with the sickly sweet smell of tobacco, hashish, and opium. Guests coasted in and out, their half-lidded eyes red-rimmed and blinking.

Declan took up position against an opposite pillar and stared into a glass of claret. He waited a beat and looked up, willing her to glance his way. When their eyes locked, he winked.

Her green eyes grew large; she arched a brow.

She looked ready to mouth something when a young woman caught her eye. The girl stepped from an anteroom and Helena pounced.

"Excuse me . . ." she began. The young woman stood just outside the door, fiddling with a crooked wing hanging limply from her costume. Declan shoved off the pillar and ambled closer.

Helena asked the girl, "Are you, Miss Lisbette Twining?"

The young woman looked up. "Ah . . ." she began, her voice tired and drawn out.

Helena tried again. "But may I help you with your wing?"

"That would be *so . . . niiice,*" drawled the girl, speaking slowly, enunciating every syllable.

"Miss Twining," Helena mused philosophically, wrestling with a wire inside the costume. The girl toddled this way and that as Helena worked to straighten the costume. "What a pleasure to meet you. You do not know me, but I've . . . I've heard so much about you."

"All wicked, I assume," the girl drawled. She giggled.

"Nonsense. But I don't suppose we've been properly introduced. I'm Lady Helena Lark. I am betrothed to the Duke of Lusk . . ." She enunciated the duke's name formally and let it dangle.

"Oh, I know you," rasped the girl. Her words came out in a kind of extended yawn, as if she'd only just awakened. She spoke as if she was talking more to a pet cat than another girl. "Bradley's future wife. *Charmed.*"

"But are you acquainted with the duke?" Helene asked, stepping back from the wing, now hanging at a more upright, but still very odd, angle.

"Oh, Bradley and I have known each other since we were in the nursery," she told Helena slowly. "And we share a bevy of maddening friends. He's a *lark.*" She drew out the word *lark* as if it contained five *a*s and *r*s.

"Of course you have," said Helena defeatedly. "It is a pleasure to meet one of Lusk's friends."

"The pleasure is all mine. But aren't you gorgeous? Bradley loves pretty girls. But will you excuse me? I'm just stepping away for some . . ." she searched for the correct word, ". . . air."

"By all means," Helena said, pointing the general direction of the terrace. Miss Lisbette walked away with the uncertain toddle of a child.

Declan took up position behind Helena. "She was out of her head," he said. "We could try her again on—"

"No," Helena cut in. "If he already knows her, and he's never shown any serious interest, he'll not make a bold gesture to show a preference for her now."

"You're probably right."

"There is no guarantee he will like any of the girls," she said, her voice very low and very sad, "but certainly not one he's already had the opportunity to consider, and done nothing."

"Don't let it defeat you," Declan said, surprising himself. He'd expected defeat with every girl upon whom they embarked.

"Things are running very thin, aren't they?"

"We still have the two strong contenders. And another girl tomorrow."

Helena nodded, staring into the bouncing, bounding dancers in lines on the dance floor.

"Are you ready to go?"

"Yes," she sighed. "But I'd like to catch sight of those two contenders you mentioned. They're both meant to be here; they hope to lay some foundation, if they can. Ingratiate themselves with Lusk." She glanced at him. "I would feel better if I saw some progress on that score. Anything. I'm terrified the two girls will catch sight of him and beg off."

"They won't," Declan said, but he had no idea. He'd had so very little idea about any of this from the start.

"Declan, look," whispered Helena suddenly, standing tall. "That person in the black cloak. Do you see? To the right, just beyond the man dressed as Big Ben? I swear this person follows us, hovers until we see him or her, and then bolts. Look they're getting away again!"

Before Declan could see the person at whom she pointed, Helena was off.

Chapter Nineteen

The Seven Duchesses (Potential)

Happy ✓
~~Sneezy~~
~~Doc~~
Sleepy ✓
~~Bashful~~
~~Dopey~~

There was no small number of hoods and capes in the ballroom; considering this, it was a miracle Helena spotted the cloaked person at all. But black was not a pervading color among the revelers, and the cloak stood out like an inky stain in a wave of blues and oranges, golds and pinks.

Helena darted toward the person, dodging lines of grinning dancers, rounding footmen with buckets of champagne. The sunken design of the ballroom effectively trapped all guests in the lower level; one could only truly escape by mounting the substantial open stairwell.

To Helena's delight, the cloaked figure strayed very little from what seemed like a straight line for the stairs. She didn't know what she would say or do when she reached the person, but she was determined to catch them. At the very least, she hoped to expose a face.

She'd just rounded the buffet when Lady Rodericka Newton, the potential duchess she'd met first that night, charged into her path and caught her by the arm.

"Lady Helena!" chirped the towering heiress. "Your betrothed is embarking on the most amusing parlor game, and look at you here near the food! You've nearly missed it. You must come at once."

"What?" Helena strained to see the stairs around the imposing figure of Lady Rodericka.

"Lusk, your fiancé!" enthused Lady Rodericka, her sharp Yorkshire accent rising above the band. "The card room's been given over to the most diverting game of Mirror-Mirror. You cannot allow him to play it without you." The girl began to tug her by the arm.

"Oh, well, actually," began Helena, pulling the opposite direction, "Lusk and I have a habit of going our separate ways at parties. We are loath to pair off and seem exclusive." She reared, searching for the black cloak. When, finally, the view cleared, she saw the person stumping their way halfway up the stairs.

Helena swore under her breath. She had to be so very careful about giving off the appearance of *running* in society settings. Her reputation as a bolter had, obviously, preceded her. Except when absolutely necessary, she tried to minimize her visibility in the *ton*, appear reasonable and content, and above all, not *run*.

She pivoted, trying to locate Declan, and—oh thank God—spotted him immediately. His black-leather hood loomed a foot taller than everyone else. He was already in pursuit, brushing past her with a hidden pinch to the arm.

Helena leaned against the sharp clasp of Lady Rodericka's hand and watched the room part as he approached. Women turned to stare, men skittered out of the way. If her parents caught sight of him, would they know? Would her sister Joan? What of Girdleston? Helena couldn't imagine catching even a glimpse and not recognizing the Lusk stable groom. Regardless, she knew she could not follow him. Even if she could wrestle free of Lady Rodericka, he attracted far too much attention. In a room of spectacle, watching Declan Shaw, shirtless, in black leather, was the only show worth watching.

"It's *this* way," Lady Rodericka was saying, pulling her in the direction of the anterooms. "But how could you allow him to play such a naughty game without taking part?"

"Really, Lady Rodericka, it's not—"

"Here we are," sang the heiress, coming to a stop in front of the card room. "Oh, and look, we're just in time. Lusk will have a go, and then perhaps you may take a turn!"

The tall woman thrust Helena forward, propelling her into the card room like a sack tossed from a horse.

Bashful indeed.

Inside the card room, all activity and conversation stopped.

After a long moment, a thin man said, "And what have we here?" He stood beside a table with a mirrored contraption.

Helena waited for him to say more, to introduce himself, to invite her from the threshold, but he merely stared.

She searched her brain for something to say. *Hello* seemed too hopeful. *I beg your pardon* too apologetic. She was just about to say *Good-bye* when the man let out a sputtering, can't-hold-it-in laugh. Snickers and snorts followed from around the room. It was as if the population of the card room had been holding their breath, waiting for her to turn up and amuse them.

Helena glanced at each of them, searching for some common ground. She'd had very little contact with the men in Lusk's circle. She knew them only as the crowd collected in the entryway, boisterous but aloof, before he went out; or as whispering, snickering interruptions to the opera when she'd been dragged to the ducal box.

Tonight, the men were splayed in chairs or leaned against the wall, the posture of someone without sufficient motivation to hold themselves upright. There were women, too; they roosted more than lounged, their hips perched on card tables or balanced on the laps of men. The Duke of Lusk was seated at a center table, his cravat hanging loosely open, his hair mussed. A woman dressed as something like an ice storm stood behind his chair, her gray-blue gloved hand across the back.

The other women were dressed as a feathery tropical birds, the goddess Aphrodite, something to do with a rainbow or prism, and the most voluptuous Mona Lisa Helena had ever seen.

The costumes of the men seemed to be less literal and more ironic. Most wore the usual evening attire with a simple mask. Lusk had, in fact, approximated the look of sturdy English limestone, although Helena would have never guessed. His evening suit was creamy white (the color of stone? she assumed), with bits of crushed rock affixed to a matching hat. On the floor, propped against a chair, was a forgotten pickax.

When the laughter died, the room fell into the expectant silence of an audience. Ice clinked in a glass. The women's bangles rattled. Someone cleared his throat. No one said a word.

"Forgive me . . ." she began.

There was no reply, no reassurance or introductions or welcomes. A deep blush burned her cheeks and her stomach twisted into a tight, bobbing knot. She felt small and plain and provincial. Her confidence, typically as reliable as the sunrise, sunk under their collective, silent stare. She wished for a mask, she wished Meg had pinned her hair up, she wished for a fan to snap open or, at the very least, squeeze in her fist.

She wished she was at home in Castle Wood, reading by the fire, far away from disingenuous people and a fiancé who sat back and allowed her uncertainty to be the source of amusement for strange men.

But she was not in Castle Wood, and she had little choice but to stand straight and raise her chin. She looked to Lusk, the only familiar person in the room, and he stared back with flat eyes and a snarled lip. His indifference took her breath away. Her eyes began to sting, and she glanced over her shoulder at the doorway. Lady Rodericka hovered just outside, watching with wide, horrified eyes. She saw her error now, and she was slowly backing away.

Helena gritted her teeth and turned back.

"Forgive my intrusion," she said, forcing volume. Her voice came out nervous and airy, and she cleared her throat.

"I was led to this room by mistake. Please continue your game." She inclined her head to Lusk, a show of respect, and farewell, and (hopefully) *Go to hell*. "Your Grace," she said as she took a step backward.

"Oh, but you cannot go now," said the man beside the table with the mirror device. "You'll miss your betrothed's spin. Really, you must stay. It's one of our favorite little games."

"I feel certain the duke can carry on without me," she said.

"Nonsense. Who would like the future duchess to stay?" the man called.

Hoots and whistles and *Here-heres* confirmed him.

"You're not *afraid* of us, are you, dear? As the bosom friends of His Grace, we'll want to get off on the right foot, considering the Wedding of the Century is set to *finally, really,* happen. That is—if no one among the key players *runs away*." He stifled a laugh. More titters from around the room. "Don't tell me you're looking to run even from our little game?"

"Leave it, Bearington," drawled Lusk, dropping his head onto the woman's arm at the back of his chair. He stared at the ceiling.

"Don't be a coward, Lusk, it's all in good fun," teased the man. "Who can say, maybe the future Duchess of Lusk is wicked enough to join our merry band, after all."

"She's not," Lusk said to the ceiling.

"Come and have your turn," the man said to Lusk, giving the mirrored device on the tabletop a spin.

Helena stared at the unfamiliar contraption revolving in the center of the table. It was shaped like a large cylinder lantern with five flat sides. Each side was a rectangular mirror that reflected the room at different angles. When the man jabbed it with his finger, the device spun crookedly on a metal base, blurring the reflections and splashing the room with spinning light.

Helena glanced around, trying to ascertain what her role in this game could possibly be. Would she operate the device? Interpret it? Or perhaps they meant for her to touch it and they would examine her reflection and . . . and . . . call out things about her?

Contempt roiled in her stomach. She detested not knowing what to expect or what to say. The humiliation would be greater now if she fled. They were waiting for her to run. She had no choice but to simply allow the moment to pass.

"What do I do?" Helena heard herself ask. On cue, the room dissolved into laughter.

"Oh, you do nothing, dear," said the man. "It's not your turn." He turned to Lusk. "Lusk will not ninny out, I hope, just because his betrothed has come to look in on her duke."

"It's a stupid game," Lusk said, repositioning his hat.

"You say that about every game. Go on. Give it a spin."

Helena was relieved. Nothing would be required of her. Lusk would have his turn, and she would go. She glanced around the room. Lady Rodericka had abandoned her. There were only—

She saw Declan.

He stood just outside the door, hands open like claws at his sides, jaw clenched, eyes like daggers. Their gazes met, and the look of desperation and anger on his face made her eyes swim with tears. He made a barely perceptible half nod of *You can manage,* and *Keep calm,* and *I'm here.* She blinked in understanding, feeling a surge of longing so deep she almost reached out to steady herself on a chair.

But she mustn't stare; she mustn't do anything but appear impervious to it all. She *was* impervious to it all.

She breathed carefully and turned from Declan's strong, familiar face to the pale, weak-jawed profile of Lusk.

In the chair beside the table, Lusk said in a loud, showy voice, "You're an arse, Bearington," and leaned forward to give the mirrored device a spin.

"You must say the words!" called the woman dressed as a tropical bird.

"Mirror, mirror on the table," droned Lusk, "show me my mate if you are able." He sat back in his chair, lacing his hands behind his head. "It was always a stupid game," he muttered, but the room burst into applause, stepping in to watch the spinning mirrors streak the room with a whirl of refracted candlelight and the blurred reflections of ecstatic faces.

When the spinning mirrors began to slow, Helena realized that one mirrored surface would always reflect Lusk's face, seated in the adjacent chair. The other mirrors hung on small hinges that changed their angle with the force of the spin. They reflected a range of random points around the room—the faces of other guests, or the pink-papered wall, or a chair leg, or someone's elbow. The slower the device spun, the more clearly the reflections could be seen. While it spun, a new reflection came into view every half second, along with one fixed reflection of Lusk's bored, half-lidded face.

She saw the face of his friend, his expression distorted into a monster's leer; the carpet; half of a gutted candlestick; the enrapt face of one of the women; the bulging bodice of still another woman. Every reflection was met with hoots of laughter. On and on it went until, at last, the device creaked its final revolution and the mirrors were still. Collectively, the room leaned in, watching the mirrors as if they would reveal the secrets of the world. Helena held her breath.

When the spinning finally stopped, the reflections in each mirror revealed the following: Lusk's face, an empty goblet, someone's leg, the carpet, and finally Helena.

The room burst into a wild eruption of approximated boos, laughter, hisses, and the word *Oy!*

Helena, shocked at the paleness and trepidation seen in her own reflection, stepped to the side.

"Sodding bad luck, Victoria!" someone crowed. "The mirror never lies!"

"Now be a good girl," the man called Bearington sang, "and kiss your mate! There you are, none of those virginal nerves here. Christ, can someone get her a drink? She looks like she might swoon."

Two laughing women were suddenly behind her, herding her in the direction of the duke's chair. Helena dug in, but they swept her along on a wave of tinsel and petticoats. Before she could pull away, the women propelled her into Lusk's lap. The room erupted again into laughter. Helena recoiled, scrambling to get up, but he latched an arm around her waist and held her to him.

The pinch of his bony fingers flooded her with panic. She went stiff, lurched, and finally opened her mouth to scream. He squeezed harder, forcing the scream into a yelp. She coiled her strength, ready to lurch again, but Lusk leaned his head into her ear and whispered, "*Get out* of here."

His tone was flat and irritated and he jolted her with his hands when he spoke.

What?

It was the last thing Helena had expected him to say. But had he really just ordered her to go?

All around them, his friends hollered and toasted. Someone spun the mirror again, and the room was a swirl of dizzying light.

Helena tried to turn her head, to look into his

eyes. He evaded, leaning into her ear a second time. "Did you hear? Take your bloody groom and go."

She was about to try again to jerk away when she heard a gasp and the room fell silent. A goblet dropped and shattered. Helena looked up.

Declan.

He walked to her as if the room was empty. The crowd saw only him. Their faces were lit with fascination. He was unknown, of course—a towering, muscled highwayman. His expression was taut with silent fury. He looked only at her. Helena stared, choking back a sob. She pulled out of Lusk's grasp, and he let her go.

She wanted to run to Declan—it was her only thought—but a cautionary word rose behind her.

"Discretion," Lusk whispered.

A reminder and warning.

The three of them were being watched by a roomful of people who wanted nothing more than a riveting story to tell.

Helena slowed her step and raised her chin. She walked to Declan but did not touch him. With her eyes, she said, *I am all right.* He hesitated. She nodded at the door and put one foot in front of the other. He fell in beside her and they walked from the room.

Once outside, Helena navigated the ball through burning eyes. She would not cry, but she also would not remain. Her time at this ball had come to an end. She felt Declan fall back, following but not flanking. She must pretend to be alone. Inside, she ran; outside, she was simply wafting through the ball. She circumvented the dance floor and ascended the steps, weaving through revelers.

At the top of the stairs, she fixed her eyes on the front door. Footmen stepped up to offer her pelisse, but she ignored them. When a butler fumbled with the door, she reached for the knob and threw it open herself. She was down the steps in an instant, gulping in the cold night air.

She turned left without thinking and walked to the end of the block. Carriages idled in the road, their grooms and coachmen smoking or throwing dice. Helena kept moving, turning first one corner, and then the next. When, finally, she outwalked the last of the carriages, she stopped. She was panting, energized by exertion and misery and fear.

"No. Not here," clipped a voice behind her, Declan's voice, and then suddenly he was there. He took her by the hand and led her deeper into the dark. They went another half block, and the sidewalk opened up into a small square, bordered with an iron fence. Declan swung the gate and led her inside. She followed along, exhausted now, dazed, her steps dragging.

"Not yet," he said, leading her deeper into the shadows, away from the last streetlamp.

Finally, when the sounds of horses and carriages and barking dogs faded, and the dark chill of the park closed in around them, he stopped. He took a deep breath, checking around them. He turned to her.

"Helena," he whispered.

She fell into his arms and he swept her to him. "Why?" she cried, for the tears falling freely.

"Why is this my lot? What sort of family would subject their daughter to this?"

He squeezed her, tucking her against his strong chest, his chin on her head. He dug his hands into her hair and wrapped a secure arm around her waist. She burrowed in, leeching his strength and his warmth.

"They do not know you," he said.

"They know that I am uncooperative and embarrassing and annoying. It's almost as if my stubbornness ignited *their* stubbornness, and we were locked in a kind of spiral. They could not allow me to prevail."

"I cannot believe their stamina, honestly," he said. "Why not simply shackle your sister Joan with the duke?"

"Because my grandmother left the forest and cottage and river *to me.* If Girdleston wants the river for his mining boats, Lusk must marry me to get it. Joan will have only a dowry. What would Girdleston want with a pot of money when he could make an endless fortune instead?"

"I'm so sorry," Declan sighed, kissing her hair.

"The sad thing is, Joan would likely do it. She would marry Lusk and find a way to survive as his wife. Not Camille, thank God, but Joan covets the title of duchess as much as my parents. To make matters worse, we are indistinguishable to Lusk. He doesn't care which unsuitable girl he marries for money. And oh!" she exclaimed, pulling away. "He *knows*!"

Declan peeled off his mask. "Knows what?"

"Declan, in the moment you came for me, Lusk told me to run from the room. He whispered in my ear, 'Get out of here.' "

Declan's face went white.

She held up her hands. "He told me to go *to you*, in particular."

Declan took a step back. "No."

"Yes."

They stared at each other in the dark. She continued, "He's always been an enigma to me, but I promise you, he knew I was miserable, and he sent me away. He sent me to *you*."

"Was he angry?"

"I don't know. He wasn't happy. But . . . but I almost felt he was more irritated with his friends. He was barely sober, as always. His breath reeked."

Declan began to pace. "Is it possible that we've evaded Girdleston with our . . . our connection, but not the bloody, sodden duke?"

"Connection?" Helena repeated. "Is that what we have? Good God, Declan, I told you tonight that I love you."

"Listen to me," Declan said, spinning to take her by the arms. "If Girdleston discovers that I am working against him and not for him, then we are . . . we are finished. I will be sacked—"

"I know—the money. You'll not get the money."

"It's more than that," he growled.

"How? How is it more than you being sacked and not getting the money? I've told you I'll look after your fami—"

He shook his head with such defeat and agony she stopped.

"Declan, what?" She watched his profile slump. He breathed in, slowly closing his eyes.

"There are things you do not know," he said. "But your focus at the moment needs to be only saving yourself, not me. I will not make your lot worse."

"*This* is worse," she said simply, speaking more to herself than him. "I thought tonight could not be more terrible than it already was, but *you* . . . are making it . . . *worse*."

"I know," he said. "But your challenges are great enough without taking on my problems as well."

"Your problems *are* my problems," she said.

"No," he said, "they are not. They are mine, and I have tried very hard to keep them from you. I've tried so very hard to not entangle my cocked-up life with yours, but I have not . . . been able . . ." he mimicked her same angry gusts of speech, ". . . to keep away. From you."

She spun from him and came to stop on the edge of the clearing. The night was cold; she felt it suddenly to her bones. She began to shake. She wrapped her arms around herself. She stared into the murky green shrubs.

"Did he hurt you?" Declan asked softy. He came up behind her. "When you were pushed onto him."

"No."

"Their behavior was unforgivably cruel," he said. "I risked everything by going in, but I refused to leave you to their ridicule and . . . and whatever came next."

She fell against him again and he held her. After a moment, he said, "I cannot believe Lusk gave you a way out."

"The duke hates me," she yawned. "But his hatred is the least of my problems. If nothing else, it means we rarely have to interact. Before I met you, I considered his hatred to be one of the few things I had working in my favor. It fortified me: *at least he doesn't press himself on me*. But now?" she asked, looking up, searching for the comfort of his familiar brown eyes. "Now I am fortified by my love for you. It is far better. To enjoy love instead of thinking, *At least he won't touch me*."

He whispered her name—soft, so softly. She went up on her toes and lifted her face. She didn't have to wait. He descended immediately, a reflex now, his lips as known to her as her own. He began soft, and she followed, receiving; she was too exhausted to do more than allow him to lead.

They fell into a kiss that vanquished every bad thought of the night and every terrible fear for the future. They were consumed with each other; their hands grasped like they were sliding down a cliff. Their bodies pressed so tightly together they breathed as one.

A stone bench sat on the edge of the clearing and Declan swept her up and carried her to it, dropping down. One minute they were standing, and then she was in his lap. She wrapped her arms around his neck, climbing him, and he scraped her skirt into a bunch at her waist. He scooped her bottom against him and devoured her mouth.

She squeezed him, the anxious coils of her insides finally slipping from their heavy knots. She could feel Declan's heartbeats inside his chest, too fast to count. It was a drumming she could listen to all night—all her life. How she wished she could leap over the obstacle of escaping Lusk and dive into a future with Declan. This wasn't greedy, was it? He was conflicted about their rank, he had some extenuating circumstances, but she knew they could sort it out.

If only she wasn't forced to extricate herself from Lusk first. Just when she thought she could resent her betrothal no more, the impending dukedom felt like a closed door with a double lock. If only they could—

Helena stopped.

She ran the sequence in her head again.

Oh my God, she marveled. *Why hadn't I thought of this before?*

"Declan," she said breathlessly, pulling back.

"Hmm?" he said, kissing her.

"There is one way to make certain that I cannot marry the duke."

"Marrying him off to one of these other girls," he recited.

"Yes," she said, kissing him again, "but if that doesn't work."

"It must work," he moaned.

"It might," she said. She gave him a hard kiss. "But regardless of what happens with the other girls, the Duke of Lusk cannot marry me *if I'm married to someone else*."

Declan went still.

She finished it. "He cannot marry me if I am married to you."

Chapter Twenty

The seventh and final potential duchess was a baron's daughter called Miss Tasmin Lansing. Most mornings, she was said to ride her horse in Hyde Park, and Declan and Helena had planned to approach her on Saturday morning while the rest of the household recovered from the masquerade.

It was meant to be the simplest and most straightforward of all their duchess encounters. The equestrian-minded men and women of London routinely rode in the park, many in the company of their grooms. Helena could approach Miss Lansing as any young woman might reach out in casual friendship to another.

Declan had never dreaded a meeting more.

The masquerade ball had not been a disaster so much as a cascading torrent of freezing panic that plunged him under again and again. The final dip had nearly killed him.

After Helena's . . . well, it wasn't a proposal of marriage so much as her announcement of the next, most natural course of action.

A proposal he could decline.

The natural course of action he had to discredit and disprove, all without crushing her spirit or without revealing that she was trying to marry a man who would likely spend the next twenty years in prison.

Ultimately, she'd been too exhausted and too cold to carry on discussing it, and they couldn't remain away from the masquerade for more than an hour. When she'd had enough, he'd walked her as close to the party as prudence would allow. From the shadows, he'd watched as she slipped back inside.

Her plan was to locate her sister Joan, remain close, and bide her time until a carriage to Lusk House departed. Declan hadn't left the street until he'd seen Nettle tuck her into a carriage with her mother and sister.

And he had not seen her until now, when he was meant to accompany her to Hyde Park, when they would be alone for the morning. Their discussion would, undoubtedly, resume. Declan hadn't slept all night for dreading it.

"Good morning, Shaw," she said cheerfully, mounting the gray mare he'd saddled for her. They met in front of Lusk House, Helena in a snowy ivory riding habit, black gloves, and cream-colored hat. She was accompanied by her sister Camille.

Declan had not expected company, and he had the fleeting hope that her sister would ride with them until Helena approached Miss Lansing. With Nettle there, too, Helena couldn't speak freely. He would have more time to think, to fortify, to finagle the plan in such a way that his family was provided for and she was free of Lusk but also not married to a mercenary. Avoiding prison felt like a very distant and very vain hope at this point, but if he had more time, perhaps he could discover some way to provide for everyone else.

More time was not in his future. Within moments of loping into the park, Helena said, "Camille wishes to explore the trails around the Serpentine. Nettle? Would you mind looking after her?"

"Very good, my lady," said Nettle, and Camille took off like a shot. The older groom dug in his heels, trying to keep up.

Declan watched them ride away like coins sinking into the sea. They were not coming back.

"Tell me," Helena said. No preamble.

"What?"

"All the reasons."

"Helena," he began.

"And do not tell me I've not considered all the ramifications of life as your wife. My regard for you from the beginning has been very clear."

She wouldn't look at him. Her eyes were trained on the open field of green winter rye.

He remembered that he was meant to be escorting her as her groom, not riding beside her as a companion, and reined his horse to follow a few paces behind.

"Where, I ask you, am I meant to find a vicar to marry us with no license?" he began. What choice did he have but to answer her? "And what of the banns? I haven't the money for a special license."

I haven't the money . . .

How many times would he be forced to say these words to her until he was able to work as a free man again?

"I've heard some priests in the Roman Catholic church would marry us without the banns," Helena said. "We needn't keep to the Church of England."

"A Roman Catholic priest would *not* do it," he said, but he realized he had no idea if this was true. His family was of Irish descent and his religion was, in fact, Roman Catholic, but faithful church attendance was hardly part of his life. He couldn't remember the last time he'd been to church.

"Let us assume we found some priest to do it," he said, "fine. We're married in the eyes of God, perhaps. It would not be *legally* binding with no license."

"It would be *enough*," she said. "It would buy time. No duke will risk the crime of polygamy until they sorted the paperwork. Sabotage, just as you said. A complication that stalls the marriage to Lusk."

"Helena," he said, "this is direct defiance. What of your parents? Likely they would never forgive you. Your father would act upon his right as your guardian and grant Girdleston permission to use the river and woods. Or they might very well toss you out, disown you. I . . . I cannot provide for you—not right now." It strangled him to say these words.

"I don't need provision—"

"You cannot say what you need. You're the

daughter of an earl, you've been fed and clothed and housed by your family's estate for your entire life. You know nothing of what it is like to work—"

"I am an apple farmer."

"Perhaps you are, but what if your father throws you off your land? And chops the trees to make way for the mining wagons? I . . . I won't have the liberty and resources to keep you safe and comfortable. I've been trying to say this all along."

"I have some money," she said. "If they take the land, I still have Gran's jewelry. And some gold. We will get by."

"Helena," he said, "think beyond this year to the rest of your life. The reality of my not being able to provide for you is a knife to my heart. I feel the same way about my father and sisters. Does my anxiety mean nothing? Do you not hear my distress? I am tortured, thinking of you cast out from you family. And your reply is a hidden bag of gold?"

"You would rather see me married to Lusk."

"I die to think of you going to Lusk," he growled. "But better than *you* dying in earnest—cold, hungry, cast out from your family."

"You've no faith in me," she insisted.

"Helena, you are a marvel to me. Truly. Never have I seen such courage, or resilience, or the cool ability to operate under extreme pressure. Not on the field of battle or among rival gangs on the crime-ridden streets of London. But you are still a young woman, and the duke's family is unbelievably powerful. You've no idea of their far-reaching power." He thought of the door of his prison cell swinging wide on Girdleston's command. Then he thought of it clanging shut.

"If your family does not cast you out, Girdleston can make your life miserable, and that says nothing of what he'd do to me."

"Titus Girdleston," she said, "is a petty man who resents that his brother's son is duke and not him. He is forced to pander to the very authority that, by fluke of birth, has made him second-in-command. His greed will eventually consume him. He wants too much, and if we are careful and watchful, we can bring about some misstep or expose cheating that will destroy him. He is not the duke in earnest. And Lusk, as pitiful as he is, gave me some hope last night. He *can* summon cogent thought. He is not completely dead inside."

Declan was shaking his head. "This 'authority' of which you speak? It is designed to protect landed men like Girdleston and your father. You have fought valiantly, Helena, but you have been powerless."

She was silent. After a moment, she said, "I am *not* powerless. I refuse to think of myself *without power.*"

Declan studied her back. She sat upright in the saddle, her shoulders tight. She held the reins with stiff arms, her elbows at sharp right angles. She was correct, of course. She'd refused to allow her parents or the dukedom or the aristocratic "wedding mill" to force her into a future that she did not want. How fierce she was.

And now, ever so fiercely, she pursued what

she wanted. Or what she thought she wanted.

Which was him. Unbelievably. Remarkably. Whether he liked it or not.

Did he like it? In a perfect world, without the threat of prison, without his current penury—yes, he would like nothing more than to take Helena as his wife.

But this was not a perfect world. And that said nothing of their world in four or five years, when she might wake up and realize she was married to a mercenary instead of a duke.

Helena reined the mare left, leading them down a long, wide path lined with mature trees. The canopies formed a tunnel of autumn color. Fluttering leaves of gold, red, and burgundy dropped intermittently, a soft rain of wafting color. The filtered sunlight cast the trail in golden light.

She captivated him. The collective weight of his feelings for her felt like a mountain. He stood at the bottom, barely able to climb the first rise.

"I'm tired, Declan," she said. "I'm tired of trying to convince you and tired of being with you only in wet carriages and dark gardens. I'm not made of limestone. I'm simply a woman, and I have my limits. For now, I will carry on, trying to marry Lusk off to someone else, but if he doesn't take to one of them, I'll run away again. In earnest. Gone without a trace."

"You will not," he countered.

"Then I will marry Lusk," she said.

"You *will not*." His voice sounded like gravel. "We will continue with the plan. You said yourself that Lusk has some spark of a soul. One of these girls will manage to ensnare him. Your parents' bad behavior and Girdleston's every move is motivated by greed for Lusk's money and title. These potential duchesses will be driven by the same. *It is enough.*"

"And then what?" asked Helena. Anger radiated from her ramrod posture in the saddle.

Fine, he thought, let her be angry. Simply—let her not be defeated or rejected. Let her not be hurt by him.

"Meaning?" He was afraid of the answer.

"I mean," she explained, "after one of the girls enchants him, and he throws me over. And I'm finally able to go home. Then what happens? Between us?"

"Helena," he growled. "What do you wish to hear? That I love you? Alright. Fine. *I* love you."

He took a breath. If he stopped to examine this statement, he would lose heart. Instead, he kept talking. "I've loved you since the moment you stepped into the duke's house and turned down three private servants but chose me.

"I've loved you since you sailed into the stable in the white gown, and I've loved you for every ridiculous debutante you've cultivated for your own jilting.

"I love your beautiful peridot eyes, and your lithe body, and your onyx hair. I love that you are an apple farmer, and I love that you are relentless. I need relentless. I can see that now. I need you."

He was breathing hard. Sweat trickled down his neck. The horse danced beneath him, confused by his tense thighs and taut rein. The words poured from him like blood from a wound.

He thought of his mountain of unexplored emotion. He hadn't climbed it so much as jumped off the top.

"Love," he finally finished, "is not our problem. It is simply not enough."

He'd said this to the back of her head, riding four paces behind. Finally, after what felt like an eternity, she reined her horse around. Her face was lit by a sunbeam through the trees. Smiling lips. Bright eyes. Glowing cheeks. She shined brighter than the autumn morning. Tears streamed down her cheeks. She breathed in small, tight breaths.

"We should kiss," she told him, reining up.

"We cannot kiss," he told her. "I am your groom, and you are my charge, and we are in a public park."

"You are a terrible groom," she teased, smiling through her tears.

"There are so many commonplace things that we won't be able to do, Helena. Not for a very long time, perhaps not forever. My love for you is real, but please begin to consider the challenges we face. I may be a terrible groom, but I'm in no position to be a good partner to you, not for years, perhaps."

"If you can imagine the worst for us, then I can imagine the best," she said, reining around. "Perhaps the reality will be somewhere in the center."

"I pray to God you are correct."

She shot him a sweet smile, full of love and hope, and dug her heels into the mare. The animal sprang forward, galloping ahead, tossing bright leaves into the air.

Declan tried to think of the task at hand, of finding this seventh potential duchess, of Girdleston's impeding party, but his mind was consumed by the unlikely prospect of marriage to Lady Helena Lark.

Is that what came after proclaiming love? Marriage? He'd never said *I love you* to woman in his life; marriage hadn't ever crossed his mind. He was too busy. His father and sisters required too much. No girl had been worth the upheaval of his life.

But his declaration of love had been real—nay, it had been urgent and necessary and long overdue.

But to Helena, it would not be enough. He knew this. She'd already asked what came next. To her, these last five years had meant one, long evasion. She longed to live life, not run away from it. As well she should. And that said nothing of what he longed for.

Declan hadn't allowed his mind to indulge in the fantasy of marriage to Helena Lark. The probability of success felt too narrow, as thin as a keyhole to his jail cell.

And yet—

And yet he wanted it.

He ached with wanting it—a new and alarming pain. One of the many benefits of life as a mercenary was freedom from want. His clients paid well, the work was active and exciting, and he'd earned the respect of prosperous men. He hadn't known true, unrequited want until he'd met her.

He would fight that want forever if it meant

keeping her safe, but *his desire* was not the struggle. The struggle was with what *she* wanted.

From the beginning, he'd not been able to deny her a single bloody thing.

And now she wanted him. Presumably forever.

God help them.

Forgetting the threat of prison, overlooking the differences in their rank, how could he possibly arrange the logistics of a wedding? In a matter of days? Could a Catholic priest be convinced to do it?

Not thinking of it should have been far easier than the mental contortion of sorting it out, but his mind locked on to the notion and would not let go. Now that he'd professed his love, marrying her felt as natural as putting one foot in front of the next.

And perhaps that's how she'd achieved the daily evasion of her parents and her future with Lusk all this time. One foot in front of the other. One heartbeat after the next.

A quarter hour later, they came upon Miss Tasmin Lansing and Declan was forced to concentrate. The young woman stood alone in a clearing, taking refreshment from a saddlebag while her own liveried groom stood guard.

As they grew closer, Helena observed, "But she's very pretty. Don't you think she's very pretty?"

Declan squinted at Tasmin Lansing. Even from a short distance, he thought she projected a very pretty sort of "difficultness." She had an *I require soothing* pout. Her mahogany hair was tucked beneath a sleek green hat; penetrating eyes looked out coolly against alabaster skin. Her expression seemed to dare the world to amuse her.

"She looks guarded," he said. "Pretty enough, I suppose. Maybe a bit sour?"

"That's quite an assessment from two yards away," Helena said.

Declan glanced at her. He'd given the wrong answer. He cleared his throat. "I gave up assessing women when I met you," he amended.

"Clever man," she said, trotting away.

Helena sidled up to Miss Lansing and made an eager, chatty introduction. Five minutes later, she was asking if the young woman would ride for a stretch to become better acquainted. Miss Lansing agreed, and Declan exhaled in relief.

One step closer. Another foot in front of the other.

When the women were gone, Declan struck up conversation with Miss Lansing's groom.

"Your mistress sits a pretty horse," he said, nodding at the path down which they disappeared.

"Third one this month," said the groom. "Miss Tasmin can be finicky, like. She misses her horse from Chadwick Hall in Devon, but her father doesn't want the country livestock in London. She's demanding, that one."

"The horse?" asked Declan.

"No, the girl. I've learned to stay out of her way, but there's no pleasing her when things don't go as she imagines. Temperamental, I'd call it?" A weary sigh.

"Unmarried, is she?" Declan asked. "Maybe a husband will settle her."

"Maybe," considered the groom. "I'm not privy

to her aspirations, but it's plain to the staff that she's in search of a brilliant match. Her sister married an earl and moved to a castle in Wales. She is determined to outdo her. They never got on, the two sisters. Only a chosen few get on with Miss Tasmin."

"Perhaps my lady will befriend her."

"Not likely," sighed the groom.

Splendid, thought Declan, and he said no more. They sat in silence until the women cantered back.

When Helena reined her mare abreast, she gave Declan a quick, knowing nod.

To the young woman, she called, "It was lovely to make your acquaintance, Miss Tansing! I'll look forward to your very best effort at Titus Girdleston's birthday party Monday afternoon."

"I'll see what I can do," replied Miss Lansing, examining her gloves.

Helena studied her for a moment longer, nodded to her groom, and galloped away. Declan followed, and when they were out of view, Helena described Miss Lansing's cool unpleasantness but also her incredible motivation to marry a duke. She was even more beautiful at close range, a circumstance of which Miss Lansing was wholly aware, and Helena believed she knew how to flaunt it. Best of all, Miss Lansing wanted to give Helena's plan a go, and she admittedly loved to win.

Their third potential duchess had fallen into place.

"Helena, there you are," said Camille Lark, joining them at the edge of the park. "We've just seen the oddest thing. There is a very strange person in a dark velvet cloak, lurking in the trees, *watching you.*" Camille shaded her eyes with one hand and pointed to the tree line with another. "It was just . . . there. The person saw every turn you made as you rode out with your friend."

"You're joking," Helena said, reining around. She was already looking to Declan. Her face had gone white. "Shaw, the cloaked figure again."

Declan gathered his reins, scanning the tree line. "Was the person on foot or horseback?"

"Mounted," said Camille, breathless.

"Astride or sidesaddle?" Declan's thighs dug into his horse. The animal began to dance.

"Astride," said Camille, "like a man. But it was a slight person. I never saw a face."

Declan glanced at Helena. For the first time ever, her expression conveyed the beginning stages of fear.

"Nettle," Declan called, spinning around, "will you take the ladies safely home? Use very special care. Do not let them out of your sight. Keep to the main roads. I must pursue this."

Nettle assured him, and Declan spoke to Helena. "Go with Nettle, my lady. Stay close to your sister. Be watchful and do not deter from the shortest route home."

"But, Shaw?" she called, worry in her voice.

"Go," Declan said, digging his heels into his horse and bolting for the tree line.

Chapter Twenty-One

The Seven Duchesses (Potential)

Happy ✓
~~Sneezy~~
~~Doc~~
Sleepy ✓
~~Bashful~~
~~Dopey~~
Grumpy ✓

Declan came to her in the middle of the night.

She was in a deep sleep. Something about the very real, very near smell of him elevated her achingly sensual dream to a vividness that made her body hum. He was in her dream, but now she could taste him, she could *feel* him.

He shook her gently. "Helena?" he whispered. He put a palm over her mouth.

Helena's eyes popped open.

"It's me," he whispered, hovering above her. "Shhh. It's Declan."

She blinked into the darkness. His face was

clear, but his body blended with the shadows. He'd dressed again entirely in black. Not the black from the masquerade, but a black overcoat, dark shirt, and buckskins. Without the yellow livery, he looked like a thrilling stranger—an achingly familiar, very thrilling stranger.

"Can I move my hand?" he asked lowly. "You won't scream?"

Helena nodded and he slid his hand away.

She gasped, "What are you doing here?"

"Does your maid sleep in the anteroom?"

"No. Belowstairs."

"Good. Will you get up? Can you dress yourself?"

"Of course. But how did you get in?"

"The window. Which is the way we're both going to get out." He nodded to the fluttering drapes at her window box.

"Did you locate the cloaked figure? Do you have—"

Declan shook his head. "I searched the park for an hour, but there was no trace. I was afraid to spare any more time. I've . . . I've had a change of heart, Helena. That is, a change of *plans*. I used the time to make arrangements."

Helena's rapidly beating heart seized. She stared at his face in the dark. "What change?" she asked cautiously.

"About our future. That is, your future with me. I agree that we should get married. If you will have me. I've located a priest who will do it."

For a long moment, Helena did not move. She examined the words, making sure she had heard correctly. She hesitated, waiting for him to reverse what he said.

He stared at her. "Helena?"

She threw back the covers and leapt up. Working quickly, she began to gather her garments. A dress—she would dress darkly like him—stockings, slippers . . .

"But where will we go?" she asked, dropping into a chair to slide on her stockings.

"To his church," he said, watching her ease the silk up her legs. After a long moment, he spun around, staring at the wall. "But we must go now and be back before sunrise."

"You've located a priest who conducts weddings in the middle of the night?"

"Actually, it's early morning. Father Thomas—this priest is called Father Thomas—has parish commitments on Sundays. And Monday is Girdleston's birthday. It's tonight or—"

"Tonight," she proclaimed, pushing from the chair.

Years later, she would amuse herself by looking back on her wedding night. How he came to her through the window, told her they would marry, and carried her down the side of Lusk House on the trellis. He'd turned his back modestly while she'd dressed. They spoke so very little, afraid of awakening the house. They'd already said so much, and the ramifications of what they were about to do felt too significant to say out loud.

When they left Lusk House, Declan hailed a hackney cab and they clattered across London squished beside each other on the seat, clutching both hands.

"What made you change your mind?" she finally asked.

"You don't want to know."

"Ever the romantic," she said. "I do want to know. Tell me."

He looked down at her. "If I marry you now, in the Catholic church, and if we *do not* consummate the marriage, then you may annul the union later."

"I will no—"

"Stop. You asked for a reason, and I'm giving it. I'll only do this if you have choices. You cannot predict what you'll want."

"I can predict what I want—*how very hard is it to know one's own mind?*—and I've been predicting it from the beginning. You've been the only one to listen. Until now."

"I am listening," he said, "but so must you. For once."

They traveled another block. Helena weighed the odds of challenging him. Finally, she said, "Is that what you want? To marry now and seek an annulment later?"

"It is the best I can arrange for now," he said. "I cannot, in full conscious, bind you to me in my . . . current situation. I want you to have a way to be rid of me, just in case you—"

He stopped. Finally, he added, "Just in case."

"So you are marrying me *for the moment*?"

"I am marrying you, Helena. Please let us leave it at that. The decision to do it was exceedingly hard-met, and very soul-wrenching, but I've found a way.

"*And* I've located this priest," he added. "He even knows a clerk who will sign the license.

"*And* we don't have much time," he finished. "Unless you've changed your mind?"

"No," she said at once.

She elected to leave it. She would not needle him about his "hard-met and soul-wrenching decision." She would not demand that he explain his *current situation*.

If she was married to Declan Shaw, even a rushed-up marriage, in total secrecy, by some middle-of-the-night priest, she would be safe from marrying the duke. It would be enough.

And Declan would be hers. Whether it was "for the moment" or forever—fine, he couldn't say for sure. Helena could.

She knew.

As for consummating the marriage, she would also say nothing.

Here again, she knew.

They arrived at St. Patrick's in Soho Square. Just as Declan said, the church was presided over by a priest called Father Thomas. He was a slight, irreverent man who was putting cream in bowls for mewing alley cats.

Declan called out in greeting. The priest squinted at him as if he'd forgotten which midnight favor he'd promised this night.

"It's me, Father. Declan Shaw. Peter's son?"

"Oh yes, so it is," said Father Thomas. "The couple in the very great rush. I remember now. Lovely. So be it, better rushed than wasting anyone's time. Right this way. Do mind the cats."

The small church bustled with activity. The corridors were crowded with what appeared to be street urchins asleep on cots, watched over by a snoozing nun. A bright kitchen bustled with more nuns serving hot soup to exhausted, ragged-looking vagrants. The door to a room marked "Infirmary" opened and closed to admit a ragged-looking doctor. More nuns followed, carrying basins of steaming water, bandages, and finally a red, mewling infant.

"But your church is so active at this early hour, Father?" Helena asked.

"Oh yes. God's children sometimes feel the most desperate in the middle of the night. If we intend to be 'a light in the darkness,' midnight is our busiest hour."

"So very noble," she said, "thank you for . . . accommodating us."

"There are all kinds of desperation, isn't there?" He winked at them. "We don't stand on ceremony at St. Patrick's. I became a priest to serve. Now, should we have a witness?"

Helena and Declan were married in view of two nuns, three street vagrants, and a prostitute with hair the color of an orange. Father Thomas managed the whole thing in thirty minutes.

Despite the rush, despite Declan's clear preference for the reversibility of the thing, tears filled both their eyes when they spoke their vows. They repeated the ancient words solemnly, with the feeling and emphasis that sounded like a Heart Oath to God and each other.

When they finally spilled, hand in hand, from the walled churchyard and into Soho Square, she whirled on him, took his face in both hands, and kissed him.

He sighed blissfully and pulled her to him. She

whispered, "Make love to me."

He answered was an anguished moan and kissed her again. They fell against the church wall, locked in an embrace.

"You'll see your error now," she teased, rolling away from him, panting against cool stones. "You've married me. You'll not escape my . . . my—"

"Relentlessness," he provided. He sought her hand between them. They leaned side by side on the wall.

"I was going to say 'superior reasoning and clear logic,' but alright. You cannot drive me away."

He did not answer, which meant he did not deny it. She smiled into the moonlit square. After a moment she said, "Declan, I want you to tell me whatever it is. This *thing*. Whatever you feel would cause me to annul this perfectly lovely wedding."

He turned to her on the wall. "You deserve a real wedding. Befitting the daughter of an earl."

Helena stuck her tongue out and made a gagging sound. "I deserve to know what great horrible secret you harbor that will drive me away." She made the gesture of her fleeing in terror.

Another silence. He turned away, studying the stones of the wall.

She said, "What Great Terrible Thing will keep me from going to bed with you just so that one day I can undo all the things I've just sworn to do?"

He looked at the sky.

"You are mad, Declan Shaw," she said, "if you

believe there is anything you can tell me that will drive me away. I love you."

"I haven't told you, because you've enough of a struggle already. It is *out of love* that I haven't told you." He pushed off the wall. His playful mood had dissolved, but he held tight to her hand.

They began to walk.

"You knew it would come to this," said Helena. "You knew I would insist."

"Yes. That is—I didn't think one way or the other. It took effort to find Father Thomas. It is why I stopped searching the park. If we meant to do it, I had only this afternoon to arrange it. I allowed the details of the priest and the church to carry me away. I didn't want to reckon with . . . with your relentlessness." He glanced at her. "But I am inclined to tell you. I am so bloody exhausted from telling you *no*."

"On this, we are completely agreed."

"Fine," he said, pulling her down the street. "We have several hours before sunrise. We'll keep to the shadows, we'll keep our voices low, and we'll walk. I will tell you."

They walked half a block, and he said nothing.

"If you're trying to frighten me," she said, "it's not working."

He leaned down and kissed her once, hard; and then again harder. "God, I love your courage," he said. "You will need every ounce of it."

Chapter Twenty-Two

Perhaps, Declan thought, he'd always meant to tell her tonight.

Deep down.

If she demanded to know, and if she went so far as to marry him, he might as well tell her the stakes.

He'd done his part and given her a way out. After she knew, she would stop asking to consummate the marriage.

He took a deep breath. "When Titus Girdleston hired me— No, let me go farther. The *reason* Titus Girdleston hired me is because I was incarcerated in Newgate Prison. That is, at the time."

"What?" she asked. "What time? When was this?" She stopped walking. He tried to release her hand but she held on.

"The day you arrived in London," he said. "I came to Lusk House from my cell *in prison*." He spoke to their joined hands. "I am an accused felon—not convicted, but accused. Girdleston hired me for money, I've said this. But he also holds the threat of returning to prison over my head. A sharp ax he threatens to drop."

He looked up, bracing to see fear, revulsion, disgust.

Her green eyes were bright with . . . excitement?

Oh God. Well, he thought, at least he always had that.

She asked, "But in prison for what?"

"Nothing I did. And if you believe that, you are among a very small group. But it's true."

"I do believe you."

"I've been accused of kidnapping a young noblewoman," he said.

"No." There was heartfelt pain in the word.

Declan nodded. "A client of mine went missing, the woman I mentioned at the Wandsworth market. Knightly Snow."

"The girl you were hired by St. James Palace to escort to France?"

"Yes. It all happened very quickly. Too quickly." He chuckled bitterly. "One moment I was being summoned to the palace to meet with the sons of the king, the next I was en route to France with this volatile young woman."

"And she—what? Opposed you?"

Another chuckle. "If only. She was difficult, but she never challenged me. If we'd gone toe to toe, I believe I could have made her see reason. No, it wasn't her. Or at least I did not believe her to be the opposition. The palace hired me to take her away, but what they really wanted was for me to *get rid of her.*"

"As in . . . kill her?"

"Probably," Declan said. "Which perhaps she knew. I would have never done it, but maybe she ran away because she feared for her life? I cannot say. I've not been allowed to investigate what happened because they tossed me in jail."

He thought about the night he was summoned to the palace and his meeting with the brothers of the future king.

"The royal dukes have denied that they wanted her killed. Not that it matters. They are sons of the king. I am hired staff—or more accurately, I was a pawn."

"But what do you mean?"

"The prince's brothers were intentionally vague with their orders. This is not uncommon in my work, so I wasn't alarmed. Sometimes I'm hired to make something happen with detailed precision, other times my employers prefer that I work out the details and don't tell them how it happens. This was one of those times. The suggestion was essentially, 'Take her to France and make certain she doesn't come back.' "

"Oh dear."

"Indeed. But I made it very clear that I would not harm an unsuspecting young woman—I would not harm any woman." He sighed. "I'm not in the business of violence toward innocent people, no matter how ingratiating."

Helena snorted. "Was she horrible? Totally unsuited to be the future queen?"

"So horrible," he confirmed. "Based on my very brief time with her, I'd wager she'll be a disruptive force, whatever she becomes, and that includes time on any throne. But I've no interest in palace intrigue. I told the dukes that I'd escort her to France but I *would not harm her.* They assured me that harm was never their intention.

They told me Miss Snow had *agreed* to go. She was excited to travel to the Continent and enjoy her aunt's villa in Nice. Honestly, I think they gave her money to go away."

"So, you escorted her, and—"

"And when we reached the French seaside, she gave me the slip."

"This I cannot believe," said Helena.

"It does no good to deny it. Believe me, I've tried. The crushing regret will be with me forever." Declan stared into the dark street, shaking his head.

He went on. "Knightly Snow was a difficult charge but hardly someone I considered a flight risk. I underestimated her, a stupid, amateur mistake."

"But how did she do it?"

"Bribery. The cover of darkness. And I suspect she had collaborators." He exhaled heavily. "We'd been under way for nearly two weeks. We had another day's travel to reach her aunt's villa—this was near the town of Marseille. I'd arranged for rooms at an inn just south of town.

"Like every night along the journey, I'd posted men outside her door for her own safety. It never occurred to me that she would bloody run away. She'd given me every indication of being a willing traveler, eager for a holiday in the care of her aunt."

"Declan," Helena pleaded, "why didn't you tell me all this before?"

"My legal problems are not yours to bear, Helena," he said. "You've enough to sort out."

"I piled my burden on you. I didn't give it a

second thought."

"Yes, but—"

She held up a hand and interrupted. "Tell me the rest. Say what happened, and we shall bear it together."

Declan took another deep breath. "I took the first shift outside her door at eleven o'clock and the last shift at sunrise. She slipped from her room in the intervening hours. The men guarding the door were trusted members of the palace staff. They'd been added to her retinue to smooth the way. The dukes wanted her gone, not uncomfortable. We traveled with ten servants in all. I'd not worked with these men before—they were glorified footmen—but they'd proven themselves trustworthy to this point. And again, she'd given no indication of anything but compliance. It never occurred to me that she needed to be contained."

"So these men abducted her?" Helena guessed.

"No. They allowed her to leave the inn. They denied everything and claimed she crawled out the window, but I scoured the room and saw no sign of this. I believe she paid them to allow her to go. They resigned from service as soon as they returned to London and both men are currently enjoying a pleasant retirement with a fat pension no one can explain."

"But what did you do when you discovered that she was gone?"

"I did what I've always done: I began to hunt her down. But first I sent word to the palace. It felt like the responsible thing to do. What if she turned up back in London?"

"Did the royal dukes seem . . . alarmed? I suppose they'd wanted this all along."

Declan shrugged. "I was occupied trying to find her . . . drumming the ground, shaking every tree. They made no reply."

"So why were you arrested?"

"When I failed to deliver Miss Snow to her aunt's, her family became distressed. They appealed to the palace first, and the royal dukes feigned ignorance. When the family became incensed and demanding, the palace cast around for a scapegoat."

"And they chose you," realized Helena.

"It was so very convenient. They dispatched royal guards to Marseille to arrest me. My defense fell on deaf ears."

"In France or in London?"

"Everywhere. I am hired muscle and my accusers were the sons of the King of England. A girl in my charge is missing, and I could not account for why or how. Arresting me appeased her family and stifled the story of the future king's vanishing paramour. The entire incident was deescalated, and I was stashed away in Newgate with very little access to my lawyers. Hell, they barely allowed me to speak to my father. I poured my entire savings into my defense, but the palace's accusations and cover-up trumped anything I tried. Things were simpler if Knightly Snow remained a missing girl, likely kidnapped by her bodyguard, now safely in jail. The king's son mourned her 'death' and moved on to a more suitable courtship. Her family held a funeral. And I sat in jail awaiting a long-postponed trial," he finished. "Until the day Girdleston turned up to hire me to 'contain' you."

"My God, Declan," she breathed, "it's unbelievable. And entirely unjust."

Declan shrugged. "It is yet another example of the upper class orchestrating what they want, when they want it, with no regard for damage to inconsequential people along the way. As far as I know, Knightly Snow is alive and well and frolicking about France. As far as I know, no one has even bothered to search for her since I've been locked up."

"You think she . . . survived? But why did she run in the first place?"

"Yes, I think she survived," he exclaimed. "I had almost tracked her down . . . I was half a day away . . . when the palace sent guards to arrest me."

"But did you tell—"

"Helena, I have told anyone and everyone who will listen. I've explained what I believe happened and where I think Knightly Snow might be found. No one cares about anything but keeping this girl away from the future king. They *don't want* to find her. The more lost she is, the better. My freedom means nothing."

"But her poor family . . ." whispered Helena.

"Think of your own family, Helena. I'm sure they do not wish you dead, but they are focused on their own prosperity. Surely Knightly Snow's family mourn her, but they'd allowed her to enjoy life at court with no chaperone and then waved her off to France without coming to London to say a proper farewell."

"That poor girl," said Helena, shaking her head.

"Oh no. Do not seek a victim in Knightly Snow. She is impetuous and demanding and self-involved. If she'd not run away, I'd not be in this predicament."

"But why would she run?"

"God only knows. The South of France is a playground for European society. The closer we traveled to the seaside, the more revelry was on display. She begged me daily to pause our journey so she might cavort with holiday seekers—men she met in the dining rooms of inns or at scenic overlooks where carriages clustered to take in the view. We passed castles that she wished to explore, and she read notices about country assemblies she wished to attend. I refused because I'd not been hired to squire her around France on a whim. The aunt was expecting her and I intended to deliver her. I told her repeatedly that she could do what she liked after I'd gone. Best I could tell, based on locals I spoke with after she disappeared, she could not wait."

"My God," marveled Helena. "It's no wonder my grandmother wanted me raised in the forest."

"No forest could contain Knightly Snow," grumbled Declan.

They walked a moment in silence and then she asked, "So, in the end, what was the charge against you?"

"Abduction and foul play." He exhaled. "My lawyers were able to have the charge of murder removed because there was no body. I've been in

Newgate since summer, awaiting trial. And then, as I've said, Girdleston turned up."

"But what could he have to do with any of it?"

"Nothing. Or rather, I should say, who knows? It was Girdleston who told me Miss Snow's family had dropped the charges because a cousin had made a sighting of her in France. Which is what I've anticipated all along."

"And Girdleston knew?"

"I suppose? Honestly, I cannot say. He arranged for me to leave prison, but he never fails to remind me that if the cousin's sighting of Miss Snow does not come to fruition, I will go back."

"What?"

"If this cousin cannot locate her—if *no one* can locate her—then Girdleston suggests that her family will revisit the charges."

"But *you* believe that *you* could find her."

"Yes. I could find her. I was this close!" He held his thumb and forefinger.

"But you've not been able to search," she realized, "because you were hired to mind me."

"Girdleston offered me enough money to provide for my father and sisters for the rest of our lives. It is an inordinate sum. I need that money, Helena. There was no option but to take this job."

"No wonder you resisted helping me," she repeated.

"The money did not keep me from helping you." He stopped walking and ducked into the shadowy gap between two buildings, pulling her with him.

"The real reason I didn't help you," he whispered, taking her by the arms, "is Girdleston's threat of returning to jail."

"But how can he—"

"The duke's family is so powerful, Helena," he exclaimed, his voice a harsh whisper. "This is what I've been trying to impress upon you. I'd been fighting for my innocence and he turned up with a story about someone seeing a girl resembling Knightly Snow—and I'm released *in a day?*"

Helena said nothing. She shook her head like a person denying the inevitable.

Declan continued. "I've been a pawn in their game since the beginning, and justice and fairness have no meaning. Who's innocent or guilty makes no difference. Girdleston couldn't care less about any of it," he finished, "but he reads the papers; he keeps up with life at court. And when he needed a very desperate man to do exactly as he asked, someone with no sympathy for a very sympathetic young woman who is too beautiful for any sane man to resist, he knew who to ask. *And* how to manipulate me. His job offer was very clear: 'Do just as I say or you won't get paid. Oh, and you might also go back to jail.' "

"*No,*" said Helena.

"Yes," he said. "And now you know."

"But is that . . . it?"

Declan looked at the sky. *Only this girl. Relentless.*

"What do you mean, is that it?" he asked. "Helena, do you hear? Your husband might spend the next twenty years in prison. I had one job: to see you marry Lusk. I have obviously failed at that job.

"Whatever machinations Girdleston played to get me out of prison will snap back into place as soon as we're discovered," he said. "If you fail to marry Lusk, I'm going to prison, likely the very same day.

"And *that's* why I won't be able to provide for you or protect you or even bloody see you. I will be locked up. Powerless. My father, my sisters—" His voice broke.

"Declan," she said softly, putting a hand to his face.

"It's terrible in prison, Helena. It is hell on earth. But I would have done it in a second if it meant keeping you from Lusk. I am running mad, worrying that nothing we've planned will work."

"Declan," she repeated. "We will sort it. We will hire new lawyers. We will send an investigator to France. *I* will go to bloody France. Girdleston is not God. He may've gotten you out of prison but there is no guarantee he can send you back."

"Helena, you have been fighting him for five years. He hired an *accused felon* simply to get you down the aisle. The only reason he's not won so far is because his accused felon is in love with you. But I assure you, our love is no match for the dukedom."

"No. Stop saying that. The reason he's not won is because his greed and entitlement have finally caught up with him. I will turn his nephew against him. See if I don't."

"Helena," Declan sighed. "We cannot hinge everything on three young women who, based on everything we've seen, will be completely ignored by Lusk in a drunken haze."

"They won't be," she insisted.

"They might. And then you will be forced to carry on with the wedding, until the terrible moment when you reveal that you cannot marry the duke because you're already married—*to me.*" He dropped his head against the wall.

She slid into his arms, holding him tight. "We'll run away."

"What of your orchard? Or my father? If I return to prison, you must be able to provide for yourself. Your parents will disown you."

"Stop," she said, slapping both hands against his chest. She brought her face nose-to-nose with his. "One thing I will not do, even if you are in prison for the next thirty years, is annul this marriage."

"You don't know what you say." A whisper.

"I know exactly what I'm saying. And hear me now: we will consummate this union." She grabbed his overcoat by the lapels. "Tonight."

"Oh God."

"Do it," she demanded. "If you're bound for prison—which I highly doubt—then we'll enjoy this before you go."

"Helena," he said.

"Do you love me?"

"Helena."

"Do you love me?"

"Yes, I love you."

"Then *do it.*" She kissed him, employing everything he'd ever taught her about kissing, plus eagerness and the earthy sensuality that he associated only with her. It was the most soul-searing kiss of his life.

He pulled away, panting. "Here? In the alley? Absolutely not."

"Then find somewhere." She kissed him again. "Declan, please."

He tried to resist, God help him—he tried—but he hadn't slept in nearly two nights. His emotions were raw. And most of all, he wanted her. He'd wanted her since she'd come to him in the stable.

He kissed her, forcing his mind to work. They had little more than an hour before he must deliver her to Lusk House. He refused to make love to her outside, on the streets of London in the cold November air.

His rented flat in Charing Cross had long since been given up.

He wouldn't take her to a coaching inn.

He saw little help for it but taking her home, to Savile Row.

Chapter Twenty-Three

Declan led her by the hand through the intermittent traffic in Oxford Street and hired another hackney. Again they rode in silence, this time locked in a passionate embrace. When they reached his father's shop, he threw a handful of coins at the driver and they half ran, half staggered up the walk.

She fell against the door, breathless and reaching for him. He made a growling noise, falling to her.

"Shhh," she breathed, giggling.

"It's alright," he said against her mouth. "The family is next door. This is the shop. These buildings are five hundred years old and the walls are as thick as a fortress. No one will hear." He kissed her. "I do hate it that your wedding night does not include a proper bedroom."

"You stole me out of a perfectly good one," she said, kissing him back.

He gathered her up. She had some vague notion of him retrieving a key from among flower pots and unlocking the door. She stopped kissing him long enough to peer into the dim shop, but he looped an arm beneath her knees and swept her into his arms. He carried her inside and kicked the door shut with his boot.

Helena let out a little yelp, thrilled by every part of it: the makeshift wedding suite, his strength, even the terrible truths that he'd just shared. They faced so many obstacles, but they would do it together.

Declan set her down long enough to whip off his coat and peel hers away. Working quickly, he lit a candle, took her by the hand, and tiptoed from the showroom, through a workroom, and finally to a small room stacked with bolts of fabric. The grate had been laid with fresh wood for the morning, and he knelt to start a crackling fire. When the flames took hold, the small room was cast in jumping orange light. The colorful fabric glowed, and Helena pulled off her gloves to run her hands across bolts.

Declan was far less reverent. With wild abandon, he began to unfurl the material. Bolt after bolt fluttered to the rug on the floor. Wool, silk, linen, cotton, silk again.

"This is truly pathetic," he said, "but the best I can do. Have you changed your mind?"

Helena shook her head, speechless for once. The fabric and the fire, the small, private room—she wanted for nothing more.

"I want for nothing more than this."

Declan shot her a smile that expanded her heart and huffed out a breath. He put his hands on his hips and stared down at the colorful nest of fabric.

Helena followed his gaze. "Now . . . ?" she

asked, feeling suddenly bashful.

"Now, Mrs. Shaw," he confirmed. "And please be aware, you will do nothing. For once, I am in charge." He clicked the door shut and bolted the lock.

She laughed, a nervous, breathless sound. She watched him pull off his boots, thrilled by the sight of his determined profile and the athleticism of his body. She thought of him dragging Lusk that first night, inventorying her ridiculous wedding gifts, chasing her down the street in the rain. He was so competent, so certain of his physicality. It was like watching a Greek marble statue come to life.

Without taking his eyes from her, he dropped the boots to the floor.

Helena bent to remove her own slippers.

"No. I will serve you." A wink. "My lady."

She giggled, and he answered her with a smile, whipping his shirt over his head. His bare chest glowed in the candlelight. Helena gasped. His body was a taut, muscular landscape of bulging shoulders and biceps, flat stomach, and razor ribs.

"Declan," she whispered, reaching for him. He ignored her, shucking his pants to reveal powerful thighs in loose drawers. His erection was visible through the white linen.

"Now you," he whispered, coming to her. "Is my lady warm enough?"

"I am on fire," she whispered.

She wanted to touch him—she wanted nothing more than to touch every part of him—but she felt uncertain. She raised her arms to touch his shoulders, but her fingers hovered just above his skin.

He chuckled and clasped a hand around her waist. He gave a little yank and she toppled, colliding with his bare chest. Her hands made contact, filling with his muscular shoulders. She squeezed and slid down the smooth hardness to rocklike arms.

"May I help you with your dress, my lady?" he asked, reaching around to loosen the fasteners at her spine.

She looked up, and he captured her mouth, kissing her gently as he worked. Helena sagged against him, spent by the sweet softness of his mouth.

When her dress was open along her spine, he peeled it slowly from her shoulders, moving his mouth from her lips to her neck, nibbling her, grazing her skin with the scruff of his beard. The dress fell forward, rolling from her arms and sagging to the floor. Declan stepped back, his eyes hungry, looking at her body where the dress had been.

For a moment, he went very still.

"No corset," he rasped, staring at her breasts through the thin fabric of her shift.

She shook her head. "There was no time. No stockings or petticoats either."

He nodded, swallowing hard. He drank in the sight of her. Then slowly, reverently, he came to her. The heat of his bare skin singed her through her shift. Every cell of her body went on high alert, throbbing toward him.

He dipped his head, nuzzled her neck, and then

stooped, kissing lower. He pressed his face to her throat, pressing kisses on the indentation above her clavicle. Then he bent lower, sinking, passing over her breasts. He went down on one knee and paused, nuzzling her breasts through her shift. Helena cried out and grabbed his shoulders to stay upright.

He sunk farther still. She felt his breath on her belly, and lower, past the most private part of her. Here he breathed in deeply, his mouth sliding across her core. She startled; her body pulsed with a bolt of pleasure so intense she almost collapsed. But his hands were on her hips, holding her up, massaging, sinking with him.

Now he went lower, dragging his lips down her leg, over her knee. He sat up and allowed his hands to finish the journey, sliding firmly down her leg. When he reached her ankle, he encircled it, taking hold like a cuff. After a moment, his palm brushed the top of her foot while his thumb ran beneath her heel. Her slipper loosened, hung, and then popped off. He repeated the movement with the other foot.

When she was barefoot, he reached for her hand, and tugged her down to sit on his one raised knee. She sunk like an apple falling from a limb.

"Are you well, my lady?"

She nodded. Words evaded her. Her hands had been on his back, holding on, but she was secure on his knee and began to feel her way around his chest and belly, tracing muscles. Learning the contours and textures of him.

From his vantage point on the floor, one knee

raised, his lips were too low to kiss her but perfectly aligned with her breasts. He nuzzled and nipped, licked and sucked, teasing her through the shift. Each swipe of his mouth brought escalating waves of pleasure. It was pleasure that begat need; need that shimmered in pleasure. She wanted more, she wanted everywhere, she was a vessel of want. She made whimpering noise, digging her fingers into his hair, pressing his face to her breast.

"What does my lady like?" he rumbled lowly.

She could but cry out.

He held her securely at the waist, large fingers splayed wide, but now he slid his hands down, tracing her legs, and caught the hem of her shift.

"Raise your arms, my lady," he whispered. She complied and he slid the thin fabric up, up, tugging it from beneath her bottom, dragging it over her breasts, sliding it over her head.

In her dazed peripheral vision, she saw it flutter to the floor.

"Now what shall we do?" he teased, returning his lips to her neck.

Helena didn't know much of the mechanics of lovemaking, but she knew what came next. Slowly, she unfolded her body from his leg and slid to the floor. His hands caught her, easing her down, handling her with firm, lingering strokes.

She hit the fabric with a soft moan, his left hand hooked to the inside of her thigh. Helena gasped, pulsing a little in the direction of his wrist, his hand; he was *right there,* so very near the most desperate part of her.

Declan chuckled and slid his hand away, grazing her as he let go.

Helena whimpered, but he placed his hands on either side of her and stretched out, slowly lowering himself across her body.

"You're alright?" he asked.

She nodded.

"Are you cold?"

She shook her head.

"Are you enjoying this?"

She nodded again.

"Will you remember it when I am in pris—"

"Do not," she said, clamping a hand over his mouth. He pulled it away and kissed her—kissed her like she was accustomed to be kissed. But now there was the added pleasure of the weight of his body, the feel of his naked skin up and down her own nakedness; every nerve ending sung with the contact. His hardness, impossible to miss, nudged hotly in the precise spot she most needed heat and hardness.

And there was so much of him to touch. His broad back, rippled with muscles. His bottom, hard and round. His hair, his cheek, his back again.

"Are you—" he rasped, and Helena smiled, because he'd lost some of his teasing control. His voice was broken. He panted.

She arched her hips, wordlessly answering him.

"Yes," he hissed, and reached between them, jerkily sliding away first her drawers and then his.

They were naked now, and when he laid back down across her, Helena spread her legs, but it felt like the most natural thing in the world. She could not imagine *not* falling open for him.

His answer was a growling sound, and he came up on one arm, staring down at her.

"Helena," he whispered, all playfulness gone. "My love. I cannot believe that I've found you. That someone as singular in every way has been given to me."

Her vision blurred; she saw only the shape and color of him through her tears.

"If you ever leave me . . ." he began.

"Declan," she said, her voice clear. "Declan, I will never leave you."

"I would understand," he pressed. "I would be no different from my father. I would welcome you back, simply to be in your realm."

"I don't have a realm, Declan," she said, cupping his cheek. "I will never leave you. And you will *not* go to jail. We will prevail."

He nodded and lowered himself to kiss her. "I love you."

"I love you, too," she whispered into his neck.

He moved then, entering her in one, forceful thrust.

Helena gasped, unprepared for the tension and pain and fullness of having him inside her.

He sucked in a breath and held very, very still, burying his face in her hair.

Helena bit her lip, trying to redistribute the discomfort. She squeezed her eyes shut. Her fingers dug into his shoulders. She made a whimpering noise.

Declan began to nuzzle, moving his nose to her neck. He sucked her earlobe. He kissed his way across her jaw to her mouth. He held his body perfectly still.

Slowly, he began to kiss her, working around her bit lip. In time, she loosened her teeth and he swiped her with his tongue. She kissed back. He swiped again, deeper and deeper, until the pain and pressure subsided. She forgot it or it went away, but it was less important than all the lovely things he did to her mouth, and her ear, and her mouth again.

Gently, without realizing she moved, Helena's hips began to rock upward, seeking. Declan's mouth froze against her lips, and she whimpered a *no, don't stop* sound.

She rocked again and Declan made a strangling noise.

He moved a leg, dropping his knee beside her leg.

Helena tried again to engage the kiss. He followed, although without focus, or intent or even much skill.

She rocked her hips a third time and he answered her with a small thrust of his own, and Helena understood.

Now her kisses fell off, and she turned her head to the side. "Yes," she said, and he growled.

"Truly?" he gasped, and she repeated the word.

"*Yes.*" Not an answer, an affirmation.

Declan made a vague sound of praise and relief combined. He resumed kissing her, really kissing her, and rocking into her.

Helena gasped at the pounding, pressing shock of it all, but then she laughed, delighted—this was so lovely—and she kissed him back, meeting him thrust for thrust.

She wrapped her arms around his neck and lifted her knees, first to his haunches. He reached back and took one ankle, showing her, and she wrapped her legs around his waist.

Declan rolled them, flipping her on top, and then rolled them again, driving into her when she landed on the bottom again.

"More," she huffed, and he flipped them again, rolling and rolling, tangling the fabric, fusing himself to her.

Her climax took her by surprise. One moment she was kissing him, pressing against him, and the next she thought, *Wait, wait, wait, I will—*

But she couldn't say what she would, because she didn't know—but then she did. Her world imploded from the junction of their bodies, pleasure radiating like a star, like a thousand stars, through every limb, shimmering and buzzing. She felt it under her skin, inside her belly, up her spine. She even felt it in her toenails.

She cried out and Declan matched her cry, pumping into her once more, twice more, and then collapsing on her with a groan.

For a moment they lay there, hovering somewhere between the soft fabric beneath them and the transcendental realm of glowing, pulsing pleasure mingled with pure, selfless love.

Finally, Declan raised up. "Are you well?"

She nodded.

"Are you hurt?"

She shook her head.

"Have I pounded the voice from your lips?"

"Yes," she whispered, and she turned her head

away. Without warning, tears filled her eyes. "Please do not go back to prison," she whispered.

He sighed wearily. "We shall make every effort."

She nodded. "Considering the threat of it, I can't believe we waited so long to do this."

"Liked that, did you, my lady?"

Another nod.

He moaned and kissed her neck. "Do you know when I found it most challenging to keep my control? Around you?"

She shook her head. "The masquerade?"

"No."

"The wet carriage after Lady Canning's?"

"No. My God, I'd only just met you. At that point I was blaming our attraction on prison."

She laughed. "It was Madame Layfette's?"

He nodded. "There was something about our coming together to make the plan happen. I'd just managed to admit that I was a mercenary. And then seeing you in that . . . in that—"

"You know I can likely bring that negligee back—"

"Nothing intended for Lusk," he said. "Please. Only you. I want only you."

"And you shall have me," she said, wrapping her arms around his neck. "One of the girls will work out. Lusk will throw me over. We will go home to the forest."

Declan buried his face in her hair and breathed in, flipping them over again.

Chapter Twenty-Four

Titus Girdleston celebrated his birthday, Declan thought, like a five-year-old girl.

The room swelled with pastel bunting, streamers, and pink roses. In *December.* Attendees were expected to bring a gift; each of which, according to Helena, he would open while they watched.

The guests included friends, business associates, political allies, and all hangers-on to the Lusk dukedom by blood or marriage. Luckily, this meant that Helena had been free to invite her three potential duchesses.

Declan had kept away on Sunday, the day after their (God help him) wedding and the night in his father's shop. He'd left a note before they'd left Savile Row, tidied the shop as best he could, and returned Helena to her bedroom just before sunrise.

Two hours later, all grooms were expected to help the footmen set up for the birthday.

He saw Helena only in passing. He'd expected the encounters to be intense or steeped in longing, but he felt very much the way he'd felt every time he'd seen her within Lusk House.

There she walks, the most beautiful woman I've ever seen.

Is she safe?

Is she comfortable?

When will I see her again?

The sameness of it, by no means insignificant, caused him to realize how very long he'd been in love with her. Being married did not change the strength of his love, but their shared secret did drive his anxiety to new heights. Their love should feel safe and accepted; instead, he scribbled down contingency plans and escape strategies, he thought of ways to hide her or abscond with her abroad.

He thought of his family, too, and dashed off a letter of explanation, telling them what they must do to survive in London if he was on the run.

It was terrible, and uncertain, but also so incredibly worth the risk. Helena Shaw was worth taking his already upside-down life and lighting it on fire.

Guests to the party began to arrive at 2:00 p.m. The family received them in Girdleston's beloved green salon, the large formal sitting room that housed his tabletop collection of miniature houses, carriages, and village buildings.

Because Girdleston hoped to receive more of his beloved miniatures as gifts, and because child guests were prone to meddle with the display, he appointed two grooms to stand guard beside the tiny village. It was a stroke of incredible luck, and Declan volunteered immediately. Nettle partnered him across the table.

At the appointed hour, guests began to arrive. Declan, his heart lodged in his throat, watched the salon fill like a soldier watches a battle unfold.

Helena, in the pale-green dress she'd worn the day she'd arrived, stood beside her sister Camille, keeping a close eye on Lusk.

The duke, a drink already in hand, stood beside his uncle, his flat eyes staring above the heads of the guests, engaging only when addressed. On occasion, he yawned. A footman assigned to his personal care stood nearby, a refresher drink ready on a silver tray.

Miss Tasmin Lansing, the potential duchess they'd met in Hyde Park, was the first to arrive. She was accompanied by her mother, a baroness, and she brought a brightly wrapped gift. Declan exhaled. She'd come to play.

Helena stepped up, nodding to the baroness's smiles and gestures of gratitude, *blah, blah, blah*—Declan marveled that Helena could remain so composed. Miss Lansing, too, looked unruffled and fortified. She made little effort of cordiality but stared openly at the duke instead. She'd worn a golden dress, a stark contrast to her dark hair, distinctive and modern. Was it too tasteful and refined for the duke? Declan had no idea what Lusk wanted, but other men in the room stared.

After a quarter hour, the duke drifted from the receiving line to a chair beside the fire. Miss Lansing saw the shift and smoothed her skirt and patted her hair. In two blinks, she transformed her face from impatient and suspicious to sugary and ecstatic. The change was mystifying. He had the errant thought that Helena had been true to herself, wholly authentic and open, from the beginning and the duke was a fool. *Thank God.*

Across the room, Miss Lansing glided to the fireplace and lit on the arm of the duke's chair. Declan took a deep breath. He'd stalked highwaymen through haunted forests with less anxiety.

Another dozen guests arrived, along with them the next potential duchess, Lady Genevieve Vance.

While Miss Lansing looked striking and aggressive, Lady Genevieve sparkled and flitted. She'd worn red, like she had that day in New Bond Street. Today's dress was a shade darker, more rose red, but it was just as fitted and it stood out in the green room like a berry.

Helena spoke to her briefly—she'd warned each girl in advance that there would be other contenders at the party—and left her to circulate.

Lady Genevieve descended on the duke within five minutes, her carousel of cheerful expressions calibrated to somewhere between loopy smile and ecstatic grin. The duke gestured to his footman for another drink, and Lady Genevieve was there, laying a gloved hand ever so lightly on his sleeve.

Ten minutes later, the third and final potential duchess arrived: Miss Marten from the museum. She looked the least certain and most out of place; but Declan felt she was, by far, the most provocative. Her flaming red hair was swept up in a loose chignon. She took in the party with large, excited eyes. She'd worn pink, the perfect color to accentuate her hair. She glanced around the ornate salon with a look of someone determined to toss a ring at a country fair and win first prize. Covet, thy name is Jessica Marten. She wanted all of this.

Helena greeted her, whispered some encouragement or strategy. Miss Marten located the duke, squared her shoulders, and moved in.

Declan looked away. It unsettled him to watch. He sought out Helena, sitting among the family beside her sister Camille. When she looked up, her expression was anxious and pale; her cheeks were taut with worry.

Declan's chest hurt, seeing her distress. He forced a look of confident reassurance, caught her eye, and he gave her the slightest *we will win this* nod.

She answered back with a heartbreaking tiny headshake. *No.*

Declan looked back, not blinking. *What's happened?*

She shook her head again, blinking back tears. She mouthed one word.

No.

HELENA COULD NOT control what the girls did or said, and it was killing her.

It wasn't their fault. They were trying, she could see them trying. Any normal man would have slipped away from the party for an easy assignation with any of them by now.

Miss Lansing was witty and droll and rather naughty. She whispered dirty jokes and made sarcastic fun of other guests.

Lady Genevieve was purer; she went straight for his vanity and his lust. She rubbed him like a shedding cat against a sofa, employing hands, shoulders, hips, and once she'd even inclined her head and leaned it against his shoulder.

Not to be outdone, Miss Marten, shy at first, but clearly in possession of the most to lose (or rather, the least to return to), did it all. She laughed with a trill of a bird, she touched his knee, she fetched him drinks and fed him cake.

Working together and separately, the girls were like a lesson in flirtation; they were so overt almost every guest noticed. What else was there to do at a party as boring and pointless as this one? Three beautiful women beguiling a duke was the only spectacle on offer, especially as the duke seemed wholly unaffected. He was, in fact, so inattentive Helena was forced to stop watching. The prospect of obvious failure frightened her too much. These three girls had been their key to freedom, her greatest hope. And now—

She shoved from her seat to make a circuit of the room. A table of gifts stood near the door, and she snatched up a toy bridge and carried it to Girdleston's doll village. By sheer force of will, she glanced only once at Declan.

When she passed him, Declan said, "You'll have to engage with the four of them. They've made a scene, and the future duchess must acknowledge it. If people see you laughing with the girls, it will give them less reason to talk."

"Really?" she asked. She balanced the bridge on top of the cottage.

"It will give them something different to talk

about."

Declan was right, it couldn't hurt. She left the miniature village and settled among the three women and sleepy duke and endeavored to engage them like old friends.

That is—the women chatted, while the duke said to no one in particular, "I'm only required to remain here for two hours. Does anyone know the time?"

On cue, the three potential duchesses twinkled with laughter—such good sports, all of them—but Helena's chest collapsed. They'd failed. The duke meant to go. There was no girl here who would cause him to throw her over and stand up to Girdleston. These women hadn't even broken the surface. Forget beguiling him, the Duke of Lusk seemed annoyed.

The more he ignored them, the more Helena wanted to take each girl by the shoulders and tell them, *Save yourselves. No dukedom is worth this. Obviously he's dead inside!*

But then she looked around, and she saw steely determination on the faces of each woman.

So be it, she thought.

She glanced at Declan. Her husband. The sight of his strong, handsome face—her face, her strength—should have filled her with such joy and hope. Instead, she felt as if her heart was being torn apart, piece by piece.

Why had fate set him in her path only to keep him forever out of arm's reach? What had she done to deserve the machinations of Girdleston, and St. James Palace, Miss Knightly Snow, and her own parents? Must limestone and money and power fuel everything?

Tears began to tighten her throat and she excused herself, quitting the room. Before she slipped out the door, she caught Declan's eye. He winked, but the playful gesture felt like an arrow to her throat.

She wanted to weep. She wanted to fling herself at the duke and shake him until he awakened enough to see these women, to *really* see them, and to acknowledge their ambitions perfectly aligned with every trapping of his life. If he could attach himself to one of them, if he endeavored to form some bond, they could build a life together. They could attend limitless parties and spend the year traveling in sequence to each of his lavish homes.

Five minutes later, Declan sought her out in the corridor.

"Helena, don't," he said, coming upon her two corners away from the green salon. He held a miniature chapel that appeared to have been snapped in two.

"Don't what?" she said. Her voice was thick with tears.

"Do not lose your composure now."

"What could it possibly matter? Lusk has the same regard for these women as he does for my father's dogs. Either he doesn't enjoy women, he's faithful to some paramour that I haven't discovered, or he wants to move limestone on my river as much as his uncle. *He will not budge.*" She dropped her face in her hands.

"Actually, the four of them look to be having a pleasant time," said Declan. "Is Lusk ever excited about anyone? Perhaps we are striving for a reaction that does not exist."

Helena ignored him. "I cannot express how suffocating and trapped and *bound* it feels to extricate myself from this wedding! I've tried, and tried, and tried—and nothing works. No one listens except you. And what good has that done for either of us? Now I've pulled you and your family into greater peril. I've made you marry me—"

"I married you because it was my greatest wish on this earth, Helena. Do no deceive yourself. You are frightened, you are disheartened, but you must not give in to despair."

"Why not?" she demanded. "I've not a single card left to play. Our only choice is to come to them with our marriage. The promises we made last night are so precious to me. They are pressed into my very soul; it sickens me to use our union as a bargaining chip." She sucked in a breath, swiping tears from her eyes. "And you'll be punished. And I cannot protect you."

"It was never your job to protect me, Helena. I am the protector."

"But you cannot protect me *and* yourself," she cried softly. "And what of your father and sisters? They should come first. You've only just met me."

"You are my wife," Declan bit out. "*You* are my family."

Helena did not hear him. She went on. "The men in charge of these aristocratic fiefdoms, and these mines, and the whole bloody world, will do as they wish. We are pawns. You said it yourself." She cried into her hands.

Declan swore. A nearby alcove housed a statue of a woman in a toga holding a basket of fruit. He dropped the miniature chapel, now snapped in two neat pieces, into the marble fruit and reached for her. He pulled her close, kissing the top of her head.

"Do not lose heart," he whispered. "You are relentless, remember. My relentless wife. I'm not in prison y—"

He stopped talking.

Helena looked up, wanting to hear more, drawing hope and comfort from the very sound of his voice. He wasn't looking at her; his eyes were trained on the corner. Gently but swiftly he set her aside. He walked two yards and edged against the wall, flattening himself. Carefully he looked around the corner in the direction of the party.

"Bloody, bleeding—" he mumbled, baring his teeth.

"What is it?" she whispered.

"The person in the black cloak is here. At this party. I've just caught a glimpse."

"At Girdleston's birthday?"

A quick nod. "I may not be able to extricate us from the Lusk dukedom—yet—but I can bloody well discover who has been following you."

He was off the wall in the next instant, striding around one corner, then the next. Helena hurried after him, wiping tears from her eyes.

When the entrance to the green salon came into view, she saw the lurking figure hovering outside the room.

Declan walked faster, nearly running now.

"Stop," Declan called, his voice chillingly lethal. "Do not move."

The figure spun toward the sound. Declan closed in. Helena darted right, trying to see around his large body. Without warning, Declan threw his arms up. For a long, breathless moment, he was frozen in this position, his arms outstretched like he was breaking a fall.

"Knightly?" he rasped.

"Declan!" answered a squeaky female voice, dizzy with delight.

Helena stopped so fast she almost lost her balance. She reached for the wall.

The cloaked figure threw back her hood. The face revealed was female, young, and stunningly beautiful. She had pale skin, short ebony curls, and light brown eyes.

Declan stared at her, still not moving, and the woman laughed and threw herself into his arms.

Chapter Twenty-Five

"No," Declan said, his brain churning to comprehend. Knightly Snow was standing before him—rather, she was hurling herself at him.

"No. No. No. No," he repeated, his voice more hushed. His reflexes kicked in and he caught her, just as she crashed against him.

"Oh, Deck!" she whined, clasping to him like a crab. "I've waited so long for you to discover me."

"Stop. Talking," he growled, looking right and left.

By some miracle, no one had seen. He stalked from the door, unable to peel her from his body without considerable effort. When he passed Helena, he reached out and grabbed her hand, pulling her along.

"Oh, your friend!" sang Knightly Snow, still clinging to him. "She's so pretty."

She was here.

Knightly Snow was here.

In London.

She was not dead.

She'd not been abducted.

Hope swirled inside him with cyclone force.

He disappeared down the warren of corridors and stopped in the alcove with the toga statue.

"Miss Knightly Snow," he recited formally, detaching her from his body, "meet Helena La—"

He stopped, considered the ramifications and thought, *To hell with it*.

He continued, "Meet Helena Shaw. My wife."

He turned to Helena. She gaped at him. Her eyes were larger than he'd ever seen. "Helena, meet the girl whose disappearance sent me to prison. Miss Knightly Snow."

"H-how do you do?" stammered Helena. Her voice cracked. She squeezed her eyes shut and looked at the floor, breathing hard. Declan took her hand and laced their fingers.

"Your wife?" accused Knightly. "Declan! You told me you would never marry!"

"No," he sighed. "*You* told *me* that I must not ever marry."

"Silly Declan," said Knightly, swatting his arm. "Why would I say something like that? I adore weddings!"

"I cannot begin to imagine," Declan mumbled. If memory served, she'd been trying to enlist him as her own paramour. But there was no need to recall that now. Or ever. He'd not touched Knightly Snow, not once, despite her repeated attempts at seduction.

"Miss Snow," he sighed, trying again, "let us start over. Where the bloody hell have you been? I've been looking for you for the good part of a year. Your parents accused me of *abducting you*, and *I went to prison*."

"*Stop!*" cooed Knightly. "They told me you'd be

investigated but not charged. That you'd be exonerated in the end."

"Who told you?" asked Declan. "Are you saying you *knew* I was being accused of abducting you?"

Knightly Snow sighed as if she was being asked to recite a familiar poem for the entertainment of grandparents. "Those savages at the palace gave me a bit of money . . ." she winked at Helena and made a pinching gesture with her thumb and pointer finger, ". . . if I promised to make myself scarce when we got to France. They were so insistent their precious Crown Prince should recover from his heartbreak. Poor man, he loved me so very much."

"They paid you to evade me?" Declan hissed. He spun away. "They knew all along. I should have known. What a fool I have been!"

Knightly Snow laughed as if it was the most hilarious prank. She told Helena, "They felt the prince would cling to the vain hope of my return if I wasn't . . . in a manner . . . dead."

Declan spun back. "Let us forget for the moment that an innocent man was accused and sent to Newgate, Knightly. But you've let the world believe you'd been kidnapped and . . . and done in. Even your parents!"

"Shhh," said Knightly, holding a finger to her pouty lips. "I'm not meant to talk about it. But of course I had to tell you. I felt honor-bound to relieve any great guilt you might harbor. For killing me."

"I did not kill you! Obviously."

"That's why I've been following you," she continued. "Also, the South of France in winter is such a bore."

"Why did you take so long to reveal yourself?" Declan demanded. "Why stalk us for weeks?"

"Oh, that. Well, the palace put a date on when I could 'reemerge' in London if I wanted the balance of my lovely money. But I wanted to come home. And I thought to myself, I know, I shall fashion a disguise. Something mysterious and ominous. Like a little witch. A beautiful little witch." She smiled and drew up her hood, and then let it fall. She giggled. "Clever, don't you think?"

Declan stared at her. Did he feel relief or rage? The two emotions roiled inside of him like the fires of hell. Helena must have seen it on his face, because she clasped his hand.

"Knightly," he began, trying to remain calm, "you cannot fathom the agony you have put me through. You are— You are—"

Helena stepped up. "Let us not insult Miss Snow," she said carefully. "It's clear she meant . . . no real, er . . . harm." She forced out these words like she was swallowing bad milk.

She cleared her throat. "We'll need her to travel to her family and show herself. We'll need everyone to know that she is alive and completely unharmed by you." She looked at Knightly. "Am I correct in assuming that you'll attest to being unharmed by Declan?"

Knightly Snow let out a breathy sigh. "Of course."

Helena added, "And that Shaw and you are very . . . friendly." She shot Declan a raised-eyebrow glance.

"Oh, we are the very best of friends," confirmed Knightly, throwing herself against him again. Declan stood like a post and allowed her to hang.

"Lovely," said Helena, dropping his hand. "Are you such good friends that you would be willing to tempt the . . . disappointment of the palace by dropping the disguise and showing yourself? Now? For the sake of Declan's exoneration?"

"Of course!" she said, hopping back. "The disguise was diverting for a time, but I've grown rather bored of it actually. And I bought so many lovely gowns on the Continent . . ."

In what Declan remembered as one of her signature gestures, Knightly Snow flung off her black cloak to reveal a tricolored dress, with yellow skirt, bright-blue bodice, and red sleeves. The bodice was cut so low on her ample breasts Declan squeezed his eyes shut. Beside him, Helena was laughing. He opened one eye. Yes, it was true. His wife was so amused she'd put a hand over her mouth to hold in the laughter.

The hem of Knightly's skirt was short enough to reveal trim ankles and a good part of her leg. He'd never seen so many vivid colors on such a small garment in his life.

"Do you like it?" Knightly cooed.

"Knightly?" he clipped. "Helena is correct. You owe me the, er, 'favor' of exoneration. We will go to your parents and show them that you're alive—nay, that you are veritably bursting with life."

"I've already been to Cornwall," said Knightly.

"Where do you think I'm staying in London? In our townhome. You are exonerated, Declan—*and* you're welcome. I dare the palace to try and threaten me. I was exiled, plain and simple. And no amount of money is worth cooling my heals in a deserted French ocean village *in winter.*" She made a face.

Declan stared at her, trying to believe what she said. He looked to Helena. She was smiling a faint, cautious smile.

"Were you surprised?" Knightly now asked, jumping up and down. "Even a little? You were such a gentleman, so handsome and strong, on that dreadful journey to France. I couldn't put it out of my mind, the thought of returning to England, surprising you, and . . ." she said as she extended two fingers and walked them up his arm like a spider, ". . . learning if you might like to—"

Declan grabbed her hand and detached it from his sleeve.

Helena said, "That is quite out of the question."

"Well, there's no need to be rude about it," pouted Knightly. "I can see that you are married. Even if you have no ring." She whispered to Helena, "Something I'd look into, if I were you, love." She brightened suddenly. "But perhaps the three of us could have a bit of fun together—"

Declan said, "Oh God," and ran his hand through his hair. He spun away.

Helena began, "And I think perhaps we've said all we need to say for this moment. How can we help you?"

And now Helena floundered. Declan opened his mouth, just about to suggest they escort her to the door, when the Duke of Lusk rounded the corner.

Declan turned to stone.

Helena made a small gasping sound.

The duke came to an unsteady stop before them and stared.

Knightly Snow said, "Oh, hello there!"

"Hello," said the Duke of Lusk.

It was the most cordial thing Declan had ever heard the man say.

Seconds ticked by. The four of them were as still as the toga statue.

Finally, slowly, ever so slowly, Helena turned her head. She stared at Lusk.

Declan followed suit.

The duke ignored both of them. He was gazing with a startled sort of amazement at the colorful, bulging, preening Miss Knightly Snow.

Helena found her voice. "Your Grace," she said carefully, "may I introduce you to a new friend? This is Miss Knightly Snow, most recently returned from the South of France. By way of Cumberland."

"Cornwall," corrected Knightly. "What a pleasure to meet you . . ." She let the introduction trail off because no one had had the presence of mind to introduce the duke.

Helena leapt to finish. "Forgive me. Miss Snow, please meet His Grace, Bradley Girdleston, the Duke of Lusk."

"Oh, a duke!" enthused Knightly, and she dropped into a curtsy that somehow revealed more of her bosom *and* ankle at the same time. Watching Knightly Snow affect even the most common posture was like hearing a trained soprano sing "Drink Another Round Before Sunrise."

"How do you do?" said the duke—the second most cordial thing Declan had ever heard the man say. "Are you enjoying the party?"

Declan looked at Helena, and she stared back with their future in her eyes. He'd never seen a more beautiful sight.

"I don't really like the birthday parties of old men," proclaimed Knightly Snow. "If I'm being honest. But I do like dukes." She gave him a smile that said very plainly, *What do you like?*

"Well . . ." began the duke, and now Declan witnessed another first. The man was nervous.

Helena saw it, too. "Miss Snow," she began, "would you mind very much if I said two words to the duke before we continue this conversation? Perhaps you could say your farewell to Shaw. I'll steal the duke away only for a moment?"

Knightly narrowed her eyes, preparing to challenge this. Declan knew she hated to be obstructed when she'd honed in on a new prospect. He slipped his hand around her arm and yanked her down the corridor. "Novel idea, my lady. Miss Snow and I will say our farewells."

"Declan," Knightly complained, but he shepherded her away. Looking over his shoulder, he saw Helena rounding on Lusk, whispering as if her life depended on it.

Declan did the same. "Listen, Knightly. I need you throw your considerable . . . 'enthusiasm' toward this duke and . . . and make him fall head over heels for you."

"What?" she said, pulling free of his grasp.

"You owe me, Knightly. You owe me so much more than simply coming back to England. I was in jail. I have had to marry my wife under the cover of darkness, with strangers, and keep it a secret—"

"What does any of that have to do with *me*?"

He took a deep, frustrated breath. "More than you'll ever have the patience to comprehend. Look, this man is so incredibly wealthy, and so incredibly indulged, and so incredibly cynical, that no woman—*no woman*—even phases him. But he perked up when he saw you. Did you see it?"

"Well, naturally . . ."

"As a *favor to me*, because you owe me, I'm imploring you to captivate him. Bring all of Knightly Snow's considerable charms to bear. If you can get him to marry you, even better."

"Marry me?"

"You have to marry sometime, Knight. Even I've done it, and you were correct. I swore I'd never marry anyone."

"How rich would you say he is?"

"You see this mansion? It's one of three he has in London alone. There's one in Somerset. He's a duke, Knightly; he'll have homes all over the country. And carriages. Your every whim would be indulged. Best of all, the two of you have the same interests. You could be Duchess of All the Things You Love to Do."

"I cannot commit to *marrying him*, Declan, even as a favor to you."

"Fine. Just get him to break away from his family and release Helena from their clutches. They want him to marry her."

Knightly wrinkled up her nose "Oh, they would never suit. She's far too . . . thin. *And* she's married to you."

Declan held out his hands, a gesture of surrender. "I've done what I could to pry her away from the combined ambitions of the two families. Now you can do what you can for me. If ever you cared for me. If you are up to the challenge. When you meet his family, you will see. I guarantee it will be a greater challenge than ever you have faced. Greater even than the palace. He's got an uncle just begging to go toe-to-toe with you."

"Really?" Now she sounded intrigued.

"The uncle will deplore you—but he's not the duke. There's the lucky bastard who's 'Your Grace.' " Declan pointed at Lusk. "And he is in dire need of someone to liberate him in a very particular, very Knightly Snow sort of way."

Knightly stared down the corridor at the duke, his hands in his pockets, his head down, as Helena spoke quickly and urgently.

"Fine, I'll do it," said Knightly, tugging on her bodice. "For you. And because I think he's handsome. In a dazed, malnourished sort of way. It makes me want to fatten him up."

"I'm sure that you will expand him in every known way," said Declan, and Knightly, who was far smarter than she let on, snorted.

She took a deep cleansing breath. She patted her hair and gazed down the corridor.

"Your Grace?" she called.

Lusk looked up, his eyes drinking her in.

Knightly strode to him. "You look like you could use something I like to call 'true love's kiss.' "

"I beg your pardon?" said the Duke of Lusk, freezing in place.

Helena hopped out of the way just in time, and Knightly collided with the Duke of Lusk. She fell against him with enough force to push the two of them three steps back. She went straight for his mouth, kissing him full on, wrapping her arms around his neck, and kicking her heels behind her. The duke widened his stance, staggered, and then kissed her so hard they fell in the other direction, colliding with the wall. A painting of a dead pheasant bounced with their impact.

Helena rushed to Declan's side. "Oh my God," she said.

They watched in shock as the two strangers embraced.

When at last the duke pulled back, placing his hands on either side of her head, he repeated his original line. "Hello," he said to her.

"Hello," she said back, taking his cheek in her hand.

And then the flat-eyed, indifferent duke raised his head to the ceiling and howled.

Declan took Helena's hand and briskly pulled her away . . . down the corridor . . . around a third corner . . . out of sight.

"He's *awakened,*" Helena marveled, allowing Declan to pull her along.

Chapter Twenty-Six

Declan led Helena down the corridor, up a set of stairs, and through a door that led to the alley beside the house.

"What now?" he asked, collapsing against the bricks. "Knightly Snow is smarter than she looks but she is hardly reliable. Anything could happen. What is our next play?"

Helena nodded. "For now, we wait and watch. But only I should go back in. Perhaps you should vanish for a time? Not entirely, but go to the stables. If anyone asks, say you're ill. The two of us disappeared from the party for too long to now reemerge together. Camille believes we're off alone too frequently."

"Yes," he agreed, tugging her to him. "Meet me tonight after the house is asleep."

She nodded against his chest, listening to the drum of his heart. "The stable. Like before."

"Only well after midnight," he said. "I'll wait for you."

She reached up on her toes and kissed him again. "We almost have it."

"We cannot say this yet. There is more hope

than before, but no guarantee."

"Everything I've known since I met you has been more hopeful than it was before."

"If the situation with Lusk resolves itself—"

"*When*," she corrected.

"When Lusk is resolved, and you wake up married to a mercenary, you may not think this."

"I will," she said, and she kissed him again and disappeared down the steps.

ALMOST TEN HOURS later, Helena picked her way across the garden, through the rear gate, and slunk to the half-open door of the stable. Moving carefully, she peeked her head into the dark, musty barn.

"Thank God," came Declan's voice.

She couldn't see him, but she slipped between the open doors and pulled them shut behind her. When she turned, he was there. She leapt at him.

"Sweetheart," he said, tucking her against him. He kissed her hair, her ear, her neck, her mouth. The kisses came fast and hard, like he meant to get them all in before she disappeared. Helena kissed him back, trying to keep up.

"We're alone?"

"Only the horses." He led her through the same rear door. He'd lit the carriage room with a lantern and put wood in a stove. It burned low and hot near two chairs.

"What happened?" he asked, walking to the fire.

Helena saw the workbench where they'd first kissed. It stood empty, cast in low light. She bypassed chairs and went to it. "Well, the party ended," she said. She propped her hip on the workbench. "As usual, no one cared that I'd been gone for half an hour."

"If nothing else, they are consistent. Their ability to completely ignore their golden goose is unprecedented. Albeit useful." He reached out to brush a lock of hair from her face. "I will ever ignore you."

"It was one of the chief reasons I attached myself to you." She turned her head to kiss his hand.

"Hmm. And I thought you found me strong and thrilling. I thought I was an 'adventure.' "

"Well, that goes without saying," she said.

"Or you could say it."

She laughed and dropped her head on his shoulder. Even though he'd just kissed her, even though they'd made love last night, she felt jittery and . . . not *nervous,* that wasn't the correct word . . . she felt eager but untried at the same time, like she'd learned to fly but wasn't certain of landing.

"But what of the potential duchesses?" he prompted. "And Knightly Snow?"

Helena let out a long-satisfied breath, remembering the triumphant afternoon. "Will you sit?" she asked, patting the workbench. Declan hopped beside her and took her hand.

"Say all of it," he said.

Speaking quickly, gesturing with their joined hands, Helena recalled what happened after she returned to Girdleston's party.

"I gathered the potential duchesses together . . ."

HELENA HAD SAID to them, "Ladies, I'm so sorry. The duke has gone."

There was a collective straightening of backs. Expressions hardened. They weren't disappointed so much as . . . affronted. Even Lady Genevieve stopping smiling.

Helena told the young women, "We've tried. All of you have tried so ardently. I will be forever grateful. He . . . he . . ." And here she faltered, casting around for some excuse. She settled on, "He doesn't seem to be interested in women of his own rank."

"He was horrible," stated Miss Lansing. "No title would be worth enduring him. I see now why you were trying to wriggle free."

"I rather liked him," said Lady Genevieve. "And I adore this house." She gazed around the salon with an avaricious eye.

"If not him," said Miss Marten, staring at a circle of men, "then whom else might I enchant? A duke would have been convenient, but I cannot give up now."

"So you're not cross?" Helena asked them. "I was unaware of his proclivity for, er, finding love *outside* the aristocracy."

"He may seek love outside, but he must marry within," said Miss Lansing. "And he knows it." She rose and tightened her gloves. "I don't see any way around your betrothal. But good luck. I respect your creativity. Perhaps the marriage won't be so bad. Doubtless you will rarely interact."

Helena was about to tell her that no woman should aspire to a marriage that is "not so bad," that husbands and wives should interact, but Miss Lansing muttered a good-bye and drifted away to find her mother. Lady Genevieve said a proper farewell and sailed from the room with her smile in place, and Miss Marten asked if there was anyone else to whom Helena could introduce her. Helena signaled Camille, who convinced their sister Joan to introduce the young woman around.

And just like that, Helena was alone at a ducal function, just as she always had been. The duke was nowhere in sight. Girdleston was occupied with the highest-ranking guest. Her family was basking. She was alone, but not really. Somewhere in the stables, her husband—it gave her a burst of delight just to think of Declan as her husband—waited for her. And now, remarkably, unbelievably, she might actually have the opportunity to commence with their marriage. If Lusk and Miss Snow got on. If the duke could muster the courage to stand up to his uncle.

If, if, *if*. For once in her life, Helena succumbed to hand-trembling anxiety. She excused herself, eager for the privacy of her rooms to pace and worry and pray that Knightly Snow could use her considerable allure and cunning to transform the newly awakened Duke of Luke.

In theory, Lusk's metamorphosis had seemed so achievable. Now Helena thought of a hundred ways he could lose heart or lose interest or want Knightly Snow for the night and not a lifetime.

For years, she'd begged him to do the simplest thing, to set her free, and he had refused. Now she was asking him to engage himself in life and love? How much more a difficult and harrowing request. There was no guarantee.

But oh, the payout, if only he would rise to the occasion.

Helena walked a nervous circle in her room, around and around, aching for Declan, trying to guess Lusk's progress. She was alone in a boat, rowing for her life, unable to see if the shore was paradise or rocks.

She would know in a matter of hours. The party would disperse and Girdleston's second birthday gathering, a formal family supper, would commence. Lusk was expected to attend, of course. He was the duke, after all; this was his house and his dining room, and his title supported Girdleston's fiefdom. Helena could not say the duke harbored any real affection for his uncle, but one was never far from the other. It was unthinkable that the duke might miss his uncle's birthday meal.

But if Knightly Snow had managed to sweep Lusk away, perhaps he would not bother. Perhaps missed celebrations would become a matter of course. Helena honestly could not say what she hoped for most: Lusk arriving to the dinner to demonstrate new independence, or Lusk giving Girdleston the cut and not showing up at all.

What actually happened was so far superior to both. Better than her wildest dreams.

Lusk arrived to the family dinner *with* Miss Knightly Snow on his arm.

The happy couple turned up late, after the soup but before the quail, strolling into the dining room as if everyone else had arrived early. In order to reach his place at the head of the table, Lusk and Miss Snow traversed the long length of the room, quieting conversations and eliciting stares up and down the table.

The duke did not escort Knightly Snow so much as *promenade* her. Miss Snow, invoking a feat of balance previously unknown to Helena, managed to cling to Lusk while also preening beside him. She was a curved, sauntering, electric-blue-and-yellow-and-red pennant in the wind. She had the look of a woman who had been born for this very moment.

And the duke?

The duke appeared cogent for the first time in his life. His face was lit with satisfied pride. His head was high. His eyes fixed on each face along the table, alert and almost inviting for some challenge. His gloves creased where he held her hand tightly to his arm. He didn't shamble, he coasted.

As his betrothed, Helena was seated to the left of his chair. When she saw their long, stupefying entrance, she slid from her seat and drifted down the table to evict Camille. Her sister cooperated immediately and slipped from the room.

With Helena's seat vacant, Lusk easily settled Miss Snow beside him and dropped into his own seat. A footman stepped up to fill their wineglasses, and Lusk leaned forward to touch noses with Knightly Snow.

The captivated room delved more deeply into disbelieving silence. No one breathed. The only sound was Knightly Snow's giggle. Even the hovering footman was unsettled—he could not reach Miss Snow's goblet because she'd angled her ample bosom to Lusk. Meanwhile, Helena's heart exploded with hope.

Finally, when Helena thought the deep curiosity and red-faced shock in the room might actually combust, Titus Girdleston cleared his throat. In a warning tone he reserved only for his nephew, he cautioned, "Your Grace?"

The duke snapped his head up so fast his uncle flinched. Lusk stared at Girdleston as if a peasant had crept into the room and called him by his given name.

Titus paused, considered, and foolishly continued in a wheedling tone, "I was not aware that Your Grace had invited a guest. This is my birthday dinner."

"I am not obligated to make you aware of my dinner guests," Lusk shot back, his voice casual but with the bite of authority. "I am the duke. You celebrate your birthday in this house at my pleasure. At the moment, it is my pleasure to have a guest. Happy birthday, Uncle."

Without appearing to think, Girdleston stood up. In the firm tone of a schoolmaster, he said, "Your Grace!"

The dinner guests swiveled their heads to the duke. Lusk had turned away to nuzzle Miss Snow, and now he went very, very still. Helena held her breath, watching his profile. For the first time ever, Lusk appeared to be formed of muscle and bone rather than flesh and air. She watched anger tighten every limb.

After a beat, the duke slowly turned back to his uncle. His eyes pinioned Girdleston's, clear and focused and waiting.

Girdleston, seemingly unaware of his loss of control, said, "Surely you do not mean to insult your *betrothed*, Lady Helena?" He extended a hand to the table.

Helena sat still and upright, trying to look innocent and contrite and not beam with glee. Underlying it all was the thudding fear that the duke would falter, or lose heart, or bend to the pressure of his uncle. Girdleston patronized, working to remain civil. Red-hot anger veritably radiated from his face. Helena had never been afraid of Titus Girdleston, but she'd never seen him like this.

When the duke spoke, his voice was not afraid. He sounded relaxed but final. Authority rang in his lazy words.

"The betrothal is off, Titus," he said, leaning back in his chair. He took up his wineglass and swirled the burgundy liquid. "Lady Helena and I do not suit. We have tortured her long enough, don't you think?"

Grateful tears shot to Helena's eyes. She couldn't see. She couldn't breathe. She worked very hard not to dissolve into a tearful, breathless heap in her chair.

Titus said, "But, Your Grace, you've been betrothed to Lady Helena for these many years. We've an agreement with the earl and countess. Lady Helena has—"

"Lady Helena," Lusk cut in, "does not interest me. I've thrown her over. Pray, someone attend her, lest she swoon."

Helena blinked away tears in time to see Lusk shoot her a sardonic look over the brim of his glass. He raised an ironic eyebrow. Knightly Snow let out a giggle.

Every head swiveled to Helena. She felt their collective gaze like the gust of a voracious wind. For how long had she dreamed of this moment? And yet, she wasn't certain how to react. Should she feign heartbreak? Toss the contents of her water goblet in Lusk's face? Slink from the room? Her mind spun. An unwitting footman had leaned in with the salt cellar when Helena remembered Declan's advice: *Keep as close to the truth as possible.*

The truth was, she really wanted to speak to Lusk.

Unsteadily, she shoved from her seat. "Would His Grace grant me a moment alone to . . . discuss his change of heart?"

She would not rest easy until she had his assurance that this was not a one-evening stunt.

Girdleston leapt at this request. "Yes, yes," the old man enthused, "you and the duke have a word and perhaps your differences can be smoothed over. We shall set a place for the duke's new friend. Here. *Beside me.*"

Without looking at the man seated to his left, Girdleston slid his plate away and signaled to a footman. He continued. "By the time you return—"

"Miss Snow will not move from her current chair," commanded the duke, tossing his napkin on his plate. He pushed back from the table with undue force. Before he strode from the room, he kissed Knightly Snow full on the mouth.

While stunned guests watched in motionless

shock, Helena struggled to dislodge herself from the crowded table and hurried after the duke.

"She is a marvel," enthused Lusk when Helena joined him in the corridor.

"Oh yes, quite," Helena said. "I believe being marvelous is a priority to Miss Snow."

Helena had vowed to follow his lead. If he wished to profess his appreciation of Knightly Snow, she would not contradict him. She owed her future to the marvelous Knightly Snow.

"Do you think the two of you will, er, suit?" Helena asked.

"We suit," Lusk assured her, straightening his cravat.

"I am grateful that you are releasing me from the betrothal. I . . . I hope—"

"Convenient, isn't it?" he said. "Considering you're married to someone else." He shot her a look of challenge.

Helena felt her face go hot. And now she wasn't sure what to say.

The duke continued. "Knightly told me about the stable boy. Aren't *you* a little minx?"

"I—" began Helena. She was wholly unprepared to defend herself and Declan.

She began again. "Mr. Shaw and I sort of . . . fell into one another. He was hired to guard me, we were thrown together, and . . . we found love. Please believe me, Bradley, I hope the same will happen for you. Truly. I'm thrilled that you get on so well with Miss Snow."

The duke snorted. "I'd not double down, if I were you." He was looking over her shoulder into the dining room.

"I'm *not* doubling down." She stepped right, forcing him to look her in the eye. "You *should* have a wife who shares your interests and has your heart. *And* you should challenge your uncle. Girdleston takes every advantage. He serves only his own ambition, and I believe he takes a strange sort of pleasure in telling you what to do. You can throw him over and be the duke you were born to be."

Lusk laughed bitterly. "What do I know of being duke?"

"You've had the best tutors and studied at Oxford, for God's sake. Surely you learned something. Your friends have titles and somehow manage. You can hire a trustworthy steward. Or you may invoke the advice of Miss Snow. I have it on good authority that she is very clever."

Lusk snapped his attention back to Helena. "Do you think she would fancy managing the dukedom? Alongside me?"

"Ah," Helena scrambled. "I believe she is very ambitious. And she prefers to keep busy. With an estate and holdings as vast as yours, surely there will be some stimulating task to keep her occupied. *Ask* her. But do you . . ." Helena swallowed hard, ". . . intend to marry Miss Snow?"

"If she will have me," said Lusk.

"And I am truly free?"

"Yes, yes, of course. I was an arse to allow them to bind you to me for so long." He stepped around her for a better view of the dining room.

"And will you tell Girdleston to drop his agreement with my father about the barges on the River Brue? If he doesn't, your limestone shipments will destroy Castle Wood. Can you tell them to leave it as it is?"

"What?" He snapped his head back, his expression impatient.

Helena took a deep breath. As quickly and succinctly as possible, she told him about her tiny corner of their shared wood and her orchard. She implored him not to destroy it.

"Yes, yes," he said. "What care have I for Somerset?"

Helena closed her eyes, terrified she could not trust his word. Without thinking, she reached to take the duke's face in both hands, holding his cheeks in her palms.

Staring him in the eye, she said, "Promise me, Bradley. No matter what happens. I have given you Knightly Snow. Life as a sentient man is within your reach. After five years of terrorizing me, will you promise *not* to intrude on my river or forest or orchard?"

Lusk scrunched up his face, clearly unaccustomed to being confined or pleaded with or both. Finally, he jerked away and said, "You have my word. Enjoy your strapping stable groom and your wretched forest and apricots."

"Apples," she breathed.

"Right. *Apples.*"

"This is all I ask," said Helena. Her voice broke. She took a step back.

"What do we do now?" she asked in a whisper.

"I don't care what you do. I'm going back to Knightly."

"You'll have to deal with my father, I'm afraid. There . . . there may be some necessary payment—

for jilting me."

The duke smoothed his coat and tugged at his cuffs, flashing a dismissive expression. "I don't care about the money. I only care about Knightly." He paused and looked up. "But should I tell your parents about the stable groom?"

Helena's heart stopped. "I'd rather you not? I had hoped to tell them some weeks after our betrothal had dissolved."

The duke snorted and turned toward the dining room. "I'm only joking. I won't reveal what a naughty little blossom you've been . . . enjoying moonlit assignations with servants—"

"*One* servant," she corrected.

"Traipsing through country markets . . ."

"You saw us?"

". . . and your very secret business inside that Catholic church . . ."

"Er," began Helena, but the duke was chuckling to himself, walking away. He raised a hand in farewell, not looking back.

Helena watched him disappear into the dining room. She'd wished on a star and the wish had come true. She could finally look forward to the dawn.

From inside the dining room, she heard commotion. Girdleston's muffled voice, choked and outraged. Her father, braying about contracts. Her mother's tears. Above it all, as clear as shattered glass, she heard the Duke of Lusk proclaim, "The wedding to Lady Helena is off. I'll say no more on the matter and sign whatever is required, my lord. I've fallen in love with Miss Knightly Snow."

Raised voices ensued, but Helena did not wait. She fled to her room. When her family called, she feigned shock and deep contemplation. It was not difficult.

When the clock struck midnight, she waited fifteen minutes and then slipped down the stairs and out the cellar door, running to Declan in the stables.

DECLAN SAT BESIDE Helena on the bench in the carriage room, shaking his head at the story.

"Did Knightly behave as if marriage to Lusk was a consideration?" he asked.

Helena shrugged. "I cannot say what happened after I left. Before, my impression was enthusiastic hope from Lusk and an indulgent sort of preening from Miss Snow. By no means is she a *certainty* for Lusk."

"She did have a prince eating out of her hand," said Declan. "Lusk will be child's play."

"She strikes me as a very clever girl," said Helena. "Whatever her plans for him, she will keep him at the tantalizing length of an arm for some calculated amount of time. It's only what he deserves—perhaps he needs it. He is finally paying attention."

Declan wiggled his hand free and leaned back on his palms. "I cannot believe it. When you'd lost all hope before she appeared, I honestly had no idea what we would do. I was a moment away from racing us both out the door. Your original plan brought to bear—to bolt. I thought we could go to Italy. Or America."

"Yes." She leaned back so they were shoulder

to shoulder. Their legs swung from the edge of the bench. "It was nothing short of phenomenal. We could not have planned it more beautifully if we had plotted for a hundred years. If we had every girl in England from which to choose. My mother actually came to my room after the party to comfort me in my loss. She was appalled by the duke's behavior and thought I'd be suffering some humiliation or heartbreak." A sigh. "They really do not know me at all."

"I know you," he said. "And I love you." He rested his face against her ear, breathing her in.

"I love you, too," she said softly, wistfully. With no warning, tears threatened. They'd done it, they'd actually done it. They'd found a way to free her of Lusk and be together. They'd saved the forest.

"What did you tell your mother?" he mumbled into her hair.

A heavy sigh. "I simply said, 'I want to go home. To Castle Wood. To my house and my apples and the crofters.' "

"Staying as close to the truth as possible," he said. He kissed her neck and she shivered.

"It is entirely the truth. It leaves out only one thing, which is you. I reckon . . ." She pulled away, trying to see him in the dim light. "I reckon that after several weeks, you can seek me out, and we can tell them? There will be outrage, histrionics, gnashing of teeth. But it will be too late." She grinned at him. "I love that we've made it too late."

He nodded. "I'll make certain it's legally binding before we tell them."

"When the dust settles, you may relocate your family to the Castle Wood."

He gazed at her. "You are certain? About my father and the girls?"

She laughed. "When have I ever seemed uncertain to you? It was our arrangement. I would never renege on our arrangement."

He kissed her. A kiss of gratitude and possession and love.

Helena put her hand on his thigh, and it occurred to her, *I have my hand on his thigh.*

I can touch him.

I can touch all of him.

He is mine.

She could touch both thighs, and then she could slide her hands up his thighs and touch the bulge that had so intrigued her in his tight yellow livery.

Casually, as a little test, she squeezed his leg.

Declan leaned farther back. He was splayed out beside her, and he looked to her with an expression of *And what will we do now?*

Her heart began to pound.

"Just one question," she asked, holding her hand still. "Did the colorful and clever Miss Knightly Snow ever lure *you* in?"

She slid from the bench and pivoted over his knee, facing him. She landed squarely between his thighs, her belly flush with the edge of the table.

"What do you mean?" His face was playfully thoughtful.

"I mean . . ." she began, returning her hand to his thigh, squeezing, ". . . that the two of you seemed very familiar. Clearly she is fond of you. Unless I misunderstood, she's been stalking not me but *you* these last weeks."

"Ah, sweetheart," he drawled, "she's not the sort of girl I fancy."

"She appears to be the sort of girl that everyone fancies. You should have seen the men up and down the table, my own father included, watching her."

"I only fancy one sort of girl," he said, closing his legs around her, squeezing her, "and I married that girl, which is a bloody miracle."

Helena rose on her toes to kiss him, and when he leaned down to reach her lips, he hooked his hands beneath her arms and pulled, sliding her off the floor. Helena leapt, tucking her knees on either side of his hips. He plopped her down on his lap in a rustle of silk. She'd not changed out of the dress from dinner.

Their mouths met, and he traced her shoulder and back, her waist and bottom, with palms flat and fingers wide. When he reached the tangle of her skirts, he dug beneath, searching for her legs. Helena held her breath, waiting for the moment when his hands slid against bare skin.

When he moved his hands up her calves, he rasped, "No stockings?"

"Nothing but the dress," she said between kisses.

"Nothing?" he said, his voice cracking. He reached between them and undid his breeches.

She sucked in a little breath. "Nothing," she sighed.

"I was hoping for the white gown," he said,

running his hands over her breasts, kissing her again. "I cannot lie."

"The white gown was for when I had nothing left to lose. Now . . ." she kissed him so deeply, ". . . now I have everything to lose."

"God, I love you," he said, and he freed himself and lifted her up, settling her down on him slowly, so slowly. "You deserve a proper bed," he bit out, straining to hold her and love her at the same time.

"I need *you,*" she moaned against him.

"Whatever you need, my lady," he whispered into her ear, "I am here to serve."

Epilogue

Declan and Helena Shaw walked through the shady bower of Castle Wood hand in hand. Springtime had awakened colors so vivid they'd been forgotten during the cold, bleak winter. The splendor of nature glowed all around them.

Declan was grateful the verdant forest seemed to forestall speech. He was struggling with what to say. They walked in silence, enjoying the dappled sun, as he searched for the correct words.

"The duke and Miss Snow called on us last week," Helena said, breaking the silence.

Declan chuckled. Knightly Snow had been a means to an end, but it thrilled them that, six months on, the combustible couple of Lusk and Miss Knightly Snow had endured.

"Oh?" Declan said. "Any plans for a wedding?"

"They did not mention it and I dared not ask. But they appeared very happy. That is saying quite a lot, considering Lusk has always hated the countryside. I cannot believe she convinced him to leave London."

"But why are they in Somerset?"

"To host a house party apparently," said Helena. "The first and best of the summer, according to Miss Snow. I think perhaps she has elicited some talk in London, carrying on with the duke yet refusing to commit to a future. The season is not yet over and they've fled here. She mentioned she is now in the company of a chaperone."

"God bless that poor woman," mumbled Declan.

Helena snorted. "Indeed. But they were alone together when they called. They'd ridden to Castle Wood to clip apple blossoms for a bower she hopes to construct for her party. I told her she may return as often as she likes."

Declan nodded and they walked from the cover of trees to a sunny clearing.

Helena said, "They invited us to be guests at the party."

"Ah," said Declan, glancing at her. He hadn't managed to shake his fear that Helena would eventually regret her life as Mrs. Shaw, Mercenary's Wife. If she'd married a gentleman, house parties would be a matter of course. He'd rather return to battle than attend a house party at a nobleman's estate. "And what did you tell her?"

Helena laughed. "Ah, 'No, thank you,' is what I said. Naturally. I vowed never to repeat another society function after that horrifying game of Mirror-Mirror."

Declan released a breath. They came to the stump of a tree that Declan had chopped down on his last visit home. The tree was dead and threatened to fall during winter storms, blocking the bridle path. He'd left the stump, a convenient stool in the secluded haven in the wood.

In the six months since they'd been married, Declan had enjoyed some extended visits home—a week or two—while other visits were only a handful of days. His clients required different levels of security or surveillance, and he felt compelled to take every high-paying job that came along.

He settled now on the stump and reached for his wife, pulling her to him. He missed her so much when he was away, far more than he'd expected; in fact, he missed her more than seemed sustainable. He wanted to be *here,* with her, always.

Before he met Helena, he'd thought taking a wife would interrupt his soldiering. He'd not been prepared for soldiering to get in the way of his marriage. He wanted out of mercenary work. He wanted out of travel. He wanted to be home. But how could he say this? Helena had made no demands on his schedule or the travel. She was sad when he left and overjoyed when he returned, but she did not complain. In fact, she looked after his father in his absence and had taken a gentle guiding hand with his sisters. She was busy with her orchard and the crofters. She was working to rebuild a relationship with her own sisters and parents.

She was the perfect mercenary's wife; but Declan could only think: *I simply want the wife. Not to be the mercenary.*

Again, he wasn't sure how to say the words. He already struggled with the nature of his job—gritty, and common, and sometimes violent—

and how this impacted his lady wife. But to resign and have no job at all? To retreat to the forest and chop down trees and do her bidding? He saw the irony: it was almost like returning to work as her groom. It felt uninspired and lazy. There was plenty of work to do, but he would provide nothing to their living.

Girdleston had paid him a fraction of their agreed fee for minding Helena, but it had been enough to set him up in his old life. He'd bought his horse and outfitted himself to work as a mercenary. He'd hired a wagon and workmen to relocate his father to Castle Wood and renovate the gamekeeper's cottage. Whatever was left, he'd given Helena and then set out to work as hard and as fast as he could for the richest clients.

The money he earned would keep them all comfortable for the rest of the year, and Helena promised very big profits from her harvest in the autumn.

After that? Declan couldn't say.

"What's wrong?" she asked, leaning against him. Idly, she ran her fingers through his hair.

"Nothing," he lied, nuzzling against her breast. "I am drinking you in. Oh, how I've missed you."

She dropped her face against this hair. "I spend my days thinking, 'I wonder what he is doing right now?' I think about you a hundred times a day, at least. We all miss you, but I understand that your work is important. I want you to be happy."

"I . . . I would be happy here, I think," he said. The words came out in a rush. "If that is something we might . . . consider."

Helena hesitated, her hands going still in his hair. Declan listened to her heartbeat against his ear.

After a moment, she said, "The duke did say one more thing. When he was here."

The duke? Declan thought, confused. He grabbed handfuls of her skirt and pulled her closer to him. "What did the duke say?"

"He said his new foreman believes the forest in this county would be well served by hiring . . ." she took a deep breath, ". . . a sheriff."

Declan looked up. "A sheriff? Like the sheriff of Nottingham?"

"Well, like any county sheriff, I assume. As duke, Lusk is ultimately responsible for the county, and I suppose he has the power to install things like sheriffs and vicars and constables and magistrates. Apparently, at the moment, he requires a sheriff. He mentioned something about highwaymen on the New Road and stolen chickens. Poaching on his land. He wondered if you would be interested in the job."

Her voice was light and casual, but Declan could hear hope—a very tense, very cautious hope. He squeezed her more tightly, and she wrapped her arms around his neck.

Declan tried to think of conflicts or barriers but his brain leapt to the very great potential of the offer. He would be here, with Helena, with his family. He could use his experience and skill to patrol the forest, to protect, to deescalate violence and investigate crime.

He could work without leaving his wife.

"But was Lusk serious?" Declan asked. Now his

heart pounded in time with hers. He smoothed his hands down the backs of her legs. When he reached the hem of her skirt, he delved beneath, massaging her calves.

Helena let out a little yelp and laughed. "He was entirely serious. I think . . ." she dipped her head and kissed him, ". . . I think taking the job would be a favor to him—and a peace offering. After all we've been through. He's so very in love with Knightly, God help him. He can see now that our five-year betrothal was wretched. He wishes to make amends."

"And could you tolerate me?" Declan asked, kissing her, working his hands up the backs of her legs. "Here in Somerset all the time? Home every night?"

"It is my most fervent wish," Helena whispered, breathless. She'd gone slack against him. He cupped her bottom in his hands.

"Mine, too," he breathed. "I cannot leave you again. I cannot." He devoured her with a kiss.

Helena cried out, a grateful, breathy sound of delight, and he drank it in.

"Never leave me again, Declan," she breathed against his cheek. "Never leave me again."

And then they stopped talking and reveled in the soft forest floor, and mild spring sunshine, and each other.

Acknowledgments

It was a delight to tease a Regency Historical out of the fairy-tale tradition of Snow White, and I was lucky that so many people wanted in on the game. Many thanks to my daughter, who thought of casting the potential duchesses with qualities of the seven dwarves. A consortium of teenagers in my house helped me invent the parlor game of "Mirror-Mirror." My critique partner, Cheri Allan, encouraged me to play up the apples and orchard and foresaw "true love's kiss" as a Lusk-Knightly transaction. Lenora Bell suggested Declan pose as a servant rather than simply a bodyguard. There are too many, "Oh-and-then-you-coulds" to count. Every suggestion made the book so much better. Thank you to everyone who is willing to indulge me in a brainstorm.

Collaboration is one of my favorite parts of writing, and much of this magic comes from my talented editor, Elle Keck. Her barometer for winning romance and eye for the big picture takes me out of the weeds and onto the croquet lawn.

The listening ear and encouragement of writing friends Lenora, Cheri, Christy Carlyle, and Marie Tremayne is nourishing and fortifying and invaluable.

My family's support and enthusiasm is a gift that I reopen every day. Thank you to my husband, my children, my parents, sister, and in-laws. I love writing romance and you love me and I'm grateful we make it all work.

The next enchanting romance from *USA Today* bestselling author Charis Michaels in her Awakened by a Kiss series,

WHEN YOU WISH UPON A DUKE

Arrives Summer 2021